Neil Forsyth was born in Scotland i
he worked consistently unsuccessfu
and abroad. Particularly spectacula
Edinburgh led to a career in journalism that cen...
football. After discovering the Scottish fraudster Elliot Castro, Forsyth wrote Castro's biography *Other People's Money*. The book has been released in seven countries and is being developed as a feature film. Forsyth is also the author of the acclaimed *Bob Servant* humour books. He lives in London and this is his first novel. .

7797171

888 7881832

Cancellation #

D 5 A 3 C 79 F 1

Let Them Come Through

Neil Forsyth

Copyright © 2009 Neil Forsyth

First published in 2009 by Serpent's Tail,
an imprint of Profile Books Ltd
3A Exmouth House
Pine Street
London EC1R 0JH
website: www.serpentstail.com

ISBN 978 1 84668 698 6

Designed and typeset by folio at Neuadd Bwll, Llanwrtyd Wells

Printed and bound in Great Britain by Clays, Bungay, Suffolk

10 9 8 7 6 5 4 3 2 1

The paper this book is printed on is certified by the © 1996 Forest
Stewardship Council A.C. (FSC). It is ancient-forest friendly.
The printer holds FSC chain of custody SGS-COC-2061

FSC
Mixed Sources
Product group from well-managed
forests and other controlled sources
Cert no. SGS-COC-2061
www.fsc.org
© 1996 Forest Stewardship Council

To my father Stewart Forsyth, with love

Thanks to Pete Ayrton, John Williams, David Riding,
Jane Stiller, family and friends

One

'Can I tell you a story?'

She paused and her mouth parted. It closed then opened slower and she answered, 'OK,' with a little giggle and eyes jerking wide behind those daft glasses. She lowered her notes back to the table and I watched in victory when they went, taking the name with them. She hadn't said the name but it was going to be said and that's when I put down my drink and presented this dodge.

The story wasn't true. I started with the basics – my large Catholic family, my favourite uncle's death and his body being laid out in his bedroom for the wake – and she annoyed me by picking at her Dictaphone. The thing flashed red from half a dozen winking eyes and had been since the shameful little scene commenced. Her intentions were professional but it was hard for my fear not to commute to anger.

I went through the set-up – my father telling me to attend to the front door and direct neighbours and associates up to murmur regret into my favourite uncle's dead ears – while she nodded and her mouth became tight and twitchy while she pondered expressions. We shouldn't really have been doing this.

I hadn't spoken to a journalist in a long time for a very specific reason. That reason was the name that she had in her notes and what it could bring. It hadn't been a surprise to see it, at least. She was local where the name had been local. Her paper knew about the name, though they knew almost as little as they could do about the name and me. About what had happened between us and about what I had done.

The surprise lay in the fact that she was here, in a distant city, wanting to speak to me now. In calamitous coincidence, I had a return to the newspapers planned for the following day.

'…He was in a suit and he said, "I'm here to see Mr O'Donovan." So I, sorry that was my uncle's name, Mr O'Donovan, they were Irish you see, so I told him to go upstairs and take the first room on the right. Up the stairs he went and about ten seconds later I heard this unbelievable scream. It was, it was just unbelievable.'

I reached for my drink and ferried it through the air towards me. She smiled horribly and I sucked at the acid fizz. I only liked these people to see me have one drink, especially if, like then, it was morning. This is why I had sent her over to the table and insisted on ordering the drinks, which is why the drink was so strong it tugged at my teeth.

I intended to finish the drink and the story together in the hope of forcing the end. I'd fling her aside in the wrapping up, leaving her bobbing on self-doubt. Tony had promised me this was a one-shot deal, that she would go away and not come back.

From the clock on the wall behind the barman she'd had forty-two minutes. Forty-two minutes it had taken her to come squirming and stumbling at me with the name. Or the threat of the name and that was worse. But now it was departing and she was once more reduced to an earnest and ageing woman who I had no personal cause against.

'He practically kicked his way back through the bedroom door and came racing down the stairs like a man possessed,' I smiled at the memory and she joined in. And look, look at her body – the shoulders up, leaning into me, her hands stopped in anticipation. If a blind hustler had walked in off the street right then he'd have fought through the furniture to get to her. But she was *my* score.

'He ran past me and his briefcase fell open and all these forms fell at my feet but he never stopped for a second, just went off screaming down the street.' As long as she only had the known facts about the name then there wasn't much that could go wrong. It was the other information, the hidden history between the name and me, which had come for me before and could come for me again. If she had that then she'd have got there by now.

'I reached down and picked up one of the forms and I saw that they were all from the gas board. That's when I realised that the man had only come round to [*pause*] read my uncle's meter.' I gave her it slowly, laughing so she'd laugh, and she got there later than most.

'Oh,' gasped the journalist, throwing a hand to her mouth, 'oh no!' She landed her palms on the table and snorted and shook her head about with the abandon of those with enviably little pressure, little thought. I sighed to suggest an end, wedged my heels into the floor and pushed clear of the table.

'Well,' I stood before her, 'it was lovely to meet you.'

The laughing halted and she was flung into mild panic, caught between an awkward gathering of her possessions and a hopeless attempt to escape the ambush.

'Oh,' she whined, and with fair justification, 'it's just that…' she cast one limp hand back to her notes.

'Please feel free to call my manager Tony with anything else.' I slid my chair back under the table and stood square with my hands on its frame. 'Unfortunately I really have to go and check on everything for tonight's show.'

She stood in surrender and crammed her belongings into an ugly bag that spoke of financial pressure and train journeys. When they were in, she seemed to pause once more over her papers, but it was only with dismay at what she had lost and soon she was standing and I was pretending to help with her jacket.

We walked through the bar already drifting apart and I explained it was quicker for me to, yes, quicker if I went *that* way. She looked a little unsteady, for a moment I thought angry, and then thanked me for my time and produced a small wave. I wondered, walking back to my hotel, if she had expected a kiss.

And that, the interview with the journalist, is pretty much how everything started.

Two

'How long have you been asleep?' asked Tony.

It took me a moment to put together my leaving the journalist, returning to my room, falling asleep and waking with the phone in my hand. The hotel, unsurprisingly, did not provide clocks.

'What time is it?'

'Six o'clock. You're on at seven thirty.'

'Why does it matter how long I was asleep? It would still be six o'clock.'

'Yeah but then I wouldn't have known how long you'd been drinking.'

'Drinking is a problem now?'

He laughed at that because he was drinking now that it was six o'clock. He drank steadily in the evenings, worked during the day. Worked for me. Well, for us.

'No, but then I'd have known how it had gone with that journalist.'

'Tony?'

'Yes.'

'You've got to get more direct. I'll be there in ten minutes.'

The room was perfectly decent, sitting up a few floors in that hotel that only just existed. There was no restaurant, no real lobby. Just a smoked-glass door and a blonde behind a desk who didn't look up while you passed from the street, to the lift, and then those extraordinary corridors. The corridors twisted and turned, lifted up or dropped in carved sweeps round the rooms. There was a snaking belt of them round the hotel, frolicking with space when they rose and fell through floors and it had taken us a long time last night to find what they naughtily called a bar.

My breakfast that morning had been conveyed by silent hands. They had raised it on a tray outside the room, knocked and sprinted away like a nabbed pervert. Tony said that the hotel was new and part of a high-end international chain. He was surprised that they had opened there, in that particular city, and he had managed to get us rooms even though there was still building work going on. He was heavy and inelegant in his repetition of this great feat of room booking was Tony, the thief.

When I got back from the meeting with the journalist, I had been nearly at the door of my room when I heard some noise. Back along the corridor, at its distant, squint mouth, some builders had walked past in busy procession left to right. They were sniggering and had various lengths of metal hanging from their hips. We had arrived at the hotel, and the city, the day before. Other than the blonde woman at the desk, Tony and the black girl, those builders were the only people I had seen in the entire building.

Not that this was a problem. Tony was right to be inflated at his hunting down of the hotel because of the handsome twist of its position. There was the hotel, then a dash of concrete, and then the theatre. On tours, when little wins lift a fractured group of people back above the common hurt, moments like that are important.

And so, to irritate and lessen Tony, I took advantage of this situation. I filled the bath and sat stiffly in the water to begin the run-through – the plays and retreats that I ordered at this stage to give me a base for later. Through my preparations the room phone rang, stopped, then my mobile rang and stopped also.

I shaved and suited and spent long moments with a shoehorn. I had wanted to be parading the shoehorn when he arrived, to ram home the structure of the scene and our positions within it, but unfortunately I had just placed it back down when the door rudely opened and Tony walked in and said,

'You're a fucking idiot,' and I nodded in agreement and the two of us walked out of the room and down the corridor.

'There's never anyone around here, no staff or guests.'

'That's because it's not opened yet,' Tony answered, his breath shortened while he mentally counted his steps to the elevator. 'We did well to get in.'

I was overweight – only make-up (when acceptable) and decent suits kept my appearance consistent with a point just a couple of years before – but Tony was properly fat – no messing about. His weight, the bulk he'd created to carry, was democratic. Although his belly had been stretched and lowered, his fingers had also been bloated and his face pulled to each side as if straining for a circle below his greying thatch.

Thankfully, Tony had been fat before he started stealing from me. If all that, the pink wastage that quivered as he walked beside me towards the elevator, had been built and funded by me then it would be too much. I was paying for its maintenance, but I could cope with that the same way that I could cope with the stealing.

'Anyway,' said Tony in the lift. 'That's what these hotels do, they all try to be more discreet than the others, they don't want you to see anyone.'

There was a pause before what he said next, a little break in his thinking.

'But we have seen someone. Last night, when we were in the bar.'

'It's not a bar,' I corrected. I didn't want the hotel's credentials to be artificially enhanced, not for Tony's sake.

'Honesty bar. There was a little guy, remember? Cleaning the place.'

Asian, I thought he was, silently wiping and scurrying about. A child really, but busy and resigned while he worked.

'But that's a cleaner. There's no staff, no one came and asked if we were OK.'

Now we were passing the blonde woman who clicked at some unseen screen and then Tony was poised at the smoked-glass door, holding it open with a straight arm, peering out below the tense summer sky.

'There's a few there,' he said.

I reached his shoulder and saw them. They stood in a scrappy line, bowed and patient, checking their tickets and turning to companions for conversation. Tony had an unspoilt adoration for situations like this, within which he often struck some sort of *de facto* minder role, so I pushed past him and made for the alley and the theatre's side door. I walked quickly, firing a scattergun smile in response to the faces flicking to me in the lull before...

'That's him!'

'Nick!'

'My Aunt Joan, Nick, my Aunt Joan.'

'OK, come on, you'll see him soon enough.' That was Tony, finally caught up and flapping his weighty arms in my wake. I hit the alley then the block of electric light where a young guy stepped to the side and muttered,

'Good evening, Mr Santini.'

'Hi.'

I continued down a peeling passage towards the door with the taped sign:

NICK SANTINI <u>ONLY</u>

Three

I let the door swing closed to inconvenience Tony but he had kept going and I could hear his progress when he spoke to those he passed so that they would notice him. Waiting on the table were my drink and Tony's notes. This wasn't enjoyable. I didn't welcome the compelling need to push these things into me each night, only for them to vacate after I left the stage. I dragged my eyes down the sheet while I drank.

Tony knew he could only give me one page, that any more would be ignored, and so he cribbed this stuff with admirable determination. This sheet was what he did during the day, when he was working. Within his scribbles were my foundations. I probably wouldn't need them, hopefully not, but their presence was vital. They helped me spread belief beyond the fanatics to the wary. The cynics were always beyond me, the cynics really didn't matter. It was the wary that were the real catch.

On Tony's single sheet were the demographics of the city. It was little different to any other in the north of Britain, which was largely a bad thing. Eighty-five per cent white then the usual add-ons. The handier touch was that, like most British cities, they had a mini-explosion of Poles on their hands.

At the time this was happening (which was not long ago), the Poles were fairly chucking themselves into the UK. Every so often they would pop up at one of my shows, looking eager but baffled like the other foreigners I got in tourist months. I could usually pick them out, snow-skinned and blinking at me while replying 'No, not local.'

I'd say, 'You are at an exciting time in your life,' or, 'You are at a crossroads,' or 'You have just embarked on an adventure,' or, 'You take risks, don't you?' to the Poles, sitting with their clothes still creased from being folded in suitcases, who would say, of course, 'Yes.' I'd leap into how I sensed they were worried about their families, and so on. If they were old enough I'd sometimes take a punt on a dead grandmother who, I affirmed, was gamely willing them onwards in their overseas quest.

There were other points of interest. The city's industrial staples were clinging on, though the car factories had gone. There was huge development in the docks area and a few months before a paint depot had burnt down and taken half a dozen workers with it. Most useful was the news that the previous summer a sixteen-year-old boy was mistakenly shot by a drug dealer. There had been two thousand people at his funeral. What Tony had written here was:

THERE WERE 2,000 PEOPLE AT HIS FUNERAL

He was good at his job, Tony, if you were to look only at that single element of it. Two thousand at the funeral and maybe the same again who would claim to have been. That's four thousand people. I didn't even need to have one of the four thousand in the theatre, I just needed to have one of their own private circle – families, friends, workmates who had been told, in breaking voices, of the ceremony. In went the boy's name, date of birth, local area and, brilliantly, his nickname.

'Five minutes,' shouted Tony for other people's benefit as he lurched into the room. I finished my drink, waiting for the last instalment. He'd been to speak to those he called his *team*. They were a group of bored backpackers and students with whom he fought a constant battle to maintain some form of control. They came and went over the course of the tours, with Tony patching up the best he could from agencies along the way.

I had little to do with them and it was very clear they were to have little to do with me. All I asked was that Tony picked out the two most capable, and least likely to be stoned, for my jobs. The first sat at a video camera behind me on the stage and fixed it on whoever I was working with at the time. The second stood flexing down in the stalls, holding a radio microphone and ready to hurtle to the hand I picked from the fluttering masses.

Tony sent the rest of his shabby band out into the foyer and toilets in their own clothes to hit the crowd and pick up what they could. There would be occasional gems – two waiting widows naming their husbands in communal hope of later reappearance, or a young girl prodding her mother about a dead pet at the sweets stall.

One time a Second World War veteran had dropped a handwritten wish list of fallen comrades complete with ranks and place of death. As I stood later, with the room rocking to patriotic delight, and told him what Archie was telling me about the fight for freedom, that list was in my jacket pocket. In the audience had been the television men, who gave us that first series that did so well and the second that had to go, when the rumour came about the name.

This particular evening, Tony came back not with good news from the foyer but with something else.

'She's not here,' he said, 'no one's seen her.'

'Who?'

'You know who.'

'The black girl? Surely not?'

This made me laugh and Tony smiled.

'Thought you'd like that,' he conceded.

Tony, myself and the black girl had spent the evening before on a little expedition. We'd visited a bar, we'd come out when Tony instructed and fulfilled what he and the photographer requested. We'd all gone back to the hotel's honesty bar, had a drink and then headed to bed on individual missions through the corridors.

The black girl, who Tony had added to his feeble collection of workers a few days before and I was fairly confident that I would soon sleep with, was Tony's *big idea*. A few years before, according to Tony, she had been one third of a girl band that he had somehow steered to fleeting success.

Their exposure had come and gone in months. Tony blamed the record company. I, despite knowing nothing about the situation and being comfortably unaware of the band, blamed Tony. Now this unfortunate girl was skint and widely forgotten and therefore part of Tony's *big idea*, which didn't seem to be going very well.

I rose and Tony lifted the box with its strand of wire. He bolted it to the back of my belt and looped the wire up the inside of my shirt from where I collected it at the collar and clipped it to the wing. I pulled my jacket together, to shield my awful torso, and buttoned it twice.

There wasn't going to be any make-up because recently the black girl had been the one to apply it, choosing to work in silent dabs with Tony pretending not to look at her. She hadn't shown up and Tony clearly hadn't made the connection that this absence needed to be filled. It's hard to know why I wasn't more irked by these collapses in procedure. Things had fallen a long way since that second series was abandoned and the journey back was slow.

'Anything else?'

'Yeah,' Tony answered. 'There was a woman in the toilet, sneezing like a bastard apparently, eyes going as well.'

'Seat?'

'Four up from the front, two in from the left.'

'Good.'

I led Tony from the room and walked between the industrial walls. People moved from my way, looking sideways or offering ignored support with Tony pounding along behind. I knew he wanted to ask me the question but was surprised when he did. I could have destroyed him for the distraction, in front of lingering members of the disinterested crew, but it was good to get it done when it could not be extended. He spoke when the curtain was in front of us, when the young Australian who would soon be handling the camera was reaching for the microphone.

'Did she ask?' His face was urgent in the darkness.

'What?' I had to shout above the booming delivery of my name.

'The journalist, did she ask?'

I thought briefly of not telling him, of leaving him with eighty-five minutes of not knowing, but he understood what he was doing by asking at that point – when I had to focus and rigidly split the real from the unreal so I didn't come unstuck.

'No,' I told him, moving to the flood of light. 'She never asked.'

Tony smiled and rocked gratefully and I looked away at the heavy curtain, then a wall of faces that twitched with noise. Beneath the splintered acclaim, the wire on my shirt hissed when it came alive.

There was a time when I saw Tony very differently. As a saviour even, back in Soviet Street, at the end. The Soviet Street in question is in Soho, a dispiriting leap from the theatres and the tourists. It's short and neglected and dirty and the little action that it sees is not of any great worth. There's a Chinese supermarket, a newsagent, a brothel and an angry little pub called the Green Giant. There is also a laundrette called the Lost Sock. And above the Lost Sock, six years before I took to the stage that night, in that city, I rented two rooms for £75 a week and stuck a piece of card above buzzer number eight that read:

SPIRITUAL GUIDANCE/MEDIUM SERVICES

I took ads near the back of grubby newspapers, amongst the wank lines and the baldness cures, and spent a week sweating on the tube and working my way round the city. In the leafy spots of London where people have the space and time to worry about such things, I stuck photocopied notes in natural therapy centres, health food shops and willing cafés. When I had completed my tour I returned to Soho and despatched the rest to the phone boxes, sandwiched between the hookers' postcards.

I persuaded the Gentle Touch brothel, who had the door across the landing from my rented rooms, to stop leaving their door open. I didn't want customers wandering in there for spiritual salvation. Finally, I brought my grand plan to an end by pinning up another declaration, this time in the Green Giant, that said:

RECEPTIONIST NEEDED. HONEST, RELIABLE, C.I.H.

I had meant to be more ambitious in my staff search but the thing was that I didn't have many customers those first weeks. I didn't have any at all. This left me enduring my afternoons in the Green Giant and so I decided that it was a tolerable place for my receptionist hunt to begin.

The mornings were spent boldly preparing the office for the future custom. The rooms were cramped, both around ten feet by ten feet, and connected by a thin door that I coated in felt to dull noise. I fashioned the room that came off the landing into a reception of sorts and cleaned up the little toilet that led off it.

I purchased two plywood atrocities for desks and jammed one into each room. In the room that was meant for consultation and the conjuring of distant voices I added a leather chair that I got for £20 because it was fire-damaged. In the other room, on the desk, went an ancient answering machine that I had taken from Dad's pub some tough months earlier, when I left the same way that Mum had left – vanquished, broken.

From a charity shop came a faded couch and unsatisfactory chair for the reception room, where I banged some hooks into the wall and then stopped. That was me nearly out of the money that Mervyn had given me, so I adopted a strict, limiting timetable. I got up late in my flat in Earl's Court, caught the tube to Soviet Street, checked the answerphone, and then retired to the Green Giant. I followed that schedule for a couple of weeks and then two things happened one after another. I got a receptionist and I got some customers.

I was in the Green Giant at lunchtime, drinking pints of lager topped with lemonade in cheerful testament to the early hour, when I saw a podgy woman reading my advert that was pinned beside the phone.

'You interested love?' I shouted over boisterously and she turned round and drifted over to me, smoking and sporting the diluted remains of what must have been a decent black eye.

'Cash in hand?' she requested flatly.

'That's what C. I. H. stands for.'

'Right.'

She looked unimpressed, gazing down to her fingers on the bar that fluttered involuntarily.

'Would you like a drink?'

'Do I get the job?'

Christ, I thought jauntily, to buy this awful package a drink I've got to give a job with it. I didn't really think that. I was only seventeen years old, I was struggling to even talk to her. What I really thought was, I am going to offer her £200 a week, but I have no way of paying her.

'£200 a week? Start at nine on Monday? It's over there,' I pointed through the window and the empty street. 'Buzzer number eight.'

'OK,' she said, defeated and already shuffling towards the Green Giant's difficult front door.

'Don't you want a drink?' I called after her but she didn't answer, just walked right out of the Green Giant and away.

On the Monday I got to Soviet Street and she was coming down the stairs towards me. We were both surprised to see the other and I called a staff meeting in the Green Giant to smooth things along. She accepted a drink (Midori and lemonade) and even told me her name. Tiffany.

Tiffany and I sat in front of my lager tops and her Midori and lemonade and a dreadful muteness engulfed us in stages. I sucked my teeth, pulled heavily at the lager tops and then, in a flash of creativity, came up with,

'It was good of you to come in.'

She was lighting a cigarette but kindly paused to frown and slip her eyes hatefully around the Green Giant.

'In here?'

'No.'

I chuckled but she didn't and it was with worry I deduced that this was not a joke. Her eyes, I observed with some concern, were permanently dulled with cruelty. There was also some grazing on her arms that I presumed had arrived around the time of the black eye.

'That you came in for the job, I wasn't sure if you were going to come back.'

'I didn't.'

Her dearth of empathy was incredible. Her assailant – that had done the eye and possibly the arms – he was probably only looking, with emptied intelligence, for a smile. 'I was fetching my wages from my old job.'

'Sorry?'

'At the Gentle Touch.'

A hooker, I'd hired a hooker. While she sat and smoked in mild disgust, I drank my lager tops in astonishment and watched her. She was on a downward slide for sure, she must have crashed into her forties and her body was past surrender. Her face was gone, even without the temporary handicap of the injury it was pocked and squalid with years of cheap upkeep. Above it sat a tangled mess that lanked its way down on to her burly shoulders.

But still. A hooker. I was young, though not as young as I should have been, and now I was faced with this bonanza. Her tits were heavy and managed to strain even the shapeless sheen of her forgettable clothing. She didn't have too much of a gut either, and her legs...but no, none of that really mattered. She was a hooker. I couldn't not think the obvious and I couldn't not act on it.

I drained my lager tops and stared at her Midori and lemonade until it had gone the same way, then proposed we retired to the office. She sighed and drew what seemed like an inch off her cigarette then stubbed it and stood up. I shepherded her to the door and across the road then hung to the side when we reached the stairs, in a sham suggestion of chivalry that allowed me to study her rear during the upwards ascent.

Her jeans were tight enough around her square tail to cement my dedication to what was about to unfold, and I climbed with a flighty innocence behind Tiffany's corrupt, and no doubt corrupted, rump. My adventuring at this stage had been sparse – the girls from the summer camp at Glendoll College and Ayako. Now I was to be involved with a *pro*.

When we got into the office she went through the motions admirably, hanging up her plastic jacket and inspecting the room with a fake professionalism and an authentic bemusement. (I had bought some black paint with the last of the interior design budget. After painting the back room there had been a decent drop left and, caught in the moment and drunk from the Green Giant, I'd used it for a huge question mark behind what would be her desk.)

She stood with her back to me, studying this handiwork, and I stepped things up dramatically by briskly scooping my arms around her and on to her vast breasts.

'We both want this,' I whispered and massaged them tenderly with my fingertips. She remained conspicuously unruffled, no word, no reaction. I pushed a little closer, so she could feel my erection through her jeans. I rocked into her daringly.

'How does that feel?'

My probings around her front grew somewhat agitated. At last she moved, indifferently freeing her right arm from beneath mine. *Here we go.* I pushed my chin over her left shoulder and gleefully kissed her sweaty neck. I waited for her hand to alight somewhere upon me or, possibly, upon *her* but I couldn't establish its saucy route. She was fiddling somewhere out of sight and then I saw her hand reappear holding something. A cigarette. She put it in her mouth and went back for her lighter.

Well, if that's how she wanted to play it. The lighter clicked. I let my hands roll to and fro over her tits. I cupped them while she drew on the cigarette then let them drop tantalisingly as she pulled it from her mouth. Lightly and playfully I lowered my devilish hands down her belly's shaking course...and then she spoke.

'The receptionist.'

Something, something made me stop while I queried.

'Sorry?'

'At the Gentle Touch. I was the receptionist.'

I snapped my hands back to my side. Unfortunately I had to then place them apologetically on her hips to lever my erection down and free from the crease of her jeans. A yard back, I swallowed and spoke.

'Is everything OK,' I said, 'with the room?'

Understandably, proceedings were a little impaired in the opening week of Tiffany's employment. I'd stumble into the office mid-morning and she'd be there, sitting by the dormant phone and thumbing through the newspapers to check the adverts that I hadn't paid for had appeared. We'd exchange greetings then I'd retreat to my room and usually sleep, slumped in the fire-damaged chair with my feet splayed over the desk.

I was a rakish projection back then, with the washboard stomach and curved limbs of an athlete or a teenage alcoholic. My hair was thick and easily ignored, and my face young and smooth as it sprung from one enchanting encapsulation to another. There was plenty of hurt all around me, but I must have looked at least OK when I slept in the back room at Soviet Street.

When I woke I roused myself and passed by Tiffany with a nod and an anonymous noise on my way to the Green Giant. A couple of hours later I'd call the office from the mobile phone that I couldn't afford and request that she joined me. A couple of hours after that, usually in the corner table at the Green Giant, I'd suggest sex and, a couple of minutes after that, Tiffany would elect to leave the Green Giant. I would stay and at some point, in some way, I would make it home.

So then we got to our first Friday together and I arrived at the office, now a little haunted by the accelerating failure. Tiffany was looking what would pass for her as thoughtful and didn't react to my arrival, which I thought was grossly unfair with the previous afternoon's attempt having been extremely conservative (a hand slipped across her knee and a sighed, 'No more games.' She'd even finished her drink before leaving).

I'd only just fallen into the fire-damaged chair next door when she knocked and entered unprompted. She eased herself into the seat intended for the absent clients and swung a cigarette to her lips. She lit it and spoke, her mouth forming a slim triangle on its side.

'So, how the fuck are you intending to pay me?'

I was a little perturbed, lacking the energy or resources to answer impressively. Her voice, usually so insultingly flat, had located a startling edge and there was no confidence behind my smile.

'It's fine, I'll pay you tonight.'

'Tonight?' She said, her face flickering with contempt. 'I've seen you in the Green Giant, I've seen you counting your coins.' She pulled at the cigarette again but jabbed the other finger to make me wait for more. When she said it she smiled with such derision my stomach tightened in response. 'And I saw you in there yesterday.' She announced it, in some terrible victory.

The previous afternoon an old man had fired a succession of coins into the cigarette machine at the Green Giant. The coins bottlenecked in some shaft or crevice within the machine as they sometimes did and I knew that he wouldn't see the refund knob, an unidentified hook half hidden by the branding. I had watched his anger amplify, his unsuccessful attempts to attract the barman, then his wounded exit. I waited until a woman fencing stolen watches distracted Tiffany and then scooted over, pressed the refund knob and pocketed the old man's money.

'Look,' I said, fishing two twenty-pound notes from my pocket and hardly believing that I had been right to think they were there. 'I want two phones. The other one,' I waved next door to her desk and the ageing model that was part of the answer machine, 'we'll keep for external. But I want two others that can be wired together. They only need to be able to call each other. One for me, one for you. Go to Atlas Electrics on Tottenham Court Road. Ask for Mervyn and say it's for Nicky.'

At last, there was something approaching interest in her cool study.

'And then?'

'And then come back here, and I'll tell you why we need the phones.'

'OK.'

Tiffany took the money and went off to Atlas Electrics to get the phones. Just like that. Capitulation, and another lesson learnt. I took my other money, just shy of two pounds, and went and bought a bacon roll and coffee before returning to the office. I chewed glumly on the papery bacon and contemplated what I was going to have to do. No choice, though, so no great worry. The momentum had to be maintained.

Back came Tiffany with a plastic bag and Mervyn's best wishes and we began the job of wiring the phones into position with a new, needed, interaction. We handed wires to each other, making suggestion and counter-suggestion in our attempts to keep the operation as subtle as we could. Then I banged in a final tack and pulled myself out from under my desk and back onto my seat. She was already on the other seat. Facing me, waiting.

So it began. I started by talking her through some primitive set-ups. At first I was still attempting to maintain some suggestion of illusion, saying that the moves *complement my spiritual understanding*, but she stopped me.

'I know what you're doing here. It's going to go a lot better if you just tell me how to help.'

She wasn't being difficult and I thought that I glimpsed something else. Not support, but perhaps a shaft of intrigue.

'Fine,' I said in decision. 'When people come in I need you to encourage them to leave their jackets, bags, whatever they bring with them, through in that room. Then, when they come through here I want you to look for anything you can find – I.D., letters, membership cards, anything that will tell me something that they won't have told me. Then...'

'Then I call you on that phone and let you know and you pretend I'm saying something else.'

'Yes,' I said, perfectly delighted.

'Right,' she smoked and looked at me. Through the smoke and her usual opaqueness, I couldn't see Tiffany's reaction to my revelation, but that wasn't my concern. What worried me was that the buzz of this cheery unity was already wearing off, to be replaced by the return of the previous matter. The money.

Confirming the fading of the new harmony, Tiffany stood and departed to leave me fretting alone. My gifting to her of my wicked ways was swiftly appearing foolhardy, and I was wrestling with both that and the unavailability of funds for a much-needed outing to the Green Giant when I heard a knock from somewhere beyond my door. Then Tiffany was speaking to someone and then she was jutting her head back into my room. I had never seen her smile properly before, without one horrendous influence or another.

'It's a customer,' she said. 'They read your advert in the paper.'

From the inglorious kick-off, the punters arrived. Mostly we benefited from recommendation, with the first of my clients tipping off their wretched associates about the dashing young man in Soho who carried the world in his head. And once people had found me, they only wanted to return.

Tiffany fell into her role with an effortless understanding, probing the unwitting clients from the moment they stumbled through the door, and relieving them of anything that could be of help in the search for answers.

'We find it works better when you are made simple,' I heard her say while she ripped a handbag from a woman's hand. Another time she told a failing businessman that his suit jacket (with wallet within) would act as 'a shield' if he was to wear it whilst with me. Crude but effective, and beyond what I could have hoped for.

Next door to Tiffany's aggressive greetings, I was doing even better. These individual battles were what I had been moving towards, knowingly or not, since I sat in the rector's office at Glendoll College and saw where he kept his files. I knew about knowledge, about how it can be introduced by one source but made to look as if it came from another. I knew about questions laid as statements, I knew about casting your net wide. I knew that you could make certain points that anyone would fall into, and from there you managed them, ran them.

Here are two, for example:

'I sense you are sometimes insecure, especially with people you don't know very well.'

'You have a box of old unsorted photographs in your house.'

No one would say no to these questions, and no one ever did. Add the atmosphere, and the hope, and the entrance opens. With my general wins and eye for personal detail, together with Tiffany's blockbusting phone calls, the truth-seekers and life-avoiders that scrambled up the stairs in Soviet Street never stood a chance.

Within months we would be booked up days in advance. I wouldn't make it down to the Green Giant until four, five o'clock some nights, and had to jostle bitterly for room and attention with less serious drinkers. Lunchtime visits would be cut short by Tiffany, over the phone or by her newly discovered half-smile looming at the pub window.

I generously upped her pay to £250 and threw in flippant bonuses when rich targets came floundering through the door. We ran a rough-and-ready means testing over new arrivals, with Tiffany pitching for anywhere from £20 to £100 an hour depending on their dress and general carriage. If she managed to pin down some strayed aristo to a two-hour session at £200, then she got a few quid extra and I knocked off early.

I even stopped trying to sleep with her. I tried, through long looks and some general patting, to sleep with the clients, but that was curiously unfruitful. More than anything, I was caught up by my success, which was a genuine surprise. I had expected to nick enough from feeble people to survive but the rush of custom and money hit me unawares.

I threw about as much of it as I could in the Green Giant and paid for adverts and rent up front, in a race to build some protection before an assumed implosion. Still the money was there, sitting in folded assurance in pockets and drawers. The period was remarkable, to me, for possibility and safety. I had lived with neither before.

There were two years of achievement at Soviet Street before the arrival of Tony's wife. The only other note of interest, before she comes flailing in, was that during those two years I saw Dad a few times. Three times, all in Soho. Once he crossed a road a decent distance in front of me and walked with that old sureness into a bookie's. Another was in the evening, it was raining and I was walking quickly through Leicester Square when he came out of one of the cinemas with what I presumed was a barmaid. She was a bored looking Latin who walked dutifully by his side while he rattled away. His face was lit up by a streetlight, and I saw him smiling at her with his eyes pitted black by shadow.

The final occasion I'm not so sure about. I was running down Soviet Street, late for the first client through alcohol-induced medical matters. Loping the final stretch with my thin legs dividing in long, curving strides, I looked to the Green Giant through habit. There was a face at the window that my distracted mind carried through the front door and up the stairs.

By the time I reached the office, the conclusion had been reached and I accepted the mocking return of uncertainty. I waited two days before going back to the Green Giant and it took weeks for my shifts in there not to involve studying the door through the cracked mirror behind the peanuts.

Tony's wife came to me soon after I was finishing up with a man who believed that his dead cat ran over his body while he slept. It was, I said with finality and an awareness of the day's thinning, a form of protection.

'When you realise that he has visited...'

'She,' he said softly, helpfully. He wasn't concerned by the slip, but best conceal it anyway.

'No,' I said strictly, 'he.'

'But, it was female. I told you. Princess.'

'In body,' I clarified with a soothing smile, 'only in body.'

'Ah.'

That was how easy it was with these people. I wrapped matters up with a spirit word he was to silently project before retreating to his bed. I don't know what word I told the man because I made my spirit words up on the spot. Poojoobah, allafana, shoomomo, that kind of idea. Occasionally people would return and say, with great embarrassment, that they had forgotten their given term.

'Oh dear,' I'd say disapprovingly before generously continuing, 'OK, OK, I'll give you a new one. Now, write this down...'

Suitably armoured, the man thanked me and then he was gone and I could hear him arranging another appointment with Tiffany. I heard the main door and a silence, followed by the main door again and a new woman's voice. There was a knock and Tiffany eased inside my room and pulled the connecting door behind her.

'Time for one more?'

'Who?'

'A woman, rich.'

I must have still looked unsure, and the Green Giant was pulling hard, so she added, 'She's been crying,' and I nodded and she left to begin the process of lying to this new client. In my room, I sat at my desk and waited. I opened my notebook and added this new case. I trusted Tiffany at a certain level, but my records were pretty detailed in those days. I would have a page for each patient that I could use as a reminder for future sessions as well as a record of payment. Here I just wrote:

Woman, rich, crying when first arrived

Another knock.

'OK.'

The door opened, the woman entered and I smiled and said, 'Just take a seat here please.'

In the notebook I added:

Rich but money going, wedding ring, was beautiful, crying genuine

And then I closed the notebook and said softly, 'I sense a great sadness. Please, start at the beginning.'

The woman's sessions became daily and ran for two hours. It wasn't spiritual guidance she needed, it was for someone to exist in close proximity during her detailing of the incredibly diverse shortcomings of her husband – some rock band promoter who had clearly done pretty well off the backs of others, and viciously screwed over this ruined woman in the process.

They'd been married for over twenty years and he'd waged an impressively determined war of attrition against her since the beginning. In the early days this had been through women and neglect. She would surprise him in cities around the world and find him holed up with loyal tour staff or misdirected groupies. She would drop off sandwiches to a London studio and he would have some work experience girl bent over the mixing desk.

One time, she said with a battered calmness, he had told her and others with immodesty that he had arranged for a handicapped fan to visit the band backstage. Later, a band member's wife full of cocaine had told her that the wheelchair-bound enthusiast had given her husband a blowjob with the band slow-clapping him to glory. The band member's wife had laughed during the telling of the story, my new client told me with fresh bitterness, and I was uncomfortably close to laughing myself.

She had become immune to such trivialities over the two decades, and he had been an external factor for some time, only stealing back for birthdays or for some indefinite appearance over the Christmas season.

Now it was a campaign of finances. She had money (she was dropping £100 a day with me for a start), but he was valiantly fighting her attempts at a pay-off. He had terrified her with talk of lawyers, how that mob would be unable to halt their litigious ways if they were called in, and that the kids would be presented with psychologically ruinous timetables of parental attention. All she wanted, she begged, was some security. Also to know about the affairs, but was that important?

'It may well be,' I told her mysteriously on more than one occasion. 'Let's *really* get into that tomorrow.'

I did a few good numbers on her, with Tiffany's help. Early on, she went through the woman's mobile and found a stream of abusive text messages going backwards and forwards to a named adversary. Luckily from me, she hadn't told me her husband's name in the opening sessions so I was able to conjure this one up in a sudden, uncertain epiphany.

She had told me where she lived and I recalled that I had left my ads in a small, third-world-sympathising coffee shop just along the road. There had been oversized photographs of African children scattered across the wall behind the well-meaning mass of chemical-free food.

'Africa,' I wondered aloud, when the conversation had grown a safe distance from her domestic arrangements, 'Africa has brought you here,' and when she caught up she was bowled over by the deduction.

Tiffany hit me with a nice one-two. First, after a bit of handbag rustling, she interrupted the session with a phone call to say there was a trio of tickets (one adult, two children) for an approaching weekend in Euro Disney. Twenty minutes later and I was standing at the window, hands clasped behind my back and reporting evenly that she had her eyes on a distant horizon, a place she would visit for a short period with those she loved more than anyone (I was tempted to stretch this further – 'A mouse, I see a mouse,' for example – but pulled myself together). Then, one day, in fact possibly the last day that I saw the woman, Tiffany called me again a few minutes into the session.

'Sorry,' I said, frowning and plucking the cheap handset. 'I thought I'd turned this off. Yes?'

'Her handbag's full of property stuff. Flats in north London, half a million and up.'

'Thank you, Tiffany, five o'clock is fine.'

'They're two bedrooms most of them, she wants to stop wasting her money in here the stupid cow.'

'OK. Please hold all further calls until I'm finished here.'

I knocked the conversation around in an extended circle before declaring that I believed the woman was ready for a step, a big step, and was this something that perhaps she was already planning? If that did happen at the last session, then it was also the day when she looked up at me with mascara running freely over her tiring features and announced that she was going to meet with her husband that very night. She was going to reach a settlement, tell him about me, and everything that I had taught her.

'Fine,' I said quickly, 'but it's probably best you don't tell him how to find me. I am *your* contact with the other world, we do not want the balance to be disturbed,' and she seemed to accept this, as she did everything else.

The next day I walked into the office and no Tiffany. That was unusual – she arrived well before me to run through her portfolio of pitiful tasks. More unusual was the fat man with grey hair sitting in her seat.

'Nick?' he said, getting up and shaking down his shapeless leather jacket.

'Yep.'

'My name's Tony. Can I buy you a drink?' He strode to the door and yanked it open, hesitating in patient control to let me study the Tiffany-less office before following him out and down the stairs. We didn't go to the Green Giant. By this point I was avoiding it for other reasons, but it wasn't my choice anyway. I was just following this man who had been in the office instead of Tiffany and who now led me through a couple of streets into some refined spot where the waiter knew him and took us to a booth.

The table was beautifully polished. I remember this because I was looking at it a lot to try and escape the situation but, when I did, the man's face was still there. He ordered the drinks – two Bloody Marys – then finally came to some sort of beginning.

'I met my wife last night for the first time in a while. She's changed a lot, and it appears that's because of you.'

'OK.'

There was no point denying the situation, and there didn't appear to be any anger. What I was hoping for was some form of bribe, an offer I wouldn't refuse that could see this guy's wife cast aside with no complaints.

'She told me about your talent.'

'My spiritual abilities,' I corrected through habit.

'No,' he said, fixing me with a decent smile, 'your talent.'

He talked about what he called the industry, and tour structures and ticket splits. He talked about what he called *the substantial merchandise possibilities* that would lie open to someone like me. He talked about television, which he called *The Holy Grail*. And then he talked about himself, with a frantic tour through his history, and what he could do for me and what we could do together. The way he drew it, there was a world of wealth waiting for us back beyond the doors of the bar or restaurant or whatever the fuck it was.

Tony had what I supposed that I wanted and it became a process. The handing over of power was a relief in many ways. My own master plan had ended at Soviet Street and the one-on-one scraps to be fought in the back room. I said little, trapped in the fear and inevitability of the situation.

It was too relentless and I was drifting when the conversation switched to my techniques and suddenly I was more than alert. The man ambled through some of my moves, illustrating those that were transferable and should be encouraged through to this new life of mine. He told me the cruder practices that would have to be left behind in Soviet Street.

There was too much, he had *far* too much. He had pumped his wife for everything she had on me, everything she had been subjected to and witnessed without realising she was doing so. But even then, this was a long way beyond that and at first I couldn't see the real source. I didn't mind anything that he was telling me but I needed to find where the knowledge had arrived from. It was when we were walking back to the office – Tony fiddling with his mobile phone, me in a curious detachment – that it came.

'All the stuff about me, Tiffany told you that didn't she?'

'Yep,' he said without looking up, 'I paid her off for you by the way, two months worth, all sorted. She says thanks, and good luck.'

'Tiffany!' I laughed, relieved at the clarity.

'Incidentally,' he continued, following me up the stairs, 'I want all your notes on my wife. And I need you to sign this.'

He pulled a rolled piece of heavy legal paper from his jacket. I don't know if I'd have signed it, with the fifty per cent clause well hidden, if things hadn't gone as they did in the moments after. I didn't answer Tony, just kept blindly walking upwards until I saw that the door was swinging open and around the lock was an explosion of fresh splinter.

'I've been burgled,' I observed, and then I got to the landing and saw him.

'Jesus Christ.'

Tony got to the landing behind me. He reached a hand for the wall and his body swayed to a rest. I looked at Tony so I didn't have to look into the room. Tony looked only at the name, as I've been calling him, because that's what he became after that day. He was another of my Soviet Street clients but after what he did that day he became somehow reduced to a name. No. Condensed, not reduced.

His name was Joe Yakari, but I knew him as Java Joe.

Four

'Now,' I said, skating across the bow of the stage. Faces, bodies, social groups. Age, sex, race. Old ladies. There, there, there, two there, there, there, there. Old ladies. They held me up and I could never really fail when there were old ladies with their quirks and muddled brains. They occupied that welcome position right next to the generation one above, who dominated the show's later proceedings so definitively.

For now it was the opening, the first shots of wonder for the ranks of departed ambition that sat before me. The methods here came from an earlier time. They came from a time before theatres, and audiences and Tony. They pointed backwards to Soviet Street, and even perhaps to the room at the OK Corral, with Dad lurking dangerously nearby.

The opening that night started like it always did – by towing them on to the same side, so the fear of defeat could be extended.

'I need you to help me. Sometimes they will speak to me but I won't get it all. They might not want to tell me everything, they might not trust me. They might,' I said, 'be shy.'

A couple of laughs, some murmurs and jokes – *She won't be shy!* – amongst their little groups of dreamers.

'Will you help me?' I considered and they blared unevenly that they would.

'Good,' I said. 'Good. It's a beautiful city you've got here. I was out today for a walk and...'

My whole body shrunk a little. I pulled in my arms, inclined my head and fixed the woman with a frown. She was looking away, at the screen behind me that carried my face and would soon be carrying hers. Then her friend nudged her and she was looking up at me in alarm. She was definitely in her sixties, maybe older, and I had selected her within my first few paces on to the stage.

'I wasn't going to get started yet but your father, did he die,' and at this I drew my hands to my chest, 'of problems...'

She was already nodding. Already. I let her continue, with the nod and the trust bouncing back from the screen to detain the silenced others.

She was old and did not carry the shine of strong genes. Her father was almost definitely dead. Chest problems – and I would have dropped my hands to the abdomen for an even greater spread – covers heart disease, pneumonia, diabetes, most forms of cancer, and on and on.

'What's his name?'

'It's Alan. Was Alan,' she stuttered.

'*Is* Alan,' I corrected with a deftness designed to be noticed. 'Alan, Alan,' I repeated softly before a fleeting chuckle. 'Ah yes, we'll be hearing from Alan later I think.'

She clutched her hands and the audience handed up a jumble of laughs and mediocre clapping that I stopped with a palm.

'Today is the fourth of June,' I announced, walking and watching once more. 'It's a special day.' I wore a smile with little enthusiasm to unsettle them. Give them a little dip of worry before the first blast. More walking, more watching then I stopped.

'It really is a special day.' I eased myself into a hawkish concentration. They knew something was coming and all over the theatre they tightened in their seats.

'For someone in this room.'

And up went the hands, three in all, which was fine.

There are 365 days in the year and the theatre held three thousand people. Anniversaries, dates of death and, of course, the birthdays of both them and those close to them. This was just maths and probability, that's all, but these people would never seem to appreciate that. These people could always see everything but they always believed something more.

I went through the volunteers quickly. At this stage, they were as interested in the screen and the man running with the microphone as they were in me. I talked a lot about a little and they watched with novel bewilderment their features being thrown on to the wall. Their voices rang from speakers when they spoke and a jagged circle of turned heads formed around them.

After predicting that a middle-aged woman with a wedding ring had children that she cared about deeply, to her touching astonishment, I directed with a smooth point for the Australian worker to turn the camera off for effect. I dawdled about with anxious steps, mumbling just outside the wire's reach.

It would have appeared that I was sizing them up in lazy sweeps, giving each area the same unbiased study, but as my head moved my eyes corrected to stay on her. *Four up from the front, two in from the left.* And there, the tissue hovering at the face. Well done Tony. I set off earnestly and let my arc pass her by before halting and flinging out the finger.

'How's your hay fever?'

Below me the black-suited student pushed off from the stage wall and bounded up the sloped carpet holding the microphone aloft like a torch. She was speaking but he hadn't got there and then he reached her and her words arrived and bounced out around the room.

'...hay fever.'

'Sorry, love,' I said, leaning forward with my hands bound in forgiveness. 'We didn't catch that.'

'I don't have hay fever,' she repeated and my fingers dug in amongst one another. In the seats around the woman the people peeked at her with concern then back to me with faces held back in question. The silence, ugly and unwelcome, flooded in.

I smiled, laughed quickly and held my hands and body open. No threat, I told them all, no threat. Not for them, not for me. From the speakers came only the hum of their availability. Options made clinical progress through my mind but then I saw him. Over the shoulder of the woman. A fat, ginger man whose shoulders were drawn to each other in suffering and whose hand ran over his head, which looked to be glistening...

'Sorry, darling,' I laughed again. 'I'm talking to the gentleman behind you, with the red hair.'

Her eyes and mouth widened as she looked beyond me to the screen where the operator would be refocusing on the man. I watched them both straighten – her with embarrassment at her error, and him with intimidation at seeing his troubled face stretched six feet high behind me.

'Yes, my friend, you!' I exclaimed to a decent rumble of laughter. 'I'm hardly,' I added with the half-mock I used so well, 'going to get the two of you confused,' and the rest of the room joined in the fun.

'Now, sir,' I started again.

There is a historical medical debate as to whether redheads have a higher propensity for hay fever. Certainly, it is believed that there is a link to the allergy-friendly atopic syndrome. I have long settled for one in five redheaded Brits having hay fever. More importantly, it was summer and you only had to look at the guy…

'I believe that *you* are struggling with hay fever, or perhaps…'

'Hay fever,' he interrupted, 'Yeah, bloody right I am.' He dried his forehead with the shirted nook of his elbow and the audience laughed again and this time in relief.

'OK, OK,' I said, poking the words through my smile. I raised one arm, framed and cubic as it ran out then upwards. My hand shook very slightly, as if rattled by a private wind. The cameraman dutifully projected it, up close so the people saw its movement, its involvement.

It was time and I snapped into a hunched brace with my fingers jabbed to my temples. The hush had been provisional and pregnant and it was quickly cracked with a scream, a cry, a smattered applause when they recognised what was coming.

'*Please*, ladies and gentlemen,' I urged with my eyes screwed closed and face stirring in tortured stretches, 'Please.'

They held themselves back once more, and I made them wait.

Wait.

Wait.

I drew my face vertical and showed them the cleared and blissful state I had attained. I stood there as a signal while they watched upwards from the depths, swamped together in submission. My fingers were lighter now, swivelling against my skin and coaxing onwards what lay beneath. Within my calves, the readiness stirred from memory alone.

'OK,' I whispered, my neck skewed so this changed voice would carry clearly through the wire.

'Let them come through.'

And the crowd clambered on a wall of noise.

Five

The boy shot dead by the drug dealer was the hit of the night. I brought him out slowly, making sure they were with me. They knew the story and dozens were quick to call out their personal ties. When he finally arrived it was into a room so heavy and occupied by belief that I stretched it even more, giving him a purpose as well as presence. Through my agent lips he delivered an anti-drug tirade that brought them to their feet over and over again. Other than him, it was just the usual matching of names to deaths and to what must have come before.

After the show, Tony and I went for dinner at an Italian restaurant. We both got drunk, and I told him I wanted him to stop stealing money from me and he pretended that he hadn't heard me. Then we went back to the hotel and, as I walked away, Tony shouted a reminder that we had another show in that city and that theatre the following night.

Soon after I was asleep and, apparently, Tony was as well. As far as I was concerned, from me on the stage, holding the crowd like I always did, until the next morning. As far as I was concerned, nothing happened.

Six

I woke the next morning to this (Tony):

'I've got some bad news.'

So did I. My hangovers were committed to unpredictability. I could go to some gruesome party with Tony and move from champagne to beers to £20 cocktails, then fearlessly take on a minibar single-handed and wake up in the morning as innocent as a child. Other times I would nick a couple of pints back in London and spend the night rolling in my rented flat, assaulted by sweat and fear.

On that morning I woke with my hands charged with some alien buzz. They shook independently – one rustling in vague fright down by my side, the other tapping the phone against the side of my head with small, erratic strikes of warning.

There was a knock at the door, slow-handed and official.

'I'm going to have to go Tony, there's someone at the door.'

'Yeah, that's the bad news.'

His words were edged with unease. Tony's voice was the most accessible I had ever had to read. When we were on tour and the two of us moved through the world in a bubble of existence, I could tell what he was wearing when he called from his room. When he inquired in restaurants as to my dinner order I could reply with mine and also his, given away in the manner of the question and how quickly he had discarded the menu.

But that voice at that point, coming down the hotel wires, was bad. Not disastrous, perhaps, but bad enough for me to know that I didn't want it. I didn't know what it was, but I didn't want it. I wanted it to stop and not go further but I couldn't. I had to…

'What is it?' In the nothing that came back I saw him advance a hand through his grey hair.

'Best you act surprised,' he said, and I didn't hear the disconnection because the knocking started again.

I swept the covers away and levered my legs round and down. They were thinned through neglect and bore markings that were a diary of carelessness – of drunken stumbling and arrogance where I had clattered them into table legs, taxi doorsteps, stage speakers and whisper boxes. Twenty-three years old and already a body accelerating away, such is the result of having life promoted unnaturally downwards into youth.

It was a relief to confirm that I didn't have an erection while pulling the hotel's bulky, unisex dressing gown from the room's single chair. I padded to the door and jerked it open to produce a policeman. He was as young as I was and immediately the recognition was there. One full series, one pulled, one DVD and the tours. You'd be appalled at how many people that had got through to, and to what people as well.

'How can I help?' I shouldn't have had to start things, which was the first sign that it wasn't going to work out for him.

'Em, there's been an incident. An accident. Well, someone's hurt.'

'Hurt?'

'Well…' He was hopeless.

'Dead?'

He breathed, he wanted to start again.

'Where?'

'There,' he turned to his left, 'but you can't…'

I was already beyond him and striding in the dressing gown down the corridor, which was lit by thin windows raised high in the wall, with the city hiding beyond. The policeman fell in behind me on the stairs, coming again and again with alternating approaches – friendly, pleading, an unhelpful threatening.

On the ground floor I concentrated on the other voices. They deflected down the walls towards me and I followed them round a couple of bends while they moved from chopped collection to defined discussion. They were measured and denoted authority and Authorities and I turned a final corner to see the uniforms.

In the limited space before the smoked-glass door there was a tight formation of police and ambulance workers that was inverted around some unseen centre. I walked through the outer ring of bodies and wedged between two police shoulders.

In death, the black girl looked beautiful. Her skin glowed defiantly and reflected the light that hung above her. Her arms had been laid straight at her sides and twisted to keep the cuts pure. They were a violent compilation, crazed in depth and length and crusted black against the smoothness all around. A blanket climbed her chest but stopped short enough to give an inch of cleavage below her unbroken shoulders. She was, was she smiling?

'What's he doing here?'

'He just walked…'

'Get him back to his room.'

'Yes sir, em, Mr Santini? Mr Santini?'

'Mr Santini?'

I gave in and looked at the new voice. He was a policeman, a detective, and a regrettable one at that with sunken eyes and a ludicrous spread of facial hair. The job and the rank had given him a certain surety that I shied away from. I wasn't going to allow him to exert *anything* over me so I turned and walked away in the hotel's dressing gown.

The voices retreated behind us and I battled with a savage anger. It was a startling arrival of rage, all the more hopeless because of the aiming at decisions that were past and, it appeared, devastating.

When I got to my room and closed the door on the policeman's questions, I tried the phone but there was no answer from Tony's room. I found my mobile but there was no answer from his. I sat on the bed in an awful, unknowing solitude. Adrift in complicated minutes stolen from any level of understanding and untouched but aware of the mayhem approaching.

The knock came again and I hoped it was Tony but when I shouted and the detective opened the door I couldn't be surprised. He was shorter than I had appreciated but I hadn't been wrong about the conviction. He stood ringed against the whiteness of the corridor and looked at me in unhurried inspection.

There was a good frame to him, carried I presumed from substantial sport as a youth or some lingering exercise now, but he subtracted his body's benefits with some barbarous additions. His hair looked parted with a ruler and the bearded statement, that looped his mouth and hung like a tongue over his chin, had been painstakingly shaped to give him something, anything that might help in his reach for authority. It was a decent face, brutalised with low-level ambition.

Under his arm he carried a newspaper curled open to show a photo. From where I sat it was incomplete but I knew what it was. It was a photo that showed me and the black girl emerging hand in hand from a bar in this city the night before last. We were looking at the camera in a comfortable surprise, our bodies swept together in response. Below it there would be some empty commentary on our new-found love and some needed reminders on our wilting careers.

It was that morning's newspaper. It was a photo and a story that was to rectify wrongs, mask indiscretions and help launch us (Tony and I) back to where we had been. That photo, that headline. That was Tony's *big idea.*

Java Joe had the newsagent on Soviet Street. He was a quiet and defeated man who wore a heavy polo neck and stood between the till and a large map that coated the wall. One day in my early weeks at Soviet Street I pushed some aspirin across the plastic. Something came from Geography at Glendoll College and I asked, 'Is that Sumatra?'

'Java,' he said, and nothing else. I told Tiffany about this for something to say and she replied, 'Yeah, Java Joe, he's been there for years.'

I got through a few silent trips to Java Joe's shop until he spoke to me again.

'Hey,' he shouted when I stepped inside. On the counter was a paper, one of the few that were still taking my advertisements at the time, when payment was irregular in the opening, hungry, stages of Soviet Street.

'This is you then, Tiffany said?'

'Yeah, it is.'

'Can I get an appointment?'

'No problem,' I told him with only slight suspicion. 'Come in tomorrow morning.'

It's too easy to say that I should have sent him elsewhere, that I could have said we were booked up, or I was a fraud and there would be no miracles here. But I was skint and I needed customers so Java Joe became one. The next morning I told Tiffany to add Java Joe to the thin list of bookings and she produced a rare laugh and called me a desperate bastard and I smiled back in rarer union and said, 'Just noticed?' before walking through to the back room to worry about money.

He arrived with a jumble of problems. There was a wife and

kid, a loan that the wife knew about, and an overdraft that she didn't.

'When did you take out the overdraft?'

I nodded in agreement when he told me the previous month. Enough left, I realised happily, for more days like this.

Java Joe's shop was struggling and one of the reasons was his distaste for porn. He had the only newsagent in Soho where the porn was actually hidden. The magazines rattled so strongly against his religion that he used gloves when a limited delivery arrived, smothered their covers in paper and banished them to a distant corner of the shop.

'I know I could sell many of these magazines, sir,' he explained, 'but every time someone buys one, I am sick to my very stomach.'

I enjoyed the way that Java Joe called me sir, and I enjoyed how often he came to pay me money to listen. Tiffany told him that a weekly booking was the *only guaranteed way* to ensure he got to see me and as a result the appointments were regular for over a year, and repetitive for both of us. His overdraft grew, other loans arrived, and still he detested the porn and the lying to his wife. In turn, I gave him very little.

He never arrived in a jacket, only in that fucking polo neck, so Tiffany's hunts next door were impossible. It was just me and Java Joe, and I danced around some of my standard fare which seemed enough for him.

The pressure grew around Java Joe and he drifted from the individual who had first arrived. He was ageing between the sessions, and his mood became more brittle. There was some problem with his leg (he said it was hereditary through his father's side) which worsened and left him already edgy by the time he'd managed the stairs.

I knew that I had to go to Java Joe with more and I arrived without much effort on a strong play. It came when he brought out a new touch to his story. The shop, he revealed deep into a session, had come his way after an uncle's death. I excused myself, walked next door, gave Tiffany a tenner and sent her to the Green Giant to target the ancient, flagging members of the daytime content. Five minutes later, my phone rang.

'Something like Ron Geery they reckon, but you're going back twenty years.'

'Yes, that will be fine.'

I hung up and apologised to Java Joe, then waited as long as was needed before frowning and leaning forward in my chair. I asked softly for silence and fluttered my hands around my head.

'Ron Geery. Who is Ron Geery?'

'Rangiri,' he shouted, 'my uncle Rangiri.'

'Yes, Rangiri. Now let's see what he's got to say to us, shall we?'

What Rangiri had to say was quite extraordinary. Not only did he approve of Java Joe's hesitant stocking of porn, he recommended that the shop went a stage further, greatly increasing the range of the profitable magazines. Java Joe was amazed.

'He was such a religious man,' he told me, his palms gripping the sides of his head in wonder.

'I know. But your uncle is also a good man. He wants what's best for you. He wants that overdraft paid off, that loan paid back – you know what he was like about debt.'

Java Joe nodded agreement.

'What your uncle is saying,' I explained, reaching over the desk with charming closeness, 'is if you have to sell those magazines for the good of your family, then you should *really* sell them. Do you see?'

'Yes,' said Java Joe gravely, 'I do.'

'Good. That's the hour done now I'm afraid.'

It was Tiffany, a few days later, who told me of my success.

'Have you seen Java Joe's?'

'No.'

'You should do.'

If she hadn't been tired, and bored, and probably angry with me about money, she looked like she would maybe have smiled.

Down at Java Joe's an entire wall of the shop was now an onslaught of porn – a bank of promises on age, race and size that rippled with flesh and haunted eyes. Amongst the magazines were additional touches, little fluorescent stars with felt-tip boasts, stuck off-centre amongst the tits.

3 FOR 2!

'Nicky,' shouted Java Joe, spinning round the counter and pointing proudly at the display. 'I thank God for you Nicky, and my uncle.'

'You're a lucky man. These things selling OK?'

'Oh yes. Many, many selling.'

'Good stuff. Well, see you next week?'

'Of course.' He shook my hand happily.

For a few glorious months, Java Joe sold his porn. He told me that the overdraft was easing, that he'd bought a van (JAVA JOE'S – *Find Us In Soviet Street!*) and brought in someone to work on Saturdays so he could go on haphazard outings with his wife and son. Up to Oxford, over to Norfolk, down to Brighton. He'd come in to see me, and pay me, with excited tales of motorways and pubs with £9.99 roasts and a playground outside.

Tiffany gradually pushed up his fee (explaining that the *introductory offer* had come to an end, an immaculate twist that she used extensively) to £50 a pop, which he could comfortably accommodate thanks to the magazine-buying habits of Soviet Street's regrettable footfall.

At first my stealing from Java Joe was irregular. It began after his comment, during a gap in a session where I sat and wondered what Rangiri could say next.

'The stock market,' asked Java Joe, 'do you know about the stock market?'

The innocence, and the money that lay behind it, were both targets that I found myself unable to resist. The next session Java Joe gave me the first of his money and I told him I'd already had some interesting thoughts and that I had a vision of the money causing *great happiness* for his family. The next session he gave me more. It was a few thousand a time. When I told him of the rampant rises in his phantom stocks he said the same thing each week.

'I do not know, sir,' he told me with his eyes big and brown, 'how I can thank you.'

Things changed, and things changed for Java Joe, very quickly. I arrived at the office one morning with Tiffany shouting, 'Java Joe's fucked,' and holding up the *Soho Star*. The *Soho Star* had a certain influence over the area through its committed coverage of local transgressions, and they had a new one.

LOCAL NEWSAGENT RUNS 'DEN OF PORN'

'Shouldn't that be porn den?'

'He's been selling all sorts under the counter apparently, dildos and so on.'

'Dildos?' I almost felt hurt. 'Where was he getting dildos?'

'It doesn't say.'

'You can't sell porn in Soho now?'

'Not without a licence.'

'For the dildos?'

'The dildos and...' she squinted at the page. Tiffany's eyesight wasn't great. 'DVDs, sexual appliances and amyl nitrite, commonly known as poppers.'

'Fucking hell.'

'It says he's going to be shut down, criminal charges too they reckon,' added Tiffany and then, remarkably, 'Poor Java Joe.'

It was tempting to point out Tiffany's role in the downfall of Java Joe, or the disappearance of a weekly £50 contribution towards her mediocre wages. Instead I conducted some investigation. The *Soho Star*'s article was a strange affair, an attack on Java Joe's depravity that was only slightly blunted by the acceptance of his less than unique presence in the area. 'Soho's well-established and heavily monitored sex shops,' the paper called the ranks of legal outlets that had been threatened by Joe's cowboy operation.

I left the paper and Tiffany's questions and ventured back

down to Soviet Street. I approached Java Joe's from the other side of the road. It was closed but there was a light on. The windows were grubby and the light pale so I had to go closer to the glass than I would have hoped.

Inside was Java Joe, standing at the counter, looking down at his hands, which were pushed into fists on the counter's surface. He was speaking and I realised that the two stationery shadows in the foreground were people. A woman and child, standing with their backs to me and facing Java Joe.

If I was to spend time over every point that prompted regret, I wouldn't even have got this far. I think, though, it is fair to hesitate here for just a moment. If I had walked into the shop, for example, none of this would have happened. But I didn't. I walked away from Java Joe's shop and back down Soviet Street, leaving him to talk to his family.

The landlord of the Green Giant told me how they caught Java Joe. The council had received a tip-off – some grunting call by a betrayed punter or maybe an angry, legitimate sex shop owner – but it had only named the shop as Java Joe's. They searched their registrations and found nothing. Then, one lunchtime, when the council officer who had taken the call was walking to buy a sandwich he passed a line of traffic at the lights. And there it was. There he was.

JAVA JOE'S – *Find Us in Soviet Street!*

It took perhaps a fortnight for a shattered Java Joe to reappear. He arrived in the office strained but polite and asking to restart his sessions. I welcomed him cautiously and spent an hour listening to his considerable woes and offering my own confusion that his beloved uncle would place him in such peril. Java Joe asked once more how his shares were performing.

'Very well,' I told him. I reiterated that they should be seen as a long-term investment, but he didn't want his money back. The opposite. He told me that the shop was on a decent lease, that he was thinking of selling it but clearly didn't know where to start.

I'd like to think that I wanted to help Java Joe when I told him

I would look into it, and that I'd maybe even help him by buying it myself. I'd like to think that later that day, when I went to the Green Giant and looked for the man who I knew from our loose conversations was a local estate agent, I was fired by community spirit. But none of that is true.

I knew what kind of man the estate agent was. I knew from his afternoons in the Green Giant and his angry air and the betting slips that I had once seen fall from his pocket, fluttering pink notes of failure that he hadn't bothered to pick up and had instead kicked into the bottom of the bar.

I took him to a table and for the first couple of drinks I poked about with the possible sale of my office, which I told him that I owned. He was interested, and even more interested when I said:

'To be honest, there could be some extra money to be made if, well, maybe you could be a little flexible with a couple of legal things.'

He smiled with delight and held his empty glass.

'That shouldn't be a problem, can you do something with this?'

A little later I told him. Not my office but a local shop. I wanted to buy it and then I wanted to sell it. I could buy it for a lot less than it was worth and the two of us could split the profit.

'A distressed sale and a back-to-back,' he said with a jarring note of professional input. 'On paper it's legal, but I suspect the seller isn't aware of certain aspects. The value, and your plans for a resale?'

'No. Can you do it?'

'Easily,' he said, 'I can market it before you even have it. Knock ten per cent off, sell it to an investor.'

'I don't have the money to buy it, I could maybe get it...'

'You don't need it as long as he doesn't have a lawyer,' he said, warming to the crookedness, even leaving his glass to demonstrate with pointed fingers on the table where the money would go. 'Both deals can go through in the same day. The owner sells it to you, you sell it again, and then you pay the original owner. All in one day, a private sale, you see? I know lawyers that'll take care of it. Pals of mine, you know?'

'OK, then let's do it.'

I told the estate agent to be at my office the following week for Joe's appointment and bought him a final drink. He was shaking my hand when he said,

'It's not Joe's is it? Java Joe's?'

That was unfortunate. But he would see the names at some point.

'Yeah.'

He laughed, rubbed his head.

'Poor old Joe,' he said.

'I know,' I answered and I meant it, I did.

The next week I sent Tiffany out of the office before the arrival of the estate agent and then Java Joe close behind. I left them together for no more than ten minutes before the estate agent opened the door. He lifted a cardboard folder where he had scored another surname out with biro and written YAKARI below it.

'All done.'

I thanked him and joined Java Joe in the room. He spoke before I could.

'Thank you, sir,' he said. 'For buying my shop.'

'No problem, Joe,' I told him, 'it seemed like the right thing to do. It'll be useful you know, for storage.'

Weeks later I met the estate agent in the Green Giant. He gave me twenty thousand pounds in cash. It should have been more, I knew that, but I had asked for cash and nothing else. I didn't want to know any figures, I didn't want to know anything. All I asked was when Joe would be paid.

'Two days,' said the estate agent. I left the Green Giant. I never went back, not wanting to see the estate agent and consider what we had done.

Two days later Joe came to see me, with fifteen thousand pounds for the stock market.

'I'm sorry it's not more, sir,' he explained, 'I thought it would be but the estate agent said about the charges?'

'Yes, sorry, Joe, I paid what I could.'

I took Java Joe's fifteen thousand pounds. I had made over forty thousand pounds from him in a couple of months. The money stayed locked in my desk before coming back with me one night to the flat in Earl's Court. I stuffed it into a detergent box and stowed it under the sink. I didn't spend it, didn't look at it.

The next session we had after he gave me the money for his lease, Java Joe explained that he had made a mistake. He'd believed he could gain some unexplained work with family members, but his unexpected unveiling as an illegal porn distributor had left him more detached than he had appreciated.

'They are disgusted, sir,' he told me blankly, 'totally disgusted.'

Java Joe told me that his family now had little left. I said nothing and he didn't extend the discussion. At the following session he at least got round to asking for some of his money back. I told him that I would look into it. A week later I told him that I had left a message for the relevant broker. A week later the broker was still to call back. From there, things descended from convention.

It started when Java Joe announced he was living in a men's hostel. He said it with such acceptance that I thought momentarily he wouldn't ask again for the money, but he did.

'Just some of it,' he said apologetically, 'to help me.'

'I just wish,' I said, frowning at the silent phone, 'that the broker would get back to me.'

I found it unlikely that Java Joe was living in a hostel – it had happened too quickly and there were still notes of pride in his appearance – but the next week I accepted it wholly. His clothes were the same and unwashed, his hair matted, his stubble had been shaved (I recognised) with a cheap razor and cold water and his eyes were filmed with distress.

He told me that his wife didn't know where he was. That he had been unable to spend another night at home, with the questions and his family watching him and waiting for progress.

Java Joe was staying at the hostel because of pride and because of shame. I only understood the shame. He should have approached me earlier and with more force. It was my power that had stopped him. The hundreds of revelations, the sheer spread of insight. It was hard for Java Joe to push through that control to get to what he needed to do. But now he had no choice. Even then, it was the end of the session.

'I need my money, sir. All of it. I need it as soon as it can be got for me.'

If he hadn't asked for it all, then I think I would have given him some. But when he asked for it all I found that I couldn't consider giving him any. It seemed, somehow, that I needed it more. I looked at Java Joe and all I saw was further descent. I was different, I was on the up. The money had become neutral in my mind. Surely, I contrived, it would be happier with me?

'I'm afraid I have some bad news,' I said. 'I spoke to the broker. Your investments have fallen considerably in value. With the penalties incurred by selling up now, I'm sorry to say that it would make your investments virtually worthless. Now, if you can just wait?'

'How can I wait?' he asked quietly, sitting in the chair that was a stop on his return to the hostel.

I nodded, stood and led Java Joe through to the other room. He was too busy with the development to give a reaction.

'See you next week Java Joe, same time?' said Tiffany.

'Yeah,' said Java Joe, walking with dropped shoulders to the door.

'You haven't paid,' I said, instinctively, and then with contrition, 'this one's on me.' He didn't respond.

The following week I stationed myself next to Tiffany's desk in advance of Java Joe's arrival. Tiffany filled this unusual communion by telling me about a visit to the cinema with a man and I stood wondering how a man would even *meet* Tiffany.

When Java Joe arrived his polo neck had gone, replaced by a reflective jacket, the type worn by binmen and the homeless. His trousers were held up by a length of blue rope. Stronger men, and there would have been many at the hostel, had taken what they could from him.

'I don't have any fucking money,' he said, shouting the last word. 'I've not eaten since yesterday. So no fucking money.'

I felt myself shortening, drying. I held up a hand, looking for time to handle this horrific advancement in his capability. Java Joe was filthy. I didn't know, I didn't even have an idea, what was going to happen next. I wanted to say that I would give him his money, not all but some, but I couldn't say that in front of Tiffany. I was aware of her standing and moving, abandoning me to Java Joe.

'Look,' I said, 'I tell you what, Joe...'

He came at me quickly, dirty hands arcing like wings before landing on my biceps, and he leant into my face.

'You did this to me,' he shouted, 'you did it. My money, my shop, my family,' his eyes flashed with abandonment, his breath resonated and I was surprised when I realised it was drink, old and new, 'I went and spoke to a man, another estate agent...'

Tiffany punched Java Joe so fast, and with such definition, that he was down and on the floor before I had any sense of events. Java Joe was curling away, a hand to his face, and Tiffany was breathing and muttering a fluctuation between apology and the suggestion of further violence. She had missed Java Joe's talk of estate agents and I watched, petrified, in case he tried again. Clawing at the door handle, he pulled himself up.

'Fuck you, sir. Bastard, liar,' was all he said before skulking back through the door. Tiffany and I hoped the other would speak. Neither needed to, with the sound of the scene taken care of.

While Java Joe walked down the stairs of Soviet Street that day he let loose a primal piece of wailing that crashed around the bad paintwork and the stone. Tiffany and I listened and waited for it to stop. It is a little hard and indecent for me to remember that noise.

When I sat in the restaurant drinking Bloody Marys with Tony, and he told me he was going to make me a star, that conversation took place on the morning a week after Java Joe's final session. It was the day, therefore, on which Java Joe's next session would have fallen.

During Tony's description of ticket splits and merchandising, Java Joe would have been arriving at the office to find it closed. After he forced the door, splintering the lock, he would have found no Tiffany, and no me. While Tony and I made our journey back to Soviet Street, and I was finally identifying Tiffany's disclosures to Tony, Java Joe must have been making his decision, if it hadn't been made already.

By the time we were on the stairs, and Tony had pulled out his contract and told me to sign, Java Joe's tasks were completed. The shock, the snap, the end, he was already through. I got to the landing and saw him, and then Tony, from behind me, said 'Jesus Christ' and reached for the wall and we looked at each other then back to Java Joe.

He was still but moving. His body was empty and the blue rope creaked in a torturous twist that brought him round to face us. Much later, in one of the few conversations we would ever have about what we saw, Tony would wonder why Java Joe was only wearing his stained underwear. Tony was a little thrown by what he clearly saw as a late loss of dignity. I didn't answer but I knew the reason for the underwear. Java Joe's trousers had needed the blue rope, but Java Joe had needed it more.

'We need people,' was what Tony said to me while Java Joe dangled. 'Where are there people?'

I was too busy with Java Joe's curing skin, the yellow baubles of his eyes, but voices came from the Gentle Touch and Tony ran to their door. A skinhead threw it open, his eyes arrowed in anger.

'What the fuck do you—' he started, but his words ran away when he looked beyond Tony and me. 'Fuck's sake,' he said, and then, curiously, 'Why'd he do that then?'

A woman appeared, pulling some clothes together, frowning into the gloom and then screaming. The skinhead spun his head.

'Get back in there, girl, and tell the others to get dressed and out, the Old Bill will be round for this.'

Tony called the police from my office with Java Joe hanged near his shoulder and then the two of us sat on the steps of Soviet Street, swinging our legs to the side for a procession of women, in thin coats and leggings, to skip past us from the Gentle Touch. One squealed and another hissed,

'You could have shut that fucking door.'

A thought came and I started to stand.

'Just got to grab something.'

'It's here,' said Tony, pulling open his jacket. An inch of my notebook's cover, secreted amongst the leather folds. 'I was going to tell you, obviously.'

The police were bored. They swore when they saw Java Joe and said that the ambulance could deal with it and took Tony and me out to Soviet Street. I watched the morning relics in the Green Giant stir in their chairs while Tony and I were taken through some stuttering questioning.

He was a client of mine. I believed he was recently homeless after being thrown out by his wife. I only knew him as Java Joe but he was the owner of that shop, yes, that one there.

And that was that. Suicide isn't a profitable business for anyone, including the police. They'd already finished with us when the ambulance men arrived in the street with Java Joe. He was wrapped in a blanket and I was saddened that they had covered his face.

I had a stabbing worry that came to me in moments of total ending. I felt like I was on the train to Glendoll College, or in the taxi from the OK Corral, with Mervyn on his way back in to awaken Dad with punches. Now I wouldn't see this other face again, no more Java Joe, no more Soviet Street.

I looked at the windows behind which lay those rooms, bare like they always had been other than the cheap furniture and Tiffany's ashtray and maybe some newspapers piled with distaste in the corner. No more Soviet Street and now I was bound to this new man and the doubtful progression that he promised. I looked from one window to the other and realised that I didn't know which one had been mine.

'Come on,' said Tony, 'Let's get a drink.'

Hours after Java Joe and his blue rope, I signed Tony's contract half-drunk in a bar. He told me to give him a couple of weeks to set some things up and then we'd *hit the road*.

'The Midlands and up north, working men's clubs you know? Maybe Scotland as well.'

'Doing what?'

'Shows. You're going to have make a show. That stuff up there, you've got to make it into a proper show.'

'But that's what I do, it's all I've ever done.'

'Not any more.' He patted out a drum roll on the table, 'The Great Nicholas, ready to go!'

'It won't work.'

'Of course it'll fucking work,' he laughed. 'They'll love it. Listen, kid,' he tried to strike an advisory pose but he was already busy with the booze. 'You've got the talent. Now just take a couple of weeks, bash it into a show, something that will work for a hundred pissed idiots, and we'll be on a winner. I'm going to take you all the way, Nicky boy, all the way.'

'OK, Tony,' I held my hand tight around my glass. I wondered where Java Joe was now, where Tiffany was now, and, though I tried not to, where my father was now while this other man talked about my talent.

Seven

I had seen a procession of policemen come through the foreboding doors of Dad's pubs over the years, dragging with them their flaws, motives and thirst. Every one, every single one, had corruption running so close to the surface it glared in twisted solidarity with those hostelries of dishonesty.

They'd eye the barmaids through filthy, slitted glances. They'd hold hushed conversations for the benefit of my father (who spat in their sandwiches when the option arose) and talk about criminal names with a sexual reverence. And then they'd get drunk and prickly and look for reasons to project their wretched authority on anyone available. If the subject wore a recognisable badge of success – a nice suit, a pretty woman in tow, a detectable air of contentment – then all the better.

So I knew policemen and the indiscriminate threat they wielded so gratefully. And now there was this man, a detective, ready to show me the newspaper and the photo of the black girl and me and ask me questions that I didn't really know how to combat.

'Mr Santini, I am Detective Brewster,' he revealed. He called himself a detective very deliberately indeed, as though I might not have caught the distinction between the uniformed amateurs and him, ensconced in the glory of his £200 suit. He was trying to somehow level us. That, I think we both knew, was not going to work.

'Can this wait?'

'No, it certainly cannot.' The words look a lot more impressive than when he said them. He had made a mistake coming to my room because he didn't know about the furniture situation. I was sitting on my unmade bed. The chair was covered in last night's clothes, and other than that there was nothing apart from a gimmick of a wardrobe slung into one corner.

I could see him looking longingly at the chair, but I wasn't going to clear it for him and it would have been preposterous for him to attempt to do so. It was hard not to enjoy the moment. What was the bold detective to do – come and sit down beside me on the bed, question me with sideways glances while our hands nearly touched?

I watched him until I forced his eyes to the floor, where he might have seen control creeping across the carpet. I wasn't needlessly hostile, I just knew the more he struggled the quicker he'd give up. And I was worried. I mean, this was a worrying situation.

He was toiling but he still had the newspaper and, as if silently supported by the fact, began unravelling it with a graceless dramatisation. He gazed at the photo of the black girl and myself, then flicked it round to face me.

'When was this taken?'

'Night before last.'

'How long had the two of you been…'

'Listen, Detective. I need to call a couple of people. My manager Tony…'

'I've just been speaking to your manager,' said Brewster. 'Tony.'

He tried to load that with significance, hinting that even Tony's name was in range of doubt.

'How long have the two of you been working together?'

'Three years, a bit more.'

'Did you know him before that?'

'Not really, we met through his wife.'

'He said that you'd only really been on the one date with this girl.'

'Yes,' I said, and then genuinely, 'It's all very unfortunate.'

Concern was losing to anger. At Tony, and his ceaseless inadequacies that had drawn me into this. I presumed that the girl had committed suicide. She had always been a touch glum – ignoring Tony's attempts at playfulness in the make-up room, only briefly picking up when he handed her a grand in cash in the honesty bar after everything was done the night before last. It was still a surprise though, and I could do with checking.

'The poor girl,' I wondered aloud. 'I don't know why she would have done that.'

'People commit suicide for many reasons, Mr Santini, many reasons. It appears, for now, that yesterday morning she decided that her time had come. But that's what I'm trying to ascertain.'

That was probably as close to confirmation as I could have hoped for. I realised, with the black girl and me, that there was a pretty spectacular gap. I didn't know her real name, only the snappy one granted to her as part of her distant, unremarkable success. Tony had presumably told me her real name at some point but I hadn't taken enough care and in my regular harvesting of information it had been blithely jettisoned.

'Listen, Detective Brewster, can I please speak to you a bit later on?'

'OK. We're waiting for her family to get up here and identify the body. We'll have to speak to you again, but I'm happy to give you some time. It must have been a terrible shock.'

'Yeah, it was.'

He gave a criminal smile, stepped forward and dropped the newspaper on the bed.

'I don't know you myself, but the men were saying you're on the telly, doing that stuff.'

'That's right.'

'How much do you *get* for that kind of thing?'

'Sorry?'

'How much do you get for it? How much you on a year?' He looked at me as if to tell me that it was OK, it was OK for us to talk like this and about this. As if it was his decision. I flushed with anger but knew this was the pay-off for now. I didn't look at him because any reaction would have charged me further.

'Last year about seven hundred grand, I think. I don't know really.'

'Seven hundred grand?' He clucked and straightened himself out. 'Not bad, not too bad at all.' He waited for my unwelcome eyes then nodded in a deliberate dropping of reserve.

'OK, I'll see you later on, Mr Santini.'

He was walking out the door when I added. 'My manager gets half of that, though, of the money.'

He halted, I thought to respond, but instead said, 'Santini, is that Italian?'

'Yeah, I'm not though. It's not my real name.'

He remained stalled and I couldn't bear any extension so I ended it with,

'My manager, Tony, that was him as well,' and thankfully he nodded again and left.

When the door closed I waited for as long as I felt able then called Tony, the fifty per cent merchant. The phone in his room rang unbroken but he picked up his mobile with a barrage of agitation. I could hear him both through the phone and from outside. He came panting up the corridor and into my room, storming in with,

'Fuck me, what a business.'

Eight

I pointed at the chair and he swept away my clothes with his chubby hands, then wedged himself in with his arms hanging in chunks over the sides.

'Tony,' I started. 'If you had anything to do with this…'

'Don't be so fucking stupid.'

'Stupid? *That's* fucking stupid,' I pointed at the newspaper in an easy strike. 'I don't know where you went after the honesty bar, or if you said something to her. She killed herself that night.'

'What do you think I am?' He looked commendably hurt. 'She's a good girl, a bit weird but she's a good girl. Was a good girl. Why the fuck would I want her to top herself? This, this is a nightmare.'

'I'm just saying, you might have said something to her.'

'"Night, night." That's what I fucking said.'

I stared at him, at this fat man sitting sweating in the small chair with his legs jack-knifed below. At this man who had created a new disaster, which sat on my lap in the black and white of a national newspaper and, somewhere else in that city, on a slab. I looked at Tony and he looked at me and then, well, we started to laugh at the hopelessness, mostly, and the insanity of the misfortune.

After a fair bit of chortling and the occasional spluttered gag – 'Maybe she'll speak at the show tonight?' – we pulled ourselves together and combined what we had. Which was this – the black girl had unfortunately killed herself at some point during the night before last, there were no suspicious circumstances (apparently Detective

Brewster had told Tony this was a *paperwork job*), and another member of Tony's crew had just voiced a welcome belief that their fleeting colleague had been on anti-depressants.

There was a rather considerable consideration remaining, which was brought sharply into focus by Tony's phone sounding and the conversation he then had –

'Oh, hi there.'

'Yes, I'm afraid that's the case.'

'I know, it's a terrible shock. Apparently she had a long-standing history of mental issues that we weren't aware of. Unfortunately,' he added with a thick thumbs-up to myself, 'it turns out that this wasn't her first attempt.'

'Oh, he's devastated of course. I mean, they'd only just got together, so he really had no idea about all this. But he's very upset, very upset.'

'Yes, as soon as he's ready I'll be in touch.'

'OK, no problem. Oh, and thanks again for the piece. It looks great, just a shame about the circumstances.'

'Yep, bye.'

He hung up and pushed his head back, bending his neck until his windpipe appeared through the skin in squares.

'We're going to have to hold a press conference,' he announced with little courage and his eyes to the roof.

'You fucking what?'

Tony rolled his head back reluctantly. He was nervous, but not so much because of me.

'We've got no choice. In a couple of hours the two things are going to come together all over the place. That,' he gestured at the paper, 'and what she went and did.'

'Tony, how the fuck can we hold a press conference? I don't even know her. Just tell them what you did on the phone there – that she was mental, and that we'd not even really got going, that bollocks.'

'We can't,' he smiled sadly and I detested the fact that it was in these vestiges of professional knowledge that he maintained some hold over me. 'We've got to try and head things off. If we hold something in an hour, say, then you'll be talking about local and agency press. The nationals will just get what the agency send out, which will be exactly what we want because they'll send along some kid, because we won't tell them what it's about until they get to the press conference. I used to do this with the band, rehab and stuff. It's what we have to do.'

I hated it, hated that I had to agree. So I didn't.

'Just tell them that I'm too upset to talk about it, they'll soon forget about it. Christ, It's not that big a story.'

'But it could be, Nick, it could be. That's the problem. What if she's left a note telling people it was all bullshit? What if she told someone else before she slit her fucking wrists? Christ, what if she left a note saying that *you* had driven her to it? You can never get away from something like that. We've got to try and tie it all up today. Then if any of them get anything from somewhere else later, they'd have to go against their own line on it. You see?'

It was muddled and the solution was the worst part of all.

'Tony, I don't even know her fucking real name.'

Voices from outside stopped his response. The two of us watched the door. It hadn't closed properly behind Tony and so it was only a gentle push that swung it open. With relief, I recognised the little Asian, the cleaner who had been in the honesty bar the other night. He gave me a smirk of embarrassment and pointed into the room for an unseen other.

Round into the doorway they came, bewildered and broken and looking at me and Tony in a studied dejection. An elderly black couple, smartly dressed and viscerally haunted. It had to be.

'Are you,' Tony said, and I could see him swallow, 'the parents?'

The man emitted an approving sigh and they walked into the room with the cleaner or porter or whatever he was withdrawing behind them and giving me a grimace of hopelessly misplaced sympathy.

The woman stood with her head hung over her best clothes and vibrating shoulders. The man was a trickier proposition. He stood as if held back by wind, catapulted within himself by the shock. His eyes were flat and widened and his face simplified into nothing but question. He wanted, needed, either Tony or I to help him. To help him understand and find some sort of grip.

It was a look I had seen many times and usually it offered encouragement and money. That day it offered only more undefined torture. The four of us remained within our four pockets of suffering until Tony finally spoke.

When it registered that he had started to speak I felt, for one of the few times since walking into the office at Soviet Street and finding him in Tiffany's chair, real appreciation for Tony. This was what he should be doing, my complaining brain registered, protecting me from these moments. But then I heard what he said and I resented him perhaps more than I had ever done in the years since Soviet Street.

'We're going to hold a press conference,' he said. 'And I think it would be a good idea if the three of you held it together.'

In the vacuum, my conclusions worked their way quickly to defeat and I said hoarsely,

'Can you leave please, all of you?'

The parents weren't offended. For them the day was being ruled only by fate and with everything too big to come purely from people, even this request. It was being sent through my mouth by something more and they could only follow it.

'I just want to be on my own,' I explained, with something at least similar to guilt, towards their shuffling departure.

Tony saw the steel in the look I jerked at him. He rose and followed them out, stopping only to raise a final thumb in unlikely hope.

Nine

And then he texted. This was what he did when he knew my irritation with him was running at critical levels – worked his way through levels of communication in the hope that he would locate one where I might offer civility. His text said:

PRESS CONFERENCE. ONE HOUR. HONESTY BAR!!!

Exclamation marks. By this point in time, Tony's irregular capabilities were nothing more than grim confirmation of my own failure. This, the business with the black girl, was at least something new and newly thrilling in its potential finality.

It wasn't just another error, mistake or misjudged lie by Tony that would leave me with a slight ringing for five minutes while I looked everywhere but his poisonous face and refused to talk. No, if it ran the wrong way, this could potentially end the existence that I was somehow clinging on to. That sent me a little light-headed with possibilities, none of them good.

I lay on the bed in contemplation and at some point amidst the churning I slipped sadly into masturbation. With the hotel and the waiting, this was a piece of normality, but there was a grubby little matter, a repeating cameo even, that made its debut that morning.

Years of nocturnal self-destruction had left me a morning activist on this front, reporting for duty with determination in those uninhabited hours before lunch. No matter the hell with which I'd been enveloped the previous evening, no matter the trials to which I'd subjected my fading body and the diluted state I woke in, still I would battle on manfully with what needed to be done within minutes of day's bleating arrival. On this, admittedly niche, point I was a true champion and the morning's uniqueness was not going to intrude into this traditional pursuit.

Ammunition is needed for such campaigns and this incorporates recent female attendance. Perhaps it's starting to become clear. The black girl. And it's worse than that. That morning, starfished in the hotel room and sending myself to an only marginally better place, I took as company the black girl. Dead.

I would like to say that when it was over there was a heightened sense of deflation, that I lay steaming in a reflected disgust. But I rather suspect that there was a renewed vigour while I pottered around that strange hotel room, wondering what would await in the honesty bar.

Ten

·

'OK ladies and gentlemen,' said Tony, calling proceedings together. His lips were carefully pursed in what he presumably thought was strained sympathy but actually resembled a hopelessly misplaced pout. I was to his left and to his right were the parents, who were thankfully looking only at the table, their hands linked and resting upon a small mess of photos of the black girl.

A few minutes earlier, when we were setting up, Tony had selected one of these photos and propped it up in front of him using a coffee mug. I had looked at him in astonishment, which he had misread and said (honestly), 'Do you want me to make you one?' while the first of the press shambled around the corner.

He'd been right, however, about the press conference. Only around a dozen turned up and they were low-quality – youthful ambition in garish suits or dejected, ruddy-faced boozers sent here for reasons they hadn't bothered to ask about. There was only one TV crew, from the local station, who had probably seen me as a nice summing-up story, a change in gear to the utterly irrelevant.

I almost enjoyed the moment when, collectively, they realised they had stumbled into one of the more significant days their careers would bear, as damning as that was for both me and them. They straightened in their polyester when Tony went through the tragic details. Their hands raced across the papers while the parents bubbled and groaned. A few darted hunchbacked to the table and slid Dictaphones beside Tony's photo of the black girl. Others produced their mobile phones and held them ready for calls to push this story forward through the pages.

Tony seemed to be enjoying himself. I realised with incredulity that he was viewing their interest as justification of his plan for the black girl and me. They're interested because she's *dead*, I would like to have told him. Still, he put in a decent job, reading from notes he'd clearly spent the previous half an hour preparing. He walked a nice line on the mental health situation, veiling it to not provoke a reaction from the parents. They were pretty much gone though, lost in their shared freefall from immediate life, and Tony had slipped in at the beginning that they *of course* would not be speaking at all.

When he ended his opening – with some useful stuff about 'the whole team hurting and working hard to get Nick through this' – he eyed the unthreatening ensemble in decision.

'We'll take a few questions,' said Tony, which didn't worry me much. At first, this was proved correct with the only requests for my remembrance of the departed. 'She just…loved life,' I said with a doleful shrug and a squint along at the parents, who nodded back in heartbreaking harmony.

On the subject of what might have made my new-found love slash herself from the world, though they phrased it a touch softer, I was magnificent.

'She was a very intense girl. I wonder…' and this time I gave the parents a peek that was meant for all, 'if maybe life just became too much. I wish, I only wish that we had noticed…' and I lifted a hand to harbour my eyes, provoking Tony to mutter acquiescence and drop a heavy palm on my shoulder.

'Could you tell me please Nick, when did you last speak to her?'

My hand stiffened against my forehead, the fingers flattening in surprise at this move past the mundane. I waited for Tony. Nothing. I opened my face and looked for the enquirer. There had been something in the voice, a glint of recognition, but I was still perplexed when I saw her.

It was the journalist from the previous day, who I thought I had resolutely despatched from the bar with the warming story of my favourite uncle's wake. I saw again the name scrawled on her notes in the bar, leaving me to move on to the anecdote and the rushed finish. *Joe Yakari*. But if it hadn't been aired when she'd had the chance, then I knew she didn't know, couldn't know, what it really meant and what it could really mean.

'Oh, hello again,' I started, and she grinned gratefully at the familiarity, as I suspected she might. 'Two nights ago, that's when we last spoke, we'd been out for a drink. It was the night the papers had, well, caught us.' I smiled sadly.

'You didn't call her yesterday?' There was some apology, at least, in her voice when she persisted.

'No.'

'She was your new girlfriend, she was staying in the same hotel and you didn't call her?'

She was at the rear of the room, craning over the shoulder of an ancient hack who sat slack-jawed in non-wonder. He had no interest in turning and looking, despite her stretching pursuit. I wasn't disturbed by her initiative. Being here, asking these questions, it was a genuine highlight for this woman.

'I had a show to prepare for which she didn't show up to. I have to say, and, of course, this was really tragic because by then she must have…well, she must have done what she did. But I was a little annoyed she hadn't turned up for the show. I hate to say it but… so that's why I didn't call her after.'

She watched me answer. There was something unhinged about her manner, very definitely obvious enough, I noted gladly, for it to be seen by the others.

'Will tonight's show be cancelled?'

When I thought a limit had been reached she presented that. It held a level of risk because I hadn't seen its pending arrival like I had with the others. Finally Tony entered proceedings.

'Em, no, we're going to go ahead with tonight's show. The whole team are keen that it should, that it should…'

'Be a tribute,' I added, taking reluctant charge.

'A tribute?'

She was fidgeting with a pen over the shoulder of the man, who wasn't even taking notes, just sitting there and getting through the afternoon. Why not him, why could it not be him that I was speaking to?

'So what's happening to the money?'

We could have cancelled the show and we should have cancelled the show. We should have at least considered cancelling the show. But we hadn't. Tony hadn't thought of that and, frankly, neither had I. And, now that we all thought of it together (and I knew that this was happening because Tony was pointlessly shuffling his notes and I could sense the parents' faces mooning in my direction), it was too late and I was just going to have to do what I could.

'The money raised this evening will be going to a charity working with young people with regards to...to suicide and how, well, to combat it.' I could see her brace for a follow-up so I offered a scattergun of addition. 'To various charities, we're going to discuss it together.' I waved a hand at the parents and was momentarily annoyed by the thought that Tony probably thought I was waving at him. 'But the money from the performance will be going to appropriate organisations.'

'After costs,' said Tony, in reflex.

I stared ahead, my face twitching with fury. At least he hadn't said...

'The show must go on.'

He had. His ineptitude pulsed an electric anger through me. I couldn't look at him through fear of my response but, while my winded breathing steadied, I saw that the room's mood had grown transient. People were packing things away, reaching arms behind them for jackets. Only that one, that one woman, was still alert and staring with a constancy that shook me a little.

The Asian porter had arrived, plucking mugs and glasses in a welcome encouragement for the others to depart. Soon the journalist was the only person not moving. I watched her inactivity with maturing mistrust until she raised herself and walked unsteadily away to bother the porter with something. Such was her obvious disarray that he had to lead her from the room and I was pleased watching them leave, her pestering him with her banality and he moving with a professional patience that belied his young age and low role in all of this.

This is my first memory. I was sitting on a bar, perched with my short back caught between two beer taps and my feet out in front of me. My right hand was resting on top of a yellow plastic dog that held charity money for the blind and in my left hand I had a lolly. The room was loud and there were huge windows flushed with banished light. To my left, lined up along the bar, there were men.

They were spaced out along the wood, joined to glasses that rose up and down to their big faces, and they all looked straight ahead and over the bar. What they were looking at, what they were attending to, is at the edge of both the image that I hold and the memory itself. It seemed to me then that the men were entranced by a pair of waving arms. What was really holding them, as he always held them, was my father. I watched the arms and the men and those mammoth windows, before two hands came to cage me and I felt a mouth at my ear.

'Here, Nicky,' said my mother, with her hot breath of gin and smoke. 'My Nicky.'

I wonder sometimes if she said those words, if I've added them on as I go back to the memory. But I don't think I did. If I were to add on anything it would be what happened next. My mother's hands caught and stopped on my chest. The fingers ran over the bump and then jammed themselves under it, which only added to the tightness and made me squeal.

There was one last stab for my infant chest when my mother's fingers pulled the string free and then my chest nervously expanded, bruised and twitchy from the containment. Mum yelled and when I looked to my left all the men's faces were looking back at me and the only voices were the inflated attacks of my parents. I think that's what happened, I think that's my first memory – Dad tying me to a beer pump in the bar in Pimlico.

That pub was the Big Apple. It had been the Marquis of Granby until the brewery's area man had returned from a holiday to Las Vegas with a new love of themes and tricks that was to torture my father and unsettle pockets of central London from that moment on. They were ahead of the game with the theme pub scheme, and not in a good way, but Dad knew how to run a bar and leave enough in the till for the brewery and so he was selected to launch the area man's themed whims.

There were a few years in the Big Apple. I can gather together a handful of bits and pieces. My hands pushed round my mother's neck, tucked in so just one eye was left to face the men and the noise, while she swung a glass to the optic and shot some minor piece of defaming over for my father to ignore. Me through in the cellar, half in the bins to collect the bottle tops before hours of sorting them into meaningless piles.

Then came the move to Marylebone, where Dad was given the task of turning a struggling pub near the High Street into Jock's Lodge, a Saltire-heavy Scottish bar with plastic bagpipes nailed above the bar and looping tape recordings of Scottish comedians playing in the toilets.

A guy called Mervyn kept the place grimly existing while Dad patrolled a five-yard stretch of the bar and told stories in a tartan waistcoat. Mum opened the place up in the morning, turned out rounds of sandwiches, and then worked sadly through the orders and receipts at night.

I started school at a depressed building two corners away. It was a threatening and threatened place, hemmed in by high walls and barbed wire as if the residents of the looming, expensive Marylebone homes would choose to break into a school where the books came in incomplete renditions and the kids wore trousers that wrapped their shoes or halted halfway down the shin.

At the school I was nothing more than an interested observer while the wrecked teachers daftly tried to reason with the very worst of the rabble. I did what I had to do and then ran back to

Jock's Lodge. In the evenings I sold Mum's sandwiches to the men who would slap my back or rub my head and slip pound notes into my hand. Then I would sit at the stool at the end of the bar and listen to my Dad and the men swearing to each other.

Mum would come and find me at some point and direct me upstairs where she'd have me tell her tales from school while she washed her hair. I'd describe my friends and our daily scrapes with the school's headmistress and she would encourage along the lies with laughing and well-meaning reproaches before sending me to bed.

When I was eleven years old, I started drinking cider and learning magic. The two came together through a man called Jimmy Wood, a well-dressed Scottish guy who threw fivers about, in patriotic fervour, at Jock's Lodge. This caught Dad's attention and he embarked on what would be an enduring attempt to empty Jimmy's financial reserves.

When Jimmy bought a round, Dad manoeuvred Mervyn out the way and dithered at the till with his fingers dancing indiscriminately over the buttons. One time Jimmy turned up in a kilt having been at a dinner and announced drinks for everyone in the bar. I remember Dad's wolfish smile when he spun for the till and Mervyn watching, his head diverted in discomfort while Dad tapped away at an exaggerated total. Meanwhile, a forgotten barmaid assembled a flotilla of drinks on the bar and handed them out to hands that appeared from every angle.

I was in the crowd, fondling the thick plait of Jimmy's kilt in boyhood wonder when a drink was hung in the space above me. I took it without great debate and went and sat on a stool where no one seemed to mind me drinking my first cider in big, disbelieving gulps.

From there on in, I stayed close to Jimmy Wood. It got to the stage when he would add a half of cider to his order and the two of us would naturally evacuate to a table. Dad didn't mind about the cider because he charged for a pint, telling Jimmy the brewery wouldn't let him do halves of cider, which was a lie so weak I sometimes saw Jimmy smile. Mum didn't know about the cider. I'd push it across to Jimmy if I saw her legs on the stairs and had a Softmint ever ready before slinking up for our nightly discussion.

The magic came soon after the cider, when Jimmy enquired at our table in Jock's Lodge if I wanted to see a trick. He pushed a palm out flat and asked me if there was anything there. I shook my head and sipped at my cider. Jimmy brandished a coin with the other hand and placed it gently on to the open palm. When he withdrew his hand grandly, there the coin remained – straight-backed, defiant and somehow perching on its slender edge.

I enjoyed the trick but I was a child and half-drunk and magic was a stage of discovery, like the cider and the porn badly stashed in the cellar. It wasn't the trick that was the revelation, it was what happened after.

Jimmy snatched away the coin and asked me if there was anything in the palm. Again I said no and again Jimmy asked me. I looked at the palm. I pushed my eyes together and through the restrictions of the cider and the pub's smoke I saw it. Gripped tight between Jimmy's fingers, so thin it failed to catch the light and slipped to and from my vision, was the pin that had supported the coin and leant it such inescapable powers. I looked at the pin, at Jimmy's colluding smile, and the sheer beauty of the dishonesty hit me hard.

It didn't take me long to bring The Balancing Coin under my control and from there Jimmy introduced others for me to dissect and perfect. The Vanishing Coin, The Unbreakable Match, The Hypnotised Handkerchief, The Disappearing Knot. Hours were spent in my little room above Jock's Lodge, sitting on my bed and watching myself in the cracked mirror that advertised whisky.

It was a time of energy and enterprise. Some of the older hooligans at the school had gathered my enviable status as a landlord's son and I had begun punting bottles of lager in the suffocating playground. This lucrative sideline ran for an obliging stretch, with the teachers unable to differentiate between my clients' half-drunk outbursts and their usual delinquency. I was eventually nabbed with a bag full of beer and twenty quid in coins weighing down my frayed trousers and the school decided swiftly against my continuing attendance.

I put the letter in the bin on my way home, but they'd phoned the pub where Mervyn pretended to be Dad to protect me. He took me into the cellar where he told me that I had to tell my mum I'd been expelled but it was up to me the reason I gave her. Then he shook my hand and wished me luck and I felt like an adult but I didn't want to be so I ran upstairs and sobbed and told my mum that I had done what I had done but that my motivation had been bullying and its accompanying fear.

She threw me about a bit but her heart wasn't in it because, by this point, her heart wasn't really in anything. I didn't know it but Dad had been shagging like a man possessed. He'd been prowling Jock's Lodge like some medieval rapist, his cock slung sword-like while he hunted out opportunities amongst the shattered pieces of femininity that came stumbling in. At best, he was joining fat saleswomen in the backs of their company saloons. At worst, he was surprising the pub's sullen agency cleaners with his old boy poking mischievously through his opened trousers.

Each adventure would be passed straight out to the regulars in hushed renditions but louder actions. Now, I can see what Dad was doing when I watched him tell stories that involved him holding an imaginary ball while his weighty hips jerked, then rolling his eyes bashfully so the men could chortle with the right amount of respect.

I presume there was some sort of incident but all I know is that one morning I woke up with Mum standing at my door wearing a jacket that I had never seen her wearing before. She told me she was going to stay with a friend and then she walked over, kissed me on the head and said, 'I love you Nicky,' and left. I cried a little bit, then got up and dressed and went downstairs. Mervyn was opening the bar and I asked what I should do now that my mum had gone and he, I think, pretended he thought I meant what should I do in the bar and suggested I wiped the tables. No one said anything about school and so I didn't either. I helped in the bar in the mornings and in the afternoons I fell in with going along with Dad to the bookie's.

It was only now, as my days became barren and accommodating, that I learnt about this other member of his bustling list of inadequacies. I liked watching the men's faces contorting with extremism and I liked watching the horses and dogs loping aloofly round their routes. More than anything, I liked watching my dad. Specifically, I liked watching my dad because he was a terrible fucking gambler and that made me happy because he had made Mum leave.

The afternoon sessions in the bookie's became windows of joy. I slunk into a corner and watched Dad proceed from joking with the kindly women behind the counter (who turned a blind eye to my silent presence, which I thought was charity but may have been recognition of Dad's relentless misfortune) to descending into a twitching mass of persecution when the screens relayed back the true horror of his decision-making. He was prodigiously, gloriously, awesomely unlucky.

Oh, there were some good moments. The time, as an opener, when Dad had plumped heavily for a dog that streaked for home from the last bend. Only one of the inferior competitors had stuck anywhere near the leader, and it was wallowing in the wake of Dad's flying selection. Dad's arms were up in happiness. His face was bright and forgiving, with an alien edge of innocence.

'That's it, that's it.'

The dog flew for home with its legs slicing in a blur. Yards, just yards from the line, the dog's trip happened so fast and with so much speed behind it that it was sent into orbit. The cameraman had pulled in for the finish and for a moment there was nothing in the screen but the track and the line.

The two dogs re-entered the camera's range together. From above came my father's dog, landing as if from outer space, splaying itself on the dirt with a sickening crash of disjointed legs and crooked body. From the left of the screen, the other dog jogged apologetically to victory past its broken colleague.

The bookies offered a mixed response. The women behind the counter howled in alliance with the crippled faller, while from the men came laughter or escaping anger. Amongst the inferno, my dad looked smaller than usual. He wet his lips and muttered,

'You cunt, you cunt, you cunt,' with his tongue slipping around his mouth's borders like a snake.

There are many more of these. One afternoon, late in the day when the gamblers were growing sparse and time and money steadily left them, Dad approached me and my anonymous, plastic bottle of cider. He told me to stay *right fucking there* and walked uncomfortably out the door. He did this sometimes, when things were going particularly poorly. I sat and drank my cider and pictured him – deranged as he half-ran back to Jock's Lodge and made for the till.

When he reappeared, he walked directly to the counter and pressed himself against it so that the shop's inhabitants, if they had been trying and only I was, couldn't see what he was pushing across the plastic top. What I could see was the woman's face when she said 'Are you sure?' to my Dad who snarled something in response and went and stood near the door.

It was the horses that he'd laid the pub's money on. A sunny day on the flat and I appreciated the silks of the jockeys trapped in the gates. The cages flew open and the horses were flung out on to the green. It was a dash and soon a stilled jockey led his horse up the rail and free of the crowd. He had hardly moved in the saddle, just steered this superior machine away from the others who were a busy mass of whipping and cajoling behind the serene pace-setter.

Dad began to edge back into the shop's crowd. He wiped his face and the women behind the counter were watching the race, then Dad, then back to the race. From him and from them I knew that this was his horse.

Again, it was near the end that it happened. The horse was against the rail, which was a procession of tightly pulled white bars, held together with regular posts. Maybe it was the heat, maybe it was the decaying march of time, but something failed within this arrangement while Dad's horse travelled with divine belief to the race's end.

In a skim of movement, one of the fence's bars snapped free of the posting and scissored directly outwards across the track. The horse's instinct sent its head downwards while the jockey's sent his body and arms upwards. The post caught him in the stomach, hauling him clear of the horse that somehow escaped underneath only to be quickly sent to ground by the shock.

The jockey was held, cartoon-like, wrapped around the bar in the air before falling back to earth with the rest of the field arcing round this sudden chaos. The people around me dissected the incident with a similarly diverse reaction. Where Dad had been was a vacancy and the door closed behind his wounded exit. ˙

The thrill of seeing him crucified in the bookie's finished when we ended an only normally damaging outing to find Mum waiting outside with a new face and a new anger that outweighed the surprise of her return.

Back at Jock's Lodge I sat in the bar showing Mervyn the Hypnotised Handkerchief while we and the afternoon drinkers tried to ignore the shouting from upstairs. It hurtled down in crackling volleys – my mother's concentrated assaults of shrieking followed by Dad's violent bubbles of reply.

Finally their conversation withdrew into something that couldn't reach down to us and then my mum's legs were on the stairs and she was leaning over with a smile.

'Nicky. Come on up here love.'

I took a last drink of cider, handed my plastic bottle to Mervyn who sighed when the smell reached him, and then walked a little unsteadily up the stairs. The shock was that it was my dad's face that was wet and confused when I got to the kitchen, while Mum whipped round the room, pouring mugs of tea and speaking in a clip.

'I'm moving back in today Nicky, but we're going to look at getting you to a new school. A good school, but not around here.'

'Why not? Why not here?' I asked dully. I was pretty drunk.

'Because, Nicky, your father has been taking you to the bookie's instead of taking you to school. Your father did that, Nicky, because he is a fucking degenerate.'

I looked at Dad, who sat there watching my mum with an infant's helplessness. When she handed him a mug, his face folded with appreciation and he placed it on the table with unbearable tenderness, as if the awful respite of the scene would be ended if he were to spill just a drop of his tea.

It was Jimmy Wood that came through for Dad, and for me also. Seemingly, the day after my mum's return, Jimmy heard Dad detailing this latest disaster to a couple of sympathisers at the bar and declared that he would have me a school by that time the next day. Sure enough, the following afternoon Jimmy gathered my father and myself together and handed me a brochure. I looked at a photo of the biggest building I had ever seen, framed by ordered trees before it and wild mountains climbing behind.

'You're going to Scotland,' said Jimmy to me.

'About time one of us went,' quipped Dad, standing straining against his tartan waistcoat.

Jimmy, it emerged, was a loose part of some Scottish gentry. That explained the suits, the flexible working days and my scholarship to a boarding school in the Scottish Highlands called Glendoll College.

I didn't want to go, because I realised that people expected me not to want to go. Jimmy gave pep talks about glorious days spent jogging over mountains or debating in what he called a great hall. Mum told me that this was perfect, that I had to leave and it was the only way. She told me that this was the deal she had struck with Dad – that she would come back if I could go.

'Better you than me, Nicky,' she whispered one night in the dark of my bedroom.

Even Dad spoke to me about it, surprising me in the cellar when I was staring transfixed at a Reader's Wife in one of the porn magazines. He took the magazine from me calmly and was leaving the room when he paused and turned back.

'Ready for Scotland?' He raised an eyebrow, smiling at me in a way that I was pretty sure wasn't nice.

'Suppose,' I said back.

'Good. You're going up tomorrow, your mum's taking you,' and then he was off, back to the bar and the men that waited for him there.

Mum and I caught the Great North Eastern train from King's Cross up to Edinburgh. I had a new bag of new clothes and a hundred pounds. Mervyn had asked me if I knew the number of the pub to phone and I said I wasn't sure if I was going to be able to afford it and he had gone a little red and walked straight to the till and returned with the hundred pounds.

When we got to Edinburgh Mum gave me another fifty pounds and I didn't tell her about the hundred that Mervyn had already given me. We stood in the cold while she cried and said she was sorry she couldn't come with me the rest of the way but she had to get the train back to London. I travelled on to Perth where an old man picked me up in a minibus that said:

GLENDOLL COLLEGE

on the side. We spent a long time driving and talking about the college and the rugby team and jogging over mountains and how he'd never been to London but he had a brother who lived in Kent and sold insurance. We were getting ever higher and the roads became smaller and wrapped around hills. The van moved so slowly at points that I could have jumped out and run faster, before the road started dropping and we coasted into a valley that was headed by the building from Jimmy Wood's brochure.

It sat in grounds full of manicured grass and uniformed boys walking or running in pairs and upwards. I saw a row of what I guessed were rugby pitches and then we were pulling up and I was climbing out of the van, at the age of thirteen, wondering if there was anywhere within Glendoll College where I could get hold of some cider and porn magazines.

I was saved by the magic, which was lucky because I had fuck all else. The boys at that place were like nothing I had ever seen before, except perhaps in aged touches within Jimmy Wood. I realised quickly, as I was enveloped into that class and watched those boys glide through their lives, that Jimmy had not been the victim in my dad's scamming. *Jimmy knows*, that's what I thought.

They ruled their pockets of the world with an unspoken certainty. Some of them said they were from London but when they talked about London – where they lived, where they went, what they did, what they had – it was a different city to the one I knew.

For the first few weeks both I and everyone else were too confused by my unheralded arrival to properly react. I was given a uniform and books and a bunk in the dormitory. Lessons were spent trying to avoid the eyes of the teachers and the other pupils and afternoons meant standing, shivering, on the rugby pitches. I would run about half-heartedly and at least a couple of times a day I'd be flattened by some rocketing piece of moneyed muscle.

It was in the changing rooms after rugby that they finally came for me, circling and trying various avenues to my degradation. I pushed my hands into my pockets and watched them with an equal curiosity.

'What are you *doing* here?' one of them asked, with his smooth face twisted in unaffected disdain.

'I don't know,' I told them and they fell about, mimicking my accent in waves of derision. When they stopped I pulled out my hands. The left one I showed them as a flat palm, in the second I showed them the coin.

'Do you see anything,' I asked in a clear voice, 'in my hand.'

I'd found my niche, my gimmick. I became The Magician. They even took a cover story that my dad was a professional and, if I was to let slip the mystery behind the wonder summoned from coins, matches and handkerchiefs, then he would be mercilessly ejected from the Magic Circle.

After that, Glendoll became a satisfactory refuge. I got through the lessons, took up a willing role as unused substitute with the rugby (and, when Spring came, cricket scorer) and survived. I stopped thinking about cider and used evenings to run through my tricks or tell expanded tales about life with my gifted father.

When the school year ended, I spent the van journey back to Perth with spreading unease. My occasional phone calls to Jock's Lodge had been worrying. Mum had been drunk or depressed and had done little to hide either. Dad had answered once and shouted 'It's Nicky' then I heard the phone hit the bar. I thought Mum would then pick it up but it wasn't her that Dad had passed me on to. It was Mervyn.

At Edinburgh station I tried to buy some cider. The man took one look at me, still wearing my Glendoll uniform, and told me I had ten seconds to leave the shop, so it was a long journey down to King's Cross, staring at the North Sea and wondering what waited at Jock's Lodge.

I walked into the pub to see Dad sternly pouring a pint of lager and Mum swooping round the bar calling my name with arms widening. It was as good a welcome as I could have hoped for and that wasn't all. Both Mum and Dad were wearing Stetson hats. I hadn't looked at the signage when I entered but if I had I would have seen that the bar was now called the OK Corral. There was a plastic buffalo head above the door to the toilets and unconvincing lassoes nailed aggressively to the walls.

The lightness of the atmosphere should have made me realise that something was wrong and hidden from view. Mum was full of gin by lunchtime but she would linger behind the bar more than ever before, chatting and laughing with the loyalists. One time I watched, dumbfounded, Mum putting a hand on Dad's shoulder and him being kind enough not to react.

Mervyn slipped me fivers when I needed them, Jimmy Wood drained me for stories from Glendoll and Dad, transparently concerned I might be gay, asked me suspiciously how we all managed without there being any girls there. That night I went upstairs to find he'd left a porn magazine on my bed, opened at a Teens section.

It was when my Glendoll return was closing in that some

clarity arrived. Mum's comparative calmness was due to the fact that Dad had all but abandoned his traditional rifling of the till. Instead, though she didn't know this bit, he had been regularly pulling off insurance jobs.

A wealth of kitchen appliances would be bought on hire purchase, carted straight to a nearby lock-up, pronounced stolen, and then sold for half their value. Brewery deliveries were transported to friendly pubs the minute they arrived, then Dad would arrive back from a convenient appointment and deliver mystified phone calls to the police, then the brewery.

He'd even faked a burglary and pawned half the stuff from our flat, which shows his recklessness. Mum had sat down one night to watch *Coronation Street* and found that the TV was missing. When she went downstairs to confront Dad, the lock on the back door had been burst as part of his well-worked cover.

There was another showdown, another scene in the kitchen, but this time it was a repeat and as such did not have the hope of the new. I got the train to Edinburgh alone and with little confidence in how matters would progress in my absence. With a jacket over my uniform, I managed to get served two plastic bottles of cider for the onwards journey to Perth. By the time I got there I was roaring drunk and alerted the old man in the minibus to my presence by beating at the window. He drove north in sufferance, offering a touching attempt to protect.

'They'll kill you for this son,' he said. 'Let's stop, get you some water.'

'Fuck you,' I giggled and pinged his ear with my fingers.

I fell asleep and woke in the car park at Glendoll with a lot of noise and some hands on me. I was taken to the toilets where cold water was splashed in my face and I was successfully encouraged to vomit into the freezing bowl. Then it was up to an office area that I hadn't seen before and the rector put his head round a door and beckoned me in.

I recognised him from assembly and his continuing attempts to directly connect the inner workings of Glendoll to the troubles of Jesus Christ. I entered as if in a dream and fell into a leather chair. The office was wooden and enjoyable, with the sun slotting through the window. He was a nice man, I could see by the lines that smiling had struck on to his face. I felt very warm, very kind and I knew he did too. He had a big photocopier beside his desk that hummed while we shot the breeze.

'You know why you're here?'

'Because I'm pissed,' I laughed, and was a little hurt when he didn't join in. He pulled out a file and I recognised bits of it upside down. It was the boys in my year, listed with basic personal information. Very occasionally there would be a dash of biro under the type.

'When boys,' said the rector, 'do things such as you have done, I take a pen and make a mark under their names.' He sighed with displeasure and pushed the ink across the page. I was struggling to keep my eyes open.

'This pen does not get used twice.' He wasn't scary, not that I was in the mood to be scared, and I felt guilty because of that.

'I'm sorry,' I said, 'I was worried about my mum and...'

'Go to bed,' he said softly. 'Just go to bed.'

Under normal circumstances, my spectacular re-entry into Glendoll would surely have hiked my standing amongst the other boys. But unfortunately any benefit was outweighed, and then some, by another development.

One of those golden skinned high-breeds had got hold of a basic magic book during the summer months. Within it were brisk, illustrated breakdowns of my entire repertoire. Nicky The Magician was finished, shown up as a charlatan and left an object of savage ridicule.

Over time, the contempt became physical and I was cornered regularly for a decent going-over in the long months before Christmas. That short holiday gave me a fortnight of retreat to the OK Corral where I drank cider and Mum and Dad didn't exchange a word, functioning in spiteful independence while I watched in surrender. The day before I was due to return to

Glendoll, drunk and hoping for a fractional lessening of the fear, I told Mervyn about the bullying.

'You've got to hit them back, Nicky,' he said, 'because you don't want to be staying here, believe me.'

On Mervyn's trusted advice, I sought out the most determined of my tormentors on my first day back at Glendoll. I struck him with everything I had, going for his eye, but I think I caught his forehead. It was fucking sore anyway. I remember looking at my wounded hand, then back up just in time to see the bodies engulf me once again.

There were further months of punches and kicks and the indescribable pain of hair being ripped from my head before the revelation, and answer, came sheepishly sliding into view. That was my reaction, weeping and bloody in my bunk when the vision came to me. About time, I thought bitterly, about time too.

It changed Glendoll and it changed my life. It was late at night and my back ached from a deliberate studding on the rugby pitch. Seeking refuge, I was casting my mind back to the glory days of the magic's power for protection when I alighted on it – a piece of audacity that could project me back into that respected and sheltered status.

I crawled from the covers and skulked in my pyjamas up stairs and down panelled passages until I reached the rector's office. I closed the door and fired up the enormous photocopier. It didn't take me long to find the file and I crammed it face down under the copier's plastic hood. When I was done I slid the warm pages inside my pyjamas, turned off the machine and replaced the file, then ran barefoot back to my bunk.

Eleven

The great thing about that hotel was the corridors. On occasion, their lack of predictability could exasperate, but it could also help. When we left the press conference at the honesty bar as a wilted and naturally divorcing group, the corridors let me proffer the parents snatched, terrifying hugs before selling Tony a dummy and stealing twenty yards down an anonymous passage.

'I'll pick you up in an hour Nicky, for the run-through,' he shouted after me, with the compromising of my name and some jargon I deduced as an incredible attempt to impress the black girl's parents.

In my room I ran a bath and sank within the water. Any danger that existed, danger directly heading for me, was hard to gauge. I couldn't see many likely ways in which the press conference could backfire, and plenty in which it could help. The most significant peril had been the journalist who shouldn't have been there, but it was only the unexpected touch of her return that had really served to unsettle.

The parents, whose arrival had initially appeared apocalyptic, were helplessly crippled and presumably close to returning to some hometown grieving. Detective Brewster I doubted I would see again and, even if I did, his motivation would be a further attempt to gain details of my finances and wondrous existence for gossipy use in the police canteen.

Tony's performance at the press conference may have been comfortably abominable, but it looked likely to give us the time and control to leave that city to deal with matters in our absence. We should, I realised, leave straight from the evening's show and use a vague administrative error to explain an overnight exit.

With some comfort regained, I pushed myself into the pre-show programme. A flash of old professionalism reminded me that Tony's sheet of facts and propositions would be absent that evening, dismissed through the demands of the press conference. I spent my time in the bath, and an hour after on the bed, matching those moves and feints that could run on a lack of original material. This was, as always, the most soothing force of all – ordering and evaluating, lost in my crammed experience while dressing and then walking alone from the hotel to the theatre.

I neared the alley and two elderly women forked towards me, pulling me from my machinations with expressions of affinity and a newspaper. I thought they'd stumbled late on to the original disclosure of my romance with the black girl but no, the local evening rag had managed to tease in a short account of this afternoon's revelations before the presses rolled.

On a page beside a crossword and above a scandal concerning vanishing park benches, a headline too big for its space sighed:

TV MEDIUM 'HEARTBROKEN' OVER FORMER SINGER'S SUICIDE

They must have been racing against the printers because they'd gone very light. There was a brief summary of my faltering career, an even shorter one of the black girl's (which looked much less successful than Tony had suggested), a quote from Tony this afternoon, my own gracious acknowledgement of the deceased's *love of life*, and a welcome confirmation from the local police that there did not appear to be anything suspicious in the death.

The paper had bought an old file photo of me that I remembered well. It was part of the promotional shoot for my second TV series, back in that window when I was invincible. I remembered that pair of sharks from the TV channel running about after me that day like schoolkids. A month later, they'd be sitting in a restaurant telling Tony and me over champagne that the show was being pulled. Because of Java Joe.

I handed the paper back to one of the women and noticed with surprise that she was crying.

'Not too bad,' I said, without much thought, as if to perk her up.

'Here, now,' said the one who was managing to hold herself together, and fondled my shoulder with a warped hand. 'There's a reason for these things, Mr Santini, a reason.'

I edged round them and tapped both awkwardly on the shoulder. 'Enjoy the show,' I answered uselessly and made for the lip of the alley. 'He's a hero,' said one to the other, which the latter trumped with a shrieked, 'Stay strong Nick, stay strong for us.'

In the dressing room a member of Tony's team that I hadn't seen before was waiting for me, her face readied and hoping for guidance towards her demeanour. I was polite and relatively talkative to block any sympathy or, worse, any questions that the extended staff would have been mulling over. As soon as she had slipped into what passed as business-like within our strange little network, I realised that the black girl's death would rapidly be nothing but a story for bars amongst that group of fiver-an-hour mercenaries.

We were getting along fine when Tony came crashing through the door. He was wasted with ambiguous worry and I even considered a conciliatory gesture, perhaps an assurance that I wasn't expecting a crib sheet, but instead he addressed the new girl and asked her to 'give us a few minutes.' She fired me a grossly inappropriate smirk while sidling out and I was still pondering the welcome ramifications of this when Tony drifted into his panic.

It was some way to justified in this situation, though it was me that the panic should have belonged to. Tony had arrived late at the theatre (because he had gone to my room to pick me up and, although he didn't say this, had probably spent at least ten minutes knocking and cajoling at the empty door, which would have delighted me under standard circumstances) and so had only just happened across the list of complimentary ticket holders.

The list and the unforeseen names that it held had sent him scampering through to find me. The black girl's parents, Brewster and the journalist from the restaurant. All of them. All had independently slipped into the theatre and offered acceptable reckoning to whatever halfwit Tony had on the comps desk to gift them free briefs, and send Tony and I plummeting back into the day's troubles.

'I can understand the parents,' I said in wonder, 'we couldn't exactly turn them away, but Brewster, and that fucking journalist?'

'A police badge and a press pass,' shrugged Tony. He was perched on the table, his arms forming an oval frame around his gut as he hung his head. 'I don't know,' he started with little desire, 'if it's a bad thing?'

'You know it is.'

I reached for the box and handed it to him, turning away before he fastened it to me.

'It's a distraction, a fucking distraction. Her *parents*? It's sick, and then the copper. He didn't even know who I was and now he's a fan? Give me a break, what's he fucking up to? And what's the journalist hanging about for, can't you call her editor? The *Soho Star*, unbelievable.'

'I will, first thing.'

He finished his fastening and waited.

'Tony.' He looked up hopefully. 'Get this fucking sorted out. I'm serious.'

'I will, Nick,' he said in a shrunken whine and I felt a little regret that came maybe once a month. That wasn't bad going, seeing as I ripped the guy apart a few times a day. But then, a few times more than that each day, we would laugh and briefly mean it. We were somehow caught together and it was because I was the only one unhappy with this, because of Tony's steady stealing, that the problems came. Me and Tony, Tony and me.

'OK, now fuck off,' and I didn't have to force the smile.

'OK, Nick.' He grinned and was so grateful walking past that he twisted to the side so as not to touch me, to reignite me.

When Tony left the pressure rushed back. I hadn't felt it in this depth for so long that the experience was foreign and stirring. By that point, I had become a touring shadow of past invention, churning out greatest hits and nicked jokes. But now, that night at the theatre two days after the meeting with the journalist, I was momentarily reborn.

It was a pull back to those early months with Tony after he pitched up in Soviet Street, when I had been thrown into talent evenings that were kaleidoscopes of detritus and the bottomless bitterness of working men's clubs.

I was taking to a stage shorn of defence – no notes, no secret facts – and the audience had returned to hosting fear rather than the effortless backdrop they had long become. I let the knocks at the door come and go. I knew Tony wouldn't risk a return and so it was one of his team, a ludicrously ugly Kiwi who eventually eased the door open and advised, laboriously,

'Uh, I think, I don't know if, it's probably time?'

Past him and up the passage, people's faces switched to relief as they saw me. I marched to the last approach and there was Tony, talking to another man and then breaking free and starting to clap. A young guy ran for a microphone, caught unaware by my force but I kept going, suddenly arriving on the stage for the lighting crew to hurriedly flick off the wall lamps and on with the headlining pool that I entered with arms upraised.

Twelve

I started fast, on a plump woman in the second row. She was a horror case, sailing into middle age with prospects escaping in the opposite direction. I had alighted on her while she lifted a tub of drink to her wobbling mouth. Two hands, no ring. But, as I said, years slipping away and weight slipping on, and women like that (I'm talking as a student of human behaviour, I don't have room to be malicious) are utter fucking fantasists.

And so I knew that when I said to her, after getting her name at about the eighth attempt and disguising it as bad acoustics…

'Deborah, I do believe that you might have met someone special recently?'

…that she would do what she did, which was blush and turn to her mortified companions and then back to me and cover her bad face with embarrassment.

If I was forced to speculate, I would say that in the case of these women the unfortunate men that they will then hesitantly describe would not be directly aware that the woman exists. To them she will be a friend of a friend, or unremarkable office fixture, that they somehow got harpooned into an uncomfortable moment's conversation with. But for women such as this, these are the scraps of hope on which they gorge. And so there will always be a *someone special* to be tempted out.

After knocking her about for a bit I moved to the introduction, talking torturously of the uncertainty in what I did and my abiding need for their *help*. This wasted time and increased the suggestion that the show, for whatever reason, was proving especially taxing and should be covered to a degree for any future failure. However, my deliberations that night were also designed so I could scan the audience for the uninvited freeloaders.

I saw the parents first and they were much as I had imagined they would be – only partially lightened by the shift in situation, their penetrable faces bent towards me. It was a jolt when I saw the journalist, who had somehow centred herself in the front row, but this was welcome. From there she would miss a lot of my misses – those moments between my selection of an audience member and their visual response to my remarks, before the camera and microphone would catch up and give their reactions wider significance.

Brewster I couldn't see at all, which was of little concern. The parents were a known quantity (I had made a good living from the predictability and openness to suggestion of those in grief) but still had the potential to destroy if I somehow granted them the motivation. The journalist was of limited mind but was clearly enjoying her time here and given to flights of fancy, boosting her meagre capabilities.

Brewster, however, I could read unfailingly. He would be up the back with some joke of a wife, talking loudly enough for others to hear of his personal connection to me. 'Did I tell you what he makes, that guy?' he'd be repeating to his wife but watching for the reaction of others. 'Seven hundred grand, he told me this morning.' If they asked how he knew he'd probably say that I was a *mate*.

Ending the interlude, I plunged onwards and through my machinations – the temple-rubbing and the *let them come through* and then the move that sends me up in the air and the crowd up from their seats – and started with a well-proven blockbuster.

'A child, I have a child,' I said and giggled disgracefully with delight to provoke a few joyful additions from the crowd that I immediately deadened with a sudden,

'Oh. Oh *no*,' and a wince to show the inherent hurt of what was being granted. I cupped my palms over my ears in a pretty contrived touch. Quite how covering my ears was going to stop noiseless spiritual messages from the Great Beyond is a shaky premise. But these spaces in sense just didn't matter to those people.

'This child,' I continued, 'was a smashing little thing. And, when the time came…'

There were definite murmurs and I hoped that the evening's microphone bearer was aware I still had my eyes shut. It was he alone who should be monitoring these scattered arrivals of possibility.

'That child…' I broke my voice nicely and paused, swallowing spectacularly.

'Keep going Nick!'

Someone squealed, and earned themselves some claps. I freed a hand for a quick wave of (real) appreciation.

'…That child was a fighter.'

I finished and swung my hands away, opening my eyes to see a decent spread of volunteers.

Thirteen

Usually a clutch of volunteers was the target but in this particular process, the dead kid set-up, it could be a mixed blessing. Often I would choose what looked to be the most likely option, a couple already interwoven in support for example, and when I got there I would hear that someone at work had lost a nephew ten years before.

Is that *it* you imbeciles? I'd want to say. I'd abandon them and move to another case that was incomparably stronger but it's hard to transfer the original contact smoothly and so I would usually have to suddenly receive a second, remarkably similar visitor to satisfy the switch. All very untidy, despite most of the problems being secreted in the vagaries of my delivery.

Ideally, in these situations, I would have liked to gather the arm wavers into a huddled conference at the front of the stage to decide which loss would most inflate the audience's sympathy. That would have been a step too far even for the banks of idiocy that filled my shows.

I tried to filter the responses with some more direct observations. I said that the child had been *stolen from us* recently, and that they were close to someone in the audience. Amongst those who remained in the hunt with their hands displayed were what I swiftly decided was my pick, a disturbed pair of women bouncing about near the front.

There was too strong a shade of excitement to suggest that I'd get much decent heartache from them, let alone tears, but within their fervour was the desperation to be a part of this that would quietly overrule any mistrust.

'Madam,' I said, and went to the woman who hadn't lifted her arm. It was always the quieter one, the one who had the fear. 'I have a feeling the child wants to talk to you.' The two fidgeted and hugged and when the microphone got there she grabbed it with unexpected force and demanded, 'Is it baby Kevin? He was my cousin.'

Cousin was unfortunate but, in some ways, this was fine. I'd got the name and could add my little touch of looking exasperated to the crowd and adding,

'I was about to tell *you* that!' to all-round amusement.

I didn't like it when people threw dead babies into the mix. It was pretty inconceivable, even in the absent logic of my operation, for a child that died with an age of days or weeks to suddenly communicate through me in fully formed sentences. Let alone the whimsical, world-weary, cod-psychology that I liked to afford my distant callers. All well and good, you could see the sharper ones think, but from a *baby*? It would leave me having to work fast to remove the disquiet.

I'd worried too early. Presuming and dreading a relatively young death, I took a stab at,

'The child, I am sensing that he passed from us close to his date of birth.'

'His birthday, yes,' she butted in, 'his tenth birthday.'

'I was about to tell you *that* as well!' I doubled up nicely to acceptable laughter.

Revelling in my fortune, I moved abruptly into Kevin's hobbies. He was a cousin of this woman, who looked in her early forties. For his life to have made an impression, though clearly not with the rawness of recency, his death could be placed between five and twenty-five years before.

So when I saw her nod to my comment, which was really a question, that he was a sporty sort, I could follow up with virtual impunity that I could see him playing football, running after the ball and laughing with his friends.

Tony once produced, on my suggestion, some charts from the Internet

on children's hobbies. Over the last twenty-five, in fact the last forty years, football's dominance is incredible.

This got her bothering her eyes, though only with her hands. A hanky or tissue would have picked up better on the screen. I had once told Tony to arm the microphone messenger with a packet of tissues to freely disperse. We had joked about making them neon, or with some sort of flashing quality, or massively oversized like a circus clown's. Then we had gone back to the wine and Tony had never done anything about the original request. That was how it worked.

While the woman cried, she confirmed baby Kevin's great love of football.

Boys like football. Forget the charts because this is more than that – this is association, which is important. Even dead boys that didn't like football said they did to their parents. Even parents who know their dead boy didn't really like football say that he did. That's just what happens. Unless you leave the general swarm entirely, move to tiny social circles such as Glendoll College, then you can't get away from football. And I, apart from Glendoll College, moved well within the general swarm.

'Maybe,' I said, 'it was the football that taught him how to fight so hard?'

She was off and gone – wailing then tunnelling into her friend's waiting arms.

'I have him now,' I was trying to slow the development. I didn't want a collapse but I had to advance. 'And I can see him fighting and battling and never giving up. And I can see him…Love, are you OK with this?'

She broke free from her trusty pal, nodding heroically and preparing for my hinted climax.

'I see him writing a letter, in his bed. It was close to the end, and he wrote a letter didn't he?'

And she signed up with a swirl of enthusiasm, the impression of my knowledge temporarily banishing the histrionics. There were some superb confirmations – 'You're absolutely right, that's amazing,' 'How did you know that? Is he there, is he with you now? Oh, oh *Kevin*,' and so on – that the child had been a fighter and, with open astonishment shared by the crowd, that he had indeed written a letter in bed shortly before he died.

This was a great standard of mine and it couldn't have been more solid. Firstly, who is going to disagree with the assertion that a dead child was not a worthy little character, or that they hadn't shown battling reserves beyond their tender years? As for the letter being produced from a bed – people die in bed. And what's a letter? Two hasty tributes to their parents, a poem to their pals, a heroic cartoon? One way or another, young people write letters in bed before they die.

The letter-writing observation always allowed a glorious exit but I wasn't ready for that yet. The woman's friend was wearing a jacket unzipped maybe four inches. Beyond the jacket was a white T-shirt with the black silhouette of a man's head. The head was in profile and leaning slightly to the left. And that head was mine.

This was a throwback to the first tour I did with the TV recognition. Just my name would bring men and women from their houses, a magical state of progression. It was while in this daze that I caught, for the first time, Tony openly stealing. He had stood behind the stall with the DVDs, books and a humped pile of cheap, thin, T-shirts with a man's silhouette and below it –

NICK SANTINI
'LET THEM COME THROUGH'

Those T-shirts were the first time that I was forced to notice Tony's theft and now this woman was wearing one of those flimsy tenets of trust. She saw me concentrating on her and broke free from her weeping cohort, readying herself for a moment that she must have imagined so many times before.

'Hello there,' I smiled and she cooed some nonsense in response.

'Tell me,' I asked evenly, twisting so the camera would catch my face and beam back to her my conspiratorial bearing, 'about the man with the glasses. What did he do to make you angry?'

I laughed at this, which was a bit reckless as it cut the odds. If a man with glasses had done something truly horrific to her and she chose to tell this roomful of strangers, my laughter would look somewhat misplaced. However, it was, as it always was, about numbers.

Two thirds of the population have deficient sight. A quarter of the population (this is my own statistic, well formed) spend their lives with permanent, fully developed anger, looking for someone or something to project it on to. Put those two together and people in glasses manage to offend a lot of people.

And that's without the woman's unadulterated longing to please, as well as the presentation – 'a man with glasses' – that says so little. She could have seen this man on the TV for all it mattered but it worked out better than that. The two women stared at each other in wonder, screeching unattractively while the audience laughed. I extended the laughter with a comical wince and,

'I wish I hadn't asked!' while we all waited for her confirmation.

'I had a big argument with my boss today,' she said. 'He wears glasses.'

Some morons gasped at this, others clapped and I wheeled away in triumph to the centre of the stage. My eyes slid along the front row and caught a flash of notepad between the journalist's hands.

'Now, ladies and gentlemen. Why don't we see if anyone else will come and help me?'

Mistakes happened at shows, that was really the only certainty, but it was how I reacted to these slips that was important. Mistakes were incorporated, weakened or dismissed so quickly that few would even notice. The words would leave the person's lips and by the time they reached the brains of the rest of the crowd I had hijacked them and sent them onwards as neutered impressions of their reality.

But that night I was on an entirely clear round. These were so exceptional that, even in the terrible state that my stay in that city was causing, I was still enchanted by the rarity. I was floating on a high that was as welcome as it was surprising when I declared that I had someone speaking to me called William. It didn't matter what name I used. What happened would have happened one way or another.

I t took me a week or so. Early in the morning, while the other boys slept, I curled to the side and read. Through the day, at the back of classrooms or sitting on the toilet until my legs numbed, I whispered constant run-throughs until it was all there. Every boy in my year at Glendoll. Sixty-two of the bastards. Middle names, dates of birth, hometowns. Nailed in my head. It was just about waiting for the opportunity, which arrived soon enough.

We came out of Latin to find the Mathematics room locked and that left us bottlenecked in the draughty corridor. Bored, the boys turned to me and one lazily shoved my shoulder and gave me some name or other. I steeled myself against his force and addressed him as effortlessly as I could.

'Stop it, Randolph,' I said loudly and he blushed red. In the silence, a couple of others voiced the question I was waiting for. 'It's his middle name,' I told them. 'I know all your middle names. I've told you before that I'm a magician but you didn't believe me.'

There was a chorus of angry disagreement. I picked out a few of the mob in turn, relating their middle names with a point of the finger and unhurried declaration.

'I know your birthdays too,' I said. 'Just by looking at you. When I look at you,' I paused and they weakened further during the wait, 'your birthdays are written on your head.'

'Bullshit,' said one hero with little conviction. He was from the other end of the alphabet from me, which kept him out of my morning registration class and all but a couple of subjects. Perhaps this distance made him braver, but it helped me more. I studied him, smirked, visibly concentrated on his forehead and reported his birthday to the others. He gave a panicked nod before the Mathematics door opened from within and the bodies parted to let me enter first.

Onwards and upwards I went. I controlled the information carefully, knowing the need for rationing. Luckily, they seemed to equally enjoy more detail on my magical education. I told them about London buses where strangers' birthdates hovered on their foreheads, or their middle names appeared as halos, or their hometowns glowed over their hearts.

I was untouchable. The phone at the OK Corral appeared to have been cut off, but I was comfortable where I was and aware that short-term happiness was all that I had a right to expect. It was all that I was going to get. As summer approached, I was called to the rector's office once more.

'Ah, in you come. Now, Nicholas, I have a telephone number for Jimmy Wood here.' He squinted at a scrap of paper that he slid over the wood. He'd moved his phone to my side. 'I'm just going to nip outside.' He smiled and patted my shoulder as he went past. 'A good man Jimmy Wood, the very best.'

I pressed the phone's buttons. Not Mum. Not dead. Not Mum. Not dead.

'Nicky?'

'Yes, hi, Jimmy.'

'Hello, Nicky, well done on calling. I'm in the box round the corner from the pub. I've got Mervyn here, I'm just going to put him on.'

I sat alone in the rector's office and Mervyn told me that Dad had gone to prison for a year but he should be out in six months. Mum had left, Mervyn was going to run the OK Corral, and Jimmy Wood had arranged for me to stay at Glendoll over the summer.

'The phone'll be back on next week, Nicky, keep in touch,' said Mervyn, 'I can send some money if you want?'

'No, it's OK, thanks Mervyn.'

I hung up. The silence alerted the rector who bounded in with concocted buoyancy.

'I hear you're going to be keeping an eye on the place over the summer, eh?' He laughed uneasily and slapped me on the back. I don't know what Jimmy Wood had told him about my family's latest disaster, but I was fairly confident that it wasn't the truth.

That long summer – when Dad was in jail, Mum was gone and I was marooned at Glendoll – was one of great discovery. The school's baffled administrators assigned me my own room, a spacious set-up that served a teacher during term-time. There was a colour television, a private bathroom and strip windows that looked down on to the grounds. For a few days I enjoyed my fortune in peace – greedily watching my television or wandering liberated around the emptied school – until the other people started arriving.

They were a collection of international oddities. Scout groups, Girl Guides, Scripture Union, Mountaineering Award Schemes, Young Rotaries, and a compilation of foreign students. French, American, German, South African. They turned up in their buses and vans and marched about the grounds while I watched coolly through the windows of my private quarters or from some ostentatious arrangement – lounging under a tree with hands pulled behind my head, or in leisurely study from a corner table in the dining room.

I had my run of the college and turned this quickly to clandestine advantage. I loitered in the offices, charming the elderly secretaries and repeating my pilfering of information. Suitably armed, I infiltrated the visiting groups and casually tossed in my capabilities, which I had now rebranded as Mind Reading.

If they just said a single word (in any language, a nice touch) I could guess the cities that they had come from. If they walked five yards in front of me I could identify their star sign. Soon they would be ringed round me, open-mouthed at the extraordinary boy who held their very lives in his sinister hands.

In this safe and untested world I became confident and bored, leading me to force my approach beyond what I knew. I would use my information to test reactions. They were allowed to glimpse a wrong answer, then be confronted with the truth.

I'd see how their faces, and their bodies, reacted to both and I started to make guesses.

To begin, these were laughably simple. Bloody eyes from a foreign student would be translated as feeling *sad and alone*, that there was someone far away they would *like to see very much*. Grazed knees would mean a kid *liked sport and being outdoors* while I would often look for the member of the group with the cheapest clothes and least belief and say that, for them, the trip had been *a special treat* and they didn't want to *let anyone down*.

I pushed on enthusiastically – foraging through the forms of new arrivals, observing them from afar and then moving in with the certainties and the projections. I was a magnificent and mystical figure and the rewards were plentiful. With some of the girls there was glorious, hot-breathed kissing and all the boys eyed me with generous envy.

When the summer stumbled to an end and the new school year began, I attacked the returning hordes with abandon and toured the college in journeys of enlightenment. I would tell boys to imagine a number between two parameters, then stare at their face while announcing the possibilities. A twitch, a tightening of the eyes, something would let me know and I would give them the answer based on my observation alone.

I devised whole conversations that would generate reams of information without the subject being aware of the transfer. For weeks I practised the discovered art of submitting people to a barrage of useless conversation that disguised a specific instruction.

I was a fifteen-year-old who had found his future, which was lucky because it was at that point that Jimmy Wood died from a heart attack in the toilets of the OK Corral. When the rector told me, my first thought was the hope that no one had stolen Jimmy's wallet. I didn't want him to have left the OK Corral like that, wronged one final time.

His death was sad in itself and I cried with passing honesty, but it also meant my unearned scholarship was to be quietly wound up at Christmas. I waited until that came, and I had been dropped for the final occasion at Perth Station, before risking the call. I was hoping for Mervyn but there was Dad, fresh from early release.

'You coming here?'

It was a question, not a suggestion and certainly not an invitation.

'Yes, if that's OK.'

'Right, well, see you when you get here.'

I found the pub in the unexpected grip of professionalism. The only reason Dad had been allowed back by the brewery was his closeness with the area man and what the brewery saw as his success over the years. This concession was accompanied by suffocating scrutiny. Dad was being audited right down to peanuts and Mervyn was spending most of his time wading bad-temperedly through paperwork.

Suddenly Dad was a proper landlord, with responsibility and a workload, and he detested it. What he hated more was the lack of ready, unaccounted, funds for the bookie's and the various wanton pleasures that lay beyond. He certainly couldn't go back to the insurance jobs, and the events behind his capture were ludicrous. In my first days back at the OK Corral, everyone wanted to tell me the story of what had happened. This is it:

Dad had put through an insurance claim that centred on his assurance that he had bought, presumably on a whim, a second-hand car and various household appliances. He had, he kindly explained to the insurance company, then left the car still loaded with these items in a lane near the OK Corral. The next morning, much to his distress, all had vanished.

Unfortunately, Dad's borderless ambition had got the better of him while he was filling in the form and he had failed to keep a satisfactory tally of the goods he was shovelling on to the car's phantom load. And so it was that the judge at Dad's trial was reported as having turned on his bench to say to my father,

'Tell me, this car you bought, was it by any chance a double-decker bus?'

The drinkers at the bar, and even unknown men who saw me

in the street and recognised my horrible heritage, would pull me over to tell me the story. They would laugh with their red faces and wink with respect and I would stand there and wonder if they realised they were telling me the story that led to my Mum leaving my life. But I'd smile and walk away, usually to get some cider.

Dad had ignored my return until an evening when I was lying in bed and he came through the door carried by anger. He was full of serious drink and one of his undefined furies. I was a handy target.

'How much money have you got?'

'None.'

'Well then how the fuck can we live and...' He pointed downstairs.

'You want me to work in the pub?'

'No, we don't need you. We need other money, not the pub.'

'OK.'

'Well?' he demanded. 'What can you do?'

'There's something I can do,' I said quietly, looking right at him, 'That I think I could make some money doing.'

He felt behind him for the doorframe and observed me with dislike.

'Let me sort it out,' I said, 'and I'll tell you tomorrow.'

Dad murmured something about similarities between Mum and me that wasn't exactly constructive and then left the room.

The next day I spent a while down in the bar, wiping tables and finalising my plan. Dad spoke to Mervyn and watched me suspiciously. I waited until the deepest dip of the afternoon, when Mervyn had gone for a kip on the couch upstairs and the pub held only a couple of glass-eyed women through the back and a minor member of Dad's group of admirers at the bar.

That man was an unthreatening, balding worker who wore a suit and did little but laugh when he felt he should and speak to Mervyn about football. When he went to the toilet, I walked straight over to his jacket and found his wallet. Dad paused briefly while drying a glass, smiling in some ingrained response to crookedness. I looked through the wallet, replaced it and then went round the bar and whispered to Dad.

'OK, this is what I can do for money, Dad.'

When the man returned I let him settle in his stool before addressing him, my young face framed between two beer taps.

'You've got a daughter that lives in Australia but you're not married to your wife any more. You joined the gym as a New Year's resolution but you never really went there. When you leave here you're going to get a bus home. When you get home you're going to order a curry from an Indian restaurant.'

In the man's wallet had been a photo of a young couple and a child in front of what I recognised from Geography at Glendoll College as the Sydney Opera House. I knew they lived there and weren't on holiday because the child was in school uniform. There was an old photo of the man and what must have been his wife getting married. In the photo he was wearing a ring that he wasn't wearing now. There was a gym membership card that was activated two Januaries before and out of date, and a bus pass and a collection of delivery receipts from takeaways. Mostly Indian.

The man's face whitened and he looked from me to Dad. Dad turned to me.

'Yeah,' he said thoughtfully, 'that's pretty good. But you can't just go through people's wallets every time.'

'He went through my wallet?'

'If you set it up right you can. I could do it through there if you get Mervyn to put a board up or something.' I pointed at the back room that had held a pool table until Dad sold it even though it wasn't his to sell. There was an entrance but you could also get to it through the corridor behind the bar.

'Board up the entrance so people have to come round here and go in from the corridor,' said Dad, eyeing the set-up behind him and concluding, 'and they'd feel safe leaving their jackets there.'

'Especially if we made it hot in the room, really hot.'

'Could say the controls were fucked,' said Dad.

'Did he go through my bloody wallet?' The man was only asking out of sensed duty, he wasn't even standing up.

'But people would want to come back again if it went well. You'd have to have more.'

I turned to the man.

'You are having problems with a part of your legs and you're worried about getting sacked.'

'What?' He was lost and looked at Dad, but Dad was looking at me.

'How do you know that?'

'He's in here all the time when he should be at work, because he has a suit on, so he can't work nights. And look at his ankle.'

Dad peered over the bar and saw what I had seen, the trim of bandage showing above one shoe.

'Did that little prick go through my wallet?'

'OK, we'll give it a go,' said Dad. 'You should see a woman I know as well, I think that would help you a bit.'

That's how it ended, the longest conversation that we'd ever had.

The woman that Dad knew was called Rose. She was a gypsy of some strain or other but that was through choice, not birth. Rose worked from her flat, a grotesque high-rise not far from us, and Dad walked me round there while he talked to someone on his mobile phone, a new and glamorous addition that he used loudly and with language that attracted horrified attention from the general public.

When we arrived at Rose's floor Dad didn't end his call, preferring instead to wave at her and remain on the landing when she led me through to her perfumed front room. She was old and pretty grizzly with it and I was wondering how Dad could have known her when she pulled my hand to her and began to talk.

Rose spoke in long streams of detail that were delivered with a power and definition that captivated me. What she was saying was decent – mostly accurate but not hugely compelling coverage of the uncertainty of my future and tumultuous past – but could have easily come from what she knew of Dad.

It was the delivery that was the thing. Dad had seen the way I had needed the beer taps to defend myself when I spoke to the man in the pub. Rose showed me a new, stronger, defence. She reached the end of whatever it was she was doing and looked up, her old face grey and deadening in the murky flat.

'And seeing as you're with him,' she said, and I turned to see Dad bustling impatiently behind me, 'I'll stop there.'

'What would you say if I wasn't with him,' I regained my hand that had shaded pinch marks from her grip.

'I'd say that I sense you may be carrying a slight curse and then I'd ask you for some money and then I'd ask you when you can make it back so I can help you with the curse. And when you came back I'd ask you for more money.' Her eyes crept away in unlikely bashfulness.

On the way home Dad turned to me.

'Ready then?'

'I think so, yes,' I said, looking up and risking a smile. A few paces on, he looked back down.

'Maybe don't try the curse bit in the pub though. They'd fucking kill you.'

Remarkably, we both laughed. Back at the OK Corral, Dad spoke to Mervyn who spent the next day disbelievingly boarding up the main entrance to the back room, trapping a table and two chairs. I nailed a row of hooks in the corridor next to the door and Dad went on a drinking circuit of the local bars, relaying the news that his son had returned from Scotland with a gift. He came rumbling back in to find me washing glasses.

'Oi.'

He staggered through the bar, managing to collide with most of the sparse crowd. 'You'd better be good.' There was sudden menace and his face was concentrated with the drink when he headed for the stairs.

Things started unimpressively though in the back room of the

OK Corral and the problem was Dad. He would cajole pals and strangers alike through to me but his enthusiasm would get the better of him.

'Leave your jackets *here*,' he would tell them in the corridor with unnecessary threat and they would enter the room to me shaken, already glancing behind as if to check on their belongings through the wall. If I ventured some excuse to leave the room they would spring from their chairs in suspicion, and I would end up sitting back down and following the largely unprofitable pursuit of trying to guess their kids' names.

After a few confused men had left without paying and mumbled to Dad on their way out that his kid was anything from a fraud to a lunatic, I realised I had to take matters in hand. From then on, I stood in the doorway behind the bar, reading through some primitive stock readings I had prepared and waiting for Dad (not Mervyn who had forcefully announced that his involvement in the scheme ended with nailing up the back room's entrance) to land upon some impressionable specimen.

When I saw him speaking to a suitable case, usually a lone male drinker hamstrung with drink or twisted respect, I would take over the conversation and walk the curious punter round the bar. In the corridor I knew where to stand and how to open the door so the first thing that the man would see was the radiator.

'It's pretty warm in there,' I'd say apologetically, and their eyes would nearly always move from me to the doorway to the hooks. After their jackets had been dispensed with I'd guide them into the room and offer them a drink, telling them it was part of the package. Even if they refused, I'd fetch myself one and they'd be left in the room – too busy wondering quite how they had gone out for a pint and ended up in this conundrum to ponder if the weird kid could be rifling through their abandoned jackets.

I had my tools – the cards, photos, scraps and suggestions that were crammed into the cheap wallets and busy pockets of these unfortunates. I started to form extended conclusions. A plethora of condoms meant that they were single or in defective marriages, yet it also meant audacity. They wanted to hear that despite the fact they were *not in love right now* something was *going to happen soon with a woman* because that's what they thought, no matter the extreme dishevelment they had achieved in the meantime.

For those I recognised from the bookie visits with Dad I had an easy hit depending on the cash, or lack of it, in their wallets. Either *you are enjoying a lot of luck just now* or *you keep doing something that you want to stop doing.*

It wasn't just the wallets, and there were times when I'd hit extraordinary seams of precise discovery. Bailiffs' letters, torn-out job advertisements, court summonses, diaries, even divorce papers on one sublime occasion. All would leave me re-entering the room with impregnable surety.

As at Glendoll College the platform of middling trust emboldened me and allowed lines of conjecture. I did a lot of stuff with Australia and New Zealand, quickly picking up on the ease with which links to these countries could be established.

Over the years I have settled on a figure of a third for British audience members that will claim a connection to Australia and/ or New Zealand. If they've not lived there then others close to them will or will have. Or they'll have had drunken discussions about emigrating there, or they'll be romantically aligned with someone from there, or their kids will be over there or their kids will be shacked up with someone from there, and so on.

I would use this often in the future and it started in the back room of the OK Corral as I got more hits than misses by squinting at battered hands that I'd have them lay over the table (I didn't attempt to hold them, as Rose had mine, because I knew that arrangement would lead to violent disaster), saying firmly,

'Ah, Australia,' and then waiting, hoping.

Probably the two others I had most success with would stem from broad variations on:

'You're having problems with a friend or relative,'

and:

'You find your present line of work unsatisfying.'

At least one of these two would be likely to give me something, whether a nervous shift in the chair or instant, urging agreement that could then be shaped into them telling me the story while I pretended to contribute. I learnt to say phrases such as: 'Your kids are the problem' and 'It's not your boss', where the stresses on the words and rise in tone presented them as both statements and questions at the same time and, therefore, impossible to be incorrect. From there I would keep them talking and rework what they were telling me back to them with veils of added detail that would leave them abandoning their tales of woe to say,

'But how...'

And I would smile and say, 'Carry on, you've only paid for half an hour.'

Money came. Guilty fivers and bank-fresh tenners pushed into my hand or flung across the table. Some would offer hesitant praise, others told me that if I weren't my father's son they'd put me through the fucking window. But money came and would be roughly split by Dad at the end of the day. When my half grew in value he started to make deductions – an impudent seven pounds for lighting, an outrageous ten for the inflated heating – but still I was left with enough to begin morning ventures into town.

I worked through the Oxford Street chains, quickly assembling a new wardrobe dominated by black to replace my unorthodox clothing of brewery-branded fare and cheap additions provided by Mum before she left. Soon I would lead those I started calling my *clients* (to Dad's goading amusement and Mervyn's dismay) through to the back room dressed in a black pullover, waistcoat and overcoat that swung like a cape.

The coat gave me a certain swagger and also helped with persuading others to use the hooks. So much time was spent disrobing and hoisting my unneeded layers that usually my companion would do the same, unprompted, out of boredom. I was a dapper success, with money of my own and an eye for opportunity, by the time that Ayako arrived in the OK Corral.

I remember the moment she came in, a porcelain oddity that made everyone stop. She walked to the bar, to Mervyn as the obvious figure of responsibility, and I darted to his side.

'Is work here?'

She apologised for her English by lifting a hand to her mouth, as if to help shape the words. She looked at Mervyn and smiled at me and my heart stirred beneath the black.

'Sorry, love,' said Mervyn, hardly looking up from draining the drip trays, 'we're all covered here.'

'No, we're not,' I said, my voice squeaky. I looked at Mervyn, 'Lunchtimes we could have someone else, just for a couple of hours.' Below the line of the bar, I pulled my mess of notes from my pocket.

Mervyn laughed. 'Why don't you do a couple of hours tomorrow love, see how it turns out. Come in at eleven.'

'Tomorrow, OK,' she said. *Taw-mowow, hoe-kay,* she said.

'What's your name?' I asked.

'Ayako,' she told me, nervously zigzagging back to the door. 'I see you tomorrow.' She smiled at me and I grabbed a beer pump in fear of falling.

Ayako, Ayako. The next six weeks (I know it was six weeks because it's bookended by defining events, first her arrival and the second is to come) were a period that, even when I was living it, I assumed would not be surpassed.

Ayako would turn up each day with a neatness that sent her round the OK Corral leaving a trail of disbelief. Mervyn gave her a little instruction then left her to me. Dad looked vaguely astonished the first time he came down the stairs to find her smiling optimistically behind the bar, and then decided to ignore this unexpected turn. I heard him making comments that I knew were wrong about her to his loyalists in the bar, but pretended I hadn't, busy with the accelerating process of falling in love.

I would stand with Ayako behind the bar, naming object after object, and giggling with her when she tried to parrot it back. If she ventured out to the tables I would loyally tail her, introducing her to friendly drinkers and shielding her from those who had levels of perversion spectacular even in the moral vacuum of the OK Corral.

After a while, Ayako would hesitate at the end of her shift. Instead of returning to her backpacker's hostel, she and I would go for a walk or sit at a corner table in the pub and drink coffee (I never drank cider with Ayako) and talk about Japan.

One day I told her that I had bought a lava lamp on one of my Oxford Street expeditions and she asked if she could see it. We went to my room, sat on the bed and I switched on the lava lamp and put it on the floor in front of us. The lava shaped itself and I tried various arrangements that eventually left my hand harpooned round her tiny neck. When I tugged, carefully and with my fingers hot and trembling, she came to me and we kissed for a long time.

Each day would see some progression. My hands would be permitted to roam over her shirt before she would gently swipe them away with a giggle and,

'Not now, Nicky.' *Gnaw naw Nee-key.*

Next my hands would be up the shirt, flicking and tweaking at her nipples that would harden in my wavering fingers while she gasped and I felt faint with possibility. For a string of desperate days I tried to push, tease, jab my hand down her trousers only to feel her fingers round my wrist which she would pull back to her now willing, and unthrilling, chest.

But I had my eye on greater glories and eventually, eventually I got there. One afternoon I glided my hand with false confidence into her lap. She kept her arms resolutely wrapped around my back and I found myself presented with a remarkable freedom.

I undid her buttons and she squirmed and laughed when I yanked her trousers down then returned sharply to her pants, which were larger than I had been led to believe from Dad's porn. Here, inevitably, her hands arrived but it was quickly clear that this was only to block the pants' removal and not any ambitions I had to investigate their contents.

She lay on her back and I lay beside her, watching in stunned fortune as she clenched her eyes and threw her head from side to side while I rummaged hopefully amongst the hair and unexpected skin. Again, the magazines had suggested something far more clinical and exposed, but that brought only a flicker of surprise amongst the thundering heat of achievement.

Here we go, I thought, yet we didn't. I happened upon one particular bump of fluid flesh and Ayako appeared to spasm. Her arms jerked about mindlessly and her legs flew outwards as if stretched by invisible hands while she raved in what I presumed was Japanese. With my debutante cock cramming against my jeans in nervy readiness, she was suddenly stilled and blinking at me and saying,

'Very nice, Nicky.'

I nodded, flushed and speechless, watching her smile and pulling on her trousers.

That night, lying in bed and fiddling away energetically, I graphically imagined the inevitable progression. The next few days, however, I found that no matter how carefully I worked through the stages there was no development from my excursion into Ayako's pants and the disconcerting wetness that I had found there.

I would spend mornings and lunchtimes through in the pub's back room with my clients, but found myself struggling to divert my attention away from the afternoon's more pressing engagement. When the afternoon came, and Ayako and I sneaked upstairs, all my planning would end in failure. Then it was evening and I would be left facing a series of sozzled figures peering hawkishly across the table while I probed and revealed.

Not that I took defeat with Ayako lightly, or without stubborn dexterity. At what I saw as moments of opportunity within the sessions, I tried to place Ayako's hand on my youthful package, but she would switch its trajectory with a dismissive tinge that started to grate.

One time I stopped my daily rubbing just as she entered her frantic indications and smoothly lowered my trousers and pants, leaving my hopeful prick bobbing modestly at her. She smiled sweetly and shook her head and waited patiently for me to refasten my clothes and return wordlessly to my unselfish tasks.

And so I was a drained, unconfident figure when a small man left the back room one night with a pat of gratitude on my head. He had just paid me £10 to find out that the female boss he had been eyeing with unbelievable ambition at his work was, indeed, of a similar mind. The door opened again and Dad walked in.

'I've got a guy coming to interview you for the *Advertiser* tomorrow,' he said. 'Tomorrow morning. OK?' He even waited for my confirmation before departing.

The *Advertiser* was an eight-sheet nuisance that was left in bundles around the area but at the time the thought of popping up within its stained pages of local whimsy was pretty breathtaking. I walked giddily through to the bar and tried to get more information from Dad but he ignored me to discuss a football manager's defensive tactics and when I caught up with Mervyn in the cellar he didn't know much about it.

'The *Advertiser*?' he shouted above the buzz of the pipes and from somewhere within the barrels. 'That'll be good Nicky, hope you enjoy it, pal.'

I had a long night of planning my arrival into this fantastical world of public scrutiny and in the morning deliberated at length over various contortions of my new, earned clothes in front of the mirror. When Dad shouted I descended in a battery of black to be met by a flustered old man with a pad who said,

'You the kid then?'

I led him majestically to a table just before, as I hoped she might, Ayako wafted through the doors. I waved sternly and signalled the old man to sit opposite me while I settled and sighed and lifted my eyebrows comfortingly.

'So,' I said with professional kindness, 'just what would you like to know?'

The old man messed about, spending an age to locate a functioning pen and an unspoiled page of his pad, then another one deliberating over calling me a magician. I pitched in with mind reader but he reckoned that sounded *a bit dodgy* for the *Advertiser* and we settled on me being just a plain reader.

I told him how my vocation had appeared during my youth, minus the bullying and the theft of information. All the time, I would glance at Ayako who I had seen lift her palms to her cheeks in shock when Mervyn had imparted what was going on. The two stood watching me pretend not to watch them – Ayako frozen in admiration at the end of the bar, Mervyn with his chunks of tattooed arms folded and shaking as he chortled away.

Between pouring drinks for his favourites or leaning in for whispered consultation, Dad would sometimes steal looks as well. Not at me though, over towards Ayako at the end of the bar, no doubt amused at her enraptured state over the sight of me and my temporary reign over the OK Corral.

All too soon, the old man's pauses became a silence before an announcement that he had

'…more than enough. Christ,' he looked, horrified, at his notes. 'It's only supposed to be two hundred words.'

He stood up and I did likewise, rolling my eyes ruefully at Ayako. The old man waved his thanks to Dad, who ignored him, and then stopped in the doorway, turning with a finger rising in remembrance.

'Photos. They need a photo. You could come with me to the office or I could send the girl round later.'

'He'll go with you now,' said Dad with a quickness that surprised everyone. He looked a little caught when attention fell on him. 'Makes sense,' he said timidly and I blocked my smile at his unusual discomfort.

'Give me a minute,' I said with thrilling control and ran to my room where I checked on my hair and the folds of my collars. The door eased open and Ayako was there, looking at me in a new way. We kissed and then she pushed me gently away so I could see her.

'Today. Later today Nicky, OK?' *Tawdy*, she called it.

And I couldn't breathe, I couldn't breathe, I just hugged her and then I could hear my dad shout and I left Ayako, and her explosive declaration, there in my room. At the bottom of the steps Mervyn was pulling on his jacket and Dad was saying,

'A couple of hours or something, I'm sure you're due it.'

Mervyn shuffled out the back door looking a little lost at both the instruction and the kindness. I placed a hand on Dad's back and he turned to me in the half-light of the corridor. He looked around me, waiting.

'I'm off now, Dad.' He nodded grimly. 'Thanks for arranging this today,' I said. 'It's been amazing.'

He took a step so my hand fell away but that was OK because he sent out his own which flapped about my shoulders a bit while he said,

'No problem kiddo. Good luck with the photos.'

I floated to the bar and the old man but Dad called again,

'Good luck,' and I lifted a hand before wheeling happily away to follow the old man out the door.

He led me through the streets to the *Advertiser's* office which was a small room lit with yellow where a few people sat behind computers. The old man stood beside one of these people, a plain woman with short hair and too much lipstick, until she finally looked at us.

'This is the kid,' said the old man and she frowned, looked down at a piece of paper for a while and then said, 'Ah right, yeah.' She reached over for a camera, which was a lot smaller than I expected, stood up and pointed at the door.

'Come on then,' she smiled and I trailed behind her into the street, me sweating in my deep covering and her heels clicking a route to a gate in an elderly wall.

'I thought this could work, with the stuff about spirits.'

She pushed open the gate to reveal a graveyard. Old, black stones rose out of humped lines of grass which we dodged our way through.

'This place gives me the fucking creeps,' said the woman, then caught herself. 'Sorry,' she grimaced and it took me a moment to realise she was apologising for saying *fucking*.

'I'm seventeen, nearly,' I said, rattled, and she laughed and pointed at a stone collaboration that peaked with a weeping angel. 'There,' she said and I walked over to the stone, turning and leaning back into it.

As the woman bent and squinted I studied her tits which revealed only an element of shape through her jumper. The absurdity of her apology only served to amuse me and I was tickled by her misjudgement. She was not to know about Ayako. She was not to know that I could probably fuck *her* now, slung over one of these graves like the car bonnet scenes in Dad's porn.

I smirked and charmed my way through the photos and gave the woman a breezy goodbye before walking at a blistering rate back to the OK Corral. It was hard to halt a spreading intoxication. There was the intensifying success of whatever it was that I was learning through my work in the back room, there was Ayako, and there was even the meandering of my relationship with Dad into a delicate understanding.

It was an overpowering combination and I'm not sure, thinking about it now, if I have ever had the satisfaction that I had when I walked back into the OK Corral that day. Maybe some snatches from well before, sunny days in Regent's Park with Mum, but nothing as comprehensive.

The moment I walked into the bar I realised the problem. I looked at the bar – unmanned, with half a dozen men milling around the untroubled taps – and I could see the flaw in my contented picture growing until he dominated it, leaving the harmony spinning and unravelling away from me.

Warning roared in my ears, in my chest, when I walked behind the bar. By the stairs I could already see what I was going to see but up the stairs I travelled. Just another person really, but I was the only person truly existing. I had to be. What was happening was too much, too powerful, for that same moment to have meant anything to another.

Fourteen

William was a handy name, one of the strongest. William, Willie, Will, Bill, Billy and then the surnames that people would chuck in if needed – William, Williams, Williamson. But that night, to continue the luck, I didn't get past William. An arm had gone up at the back of the room with such resolution that the rented kid with the microphone had already run off when I heard the cameraman creak himself into a suitable angle.

'It looks like we have our contact,' I summarised professorially for the crowd. It was hard for me to see that far so I nicked a look back at the screen where there was a rush of faces while the camera swung into aim. Then there was a blur, and then there was Brewster with the microphone held before him, manic and happy and elbowing a female companion who looked to him then up at me.

I had no attractive alternative but to continue. For his part, Brewster didn't threaten to destruct the delicate scene from his end. He was so taken with his unexpected participation that it seemed to temporarily dismiss the fragile connection between us, and he made no obvious signs of familiarity. We swept onwards as if there was nothing there, with only a couple of drops at my end to be rescued.

'William was your father.'

'That's right, yes.'

'You called him Bill though, he's saying…'

A fair guess.

'No, more…'

'His friends, sorry, they called him Bill?'

Easy recovery.

'Yeah, his friends, yeah.'

'At the factory.'

'Sorry?'

'Bill worked at the factory.'

Using my trusted guidelines for the national averages of parental ages (lower for the working class, lower in the north), Brewster's father would have started work in the early 1960s. Brewster's accent was local, and showed little signs of having lived anywhere except this city. This industrial city, which was even more industrial then.

'He did, yes.'

'Using his hands, making things…'

'Yeah.'

'Making cars.'

This came from Tony's crib sheet the night before, and the noting of the once considerable local car industry.

'That's right, yes.'

'Now, when Bill went to the other world he had lost some of his usual sparkle?'

Dying, traditionally, takes away a person's sparkle.

'Yeah, that's right.'

'And he was struggling to breathe?'

Not quite as facetious as it sounds, I use this to angle for the follow-up and the finish.

'Yeah.'

'It was because of the smoking?'

The follow-up.

'It was, that's right.'

'You know what Bill wants to tell you don't you?'

'To stop smoking,' said Brewster, a lot smoother than I would have ever expected. I had seen his hands, when he held the newspaper article with me and the black girl. I had seen the yellowed fingers.

'To stop smoking. Please, he says, please stop. And he says that he loves you, he loves you so much and…' I stretch out my palms in defeat, 'he's gone. Bill's gone. What a beautiful man.'

The finish.

It was a decent little run and Brewster was delighted. He had been a perfect recipient of my work, with an amazement clear enough to carry to the crowd. With our interchange clearly ended, he gave me an elaborate wink through the screen and some sort of fist-waving that he probably thought was chummy. In my relief I relented and gave a personal touch of my own.

'Well, I felt like a detective there.'

I moved back along the stage, knowing that up in his row, the weak gag would have left Brewster inflated to the point of ecstasy and further subjugated to my newly demonstrated powers.

I led the show to a triumphant ending and dallied longer than usual in that slow rise and fall of final appreciation that could send you insane with its variations if you were so minded. I strode from the stage and accepted smiles, shouted appreciation, handshakes and a spank to the back on the way to the dressing room.

Tony arrived soon after and we laughed while he pulled two beers from the fridge and slumped into the faded seating. For that moment, that little moment, we were as we used to be in these rooms, at these times. We revelled in the triumphs, joked about the errors and ran through personal favourites from those who had colluded so generously in my long spells of achievement.

We would have got to Brewster soon enough if he hadn't knocked and entered in the meantime. We greeted him graciously and he accepted with deferential delight, refusing a seat or a beer and selecting an awkward stance in the corner. His shirt was straight from the packet. It leant from his body in creased rectangles.

Tony suggested that he surely hadn't bargained for being part of the show and Brewster agreed wholeheartedly, then waited and spoke again much quieter.

'Do you think I could have a quick word with Mr. Santini please? Alone?'

Tony fairly leapt from his chair, such was the camaraderie, and he and I swapped a quick expression of awareness. Brewster wanted an encore – any minute details that I may have censored from his father's spiritual communication to avoid public scrutiny. I hoped there wasn't anything too lengthy coming, no childhood spat that he wanted to stir through, listening in through me to Bill's distant responses.

Brewster closed the door behind Tony, then turned and already, already I knew something was wrong. His face wasn't right and I was pinned back with the concentration he afforded me.

'My dad was called Arthur.'

He peered at me and my response. The room seemed to disintegrate and all I could focus on was his mouth, within that disastrous beard, while what it had said travelled within me. His eyes were grey and fastened me so comfortably that I couldn't believe I hadn't previously regarded the reserve that lay beyond them. It wasn't intelligence, it wasn't even initiative, it was just recognition. He had recognised what I did. He had recognised me.

'He worked in a bank. He never smoked in his life. He died in a car accident in Ibiza in 1978. Sudden,' he added. 'No airbags in those days. Some fucking Spanish farmer with no lights on his truck.'

I felt sick, properly sick with gulping and mouth fizz. I didn't understand where this had come from or where it was going to go. Where was Tony? Where was *anyone*? Why had I let it be that it was just Brewster and me here to deal with what he was saying?

Brewster walked back towards the door, which seconds later he would open and exit through with little ceremony. This wasn't the reprieve it appeared because while doing both these things, without looking at me, he said:

'I'm going to come and see you tomorrow morning at your hotel, Mr Santini. 10 a.m. I'll pick you up from your room. Just you.'

Fifteen

I wanted to run. Moments after Brewster left the room, I left it too, unwilling to be alone with this new, atrocious arrival of understanding. If Tony had not been lurking near the stage door, telling bored theatre staff about past adventures, then maybe I would have run.

Instead, I took Tony to a bar near the theatre. He clocked my switch in mood and the blatancy of the Brewster connection worried him enough to stay obediently quiet when we got there. He watched me with admirable patience, his belly rising and falling while he drank and waited, letting me wrestle with this sudden reversal.

It was after the drinks had come and gone and more had come that I told him what had happened. Such was my panic, I even told Tony what *had* happened, rather than using the natural opportunity to shift blame to him.

'Brewster knows. He doesn't suspect it, he knows.'

'Knows what?'

'About me, about what I do. What we do.'

That wasn't a stealthy incorporation of Tony into the mess. What I did was very definitely what we did – we were captured together through the years of development, of combined success and, more importantly, of combined failure. And now, in trying to navigate away from the most crushing failure, and looking like we were getting there, we had somehow hit this disastrous run. When Tony spoke it was with an unhelpful,

'He was lying about his dad?'

I breathed before nodding to stop my normal response. Rarely, I could do without enforcing any division between Tony and me at that point, where the possibility remained that he could be of assistance. The two of us were only a yard apart, such was the table we had taken, but we concentrated grimly on our drinks and handled our internal calculations.

'What's he going to do?'

That was Tony but it could well have been me and it was the consideration of this, of Brewster's next move, that provoked us to talk. Tony abandoned his silence to give me a broad church of unlikeness. I directed his wandering the best I could and we settled on a dreadful shortlist.

'Blackmail, goes to the papers, some sort of criminal charge,' I detailed blankly. 'It has to come from them.'

'And what do we do if it's one of them?'

'I don't fucking know, Tony, do I?' I said cruelly, leaving him apologising and reaching for his wallet for another round.

Two hours later, the bar tiring around us, the drinks passing quicker and stronger, I looked at Tony.

'What if he charges me, would that be a story?'

'Charges you with what?'

'Fraud? Could he do us for fraud?'

Tony delighted in the lack of loading in my response. He graded the question, drank, thought.

'Probably, yeah. In fact, yeah. Anywhere there's money involved then that can be fraud. I think.'

An hour later and we were in a Greek restaurant near the bar, near the theatre, near the hotel.

'No, he's coming to pick me up. It's got to be blackmail or the papers.'

'But he'd lose his job.'

I put down my cutlery. Tony's face was becoming softer, I tried for the eyes but gave up and took a general focus.

'You're right Tony. But if he blackmails us, he's made that decision. With the papers he could get a mate to do it. If he wants to do one of those two, then he can do one of those two. He'll know the risks, he'll have accepted the risks. He'll just want to *do* it.'

Some time after that, in the honesty bar, back at the hotel.

'Blackmail, goes to the papers, criminal charge.'

'And what do we do if it is one of them?'

'Cry.'

And we laughed. I was flayed across a two-man couch, my hand trailing to a wine glass of whisky. I traced its edge with my finger and watched Tony rise reluctantly to make another drink. My leg was crooked and buzzing with the want of adjustment but, though I could see it, I found it hard to transmit the request. I looked back at Tony, who was surprisingly nimble round the bottles. Surprising, because he was clearly behind me in the alcohol's calling.

That's the last I remember as a clear run. After that it descends into flashes of light and sound. It's an uneven, unclear procession but there's two moments that stand separate and strong in comparison.

First, it was later and I was see-sawing on the couch with Tony facing me. He was telling me something, something that he wanted to do – a new plan. And my whole body, my whole being was saying no. As I thought about my mouth and how I could pass word to it, the memory dims.

Secondly, it was a little later again and I was alone in one of the corridors. I think that I may have been there, or near there, for some time as I looked to reach my room. The panic might have caused the memory because I was in a state of alarm when I looked into the whiteness and that boy, the Asian boy, was nearing me. He smiled and with the smile and the whiteness he looked angelic, and then he led me through the corridors to my room.

I was just inside or maybe just outside the room when he left me and I looked again and there he was, walking away but speaking as he did so. It was in that swapping of words between him and me that the memory's energy originates. I said something, or he said something, but probably I said something, and I didn't know what that was but it gave the memory a tricky, shadowy badness.

And that was that, the third night in that city stubbornly finished.

Sixteen

The black girl again. I'm called from my room, as I was before, by the young policeman and trudge to the lobby scene in my dressing room. Brewster is there, a boorish demagogue directing the mob of police and ambulance staff, and when he sees my approach his mouth begins to open in criticism. But then, from unseen speakers and with unimaginable volume, there is an eruption of tinned fury.

The alarm screams along the corridors and over our heads and it sends Brewster and his weak-willed cohorts scampering this way and that. Only myself, with my robes floating majestically around me, and the black girl, serenely incapable on the trolley, remain stationary in the distress. Soon we are alone and the alarm hushes respectfully while I push the trolley through a nearby door that, it appears, is a bedroom but the bed is somehow buckled.

My confusion at the humped sleeping arrangements means I mistakenly direct the trolley into a startlingly stiff collision. I must have misread the momentum because the black girl's corpse is somehow projected up into the air. It spins, the blanket falls from her and then she is falling downwards with ghostly limbs reaching for gravity.

It's when she lands, slung over the n-shaped mattress, that the scene's aim sharpens. Her legs face me like stirrups, her bottom smoother than even dreams should allow and I sigh and smile meekly and say 'Ah, OK. OK, I get it, I'll do it…'

Seventeen

When that ended, I lay sweating and wondering there in the bed. Brewster was coming for me at ten o'clock. That was the first threat to arrive when I woke, after I had dealt with the diversion. But it did not come alone. Patiently reworking the evening and expertly stripping away the confusion of the drink, I was left with Brewster and his phantom father, Tony telling me the thoughts I didn't want to hear in the honesty bar, and the forgotten words that had passed between me and the porter.

I ranked the dangers and swiftly elevated Brewster. The others could wait, and would reduce themselves when the hangover's lending of paranoia was repaid in instalments. I reached for my phone. Nothing. Five past nine, less than an hour.

I clambered from the sheets and walked anciently to the bathroom where I tenderly held my exhausted self while it made a meal of draining what it could. It was starting to complain when the room's door was bothered with a gentle tapping which I knew could not be that of Brewster.

I walked drunkenly to the chair, pulled on the dressing gown and then tended to my visitor. The Asian, smiling with that same godliness. He held up a glass of orange juice but I was drawn to his other arm, lashed around a battery of newspapers.

'For me?'

'Yes sir. You said last night to bring them to you.' He pushed the glass into my hand and slipped into the room where he placed the newspapers on the guilty bed. I watched him turn back for the door with my eyes hooded and weak.

'I don't…I'm sorry if I was rude last night?' I said, squinting at him passing by me again.

'No, sir,' he replied smoothly. 'No need to apologise,' he added but he looked past me and continued to travel, away and down the corridor.

Split between the brightness of the corridor and the dankness of my room, his movement briefly held me. His arms hung nearly dead straight by his sides and his legs pulled beneath him in unwilling drives that left his toes sliding bent along the ground. The combination made me stop, but not for long, and then I was back in the room's fragile sanctuary.

I fanned the newspapers before me. On one front, it was not hard to see, we had won. The coverage was satisfactorily condensed – one-pagers with either a photo of me or an old school shot of the black girl. The headlines were fine too – heartache and tragedy. I progressed into the copy and, all in all, we had done well there also.

Discrepancies arrived with the accounts of the press conference. According to the fearless observers, my behaviour at the press conference had ranged from 'a steely dignity' to being 'overwhelmed by emotion' and even, according to one reporter who had perhaps taken advantage of the honesty bar's offerings, involved me running tearfully from the room.

A satisfying minority of the reports had bothered beyond the basic facts but there were fissures of regrettable elaboration. Some of the papers touched on my dad and his unwelcome previous appearances within their pages, others on the financial results of my work (my *fortune* was the subject of some brutal inflations) with the implication clear regarding my motivation and, by inference if the reader was of sufficient intelligence, the genuineness of my talent.

The culling of my television career was treated more lightly than I expected. The cover story the television station had offered at the time was airily offered and that was more than fine with me. But there was one utterance, just one part of a single sentence in a paper with the space and scope to carry it, that made me push back involuntarily into the pillows. By chance it was folded open at the top of the pile and it was this –

> Santini's career began with him working from a London office where he offered what he called 'spiritual guidance' on a personal level. When his second television series was ended prematurely it was rumoured within the television industry that this may have been connected to revelations concerning his early practices, amid reports that one patient may have required psychological assistance as a result of sessions with Santini.

Those last seventeen words. It wasn't even clear, it wasn't even correct, yet it was enough to leave me attacked with whispers of disaster. I fought back as best as I could. I knew that Java Joe was never going to disappear from view. Because I knew this, I should see the mention for what it was – a fleeting appearance so partial and obscured as to be unloaded of potential.

Java Joe and I had survived worse scrutiny without discovery, and we had survived without discovery once more. As I had reasoned many times, the money that had passed between us – that extra bulk that had never made it to the trials of the stock market and the proceeds of my glorified theft of his shop's lease – was only known to me and Java Joe. Now, it was only known to me.

I looked for my phone once more to find the time and this need was starting to irritate. I decided to ask the Asian boy to get me a clock, now that I knew I had escaped offending him. Twenty minutes.

I wanted to phone Tony but I wanted to do it closer to Brewster's arrival to fill the last of the void. I could have ordered Tony to my room, to be with me when Brewster arrived, but I would rather gather the situation myself and then disseminate it onwards. To Tony, or a lawyer, which would again be Tony initially.

I washed and dressed and checked the time, then called Tony. He was outside somewhere, which was deeply unlikely. We ran over the newspapers and how acceptable they were. I didn't forget to ask him what he said in the honesty bar, I just didn't want to, not when it could provoke another bolt of concern when Brewster and what he might say or do was drawing so near.

I listened to Tony's encouragements, ill thought-out and brazened by alcohol, and batted them away without effort. The firmness of my position descended the conversation into near silence with Tony occasionally rousing himself with inanity such as,

'He's probably just wanting to talk to you.'

'I'd imagine so Tony, it's what words he'll be using that's the concern.'

The latest of the knocks at the door arrived. There was no doubt behind this one, with Brewster's voice calling my name through the hotel's wood.

Eighteen

He was nervous, that's when I realised that this was unlikely to progress in one of the three firm directions I had predicted. All would have required preparation and a decision that would have been definite and, therefore, strengthening for Brewster. But he was worrying himself around the room, inspecting me with a bizarrely critical eye.

'You're in a suit,' he had started with when he came in. 'Good, good.'

Now he was rushing me to put on shoes, and to remember any *notes that I needed*.

'What notes?'

'Just notes,' he said. 'I don't know. No, you'll be fine. You're a pro after all.'

He moulded a little smirk, in a disappointing warning that he was regaining momentum.

'Do I need a lawyer?' I asked and he responded, like I realised he would the moment I asked,

'I don't know Mr Santini, *do* you?' and I shook my head distastefully before yanking on my shoes.

'Ready then?' he said, grinning.

His nerves went and their replacement was a curious contentedness. I let him lead me to the elevator where he selected the basement which I presumed was the hotel's car park and it was. Through the unpainted concrete and white light he took me to a journeyed saloon.

'This is your car isn't it?' I said with sudden thought.

'Why, do you think I'm stealing it?' Brewster laughed and disappeared into the car while gesturing for me to do likewise. He must have known that I didn't mean that, that I meant that it was *his* car. Not a police car. This was confirmed when I entered and saw the absence of a police radio and the presence of family wastage – fast food wrappers, boiled sweets, lipstick and, behind me, an infant's plastic seat. A fuzzy declaration came from Brewster's jacket pocket while he fiddled with his keys, which he ended with a hand slipped into the folds and a click from the offending radio.

As he manoeuvred us free of the car park, with grunts and officious mirror work, I chose not to go to him with further narrow demands – where we were going, what was going to happen when we got there, just what the fuck he thought he was doing essentially kidnapping a member of the public – that he could easily evade and, besides, things had moved on. This was something personal and, as long as it remained personal and away from the matchless threat of legality, then I felt instinctively that it could be handled. In one way or another.

We moved into some rough banality that trundled from traffic concerns, to engine performance, to bus lanes and to property prices. In a beeping, angry squash at the head of a crossroads Brewster talked me through the intricacies of the buy-to-let market and he and his wife's skilful decision to purchase a two-bedroom flat that they had let out to Polish builders.

While we sat in the creeping queue of a motorway feeder lane he gave me a twelve-minute sermon (I timed it on the car's digital clock) on the importance of getting the right letting agent when you were an emerging property tycoon like himself. 'I don't have the time to worry about a blocked toilet in my property,' the detective generously explained, locked in traffic in the middle of a daytime morning while, presumably, somewhere in the city crimes were being committed.

The use of the motorway worried me but in the end we were only on it for a short burst before Brewster took us up a ramp into a busy car park where he spotted a space near the front with a victorious 'Ah,' and steered us in, utilising a single palm in painful showmanship. The car park belonged to a chain hotel, a hundred-room and conference hall standard set back barely fifty feet from the motorway.

'Well, here we are,' said Brewster. He tugged at his keys. His nerves had returned and I didn't know what to make of that.

I **pushed the door open** and there they were, moving with slipped synchronisation. Ayako saw me first, lying on her front and looking up dog-like with her arms divided. Only her milky bottom seeming to be connecting her to Dad – lifted as it was up from the bed and into the space between his steady legs.

He was powering raggedly away, his legs straight to the bed and his arms gripped with concentration on Ayako's ghostly sides. His belly was bigger than I would have suggested if for some unfathomable reason I had been directing the churning scene. The terror of the movements probably lasted only seconds until the fact that Ayako had stilled so markedly brought a fade-out of hostilities from Dad and then he was looking at me as well.

They both smiled, for their own reasons. Ayako in a desperate offering of hope, Dad in a deadening delivery of fact. I looked at both, wondering when what I was seeing would finally transmit reaction but all I could see was the two of them cascaded towards me. Two tiers of confirmation that this, this was something that would be remembered.

When he spoke it was with unaffected aggression.

'You been paying her wages?' he said, pointing down at Ayako's back.

I nodded blankly, looking at him so I didn't have to look at her.

'Well,' he said, releasing one hand from her side and wiping his brow. I watched a drop of his sweat, winking in the light, fall to her flesh. 'You'd better leave a few quid.' He looked at me, his face (truly) joyous, 'I can't see her coming back after this.'

With a body that felt borrowed, I made it down to the bar where I hesitated and pulled two twenty-pound notes from my pocket. After I put them on the wood and the agitated hopefuls at the bar asked me if there was *any fucking danger* of getting served, I heard my father laugh from back and above me. Then I heard, or maybe I didn't but I thought I did, a sudden combination of noise – of slapping limbs and the creak of my bed – that told me that they had started again.

Somehow I pushed a bit more down and into my loyal limbs and made it to the street and then another street and another pub where I ordered a pint of cider and took myself to the most distant space. I drank in pulls and waited for time to bring development to my thoughts and my understanding of what they were telling me.

Cider, more cider. People came and went. Sometimes I would get up, go to the toilet and piss some of the cider out. But most of the time I just sat there, jumping thoughts from Mum to Glendoll College to money to cider.

Dad and Ayako were in the mix, of course they were, but I tried to accept them only as separate entities. I thought about Japan, about what it might be like and why Ayako had come from there to here. I thought about Dad and about times when he and Mum and been together and only reasonably unhappy about it.

It was impossible for them not to join and coax me back to seeing them united as I did from the doorway of my bedroom. With darkness outside the windows and the bar easing towards close, something else from that scene arrived. It came camouflaged by the pain and the cider but then it was there, leaping out with conclusive summary.

When Dad had been speaking to me about money with his cock still holding Ayako in place, she had raised herself on one palm, sending her up until her shoulders rose and opened her exposed front. My annihilated eyes had run over it immediately before I left the room but it was only now that I saw what they had seen.

Down there, at the cusp of the arrangement that involved bits of her and bits of my Dad, the thatch that I had lovingly worked through with my hands for weeks on end had been decimated.

It was a refined shadow of its previous self, a hacked and worked reduction that was left as a dark button of hair. It had been trimmed, readied. For me. For me.

I got up from the table and walked back to the OK Corral, the business of the streets slipping in and out of my awareness while I did so. When I got there I swayed and focused and saw that the only light was a mocking glow from Dad's bedroom. I lifted the door until the faulty lock clicked open and then rested it down and walked inside for what I knew was the last time.

'Hello, Nicky,' said Mervyn. It took me a minute because I was drunk and it was dark but there he was, still in his jacket, sitting at a table without a drink. Waiting for me, there in the shadows. I looked at him and then to the doorway behind the bar, to the stairs and what was up them.

'She's gone,' he said, sliding off the leather and walking to me. 'And he's fucked.'

When he stood beside me I saw with surprise that I was nearly the same size as him. He put his hand to my shoulders and eased me onwards.

'Come on,' he said, 'I'll be with you, little Nicky. All the way.'

I got up the stairs, taking them in deliberate steps with Mervyn's hand on my back, and paused on the landing to look through the open door into Dad's room. I could only see the end of his bed but the combination of the light and the fact that his foot, defiantly erect, was still in its shoe demonstrated that his sleep had been sudden and heavy.

I went into my room and didn't know if it was a good thing or not that the bed had been made. Mervyn reappeared with two large leather holdalls, embossed with the logo of a brand of gin that I recognised from the pub's Christmas raffle. I gathered my unloved possessions and handed them in turn to Mervyn who neatly stowed them in the bags. Amongst some of the pub's overflow in the corner of my room was a battered answering machine that I scooped up as well.

For some hidden reason I sat down briefly on the bed and Mervyn withdrew respectfully outside. My eyes began to close, so

I demanded my body back up and left the room, taking once more to the stairs without a final look at Dad. I got to the bar before I started crying and then Mervyn was with me again, saying,

'Come on, kid, it's for the best.'

He told me to wait outside with the bags and I wondered if he was going to lock the door behind me. The street was steady with night-time fare and the transience of the traffic set off within me the certainty that I was about to experience a very particular type of being alone. I was crying freely when Mervyn arrived, edging through the door and holding a plastic bag out to me. It was heavy in my hand and wrapped round a soft brick of content.

'It's ten grand,' he said. 'Fuck knows you deserve it,' and he waved at a taxi that braked and swerved over beside us. Mervyn opened the door and I swung in my bags then climbed in clutching the plastic bag. He handed me a slip of paper.

'Here's your mum's new number. She's called a few times but I don't suppose he told you that.'

I shook my head. I could hardly speak through choking and trying to keep down the panic.

'Where am I going to go?'

Mervyn said the name of a bed and breakfast in Victoria loud enough for both me and the taxi driver to hear.

'I'll give them a bell,' he said to me, 'get you a good rate.' A crack in his voice made me look at him and I could see that he was toiling as well, hanging on the door and watching me retreat into my body and my fears.

'You can call me any time, you know that, don't you?'

I nodded, wiped my face, and gripped the plastic bag and the ten grand even tighter.

'But stay away from here, little Nicky, stay away from him,' and he reached into the taxi, pinched my shoulder and I thought I should maybe hug him but he was already backing out and then he shut the door and took a disconnecting pace back over the pavement.

When the taxi pulled away I heard a noise and turned to see

Mervyn still standing there. I had thought, before I looked, that he had shouted,

'You *run!*' after the taxi and me. But he wasn't facing the taxi. Mervyn was looking away and up, up to the windows above the OK Corral. Up to the windows of those small rooms where there had once been me, Mum and Dad and now there was just Dad.

He hadn't shouted,

'You *run!*'

He'd shouted,

'You *cunt!*'

He'd not been shouting at me, he'd been shouting at my dad. And his shoulders, I could just make out through the dark and the tears, rose and fell while an anger refused to subside and my life slid from view.

There was a period – a few days – of a shock so complete that I was left curiously immobile in the bed and breakfast in Victoria. It was run by a warming old Jewish woman with glasses and a cardigan and a cigarette that she held up like a candle. She smelt, faintly, of something I knew but couldn't place.

I don't know what Mervyn had told her, Miss Goldstone, when he called ahead but I was greeted like a returning hero – with a cradling grip from her free hand when we wound up the stairs to a room that reminded me of the teacher's suite at Glendoll College, with the plastic tray and pouches of tea and coffee.

'Bathroom along the corridor. Thirty pounds a night for you now, Nicholas,' said Miss Goldstone, her body heaving under her cardigan. The smell, I decided uncertainly, was kebab meat. 'It should be forty-five,' she added and I pulled the zip on the first of my brewery bags.

'Thanks,' I replied and she left me to the nothingness. Three, maybe four days I stayed in that room. Lying in the bed, trying to sleep with my legs hot and itching under the dry sheets. Sitting in the chair reading the tabloids that Miss Goldstone brought me. Sitting at the table eating the food, the kebabs and burgers, that Miss Goldstone brought me. Standing at the window and watching Miss Goldstone walking over to Cappadocia Kebab and Burger.

She was generous in her lack of probing and left me with room to accept this shift in existence. Understanding came simply at first – the realisation that nourishment could no longer be provided solely by Cappadocia Kebab and Burger – and followed to other areas. There were two women that I needed to talk to. I phoned the first with the small TV muted in the corner and a newsreader mouthing sullenly on. I would have called her anyway but it needed to be this day that I did.

'Hello,' she said in a strange voice that had been curtailed and softened.

'Mum,' I said, 'it's Nicky.'

'Nicky,' she answered, and then there was a pause and when her voice came again it was hushed.

'I tried to call you earlier, there was no answer at the pub. Happy birthday, Nicky.'

'Thanks, Mum.'

'Are you having a good day?'

It wasn't a conversation, I realised instantly, that I wanted to have. It was too big a gamble. It was my seventeenth birthday and I was living in a bed and breakfast in Victoria and surviving on Cappadocia Kebab and Burger. That was because of Dad but it was hard for me not to think it was also because of Mum.

I wanted her to know what had happened, but there was no way of doing it without damaging myself. I hadn't spoken to her since she'd left. On my birthday the previous year Mervyn had told me unconvincingly that I'd just missed her call and then took me for fish and chips. I would have been right to have given her some of my pain but I didn't.

Instead I told her that I was fine and staying with a friend from Glendoll College, where we'd both just finished. I told her about his house, a four-storey monster in South Kensington, with an attic full of pool tables and pinball, and a silent woman in white who came in and prepared all the meals.

They'd thrown me a birthday lunch. Lobster and cake and champagne and old schoolmates arriving unexpectedly with presents. Mum laughed with delight, and said:

'I knew you'd be OK, Nicky,' and, 'You're my boy Nicky, always have been,' and, finally, 'I miss you so much, Nicky,' but with nothing after it, no plans to meet, no suggestion at all.

Now, I can recognise that Mum and I together were never going to be strong enough to keep my father out. We had to split up, dodge him separately and hunt for safety. Now, I can see that. But I was seventeen, with chronic indigestion and a gaping hole where my future should have been, and it was hard to accept solitude. So I went quiet and she panicked and I only partially helped her. The conversation died with regret.

It wasn't a collapse that I wanted to be alone with. It was time to go to the other woman, the one who offered more.

Seeing me leave, Miss Goldstone suggested that if I was going into town it was the 88 bus but I had already decided to walk. Through Victoria's offices and endless traffic I trudged onwards, past the Palace and Green Park and into the assurance of Mayfair. I walked suspiciously past the silent townhouses and was glad to reach the blaring of Oxford Street.

By Marylebone I was tired and nervy, closing in to the old area. I had to get near in order to remember the route but I picked it up a couple of streets away and soon I was moving, thankfully, away from the OK Corral. It took me a while to recognise the tower and when I got there I realised I didn't have a chance with the floor number.

I stood at the door, amongst the food wrappers and dog shit, asking the sinister figures that came and went. Few answered and those that did offered abuse or blunt refusals, until a man laughed and gave me the number, telling me not waste my fucking money.

In the lift I had to accept that this was important. Walking along the patchy carpet, between the walls scarred with names and threats, I knew it had to work. When she opened the door, I realised that this was my only chance.

Now that I was little older, I could see that Rose was younger than I had thought. It had only been a year or so before that I stood at her door with Dad, but my aspects had shifted and now I could see more. It wasn't age that had dried her face and slowed her movements. It was smoking, drink, the hunt for money, life.

She took to me probably because she had no one else to take to. I told her all about my work at the OK Corral and she laughed and urged me on. I spoke quickly and vaguely of my sudden uprooting and then moved to my request. I wanted to learn more, from her, so that I could start again without the looming protection of the OK Corral.

Rose was gracious, strangely so. She discussed her own study at the charmed hands of an Irish woman in Hammersmith. They had worked as cleaners together and while they walked through the offices at night with their plastic bags, the woman had told Rose how to do what she had done ever since.

'She was a genius.' Rose pointed at me in confirmation with a wilting stub of cigarette. 'That woman was a fucking genius, Nicky.'

'Then why didn't she do it?'

Rose coughed and spat what came up into a bowl that I saw with chilling suddenness was there for the purpose.

'Because she'd been turned over in Ireland doing it. She said the wrong thing to the wrong woman.' She doused the faltering cigarette in the same bowl. It hissed softly in the saliva while she reached over to me and ran a cold finger down my cheek. 'They sliced her face, Nicky, right down there she had a scar. So she left all that, and left Ireland too. Wouldn't you?'

'Yeah,' I said, grateful at her hand beating a retreat.

'These people Nicky, you have to be careful. Nearly twenty years I've been doing this and I've been doing it here.' She waved her hand to the flat and the harmful streets beyond. 'Lots of bad people come here. They're fine with me, I'm just an old woman.'

She wasn't though. She'd made herself an old woman, for the protection. I thought of Jimmy Wood. How he had made himself a victim, just to drink in the OK Corral, back when it was Jock's Lodge, and Mum was still there. Rose's protection had been to help her body age. Everyone needed protection, and she was the only person who could give me mine.

'When do we start?' I asked.

'Tomorrow,' she picked up a ragged notebook and threw it into my lap. 'What's the first time? I haven't got my glasses.'

Below the following day's date was written

STURROCK 10.00

'Ten o'clock, Sturrock,' I said and she laughed.

'Perfect, get here for quarter to.' She plucked a bottle from the depths of her chair, and I stood and started the long walk home to Victoria.

I arrived late the next morning, after Miss Goldstone's favoured 88 bus wound its way so evasively into town that I had to jump off and catch a pricey taxi just to get there, sweating and sorry, at ten to ten (when I suggested later that day to Miss Goldstone that the 88 bus was far from the best way to get into town she told me that she found its route *fun*).

Rose was unimpressed and swore at me before throwing her hooked hands over my shoulders. I was still offering a passionate blaming of the 88 bus when I noticed with some alarm that she was guiding me towards a cupboard.

'In there,' she said sternly. 'And don't make a fucking noise.'

It made a battered sense so I slid into the cupboard and caught a vision of hung clothes before the light was swept away by the door closing. I burrowed into the corner amongst the odour and age that wrapped round me from the garments. I was steadying myself, feeling for dimensions, when the door opened again. Rose's face was shadowed by the daylight behind.

'You need to piss or shit?' Her face was tight with stress. I shook my head and the door slammed again. I could hear her sighing and swearing during a rush around the room, placing her tools – the cigarettes, the bottle, the dreaded bowl – on the table and pulling the other chair to hers, so that a hand could be offered and taken in her troubling grip.

There was a knock from beyond the room and Rose hissed, 'Not a fucking noise, Nicky,' and then she was on the move again and I could hear conversation before the voices grew and she was saying, 'Just here please, Mr Sturrock' and a man said, 'Thanks' and then, quickly, 'I did just what you told me.'

For a month or two I'd be stowed in that cupboard, up in the tower. I enjoyed it, lying there in the dark and listening to Rose talking to these people. At first I heard the conversations like anyone would. I battled laughter, embarrassment, boredom while Rose spoke to the people and they spoke so trustfully back to her.

Soon I saw the conversations as the journeys that they were. Within the opening minute of her appointments, Rose would deliver two glaring messages. There was the bashful apology, the plummeting of expectation. 'I'll do what I can for you, I hope there's something there,' she would say and I pictured her look up and push her neglected features into hope.

Then there was the sudden encapsulation of the person themselves into the search for success.

'Are you ready to help me?'

There would be a firmer note of implicit instruction.

'I need you there with me.'

And they would rush with confirmation, thrilled at the inclusion. It was a switch, a union, and much better than the detached battles I had fought at the OK Corral.

From that point Rose's voice would slip away, overtaken by the visitor's. They would talk, and talk, at the slightest suggestion from Rose, which would always be given with little loading. I had noticed this the first time I had met her, the omission of intent in sentences, leaving them pitched always between question and statement. This was an area I had already reached in my progress but now I got more and only having the voices made it easier.

Always, there was the suggestion that Rose was holding back and that her shortened inserts were purely a taste of reservoirs of understanding. The visitors would show gratitude just for confirmation of what *they* were saying, as if facts that they were producing about themselves needed to be ratified by Rose.

Any negativity of outlook was saved for those the visitor made clear deserved it – usually jilters and cheats, liars and thieves, from the person's recent past or unfortunate present. Rose offered only careful admonishment and I thought of the scar on the face of the Irish woman, who was probably still cleaning offices in Hammersmith.

Within each session there would be at least one unprompted declaration from Rose. Some shocking twist of definition that would leave me wide-eyed and waiting in the cupboard. Usually there was a pause, or gasp, before astonished confirmation from the other voice. Sometimes, which I saw was just the other side of the bet, the pause would lengthen into mumbled contradiction. My breath would be loud and hot while Rose retreated and saved something, anything, that she could.

When the people left I'd fall out of the cupboard with my questions. Rose sat and drank and talked me through the session. She told me about the person's clothing or demeanour or some other hint or trick and I'd see the missing reasoning. It was thrilling and the new spread of knowledge soon turned to ambition.

By the end I hated the cupboard, with its limitations and relegation from the action. I exited it one day with the decision made. Against rain blowing in slaps on to Rose's dirty windows, I declared that I was ready to work on one of her visitors. She laughed unwelcomingly.

'How old are you, Nicky?'

'Seventeen.'

'You ever met a seventeen-year-old male gypsy?' She laughed again.

'I thought though, that this was...'

'I'll help you, Nicky, course I will, but you've got to find your own way of doing it. Look at this fucking place, do you think I can give up a punter?'

'I don't need the money, I've got money.'

But she didn't want money, I knew that when I said it. There was something missing. Rose was entrenched in the same tangle of society that had, one way or another, bred me. There had to be some motivation.

'I was, you know.' Her eyes fluttered away and she shook her head with irritation at her momentary frailty. 'I was sorry to hear about your dad,' she said and lifted the bottle. Having it in her hand steadied her and she looked back, a little thrown at my absence of reaction. 'OK?'

'Yeah,' I said. 'Thanks.'

'That's fine, Nicky, that's fine.'

Her face was held in sympathy but I had been thanking her for the cupboard and the learning. I had already pushed the other thing away. It stayed away on the journey back to Miss Goldstone (a bewildering hour on the 88 bus) and it stayed away while I sat on the bed and counted out the remainder of my money.

Seven grand, a little more. I needed it all though. I needed to do a few things. See about getting somewhere to live. And I needed to *start*. The information and the confidence had to be begun, while they were there and sharp. I needed, also, to see Mervyn. I told myself with little conviction that I needed to see Mervyn because he would help me get somewhere to live, and that it was nothing to do with what Rose had said.

Mervyn was working in Atlas Electronics on Tottenham Court Road. I didn't have to go to the OK Corral to find out. I skirted round the pub's nearby streets one morning until I saw a familiar face, a relatively neutral drinker who had arrived at lunchtimes for some rushed salvation before returning to work. He was in his suit and frowned while he worked through the possible reasons for recognition.

'Nicky!' he said at last, then his manner slipped from relief. 'I'm sorry about your dad,' he said with a professional calmness. I could see from his suit that he had been plucked from a decent level by the OK Corral.

'Thanks. Where's Mervyn, at the pub?'

'No,' he said, backing rapidly to confusion. 'He's working in a shop, are you sure that's a good idea?'

And then I knew.

'I just need to speak to him about something, it's fine.'

'Atlas Electronics apparently, Tottenham Court Road, I've never been myself.' He thought about reaching over, to give me a touch or something, but moved seamlessly into a turn. 'Good luck, Nicky, nice to see you again.'

'Thanks,' I said but then the man flicked back and asked, 'how's your mum?'

'I don't know,' I replied and walked away from the man and towards Tottenham Court Road.

Atlas Electronics was an independent set-up, grimly clinging on amidst the chains. The windows were choked with fluorescent yellow signs, bearing two-foot prices that ended with exclamation marks, and inside sat chaotic stacks of goods. I saw him towards the back of the store, hooking plastic packages on to a display rail. He looked strange in his shirt and tie, with his tattoos despatched behind the cotton.

'Mervyn?'

He jolted into movement, taking me through the back of the store to a room of scattered chairs and a large board with men's names and sales figures. He was unbearably nervous. I didn't want to make him worse, but that was all I could do.

'Did you kill him?'

'*Kill* him? Who, your dad? Jesus, Nicky, fuck's sake. Of course I didn't kill him. Jesus.'

He sat down unsteadily, pointing for me to do the same. I looked through the sales figures.

'You're not up there, Mervyn.'

'They won't let me deal with the customers yet.' He was pleased with the diversion. 'The boss says maybe in a few months, once I've got going, you know? Sometimes I wonder if I'm just here for the shoplifters.'

'What did you do to him?'

The words were a lot harder than I thought they would be. Mervyn looked at his hands, spanning them while he thought.

'I went a bit far, Nicky, a bit far. He was in hospital for a while. He's out now though.'

'The night I left, was that when it happened?'

He nodded and stared at the carpet. I wanted to, I don't know, I think I wanted to hug him. What I didn't want to think about was Dad, under Mervyn's hands in the OK Corral, or in a hospital bed. I didn't want to think about that because I didn't know how I would react. I was scared that I would care. I knew that I would care.

'It's alright, Mervyn. That stuff, it's alright.'

He looked up with immediate gratitude. It must have been his best possible outcome of a pretty dangerous selection.

'There's something else though. I need a flat. I've still got most of that money, I just need a flat.'

He was on his feet, delighted with this easy exit, scribbling on paper and thrusting it to me. A name and number.

'He'll look after you, Nicky, no problem.'

With the note serving as a close, we walked towards the door and back through the store. I told myself not to ask, over and over, but on the pavement I asked.

'Where is he?'

His answer came quickly because he'd known it would be needed.

'Still there I think, at the pub. Except when I left and he was in hospital they went in and changed it about. It's an Australian pub now. The Wombat or some bollocks like that.'

We looked at each other and we almost laughed. Instead we said goodbye and Mervyn escaped back into Atlas Electronics and I walked into the swing of Tottenham Court Road. I felt lucky because I knew that all I had to do was move and the conversation would be further and further behind me.

That evening, from my room at Miss Goldstone's, I called the name that Mervyn had given me. The man said that he was sorry to hear about my dad and that he'd call back in ten minutes. Half an hour later he phoned and gave me an Earl's Court address.

'A nice little one-bedder. Hundred and fifty a week alright with you kid? All in – electricity, gas, council tax. That's mate's rates, alright?'

'That's fine, thanks.'

'You haven't seen it yet.' He laughed. 'Meet me there first thing, eight o'clock.'

In the morning, Miss Goldstone offered me some parting advice based around Earl's Court bus services and keeping my chin up. When I carried my brewery bags towards the frosted glass of the door she said, 'Sorry to hear about your dad, Nicky,' and I couldn't even turn round. My life was so distant from and so near to him now.

I'd never had the reason or ambition to question my living arrangements and the place in Earl's Court seemed OK to me then. It was small, and a little damp, but there was a wooden bed that looked intact and a fridge that whined a bit but was cold enough and the water came through after a moment.

The man walked about whistling over the carpet of the front room (which you arrived in, without trying, the minute you came through the door) and the lino of the kitchen and bathroom, then back to the front room where he stood looking out the window at the brick wall that lay two feet beyond.

'Fuck me,' he said. 'This place is worse than I remember. You want something else?'

'No, it's fine. How much do you want now?'

'Give me six hundred, Nicky. First two weeks and deposit.'

I went through to the bedroom and pulled out what had been ten grand. I counted out his money and jerked it from below the rubber band. When I handed the man the fifties he looked at them and said,

'I take it Mervyn gave you them?'

I nodded. I wanted to say, 'Before, he gave me them *before*,' but I was too late because he had already said:

'I should fucking well hope so too.'

And after that I just wanted the man to leave me alone.

With somewhere to live, I moved on to organise something to do. It took me a few weeks, and it was then several busy months after leaving The OK Corral that I found the rooms at Soviet Street. I used a chunk of money for the deposit and advanced rent. I put up the sign –

SPIRITUAL GUIDANCE/MEDIUM SERVICES

– and ordered cards and leaflets. I booked newspaper ads, filled and decorated the rooms, and pinned the job advertisement that Tiffany would respond to in the Green Giant. And then came Tony's wife, Tony and Joe Yakari.

Java Joe.

Nineteen

I thought, but not seriously, that Brewster might have some carnal plans for me. Perhaps he saw us locked in some furious embrace in this cheap hotel. This was only diversion. Brewster had battled through to the moral nothingness that lay behind my presentation, but I had similarly seen his own shortcomings. I had misread and dangerously undervalued his capabilities, yet, disembarking from his scrappy car, I was confident on his motives.

His interest stretched from the professional because of my occupation and the financial earning it brought. It was in these two areas that Brewster felt my value lay to him. I walked into the hotel anticipating something that wasn't too far from what I got.

I predicted a charity function where the local detective would instigate widespread rejoicing by pitching up with a fast-fading television personality. Perhaps a speech where Brewster spoke chummily about me and then invaded the photos, with he and I draped together like brothers. I had overestimated him, there was no charity involved. Through the lobby was a set of twin doors guarded by a sandwich board with plastic letters shabbily inserted. It said:

D C I Milne – RETIREMEANT AT LAST! – GOOD RIDANCE YOU
OLD B$%*£*D!!

From this I knew, more or less, what to expect by following Brewster into the hotel's conference room. There must have been some warning of our entrance because we emerged to a deep spread of faces and applause. They were all men, all in cheap lounge attire and flushed with the daytime drinking. Embracing the entrapment, I slipped into a familiar role, flashing smiles and accepting the hands that snaked out from the tables.

Every so often Brewster would stop for a bit of rough-housing with one particular specimen, hurling his arms around the other man for a grope or tickle accompanied by a bit of bellowing. He'd lean into tables and deliver an awful one-liner, often at my expense, or he'd simply point back at me – grinning like a competition winner in his wake – and add some coarse qualification.

By the time we reached what was apparently our table, which headed the room and the rest of the men, I was in a deepening despair and yet the nightmare wasn't complete. A buffoon in a brown suit came bounding over delightedly and pumped my hand.

'A pleasure, Mr Santini, an absolute pleasure. My wife and I are big fans of yours, though I don't know what you're doing being mates with this bastard!'

I turned to see Brewster doing a faux-surrender pose with his palms.

'We're not friends,' I told the man and he erupted in laughter, slapped my back, pretended to punch Brewster, and finally retreated sharply to the centre of the table with a wink to me and what sounded like, 'Ten minutes.'

'Did he say ten minutes?' I asked Brewster but he was busy shaking down our chairs while pointing out associates at the facing tables and shouting obscenities to them. The man in the brown suit spoke into a microphone and a weak order was achieved when he ran through some individual greetings and then, with no switch in tone, a number of startlingly racist jokes that had the half-pissed coppers fairly roaring.

'Here he goes,' whispered Brewster and nudged me. 'Can you beat this?' he challenged, while drinking greedily from a tumbler of whisky.

'What?' I said sharply, turning in my chair towards him. 'Can I beat fucking racist jokes? What are you playing at?'

Brewster laughed – maybe at me, maybe at the joke about a black golfer.

'What's this ten minutes shit?' I demanded. 'Ten minutes till what?'

'Till you're on,' he said casually, toasting a bald man near the back of the room with his glass.

'Fuck that,' I said, as much out of curiosity as anything else. I had suspected that this was coming and it was a pretty detestable development, but I needed to know how Brewster would represent both his threat and the required forfeit. If he wanted me to agree to this disturbing settlement, he was going to have to provide a worse alternative.

'You'll do it,' he told me.

He didn't even look at me, just instigated the whole room's clapping after the man in the brown suit reached the end of a joke involving a Chinese taxi driver. I caught the corrupt comedian glancing to Brewster for a confirmation which he offered with a quick nod, then tugged at my chair while flipping a palm to the room in encouragement. Their attention and applause switched smoothly to me.

'I'm not going up,' I said flatly to Brewster and he leant in close in response, the smell of the whisky swimming round my head.

'You'll do it or I'm going up there to tell them about last night. About my father. You wouldn't get out the fucking room.'

It was the hopelessness that hurt me more than anything, and I was breathless with fury when I stood and walked to the microphone with a sickly smile.

Twenty

There were several complications within this arrangement, other than being ensnared in a motorway hotel full of half-pissed policemen. For my work to glide as it might, I depended upon an audience that was attentive, loyal and suggestive. But already when I took to the stand there was overly confident cheering and less helpful jeering. The room teemed with wags battling for attention and every table seemed to possess one amateur joker bellowing clumsy offerings to pockets of appreciation.

I stretched the silence while I watched. It was the only course, I knew that immediately. Amongst the mayhem I was going to have to try a savage chance. More than a chance, even. I didn't have time for my usual upward trend of discovery, and there wasn't the patience available within the room for only glimmers of achievement.

I surveyed them steadily with my hands safe in my pockets. The shouts stopped soon enough and then the only breaks to the silence were coughing and occasional bits of rallying. I freed a hand and took the microphone. Someone shouted some trite remark – 'At last!' – and was rebuked by others. I pulled the microphone to me and spoke in a voice that would have sounded to them like a whisper but wasn't.

'When did Dave die?'

Nothing, then reaction from at least half the men in the room. It was a moment, one of those moments, and for it to happen then made it perhaps the greatest lie of all. I had been looking for my standard rate

– for a handful of the maybe two hundred before me to have lost a brother, dad, uncle, friend, milkman or anyone who had the common name. In actual fact, I had strayed upon a ludicrous angle.

A few months previously, I pieced together from the testimonies shouted back, a popular policeman called Dave had keeled over whilst playing golf. All this I took with nods of confirmation and 'I'm getting this' or, 'Yes, Dave's just telling me about this as well,' while I ran through what was fast approaching.

For twenty, thirty minutes I took that room on a hurtling non-journey that left them hanging on with grateful desperation. A fast-moving whip of worthlessness that had them rising from their seats in response, to will on the genius in the midst of their smashed afternoon. They ascended on a spiral of belief and noise – roaring endorsement and banging palms on the tables in answer to my great pronouncements, that:

Dave was a very generous person. Sometimes he could be a bit selfish, but you could always tell he felt guilty for this later.

Dave tended to be a bit more honest than some people that he met.

Dave swore a lot, which could occasionally be embarrassing.

Sometimes Dave had problems with authority. I'll tell you one thing, he never let his mates down.

With each edict there would be trimmings of pretend detail when Dave and I concurred and his former colleagues hyperventilated in response. But it was built on those four plastic facts that, if they only stopped and thought, everyone in that room would have realised might just stretch to anyone. Instead, they chose delirium, which I eventually dissipated with a grinding change of pace. A hand brought quiet and then I told them grandly:

'Dave wants to say that he's watching you all right now. He's saying that a couple of you' – I threw out a gesture that comfortably covered a majority of the room – 'should take it easy with the booze, because he knows what you lot can be like with a drink in you!'

While they laughed and jostled I added,

'And what's this thing about a stag do? Dave says he's still embarrassed about that?'

This was an easy piece of work. Any man who died at thirty or above and I have gained is a heavy drinker, or associate of heavy drinkers (and it looked very much that Dave was both), can be linked to this nameless stag do embarrassment. At my regular shows the crowd laugh along in universal understanding anyway, even if the former wife is looking openly aghast at my claim against her departed husband.

They hooted and yelled confirmation and then I eased them down again.

'But he wants to say something,' I adopted a paternal leaning. 'He wants you to enjoy yourselves. That's all. Because he says, what he says—' I drooped into the microphone because – it would have appeared to them – my knees were overcome. The tears came easier than ever and the response of my palms to clear them was authentic.

The room was dead, not a word.

'He says, and I apologise for the language, gentlemen, but this is Dave after all,' I smiled heroically through the hurt, 'he says you're the best fucking force there ever was, and he has never been as proud in his whole fucking life as when he walked amongst you.'

And the room erupted. There was shouting but it was more than that, with no control and an anarchy that caught me by surprise. There were men leaping on the spot, pogo like, and punching the air, thumping the air with their fists. Others collapsed into frantic combinations of bodies – hoisted on shoulders, wrapped in complicated, multiple hugs, or just holding each other with unlikely tenderness.

Everywhere I looked, men cried. Some tried to shield this unexpected display, some implored towards me as if I could halt this mortifying turn, while others stood trapped in utter confusion while the alien tears scoured their cheeks.

I gave a general wave and started the slow slalom back to my seat, allowing the members of the top table to launch various physical assaults. The man in the brown suit swung at me wildly while wailing like a newborn baby. He ended up hooking me round the waist and I ruffled his hair before corkscrewing my way out. I had only just escaped when Brewster enveloped me.

I felt his stubble and smelled the whisky before he pulled back to shout,

'You lucky bastard!' When I pushed him away it was all I could do not to smile but instead I said,

'We're going. Now.'

And then, I couldn't stop myself, I smiled too and he saw this and relented and said,

'OK.'

Twenty-one

Both Brewster and I required some time in his car to recover. There had evidently been a rapidness to his drinking and he was chuckling away and loose with the driving in sweeping us on and off the motorway and back into the city's indifferent streets. I moved from the raw note of the performance to returning doubt. There was exhaustion from what had just happened and the not knowing what would happen next, so when I galvanised myself it was to an unsatisfactory pitch.

'So that's us done,' I said. 'I hope you enjoyed it.'

'You know, Nick,' said Brewster, flicking his eyes lazily to the mirror just so I could see him do so. 'I was speaking to my friend the other day. He works in a prison, near here. He was telling me about something called lullabying. Have you heard about it? It's something that's happening in the prisons these days.'

'My dad went to prison.' It was an attempt to show my immunity to the novel fear of prison stories, but it emerged sounding desperate. I was trying to work out how the balance had turned again so suddenly while Brewster continued.

'Oh, this is a new thing, it's only just got going. What they do, the prisoners that are dealing drugs, is they find out the new inmates that have money. Then they threaten or, you know, bribe the new boy's cellmate into doing this thing, this lullabying.'

He stopped talking, wound down the window and lit a cigarette. He changed gear, stole another look in the mirror that I knew was at me, and then realised I wasn't going to ask so pushed on unchecked.

'The new boy wakes up in the middle of the night and he's got his cellmate sitting on him with a razor at his throat. The guy tells him to either relax and let him find a vein, or he's going to get smack, that's heroin by the way Nick, down his throat. One way or another, they get heroin into the new boy and good stuff too, the dealers make sure of that. And, you see, that's them got a new customer, and one with money. Do you see what I mean Nick?'

This was pathetic.

'This is pathetic,' I said. Enough. I wasn't going to let him continue with this. I turned in my seat, troubling some crisp wrappers, and addressed him again.

'Fucking pathetic.'

'What?' he said, fidgeting with his indicator, 'the lullabying?'

'No, not that shite. You know I don't mean that shite. Prisons, heroin. Fucking grow up. You think I'm scared of you telling me prison stories, Brewster? Why the fuck would that scare me? I don't have to listen to this, I don't have to listen to you. What have you actually got on me? That I lied about your dad? What are you going to do me for, impersonating a *ghost*?' I sneered in powerful climax.

He laughed at that, and nodded in compliment. I had him. That's what I thought, sitting in Brewster's car and watching him groan at the changing traffic lights. I thought that I had him. I thought, even, that he was going to apologise. When he finally turned to me with red eyes, I thought that he was going to apologise.

'I'm not saying you should worry about prison, Nick. It's just that someone maybe should.'

'Why's that?'

'Because that girl, she had bruises on her arms, from the same time as the cuts. Big bruises, Nick, really big fuckers on her arms.'

'Did she do them herself?' I asked quietly, hoping. 'While she was, you know…'

'She might have done, I'll know more in the morning,' conceded Brewster. 'Seems strange though, doesn't it?'

'Does it? How the fuck should I know?'

I was sweating and the more I thought about that and how it might look, the more I sweated. I tried to open the car window, but the handle was out of synch and spun too lightly, disconnected from the door's workings.

'This car…' I said and Brewster laughed again.

I lifted my arm and pushed it over my forehead, enjoying the initial screen it gave me, then looked at Brewster with as much concentration as I could muster. I was going to tell him to let me out of his car and I was going to make some sort of threat to make him do so. But before I did all that he said,

'Shall I drop you here?'

The car shuddered to a stop and I opened the door and made gratefully to leave when I felt his hand on my shoulder and turned for more torment.

'Enjoy your day, Nick, I'll be in touch soon enough. And don't go anywhere, of course.'

He smiled, his shaped moustache offering a shadowed roof to the expression, and I got a final blast of whisky and sweat before I was alone amongst the lucky, irrelevant people who walked on the pavement.

The day after Java Joe hung on the blue rope, and I signed my contract with Tony, I woke up in the flat in Earl's Court and didn't really know what to do. I wondered about those regulars – walking up the stairs, delicate and ready for their weekly need, only to find the bolted door. I thought about their money too. But that all had to go, and I had new, immediate demands in shaping what I had for rooms full of observers.

I would have to call people up to a stage, detail the usual stuff, and hopefully generate ripples of appreciation through the remaining crowd. The problem was that it lent the process so many witnesses. I could cover slips and cracks in the back room at Soviet Street easily enough. But it would only need one person, easier on the drink or tighter on the brain than the rest of the crowd, to call out a reasoned bit of thinking and I could hit unavoidable failure.

I'd never been in working men's clubs but I knew the people that would be there and I didn't fancy my chances of dominating the atmosphere.

For the two weeks Tony had asked me to wait, and the further month that he hadn't, I practised. He would call every few days and tell me we were very close, that he was waiting on a couple of club owners here and there, and to get *on my game*.

The interlude led to the notes, my attempt to create some structure. To begin with, the notes were a meticulous study of the plays and tricks that had worked well in Soviet Street. I drew graphs with arrows and boxes of possibility. I planned entire conversations, down to jokey ad-libs and humorous conclusions, and played dangerous examples against myself until I created a grudging victory.

So when Tony called me and said that everything was in place and I was to be at Euston Station the following afternoon, I felt only partial panic.

'What's the plan?'

'Fourteen dates, Nicky boy. Fourteen nights for the great Nicholas to astound and amaze.' He laughed.

'When's the first one?'

'Tomorrow. Walsall South Working Men's Club, the big time.' He laughed again.

At Euston Tony was in the bar, drinking Guinness and reading a tabloid.

'Here he is,' he shouted and patted the stool next to him. 'The great Nicholas, take a seat, what you having?'

'Water.'

On the train, Tony was under a new exhilaration. He told me that this was what he *lived for*. When I asked what he meant he clarified with a gesture round the half-empty carriage.

'Being on the road.'

My reluctance to recognise the celebratory air, and the wearing pace of his excitement, soon left Tony spent and sleeping. He grumbled in front of me, rolling his head with his mouth hung open.

I extracted my notes and laid them on the plastic table. The sight of them was edged by fear but I kept going, reading and testing while the train ran on. It was some time later and he had to make a noise for me to look up. One eye was open, the lid heavy in a reluctant arch.

'Homework, eh?' And he smiled after the eye closed again.

By Birmingham my study had calmed me and Tony awoke jubilant. He bored the taxi driver with queries as to the current state of Birmingham venues and bands, throwing out names that he clearly had hoped to bring back more.

'You've not heard of him?!' he'd shout, leaning into the gap in the glass. 'Best fucking bass player this city's ever produced,

I did two tours with him, great guy,' and the driver would nod thoughtfully while he strained for traffic threats that didn't exist.

The hotel was bad, as I knew it would be. The room wasn't much of an improvement on my flat. What's more, it had two beds. And what's more, Tony was soon standing at one, whistling and unzipping his case.

'We're sharing?'

'Start at the bottom, Nicky boy,' he said smartly. 'The financials have got to make sense. I could have laid out myself and, let's face it, so could you, but the sums should always add up.'

I thought of the money back at the flat, still largely untroubled in the detergent box under the sink. Some of it made in the back room of Soviet Street, most of it stolen from Java Joe. Tiffany knew about the earned money, so Tony did too.

'It's not too bad,' said Tony, unbuckling his belt and walking to the bathroom. He left the door open and continued to talk over his piss drumming against the toilet's wall.

'We've got to be at the club in two hours, you want to eat?'

'Yeah, OK.'

His spray turned to stutter as it neared an end.

In a Chinese buffet near the hotel, Tony discussed what he called the tour. The fourteen dates in fourteen nights.

'You don't need a night off, Nicky,' he explained. 'You're going to get in the rhythm and stay there.'

Tony liked these musical phrases and used a number of them between happily popping cigars of spring rolls between his lips and making messes of duck wraps, building them carelessly and leaving meat and sauce dropping from the sides of his mouth. He asked, for example, if I had a big *opening number* and mentioned a *crescendo* many, many times.

'To be honest, Tony,' I said at one point, waiting until he crammed home a fist of crackers to give me a chance to complete the message, 'I'm a bit worried. I don't know how it'll work with an audience.'

He was red and frantic in his attempt to get rid of the suddenly invasive crackers, his jaw chattering.

'I'll give it a go but maybe we should set something up, have you in the audience or something?'

'No, can't do that,' he said, a palm on the table while he recovered his breathing. 'The club owners know me. Plus, these clubs, Nick, you stick someone in the audience they'd stand out, you know, and if they nabbed us then they'd fucking kill us.'

He shook his head sadly and I was jolted by the trace of disappointment. 'Just do your best, Nicky boy, that's all, I'm sure we'll be fine.'

The slip in his confidence left regret in our walk back to the hotel. I asked for half an hour alone and told him to meet me in what passed for a reception. Tony accepted gratefully and retreated to the pub next door.

Once more I went to the notes and pounded their lessons home. I showered in the cramped bathroom, speaking above the cheap water to welcome people to the stage, joke with them about their backgrounds, and slip into those first lines of easy discovery. Whilst shaving I thanked them for their participation and reinforced to the crowd just how reliant this was on their help. I heard them shout their readiness to guide me.

I pulled on my black clothing, quietly guiding myself through a triumphant ending. While I scuttled down the hotel's stairs, too charged now for the silence of the lift, I thanked the people for coming along tonight. Walking out the hotel and making for the pub, I wished them a safe journey home. And, beckoning Tony from the pub and stopping a taxi, I was ready.

The club looked as testing as I'd imagined, an unpainted shell with a wooden sign and a tarpaulin calling:

LIVE ACTS EVERY NIGHT – £1.50 PINT

Inside, it smelt of ancient smoke and drink. A sea of wooden tables topped with heavy ashtrays ran from a stage that jutted out from a purple velvet backdrop. A few tables were taken with people newly arrived. They pulled their best jackets from their shoulders, taking drink orders from each other with clapped hands and excitement.

'Where is he?' Tony asked a barman, who was old and struggling with an optic and didn't look back before answering, 'Through the back.'

We walked through the tables and towards the stage. I saw from some distance that the velvet was nailed to the roof. Behind it was a small opening that Tony led us through into a corridor and then a room that was bright and noisy.

'Here he fucking is!' shouted a man at Tony and Tony shouted something similar before they hugged and broke off into a round of slapping and swearing.

'This is him,' said Tony, pointing back to me with a thumb, and the man cocked his neck and said, 'Fuck me, how old are you?'

'Twenty, nice to meet you,' I said and wondered if I should extend introductions to the other two people in the room.

There was a man sitting smoking in a chair and staring at the wall in apparent fury, with a large puppet and a pint of beer within reach on the floor. I looked at him long enough to give him the option to look up, but he didn't so I turned instead, and with some interest, to the final member of the collection.

The woman was bent over a wooden table, pressed towards a mirror where she reappeared in reflection, coating her lips with firm strokes. She was naked, her skin dusted with brown in what I presumed had been the previous process. In the mirror, below her face that didn't move to look at mine, her tits hung in tight bunches of smeared paste. When she finally looked, I flicked my eyes away.

'Alright?' she said in what I guessed was a local accent.

'Yeah, good thanks,' I offered a smile that I hoped was something it probably wasn't. Tony and his friend finished up their extended greetings and turned to me.

'Keith,' said the new man, bald and with a silver tooth, and stuck out a hand where a tattoo crawled over the fingers.

'Nick. Nice to meet you.'

'Well, I hope you're as good as he says you are,' said Keith, flicking his head to Tony. He had a steel that Tony didn't. 'You're on in half an hour, opening act.'

The man with the puppet snorted. Keith winced with anger but didn't acknowledge it, wishing me good luck and walking out the room with Tony following loyally behind before twisting at the door and looking for me.

'Alright, kid?' His face was slightly pinched.

'Yeah, no problems.'

I turned away. I didn't mind if he saw my worry but I certainly didn't want to see his.

That last stretch, with the jilted puppeteer and the woman who reluctantly clothed herself, was expensive to my remaining confidence. Growing reminders came from the club of what was to come – shouts and glass hitting glass, then music that broke out suddenly in a taped assault.

My notes provoked noises of derision from the puppeteer and in the end I sat and studied the wall while trying to bring back the wit and ease that had sprung so readily in the hotel room. The woman was smoking and wearing a dress covered in plastic stones that were noticeably failing to sparkle.

'What do you do then?' I asked in a weak voice. She looked up, coughed, and smiled with a shocking vengeance.

'What do you fucking think I do?'

The puppeteer laughed savagely.

'Go on, girl!'

Keith came back to the door wearing a suit too big for him.

'OK, Nicky.'

He took me to the gap behind the velvet and pointed for me to wait while he walked onwards to some acclaim. The music was brought to an ugly, mid-song halt and Keith was telling jokes with an easy rise and fall. He picked a few people out for observations that brought him generous laughter. For my introduction, he explained with friendly persistence that the people, his people really, were about to be amazed.

'He can read your minds, ladies and gentlemen,' said Keith, then pausing before, 'the poor bastard!'

Once that last, warm response was easing, he finished.

'OK you lot, settle down. Without further ado. Please welcome. The. *Great*. Nicholas.'

The Great Nicholas, I thought, so that's what that is. I edged through the velvet, smiled willingly and took the microphone from Keith before he left me there alone. It was much busier now, with tables crowned with glasses and faces and smoke above them. When I looked at the faces – silent and watching – I forgot every single thing that I had wanted to say to them.

I lasted perhaps ten minutes. I started, if such a term should be used, by asking if there was anyone in the audience who would like to speak to me.

'Would anyone like to speak to me?'

That was what I said.

It was a bewildering opener that attracted a suitable response.

'Go on then,' someone shouted in anger or sympathy and they'd have been much the same in result.

That didn't help me and I'm not sure what would have. I was steadily heating under the ugly lamps and my black outfit. I couldn't see Tony. That was probably a good thing.

'I need a volunteer.'

It sounded more like a question than it was meant to.

'You need something alright,' shouted someone I couldn't see and earned themselves some laughter.

The aggression was somewhat worrying. What little of my plans I could hope to drag from somewhere required an assistance that wasn't immediately evident. I was moving smoothly towards despair when a man at the front stood up smartly.

'Come on then, mate,' he said, 'I'll help you out,' and his companions cheered him on his way up to join me. He was friendly and sober enough, with no obvious mischief about him.

'Thanks very much, sir,' I said. My hairline itched with the sweat, my chest was alive. 'So. What's your name?' I pushed the microphone to him in a wilting grip.

'Aren't you supposed to tell me?'

There was a fair bit of gratitude from the crowd for that.

'Come on, mate,' I said, with shameless pity and the microphone held away.

'Alright, alright.' He held up a hand to the crowd, which he now appeared to be controlling. 'It's Danny.'

His table chanted 'Da-nny, Da-nny,' until he stopped them.

'Danny.' I said, 'Danny.'

I'm not sure why I couldn't think of anything to say after this. I may have been left stranded by the disappearance of my several plots, and overwhelmed by the constant reality of the crowd, but you would have thought that I could have said something. Instead I looked at the man with a curious detachment, as if I was watching from afar, and interested only in what he would say next. What he did say, finally, was,

'Are you on the fucking wind-up, mate?'

Luckily my distraction had kept the microphone to my lips. Only the front few tables, therefore, received that criticism. It at least forced me to speak.

'What,' I asked, my voice fading by the word, 'do you do for a living Danny?'

'Unemployed.'

'Unemployed, eh?' I asked, in some ludicrous need for confirmation.

'Yeah.'

'So,' I said. My voice was hiding behind a whisper, too humiliated to carry the moronic loads I was granting.

'You married, Danny?'

'Fuck this,' he said, perfectly calmly, and walked from the stage. At first there was silence.

'Well,' I said to the crowd, who shared horrific shades of concentration. 'Doesn't look like Danny wants to talk, does it?'

It was this audacious attempt to switch some blame to one of their own that broke the quiet. The abuse came in flying volleys from around the room, a steady onslaught of threats and outrage.

'Anyone else fancy,' I had to shout back to them, 'coming up here for a chat then?'

It sounded like a challenge and, by progression, a threat. Men rose and jabbed fingers but their words were thankfully sucked into the general roar that came back. To the side of the room I saw more committed movement in a figure who stalked towards the stage.

It was Tony, moving with deathly steps and his head hung. He passed a man I recognised as Keith, who threw out a hand to block him, then pulled it back and used it instead to cover his eyes.

Tony arrived doomed on to the stage. He sighed and looked up with a very total terror.

'What's your name please?'

I could feel disaster coming, rushing from all angles. It was coming from the crowd, the velvet, even the puppeteer who must have been within delirium somewhere. And, immediately, it was coming from Tony. He looked as if my question was the most unexpected group of words I could have possibly assembled. He swallowed, sighed, considered and then spoke. There was, I want to stress, definitely a period of consideration.

'Danny,' said Tony.

'Danny?'

At least the anger had to take away some of the fear.

'Another Danny?'

Tony nodded, swallowed again and said, once more for luck, 'Danny.'

'That's his fucking manager!'

The shout daggered from the very back of the room, past the crowd that stirred as one. It was nearly hurtful when I saw that it had come from the barman. The noise started once more, sharper than ever, and Keith sprung from the shadows and jogged on to the stage.

'That was your fucking barman,' I said in wonder, handing him the microphone. 'What's he playing at?'

'What's he playing at?' said Keith, grabbing the microphone with blazing eyes.

I walked from the stage, through a fire door and into a handy taxi.

I now had nothing, no direction left. Forty grand, that's what I had. A year, it could do me a year at least, if not longer. I wasn't quick enough at the hotel. As the lift took me back down and opened there was Tony, panting and surprisingly appreciative to find me. He pointed at my bag.

'No need for that. You're going back on tomorrow. Same place, I've squared it with Keith. I mean,' he tilted his head in concession, 'it wasn't exactly easy, but he owes me one. More than one, as it happens.'

I managed to laugh. 'Back on there? Don't be fucking ridiculous. Tony, I'm not going back on anywhere, but back on there? They'd kill me. I'm going back to London, now.'

'No, it doesn't work like that, Nicky. Come on, let me buy you a pint, then you can decide what to do.'

'One pint,' I said, only because it was going to be the least that I was going to have to give him, and it might as well be there rather than a final, brutal meeting in London.

In the pub next door to the hotel Tony bought me drinks and gave me some rough charm. That made little impact but he had some scraps of fact that slowly worked through my thoughts and the lingering shock of my performance. The first was his insistence that the following evening at Keith's club would offer an entirely fresh crowd.

This I found unlikely. I couldn't see such an establishment attracting more than a steady nucleus, but Tony was insistent. Those men and women in sportswear and denim would pick one night, with the acts repeated over a weekend.

'Not Friday and then again on Saturday, Nicky boy, no way. Tomorrow will be a curry and *Match of the Day* for the ones there tonight. We'll get the Saturday crowd, totally different.'

It would have made some sense if I'd wanted it to do so. Tony had another pitch to go. He told me in laboured certainty how club owners from around Britain, Keith and his wider union, were linked through arrangements carved from social, business and soft crime considerations.

'These people talk to each other, Nicky,' he declared. 'If we don't go back tomorrow and do something at Keith's then that's us. That's us done. It's not like we can sit out a month or two and have another crack at it. We've got to sort it now.'

He was genuine at least in his aim. When I waited, he saw that I could turn.

'What are you going to do, Nicky? Go back to London, live off the money stashed in your flat and then what? You can't just start all that crap you were doing before at the drop of a fucking hat, Nicky. You know this is what you have to do. This is your chance, Nicky. You know that.'

'Right,' I said, tired and wanting only to leave this pub and go to bed. The closest was the slim one in the shared room. 'I'll do it but tomorrow we need to work on things properly. I need to get things right. I'll need you to help me.'

Tony was thrown with delight, his mouth open and his hands up in concession.

'And that fucking barman won't be on either, he wasn't exactly much help.'

'No,' said Tony and chanced a smile, 'he wasn't. I'll make sure Keith doesn't have him in.'

'Keith's OK with this?'

'Yeah, he's a good guy, Keith. I told him you weren't well and so on.'

'Not well?'

'I said your guts had gone, you know, the shits.'

'Great, perfect.'

'Anyway,' he said, 'let's get a couple more, I think we need them.'

'Alright, last one,' I told him, 'Get them in then, Danny,' and he laughed all the way to the bar.

I slept well and only woke because of Tony's noise. He bashed about the room, swearing and groaning his way to the bathroom. I pushed the itchy sheets from me and breathed in the room's decay, which was well-established but certainly enhanced by the two of us.

I suggested breakfast and Tony told me it was lunchtime. I showered and when I turned the thin gauge back off I heard a phone conversation from the room that was urgent mutters and illicit laughing.

'Who was that?' I asked, trying manfully to protect myself with the limited towel.

'Keith,' answered Tony. 'All sorted for tonight.'

We found a grubby café with signs showing mistrust between establishment and customer –

SAUCES MUST BE PAID FOR, <u>NO</u> EXCEPTION

– and Tony ordered a full English for us both before selecting a window table with a decent view of a roundabout.

The fragile novelty of Tony's plan – my non-triumphant return to the club – had gone. Now there were just hangovers, the roundabout, and two dishes of desperate breakfast. Tony battled on, giving what he saw as motivation as he carved and lifted the burnt food.

He talked mostly of *other times* when his acts had faced such a negative response. He spoke, in chunks of speech with a loaded fork waiting at his chin, of bands forgetting lines, breaking equipment, passing out in the dressing rooms. He told me about a drummer who was beaten senseless by a club's bouncers after he stole some cigarettes from one of their jackets. He laughed at that one and a fleck of egg left his lips and landed on the rim of my plate.

'The guy was fucked, Nicky, nothing anyone could do about it, we stuck him in Accident and Emergency and got a session guy for the next night. That's the business.'

It was comforting to see the effort but I could also see how little effort it was. This is what Tony did. A steady stream of flimsy support, with nothing behind it except for a constant desire to avoid dispute. It wasn't encouraging. The previous evening, the uttered *Danny*, that was how he met real pressure.

Tony's phone beeped with a text message and he pulled it awkwardly from his jacket pocket. He read the message and I could see, immediately, a lie forming. He frowned to buy time and chewed a lip while his face steadily darkened.

'Keith,' he said weakly, pushing the phone back to his pocket with his eyes staying on the plates. 'We should get going.'

'We have to work on stuff this afternoon, Tony, I need to get things a lot tighter.'

'You certainly do.' He laughed and I knew that his flippancy came from the text message. 'Look. I'm going to go and see Keith, get things ready at the club, I'll be back in plenty of time.'

I looked for the time and found it on a white clock nailed to the woodchip. Nearly three.

'What time at the club tonight?'

'There for seven, on at seven thirty. Top of the bill. Where you belong.'

'Top of the bill?'

'Well, not top, but...'

'Can we meet at five?'

I couldn't help the vulnerability. My mind was screaming about what was coming again, four and a half hours away. Tony fiddled with his phone.

'Yeah, no problem.'

'One thing Tony, I need a new name. The Great Nicholas is shite, I sound like a magician.'

'I'll get you one, speak to people, come up with a good one,' he answered, looking at me with sudden attention to urge me to release him.

'You'll get one?'

'Yep,' said Tony, smiling at something else and pushing clear of the table.

Back at the hotel, alone in Birmingham, I thought about the club as it had been the night before and how it would undoubtedly be again that night. The hurdle, which I had comfortably failed to tackle, had been the suspicion and easy aggression. They had to be handled and anchored. I required something to at least force the bitter mob to give me the pause to bring in the material. If I could only get them to listen, then I had a chance.

The unlikely solution was a piece of childhood diversion that came hurtling back to me from the school in Marylebone and from *Doctor Who*. It seemed impossible but there was nothing else I could think of that would get me through the smoke, the drink and the derision.

This unexpected arrival was, desperately, all I had. I would go on to use it that night and many others. The last time that I would ever use it would be in the hotel room where the black girl had scarpered from worldly concerns, where I would stand in front of Brewster and the other policeman and think of *Doctor Who*.

Twenty-two

The black girl's arms danced through my thoughts while I travelled away from Brewster and back to the hotel. Sometimes they came alone. Sometimes they were decorated with foreign hands clamped around them that gripped and advertised the flesh so the blade could do its dicing. Sometimes those hands were my hands. But no, that couldn't have been. I ran through the night in tedious repetition and still there was nothing missing, clouded or stolen by the drink. And that left, well, it left other people.

Tony, the obvious suggestion, was ridiculous. Whenever violence had leered into our lives he had wilted and subtracted himself in any way possible. Drunken teenagers shouting barely credible TV-abuse to me in the street would leave Tony loping off in a heavy jog or edging behind me with a muttered, 'Oh fuck, oh fuck, oh fuck.' If our accosters shouted from a neighbouring taxi in a traffic lights queue, Tony would duck beneath the window as if facing a hail of bullets.

The day, and the lunch, where we were told by those two imposters from the television channel that they had heard of Java Joe (and then I was told something more by one of them while the other took Tony outside) was a glaring example. When it was over and we left them laughing like ghosts and ordering more champagne, I said to Tony on the way to the airport:

'I want to kill those cunts.'

I meant it too, with the usual distance between intent and action. But Tony looked like he'd been confronted with insanity. Even though these men had just directed our lives back downwards, back into the hunted hoi polloi, there was nothing within Tony but the dip of disappointment. No stirring anger, no waking fury.

Tony wasn't an optimist, he didn't have the drive for that. He just pushed on, and he couldn't possess what would have been required to put his hands around that girl's arms, in a move connected to what then followed. There wasn't the means, let alone the motivation, and this was the conditional conclusion I had reached before arriving at the hotel to find Tony in a stand-off with the black girl's parents within the cramped excuse of a lobby.

'Ah,' he said, with a grateful smile, 'the man himself!' The parents turned to me in subjugation.

'They were just asking,' continued Tony and I knew that he couldn't remember their names, 'if you could make the funeral.'

'Oh,' I answered with a willing transparency, 'I'd love to, more than anything, but unfortunately the police want us to stay another couple of days. Just to help tie things up.'

'Ah, I'd said about the tour?' Tony countered, frowning at what he saw as a slip.

The tour was the great, universal, all-encompassing excuse for anything at all that came up during the tour. When venue owners and local agents probed me in dressing rooms, bars, hotels, with dinner invites and signing sessions, I would look to Tony and the two of us would groan and say, 'The tour…'

'Oh no, Tony, forget the tour,' I said, enjoying the reproach. 'I would miss a hundred shows to go to this,' I indicated the fidgeting parents, 'but I'm afraid there's just a couple of things with the police…'

'They said it was all done,' said the mother and I considered that this might have been the first time I had heard either of them speak. She'd done so with overriding flatness, without question and certainly nothing as crude as suspicion.

'Yes, it's just paperwork,' I chanced a hand on her shoulder and she leant to me obligingly. 'I said that I wanted to deal with it as much as possible, to save you two from, you know?'

And they nodded and the father sighed and looked at me, perhaps, with something approaching love.

'But listen,' I sadly progressed, 'I'll be in touch very soon. Once everything is over it would be good to have a chat.'

'Yeah,' said Tony, justifying his presence and reaching for the briefcase he liked to carry during the day in a cheap shot of authority. 'Let's give you something to take away with you.'

When he puffed and scrambled for what I hoped would be loose paper, to lend these two some phone numbers and contact details, I can't say I was surprised or even particularly rattled when he re-emerged with a smile and a clutch of posters and recalled DVDs.

When they left, armed with their gifts and assurances to expect my call, Tony and I slunk to the honesty bar. I told him of my stolen hours with Brewster and the drunken policemen and he muscled some unconvincing anger my way. He shouted that Brewster was a *cheeky fucker* and even banged the table in a move far too long in the planning, which I could see had hurt when his hand was snatched back regretfully.

I relayed the tactics I had activated when thrust into performance by Brewster and Tony shared my admiration. It was while I was allowing him to enjoy the lighter results of my fortune – 'Stupid bastards,' he laughed uproariously at visions of crying policemen – that I quietly passed on the other development, the news that Brewster had employed to leave me reeling on the pavement.

I didn't, beforehand, give Tony room to prepare. I didn't steady him with a new tone or portrayal that would suggest a switch to the severe. Instead I let him laugh, and I was laughing too, at the weeping coppers and then I said with no bias to the words,

'Brewster thinks someone might have killed the black girl.'

Tony looked entirely surprised. He said 'What?!' and tried a smirking gamble that it was a joke. This was what I expected, and what I hoped for, and I accepted it with no little gratitude. I needed that reaction. With everything else suddenly tinged with uncertainty, the previously depressing predictability of our connection was now comforting.

Assured of the welcome firmness, I suggested dinner and we meandered to a steak bar where I correctly guessed Tony's entire order including the manner of presentation (muttering deliberation, clipped delivery and the menu held breezily aloft without eye contact with the waiter. This was what he did in unimpressive venues) and we inexpertly considered the possibility of a killer operating around us.

It was too divorced though, too different. Tony gave a halting summary of his current team and there was no one who could be matched to the wish, or even the *energy*, for such an offence. It would require something beyond the average, an unexpected piece of unhinging, to go about something like that. In looking for a suitable display of mania it was hard to move beyond the opaque mind that the black girl must have borne when she reached for the razor.

Chewing my steak, I recalled tabloid stories of women lifting cars to free their babies, and dying pensioners suddenly reaching out with superhuman grips. Someone who had made the decision to disembark from life in a manner that promised inescapable pain and horror was surely the prime, if not only, candidate to have clutched and bruised their arms amidst the anarchy.

It was more than enough for me and I'm sure it would have been more than enough for Tony if I had felt the need to tell him. He was doing fine by himself though, offering,

'I don't even think Brewster reckons it was murder, he'd have been trying to get you going, keep you talking to him probably. The problem is,' said Tony, jabbing with his fork, 'we can't take that chance. If he wants something, we'll probably have to give him it.'

I wondered if this was the greatest insight that he had ever manufactured or if I was so wearied that I was displaced from normal reasoning. Tony was right. Brewster was taking a chance, knowing I'd have to give him something back. Another after-dinner extravaganza maybe, and then we'd be gone. We joked freely on the way back and Tony told me he'd meet me in the honesty bar.

'I've just got to check my email, Nick. I'd better warn people we might be stuck here for a couple of days. Get some drinks in anyway, my treat.'

He said this in the lift so struggled to find a distraction when he instantly realised he was talking to the man whose treat it had now been for years. In the end he had the decency for a shamed smile before the door pinged and he could escape on his floor.

In the bar I eyed the furniture and placed us where we had been the night before. Tony had hung in front of me, dodging my attempts to focus on his eyes and his words. I tried to bring back what he had said but I was ready for it not to come. I didn't have the application, or the force of true demand, to ask him. Not when things seemed to be levelling. I sat and I waited and he arrived excited.

'Look at this, kiddo!'

He was grinning and holding a print-out in a shaking hand. It was ridiculous how alien such a document was to me, but there you go. There was a name and a date and I recognised the TV station address in the sign-off. The message was what was important.

> **Hear Nick back on road and going well. We're going to have a chat about the situation but think we can get him back. Sorry to hear about his girlfriend, pass that on. Speak soon.**

'Brilliant, eh?' said Tony, his fingers tapping the paper.

'Is it?'

'Of course it is. That's them saying, "A few more months and Nick's back on the telly."'

'Is it?'

'Yeah.'

We had a couple more drinks. I had less reason than Tony to believe that a TV return was possible. I knew what he didn't. But it was difficult to argue with the email and Tony's thrill was so sustained that it was hard not to share some of it. Besides, I'd seen the shifting morals of the men behind the TV channel. A return wasn't impossible. It was unlikely, but it wasn't impossible.

It wasn't doing me any good to think this way. I told Tony that I was going to bed and he lifted the half-full bottle and said he was staying. We shook hands gracelessly and I walked wearily to my room where I collapsed into a final battle with my doubts. They tried to conjure the black girl's arms but the images were more faded than before. They had only ever been sharpened by Brewster's use of them as an ambush.

I thought about Brewster, about the bad hotel and bad policemen, and his hustling of me to the microphone. I saw afresh the drunken cynicism that had surveyed me from the tables while I weighed and calculated. I saw their reaction when I made my move, chance and value flourishing all around. I thought of the men at the TV station, sitting either side of a desk while they considered ending my banishment. And I smiled and I slept.

Twenty-three

Five days into my stay in the city and I was woken by Brewster calling my mobile phone. He didn't call the hotel, which birthed an interest hardened by his panting and murky delivery. I could picture him scuttling round a tired police station, swivelling to check the different linoleum approaches before cramming the phone into his murderous moustache.

'Nick,' he said and then, incredibly, 'it's me.'

'Right,' I answered. I was disorientated and ruled once more to direct the Asian porter to fetch me a clock.

'Listen,' said Brewster, 'we're coming to your room in about twenty minutes. Me and another guy, make sure you act surprised and everything.'

'Why do you need to come here?'

'It's a pain in the arse. I was telling some of the boys about you, and this guy, he's new and started saying he'd come and check a couple of things with you. He just wants to check, to be honest he just wants to meet you.' There was a rather touching dose of jealousy.

'Is this about the bruises?'

There was a pause that Brewster hadn't planned.

'Listen, you're not supposed to know about the bruises, remember. We won't mention it I shouldn't think. This other guy is pretty suspicious, that's why you need to charm him and luckily he believes in all that bullshit. He keeps talking about your old TV show, I never watched it myself.'

'OK, I'll answer his questions and then you fuck off again.'

'Not exactly, no. He heard about you at DCI Milne's retirement do. It's a nightmare this Nick, but he wants you to do some of that stuff. I don't think he'll even mention the girl.'

'Why not?' A one-on-one with an impressionable mind sounded fine, but Brewster's unearned evasiveness was irritating.

'Don't worry about it.' Brewster was panting again – no doubt passing under cheap lighting, back towards salaried others. 'I need to show you a couple of things afterwards.' He sounded guilty before the phone died in my hands.

I called Tony out of habit but he wasn't there. He would be heavy and hungover, curled in vast folds of body somewhere within this building.

In between trying him – and my attempts rang out resolutely, two, three, four times – I enjoyed the trumpeted visit of Brewster and some new moron. Any ending to this city and circumstance would be acceptable but this option promised unexpected ease.

When they arrived, my joviality was extended. I had to frown and pinch and relegate my mind to darker places, just to divert from laughter. They could have been twins – with the horrific suits, like the seat covers of salesmen's cars, and a similar facial hair arrangement scraped with loathing into chilling detail.

Even better, they fizzed with competition while Brewster ran through the introductions and they stood before me in the barren room. There was a division, a lack of sameness, and that was where the pressure arose between them. To my delight I saw the edge that the other policeman had on Brewster. Whereas Brewster spoke with an unrefined rough and tumble, his colleague had the holding of something else.

His voice was smoothed and underlaid with thought, though that's not to suggest there was a greater intelligence. I guessed that he had come from a schooling lifted from the usual and then through university, sitting in lecture halls during years that Brewster would have spent hustling his way up from the entry level. I still sensed greater threat in Brewster's street logic and looseness of procedure, but this man would have to be tackled separately.

He had come here pushed by voyeurism but also because he wouldn't rely on Brewster's gruff reassurance. That was fine. If it was a final hurdle to vanquishing the bruises and the arms and the dead girl and the city then, well, it wasn't really a hurdle at all. Especially when I started so well.

'So, Mr Santini,' said this new, different policeman, 'I know that our visit today has come as a bit of surprise and I apologise for that…'

'Did you have a good birthday?' I asked. He smiled in wonder, turned to Brewster.

'Did you tell him that?' he said, willing it just a little to be not so.

Brewster looked at him as disdainfully as he felt was acceptable.

'I didn't know it was your birthday,' he said, then tried to engage me in some secret look but I was waiting for the more important reaction.

'Did you…how did you know?' He stumbled but he was enjoying it. That was for certain.

His watch. It looked expensive and new, certainly, but that wouldn't have been enough. There was a discrepancy at the face that I realised soon enough was the sliver of plastic protection applied by the manufacturer. He'd left it on and, whether through accident or design, it was not a gesture that would ever last long beyond purchase. A man of clear reserve and limited salary, wearing a wedding ring as he was, would be very unlikely to have bought an expensive watch unprovoked. So then there's retirement or birthdays. Probably his fortieth, but no need for that.

'Not to worry,' I ended things with a feckless wave. 'Sorry, I should keep these things to myself, we've got work to do after all.'

He was disappointed and continued with his voice less controlled.

'Of course. Well, essentially, we are in what we think will be the closing stages of the case and really just need to finish a couple of things off…'

At this, Brewster, I could see but didn't want to, gave me a nod of confirmation. I was glad that he was in clear sight of the other policeman and so would limit these misjudgements accordingly. Any other positioning of the two of them and he would have probably risked a hand gesture.

'Now I've read your statement and everything seems in order there. So really I think that's about it from us…'

He pointed inclusively at Brewster who winced at the dismissive edge.

'To be honest, Mr Santini, my wife and I used to love your show and, well…' He laughed so he didn't have to speak and I thought I might know what he wanted me to do.

'Shall we…' he started again but was interrupted by Brewster making a play of preparing himself for departure – clapping his hands and turning for the door – and then declaring, dryly and daftly, 'Yep,' while urging me upwards with his hands.

This understandably grated, but I swallowed and did so because I was hoping that I had correctly predicted a tawdry turn. My confidence increased during the noiseless walk to the door of the black girl's room. I turned to find two very different reactions – the new policeman baffled, Brewster in the grip of panic. He hadn't seen enough of me to share my confidence.

The room smelt of chemicals and had been stripped of everything apart from the bed frame that had been dragged into the room's centre. The carpet was strangely brushed and even the walls were stained through some technique of investigation.

'So,' said the other policeman, turning to me in the unsparing light of a bare bulb, the lampshade a victim of the committed searching, 'this was the girl's room? A terrible business. Mr Santini, we really don't have to…'

'I want to help clear this up,' I spoke slowly, 'but I should say that this could be quite emotional for me. I didn't have much warning, after all.'

'Oh, Mr Santini,' he replied, 'you really don't have to.'

'I know,' I said, and I did. This was what he wanted, with his good cop slant and his fan status. He wanted it for himself and, as a secondary move, to take away the vague suggestion of the bruises.

'Well, if you two just stand to the side, let's see if there's anything we can do here.'

The move came, **first** and foremost, from *Doctor Who*. I watched it on the black-and-white television that was also a radio and sat on a cardboard box in the corner of Mum and Dad's bedroom above the OK Corral. The night that I saw what would become the move I was lying with my head on Mum's chest while she smoked and occasionally went for her gin. On the trying little screen, the Doctor stretched a ghostly hand to the doorknob that we knew had been wired by his adversary.

'No!' Mum and I shouted together.

When he gripped it there was a moment, just a second, when it looked like we had been mistaken and he had avoided the obvious threat. And then the Doctor underwent the most incredible transformation. His body digested the arrival of electricity and everything happened very quickly indeed. The Doctor snapped into a sudden, terrifying brace. His mouth gaped open in silent surprise and his limbs were thrown into a scarecrow vision of possession – one arm straight as a ruler to the charged door handle, the other flung from his body and his legs split in straight lines like tweezers. He was lifted only by his toes.

For several seconds the Doctor was held there while the camera crept closer to that tortured, distant face. Then blackness and the music. Mum stopped laughing when she saw my horror. She calmed me as best she could and took me through to my room where she let me see her check under the bed and in amongst the boxes of optics.

I wanted her to go, even though I knew that would leave me with just the Doctor. And, when she left, there he was hovering in the darkness and still visible when I closed my eyes. Frozen, electrocuted, surely dead? I got up and turned on the light. Downstairs there was whistling and no music while Dad and

Mervyn finished up. I sat on my bed in front of the brewery mirror and then, with my plan developing, I stood.

It took me a long time. I had to stop for a while and turn off the light when I heard Dad on the stairs. I waited, breathing louder than I would have liked, for him to pass along the landing and into their room where I heard him say, 'Oi,' before the door closed.

At first I was rough and far from any accuracy but slowly, slowly, I got better. Dozens, hundreds of times, I repeated. From one side, I would arrive in the mirror's sight. A nod of acknowledgment, then I would reach for an invisible door knob, grip, wait, turn to the mirror, and then do it.

Initially it was little more than a wide-eyed leap in the air. But it came. I worked out everything that was needed. The arms should flick as stiffly as they could which was achieved by investing battles into the elbows, pointing them down while straining them up. The back should arch as if a punch was taken at the base of the spine. The mouth should stretch open along with the eyes.

It was the legs that I realised were the key. To switch from standing to creaking on my toes was not easy and it was this that I practised the hardest. The excitement kept me awake and while the room lightened (there was no curtain for the window) everything began to come together.

I collapsed into a couple of hours of sleep and by the time I reached the school in Marylebone I was alert and ready. That school had a different style of bullying to Glendoll College. Not so physical but with a disjointed abandoning and a forcing into the solitary. My illicit alcohol trading would eventually save me, but in the gap before that it was this that would spare me some mistreatment.

I hunted down a couple of kids even less boisterous than myself, who I knew would offer nothing worse than indifference, and found them hiding from the wider anarchy in a silent classroom. I closed the door and waited for their casual attention before walking smartly back. I gripped, turned, waited and then...

One, with his schoolboy mouth unready for such mastery, squealed and then muffled his mouth with his hands in humiliated response.

'*Doctor Who!*' shouted the other, in an excitement that flowed, without doubt, into wonder.

I crumpled back to a normal stance and walked out of the classroom. My heart banged away while I walked through the school and my head swum with possibility.

Every night I work on my legs. I got a length of rubber piping from the cellar and tied it to the foot of my bed. I'd wrap it round my shins and puff and strain through endless stretching. My calves became enflamed and would drum with charged anticipation when I stood.

The movement become a single thought with all the parts linked in my mind. It became so that all I had to think about were those calves. When they went, pinching in perfect alignment, my whole body followed.

At school my act extended from the shelter of fellow outcasts to the playground itself. It became a request, played to laughing and clapping crowds. I gripped, waited, was walloped by the charge, wilted, then raised a hand for some rest amongst the clamour for an instant replay.

I showed it to Mum one night in the kitchen while she waded through crumpled receipts and neater bills. She laughed, as she sometimes did, and it was always a good sign, with little noise but her shoulders vibrating and her eyes wet.

'Go and show your dad, Nicky,' Mum told me and then, 'Go on, he'll like it,' when she saw my delay.

In the end she took me downstairs herself, her hand on my head to guide me through.

'Right, listen up, Nicky's got something to show you,' she shouted.

It was rare that she took charge of the pub's noise with genuine intent, rather than when her voice slowly enveloped others in building arguments with Dad.

He frowned from the bar where he was sitting on a stool at the punters' side. Mum bent down and slipped her hand round my neck, brushing the lobe of my ear.

'Go on, Nicky, you show them,' she said.

I was gasping with nerves, walking across the bar to the door. When I got there I reached out and held the brass. It was dirty, with little reflection. I swallowed, breathed, and turned. He was looking at me with his face flushed, probably with anger and the fear of embarrassment. I took a final breath and spoke to my loaded calves, which burst into action.

Laughs, clapping and shouts of acclaim. Dad jumping from his stool and picking me up. His stubble against my chin when he held me like a trophy. The lights shining in my eyes while he pushed me up in the air and shouted for more clapping and shouting, which both came soon enough, louder than ever, as I looked down at my Mum who was bouncing up and down and Dad's hands tightened around me and he called out again. It was my glory, but he made it his.

This is what I thought of, standing watching Brewster and the other policeman in the black girl's hotel room.

Twenty-four

For a while I studied the mistreated carpet but this was only to provide a contrast. I gave them a minute or so to monitor my pondering – my loose frame and the sheer unawakened nature of my being.

The manner in which I changed my body, the speed of the switch, bore endless layers of practice. This was something I had worked on from that second night in Birmingham onwards. I had reached back to the school in Marylebone and taken it with me through those cheap hotels and venues that appeared to have recently hosted bombs, while Tony dragged me round the country and lied to me in chain pubs and motorway service stations.

It had been with me ever since. The moment in my shows, on stage and television, that the people knew me for. It came in the silence after *let them come through*. The call and then the response. The hotel room where the black girl had done what she did was a difficult setting but the manoeuvre came without complaint and worked as it always did.

'Fuck me,' said Brewster in the moments after I landed, while the other policeman shouted with involuntary alarm. Both had seen it before. Brewster at the show and his colleague, I was sure, through the restrictions of television. To be this close was a new and different thrill. I rocked on my heels for a moment, then slumped my body while raising a hand in calm but also, I think it was clear, in warning.

'I hoped this wouldn't happen,' I whispered, wounded, and I felt a hand on my shoulder. Probably Brewster's, though I hoped not. 'She's here,' I declared louder and I felt the hand flutter with something.

'Go on, son,' said Brewster, his enthusiasm spectacularly unconvincing. The other policeman let out what a shiver must sound like.

'She's cold,' I told them. 'So cold. And scared. She can't, she can't see a way out.'

From behind me, from all around me, there was nothing else while they waited for more.

'She's lower than she's ever been. There's things from when she was young I think, I don't know. There's so much pain.'

I lifted my hands to my temples, hoping that this was another gesture that they would recognise.

'She's alone,' I said in soft decision. 'There's no one else there.'

'Ah,' said Brewster.

'And then she's, she's doing what she did.' It was trickier than usual to get the tears but that was hardly surprising, what with the busy, multiplying delight. I got them eventually and leant down on one knee, waiting for the hand that came again soon enough.

'That'll do, Santini,' said Brewster, who I knew would be jubilant with his overall performance.

'That was incredible, Mr Santini,' the other policeman added from above me. 'Absolutely incredible. I hope that we weren't any trouble.'

Twenty-five

Back down in the car park in the hotel's grey guts, the other policeman shook my hand for maybe the fourth time and walked away still relating, even when the gap stretched to twenty yards, how surprised he was with the lack of cars in attendance. I told him the hotel was new but he hadn't really been looking for an answer and so he ignored it when it came. In my hand I held his card. When he'd produced it, Brewster, like some rattled lover, had stirred and inched between us as if to try and block the handover.

'Thanks again, Mr Santini,' said the other policeman, his voice messing about a bit in the concrete. 'Best of luck for the future,' he added, with surprising finality.

'Cheers,' I answered with some genuine affection. I wished that policeman had been in charge from the beginning, but there you go.

'Oh,' he called once more from beside a modest car with a corporate shape, 'good luck with the doctor.' He wasn't looking at me, but at Brewster who was rooted beside me for some reason.

'Nothing trivial, I hope,' I quipped to Brewster, my relief lending me a certain robustness that ended when Brewster replied,

'I'm not going to the doctor,' and I saw that we were near a similar car to the one the other policeman was now reversing round a post. They'd come in different cars.

'I need to show you a couple of things.'

'No,' I said simply. 'We're done, matey. I wish I could say it's been fun. Your pal there pretty much just told me that it's over. All the best.'

He didn't try to stop me walking away. I heard him scrabbling for his car keys and was mildly surprised by the urgency but I was already closing in on the elevator door before he spoke again.

'Nick,' he shouted with the glow of an echo. I looked back because there was no reason not to and I saw that he was waving an envelope.

'This is the first thing,' he said, and I started my journey back to him in open curiosity.

In the hotel room in Birmingham that must have seen some dreadful scenes, I added my own. I strained and tensed, worked and practised. My body was distant from physical demands and reacted with outrage. My legs and back ached when I pushed them through the old move.

It didn't take too long for matters to define in the mirror bolted on to the wardrobe. I enjoyed the achievement and it looked far better than I imagined it would. I left it as it was, it wasn't going to improve further and I didn't want to grow doubtful, and turned briefly to those haunted notes from the previous evening. They were discarded and instead I lay on the bed and chose a simpler line.

My major fault had been to shy away from the crowd as an enemy and that had made them one. They were no different from the individuals who had faced me in the back of the OK Corral and the office on Soviet Street. They themselves were the answer and I should have been studying the club's stifling clientele with intent – looking for options, looking for openings.

There was no need for the panicked preparation of learning lines and predicting turns. What I needed, as I had always needed, were people who wanted to hear what I said.

In the club there wasn't the same dedication as with those who had climbed the stairs at Soviet Street and given me money, but there were a hundred people in that club and, within the hundred, would be some people for me. I just needed to see them, and I had seen enough of those people to know what they looked like. The final area of work was my presentation from Keith. I needed the crowd to have more definition and I wrote what I needed.

I was light with hope when I looked for the time and found

that it was after six. The alarm returned. I had to be at the club at seven, Tony was supposed to have been here at five. He was supposed to have been here at five to *help*. I called, no answer. And then, sneakily, came the text message. Apologies, he was *caught up*, the address of the club and *c u there*.

I left the hotel with anxiety. The day's gloom was deepening to darkness and when my taxi swung into the car park the club sat squat and shadowed before me. Just when I abandoned the safety of the car another vehicle reared in behind, the lights leaving my driver's face silver when he turned with the change.

Two bodies fell out of the other car, their legs flung out late and then they staggered and laughed. Neither was jolted by my being there and seeing them like this.

'Hi, Nicky, you know this one?'

He pulled on her arm proudly, to draw her closer to him. It was only after some seconds, while she swayed and smiled thinly, that I saw the stripper from the night before.

'You not on tonight?'

'Yeah, I am,' she said. 'Are *you*?'

She laughed and Tony tried, not particularly hard, to stop her with a flapping of his hands and:

'Alright, love, alright. Come on.'

We walked in and he tugged at my arm.

'Sorry, Nicky, went for a drink with this one and, well.'

Back in the threat of the club, the woman waved at Keith and walked towards the stage. Keith was standing at the bar (talking to, thankfully, a different barman) and the club was already filling with tables being taken forwards from the back of the room. No one wanted to be near the stage.

'Looks like good numbers, maybe they've heard of you?' said Tony.

That was too ridiculous to respond to. I gave Keith the paper with my new, requested introduction. He was evasive and I think we both enjoyed the diversion of the note.

'Could you read this out please, before I go on.'

He read it quickly, sighed, and walked away. Tony said 'Keith?'

to no response and then turned to me and asked, 'What was that about then?'

'Last night, I presume,' I answered, walking towards the back of the room.

Tony huffed about and followed me, making a succession of noises and muttering 'Well now' and 'Interesting stuff.' He didn't have the conviction, even, to just ask me what the note had said.

Through in the back the stripper was already down to her underwear. I felt a twinge of appreciation for what Tony must have been doing that afternoon while I flexed my way through solitary hours at the hotel. He should have been with me and I remembered one of the things he should have been doing.

'The new name?'

'Ah,' he said. 'Yeah.'

'You've got one I take it?'

I knew he hadn't but I was beginning to enjoy giving him some humiliation. Her presence adding an edge, she was listening and watching while she spread the oil over her legs.

'Yeah, I've got one for you,' he said, his voice louder. I thought at the time it was pride but it must have been to get her attention.

'Santini. Nick Santini.'

She laughed.

'Nick Santini,' I said. The joke is that I liked it from the start. 'OK, let's go with that.'

'I know this industry, Nick, and I know that'll sell. It was the best one I came up with.'

His eyes, that flick, I read it correctly as a lie.

'OK, I'll tell Keith, I'm going to wait out there anyway.'

I walked away from their laughter to the side of the stage. It was busier than the night before and this gave me a grim pleasure. It increased the depth of failure but also the possible strength of success. I watched the crowd with my new focus and understanding of what they had to do for me, before being interrupted by Keith's arrival.

'Keith, I want to be called Nick Santini tonight.'

'A new name, new intro, who the fuck do you think you are?'

He was trying to inject something into his voice but it was half-hearted.

'Nick Santini,' I repeated and he passed onwards to the stage and tapped the microphone lightly with the ring on his finger.

He was into his opening jokes when I saw what I thought I wanted. I watched and watched, and decided that I was correct, before retreating back to the corridor. From behind me I could hear Tony's voice and the stripper's laugh and from in front came Keith:

'I have to tell you something about our next act, ladies and gentlemen,' he said, his voice rotating through the room. He sounded like a boxing announcer but read my words with an impressive belief.

'When this man comes into direct contact with a spirit, he will undergo a short physical reaction. *Please* do not be alarmed.'

There was silence, which I was more than willing to settle for.

'Without further ado,' rumbled Keith, 'let me introduce Nick...'

Pause, either for effect or so he could remember, 'Santini.'

I bounded into view, slapped Keith's back and smiled at the crowd.

'Thanks very much.'

There was already just a few pairs of hands left clapping.

'I'm Nick Santini.'

From that night onwards, I never had another bad show and there are hundreds from there to here. Of course, there were problems. There were gaffes, slips, errors, misunderstandings. Yet these passed by with no lasting damage because, above such temporary concerns, I had found my power and there wasn't one show that didn't bring its own success.

That night my talent was raw, frayed and seemingly obvious, but still it was enough to stun and hold the people in Keith's club. First there were jokes about the city, the club, the stripper through in the dressing room. I told these easier than I could have imagined. They were simple pieces, adapted from the mentalities and understandings of the pubs that had always surrounded me.

Confidence came and reinforced itself with every dash of applause, every appreciative laugh and shout. With the noise still there, I moved to the very edge of the staging and pointed at the man.

This was the man that I had picked out before Keith brought me on. He was the first of the people that I would have, ready and waiting without realising it, to guide me through the success that came from that second night in Birmingham.

'What's your name?'

'Andy.'

'Andy. I think I...'

I turned so they would have the full effect. I waited, clearly concerned. I opened my mouth but the words, it would seem to the people in the club, were stolen by what happened next.

One, maybe two, seconds later I was on my toes with my body quivering like a landed arrow. It had been even easier, and certainly sharper, than I could have hoped for from my short recovery of it back in the hotel. The messages that I had rammed into my calves in my bedroom above the OK Corral passed cleanly through the years to the stage in Birmingham.

I was only starting to appreciate the risk of the silence when it was smashed by rolling barrages of noise. While I slumped back down and looked up in tortured thought, everyone in the room was on their feet.

'I'm sorry.'

I spoke faintly into the microphone and when I lifted my hand the noise fell away as one. That's when I knew it had worked.

'Now.' They could see that I was struggling, sharing their shock while I bravely tried to order my thoughts. 'Where's Andy?'

He held up both arms so I could find him amongst the busy bodies. This is why I picked him: he was a ravaged signal to addiction. I didn't know what it had been but drink or drugs were the assumed favourites. His thinness was arresting, his body a jutting connection of parts, and his skin was coarse and struck with a whiteness that didn't come without expense. When I had seen him from the shadows there was a Coke in one of his shaking hands while he laughed openly with his companions. He'd come out the other side.

I told Andy, and the rest, that I had someone speaking to me.

'A woman, Andy, who cared for you?'

I watched his eyes wetten. He smiled angrily and rubbed at his face with a sleeve.

'Mary, it might be Mary,' he said. Most of the crowd missed that, even though they all listened.

'Mary,' I declared in confirmation.

With little build-up, and pauses only where needed, I told Andy that Mary was proud of him. After the limited success of that line played out I added my calculated extension.

'She was so proud of you, Andy, when you flushed it down the toilet.'

Flushed it down the toilet. Initially that might seem specific. But it's not at all.

Andy wept with his shoulders jumping in twin points. The crowd clapped and whispered appreciation to each other, eyeing me with the welcome suspicion of the deceived. I didn't give them the time for consideration.

During my manipulation of Andy, I had been monitoring a man who was nearly out of his seat following events, bothering his companions with gestures of wonder. When I turned from the sobbing Andy and scanned the room, the man bounced for my attention and I picked him out with gratitude.

After bringing him in and steadying the crowd I told the man that I had someone to speak to him, but they were a little confused. He nodded with an inherent agreement and I tightened him to me, invoking the illusion that we were to work together.

The man reeled off various possible identities for the hesitant visitor from the other world. I let him run on and then stopped him with some playful mimicking of his enthusiasm that played well with both him and the others. Then I retreated sharply to one of the male names that he had given and he confirmed breathlessly that this was a dead older brother.

I began with the gentle observation that his brother had lost weight before he died.

People, I felt comfortable enough saying at the time, lost weight before they died. And they do, almost all of them. Even a lot of the heart attacks and the car crashes will lead to a bit of clinging on and, amongst the hysteria, weight loss. But then it was a guess.

I told the man that there was a certain smell that he associated with his brother.

'Sometimes,' I added, 'you smell cigarette smoke don't you?'

He nodded, 'I do, yes.'

I don't know if that man ever thought that he could smell cigarette smoke and then thought of his dead brother. But the important point is that it had almost got to the stage that it didn't matter. He just wasn't going to say no.

I had the option to end it but pushed on. I gave a touch of confusion before showing another revelation coming through.

'Ah. He's just telling me about his tattoo.'

The man I was talking to had tattoos. Several in fact, as did a fair section of the crowd. And the man wasn't in here by accident. His clothes, his voice, his bruised carriage, he belonged here. His brother, bar an unlikely adoption or selfish lottery win at a young age, would have belonged here also. The gamble was less than the toilet-flushing point earlier, which had been a success. But that's what happens sometimes.

'He didn't have a tattoo.' The man's smile frayed.

That's not important, it's what happened next that's important.

I laughed, waited for a silence and said, quieter.

'Sorry, he's just telling me something else,' and laughed again, with abandon, and it was thrilling, laughing into the silence and the confusion.

'He did have a tattoo,' I announced, 'but he doesn't want you bastards to know where he had it.'

They liked that – yells and belched guffaws and the man clapping above his head with his face a demonstration of deflected relief. The rest of the show I pottered and pondered, not risking the gains I had made, and then left them demanding an extension. Keith said 'Nice one,' before taking the microphone, his face gripped in a smile, and I walked off delirious with ambition and possibility.

Studied now, that second night in Birmingham seems amateurish and wanting, but it was a triumph that shocked and changed matters entirely. In the room at the back of the club were scenes of celebration.

'Get in here,' said Tony.

He had a bottle of champagne. A few days later, over breakfast in a motorway service station, he would tell me that it had been deducted from my fee for the night.

We drank in the changing room, laughing and perched on the unsteady furniture, and then in the bar, lifting bad draught lager while the stripper danced, then round a table with the lights low after the club closed. There was myself, Tony, Keith and the stripper. It became quickly obvious, through their hardened looks, that Tony and the stripper had enjoyed a day of attraction, so I was surprised when she announced her departure and Tony didn't flinch.

When she'd gone the three of us talked about crowds, and acts, and how the two can work together.

'You,' said Keith, his eyes glassy and selecting me with a wavering finger, 'got in amongst them. That's important. Show them who the fucking boss is.'

'That's it,' agreed Tony, his head a nodding ball of flesh and hair. 'That's the thing.'

The buzz and victory from the show bounced about within me while they ran through my areas of achievement.

'I have to hold my hands up,' Keith was saying to Tony, 'I thought the kid was a folder. But you were spot on Tony, spot on. The kid's got it. He's going to make you a million, another million.'

'He'd better,' answered Tony, moving in his seat to set himself up for his finale, 'my wife wants the last one.'

I laughed with them. The union was temporary and forced, but still attractive. Maybe I should have reacted to the mention of money, and where it was to go, but it was a time of encouragement and we drank on. By the end we took turns to go behind the bar, with Keith's insistence, and return with trays of piggish loads. Pint glasses of vodka and orange, tumblers of whisky, jugs of cider and beer.

When Tony and I left, Keith was sleeping on a sofa in the corner. The club was surrounded by industrial streets widened for lorries and lined with metal buildings. Night was fighting the day, bringing greys and purples, and we walked along the wide channels between the units. He was singing and clapping, darting over to slap my back and shout declarations.

'All the way! We're going all the fucking way, Nicky!'

I yelled agreement and weakly punched the air. We reached a road with some activity – the early morning mix of sullen delivery vans, sinister cars and then a taxi that stopped, grateful for our waves. I watched the yellow lights pass by on the way to the hotel and I was falling asleep when Tony shouted.

'Hey, that's it!'

We were halted by traffic lights. Tony was righted in his seat and pointing out the window. He was twisted away from me and raised, eager as a child.

'That's where we had dinner earlier, me and her.'

I slumped to the side and jabbed my troubled eyes up and out the window. It was a large restaurant and I think I saw the sign when Tony did because his body shook with the realisation and the finger he had on the glass braced, the knuckle white because of his horror pushing it harder. The taxi started and Tony tilted his head back. His eyes were clamped closed in regret while the taxi moved again and we passed by the restaurant and the sign above it.

'Santini's,' I said. 'Interesting.'

In the morning I lay awake before Tony and thought of Santini's. The absurdity and lingering drink softened it and I smiled through the haze at the sleeping rump yards to my side. But I also thought of how Tony had revealed the name to me, in the back room of the club with the stripper laughing in response. That dart of the eyes he did, that I had known was the escape of a lie. It would be useful, I thought then, in case he lied again. That feels very long ago.

When he woke he panted and coughed, waited and then turned to me, his face flattened to the pillow.

'It's still a good name, Nicky.'

I laughed because I wanted to and so he could as well.

Twenty-six

NICK SANTINI IS A MURDERER

That's what the letter said that was inside the envelope, which had been stamped and posted to Brewster at the address of a police station. Things happened before I read the letter – Brewster swindled me into the car, told me that the note might come as a surprise, at least *I fucking hope it does* he said with a peculiar laugh, and then handed me the envelope already split open – but what's important is what it said.

Seeing it there does a poor job of demonstrating the message. The letters themselves were deliberately basic, flicked in single strokes that I guessed preserved anonymity as well as adding to the basic intent. But it was elsewhere that the note delivered a neat one-two of suggestion.

There was something about the paper. I had seen the same embossed grooves, the same paper, sitting in a neat pile on the table in my hotel room. Brewster wouldn't know this but the note had come from the hotel, where everything was coming from. The envelope was different, cheaper and anonymous. But it was hard to concentrate on the stationery when, below the words, was an angry smear of blood.

Looking at the blood (and it was hard not to. I looked at the blood before, during and after reading the words. Who wouldn't?), I took a moment to move past the deliberation – shouldn't notes like this be written entirely in blood? This wasn't just frivolity but a line of thought. The blood was there as an addition. Coupled with the weighty accusation of the words, it would have to be serving a purpose of some immediacy. And yet it was alone, unattributed. So the message it carried it carried through the blood itself.

During my progress through that muddle, Brewster had charged the car and taken us out of the car park. I knew what he was going to say when I said,

'Whose blood is it?'

He was going to say, which he did then say,

'The girl's.'

He reached towards his chest and pulled me out a sheet of paper. It was some police form, lots that I didn't understand and then a section entitled Blood Identification. I recognised the look of the name, from the press conference mostly, as the black girl's.

'I had it run through this morning,' he said. 'By a pal. It's not in the file yet.'

He looked at me, in a snatched check, before steering into the traffic and lifting a hand in response to a car forced to jam and buck when we sidled unwelcome into the ordered flow. Perhaps to let me have every angle at once Brewster spoke again while he fiddled with his radio.

'It was sent yesterday, postmarked somewhere near here.'

A man's voice with a local accent broke free of the radio and began to run through the benefits of a car showroom. To put off the needed evaluation of the paper that remained gripped between my fingers I extracted my phone and called Tony. Brewster was whistling along to a song that he'd clearly not heard before. Still no answer from Tony. I texted him.

call me ASAP. important

and settled back into reluctant study of the note. It was the strength of the motive that attracted and repelled. There was a hatred and an excusing of feeling in the blood's dispersal that held a daunting intensity. This was primal, life and death. And the only death was that of the black girl who had, surely, dealt with the matter herself. I was detached from that death. That night was there, planted. I had gone to bed. The girl had died. Yet, somewhere along the line, in someone's mind, our paths had been pushed back together.

'What do you reckon?' You'd think that was Brewster, but no, it was me, defeated and desperate.

'I don't know,' he said, turning down the volume on the radio. 'It's a strange one.'

His motivation was of continuing interest. There was his official status in the set-up, which would occasionally hit me with alarming recollection, but it was hard for the fear to maintain itself when all he was giving me was untroubled support. I wasn't wearing gloves, for example, and neither had he when handling the letter. The envelope had been opened, true, but I knew that it was only he and I that could have viewed it under those unguarded circumstances.

Money left the streets around us. The buildings lost their confidence, their coat of value, and shrank and cheapened along roads that grew boisterous. Soon we were within one of the estates that tend to ring such cities. Away from the critical eyes of moneyed tourists, just before the nervous countryside. Sickly kids walked around aimlessly holding reminders of where they were – sticks, cigarettes, the leads to vacuum-bellied dogs – and angry cars were despatched in wild arrangements on the pavements.

Brewster pulled his state-owned vehicle into a space and a man and possible son rose through habit from what looked like deckchairs in a jungle of a garden. Up went Brewster's hand with the wallet and badge and back down they went in a see-sawing answer that made Brewster giggle.

The man shouted out to others and I watched what awful representation there was of humanity stir and observe and then, when Brewster and I failed to show movement, suspiciously return to their grimy endeavours.

'What the fuck are we doing here?' I asked Brewster with no small reluctance and the note feeling heavier in my hand.

'Nice spot, isn't it,' he chuckled. 'Some of the stuff that goes on here you wouldn't believe. Seriously, Nick, you wouldn't believe.'

I wasn't going to condone more of that so I waited. A shell-shocked woman walked past, nodding at us in a ghoulish affinity that had lasted beyond whatever poison had saucered her eyes with despair.

Brewster watched her departure in the mirror and I didn't want to hear his summary on her so I intervened,

'Why are we here, Brewster?'

I knew he'd leap on this piece of personalisation and he did, smiling back in homely greeting and pointing over the dashboard.

'You see those ones?'

He gestured at two young boys who stood leaning on a broken fence, spitting and watching us.

'Yeah.'

'I'm going to buy them, this afternoon.'

'Sorry?'

'I'm going to buy them, rent them out.'

I couldn't, I couldn't quite get this. Street power had certainly warped Brewster but this was surely a step beyond that faithless process.

'You're going to rent out kids?'

I could see there was a problem. He flushed sharply and jerked his head behind him to check for any listeners secreted in the back seat. For a moment he couldn't locate words, opening and closing his mouth with his arms flattened and pushed into the wheel with visceral reaction.

'You, fucking, you, what, fucking, *you what*?' is more or less what he managed.

'The kids. You want to rent out the kids?'

He lifted one hand and slapped his forehead in hard, steady beats of delirium. He was sweating too. And gulping.

'KIDS,' he shrieked, his voice raised to womanly levels with the hysteria. 'I'M NOT RENTING OUT FUCKING KIDS.'

Beyond the boys, I noticed now, were some buildings. A couple of houses I guess you would call them. Crippled with not just neglect but their original failings – square excuses clad in mottled plaster and with windows that apologetically allowed inspection of tissued curtains and cruelly lowered ceilings. It was these modern relics that Brewster had been referring to and I enjoyed my error, laughing in gratitude for the diversion, with Brewster's anger continuing with abandon.

'You've got no idea,' he said to me, his eyes narrowed in comfortable venom, 'what we do to those bastards when we get them in the station. No fucking idea.'

'I can imagine,' I said unrattled. 'So, you're wanting to buy those two houses?'

He huffed about a bit more – informing me of various, vicious holds and punches that left no bruises, and of forcing this particular brand of criminal to stand in basins of scalding water, or on tables in interview rooms with their hands not permitted to leave the ceiling, and so unimpressively on – then wearied himself into some sort of calm and turned to his plans for the houses.

He wanted to buy them on a buy-to-let arrangement, through some specific mortgage that he discussed as if he had been sold it by spies, and rent them to associates of the Polish builders in the currently sole member of his landlord's portfolio. The two buildings he referred to looked, more than anything, like they wanted to burst into tears.

'Are you sure?' I asked in a natural, unconnected response.

'They're a bargain,' he said defensively. 'Repossessions, I heard about it from my solicitor. He's as dodgy as they come,' he shook his head with wistful pride.

'Well,' I said, 'you sound like you know more about it than me.' I thought only briefly of Java Joe, sitting in the back room of Soviet Street as he thanked me for buying his shop's lease. I had other, newer pressures. With this side issue of Brewster's closing, my attention was already centring back to the note. There was only the lingering consideration of why we were there, looking at these houses. Why I was there.

'…I just need the deposit,' Brewster was saying, finishing something that I had missed. 'Eighteen thousand.'

So this…was this it? Was this why?

'For them both, that is,' said Brewster, and the gentle encouragement confirmed my reading.

The emergence of this full-blown corruption was a relief. When it was held back, no matter how roughly, it had the threat of the unknown. Now it was here, and with price tag attached, it was far more easily measured. I nodded for him and looked at the houses that it appeared I was going to buy for a police detective. A detective, no less, that was willing to ignore a note that bore the blood of a suspiciously dead girl and accused me of murder.

'Look,' said Brewster, struggling with a kindly bearing, 'I know you didn't have fuck all to do with that girl dying. I think she killed herself, so does everyone else at the station. This,' he pointed down at the note, 'is a lot of bollocks. I've got no problem sticking that straight in the bin. Straight in the fucking bin. But if I don't then, you know, with the bruises as well. We'd just have to look at the whole thing again. Could take a while, too.'

He peered at the houses in clumsy demonstration of the trade-off. The note and the houses. It was to be a deal. And why not?

'I'll get the money,' I said. 'Just let me speak to Tony.'

The brutal boys had wandered away, somehow electing that they might have something else to fill the day with. I saw that one of the tragic houses had a satellite dish bolted to the wall but that the wires hung loose below it. I wondered if that had been a piece of optimism that hadn't come to pass, or a previous enjoyment ended by dwindled funds.

'I just have,' I said to Brewster who nodded and sighed in understanding before he had even heard how I was to finish, 'to get hold of Tony, then we can get this sorted out.'

Twenty-seven

I'm knocking at the door of the black girl's hotel room but there's no answer and so I try leaning into the door and it parts willingly. The room's dark and I walk to the bed calling out softly because I can see a lump of darkness on the bed. I get closer and features emerge, her eyes stoked with revering lust and it's hard to look elsewhere because she lies in unclothed anticipation.

I pull and yank and tear myself naked also and then I'm on top of her, probing tentatively and then gliding within. She's quiet but she rocks about a bit and I think there's the occasional moan, but the real action comes from those majestic breasts. Even though she is lying flat they push up and away from her frame, stretching the black smoothness into two domed suggestions that move electively in time to my determined swinging.

And it's the breasts that finish me off – with their defiance and their little leaps – and leave me shuddering and empty above her. I retreat outwards, saying something appreciative and a touch flirtatious, and make for the bathroom. When I'm in there I take a moment to handle the new light and then look to the mirror and see that I'm covered, I'm covered, I'm covered in blood.

And this, oh dear, but this. This is when I really end things. Away from the girl and the fantasy. Back in the hotel room, an hour from Brewster and his buy-to-lets, it's the image of myself in her blood that sees me finally culminating. But I should say in wanting defence, and it's true, that it wasn't the blood that got me there, I was already arriving. And, also, when I got there I did think – this is a bit much.

Twenty-eight

Before that unfortunate event (and it's good of me to include these) I tried to phone Tony who remained resolutely out of touch. After Brewster dropped me off, I had tried Tony in a rapid, unsuccessful sequence and my irritation had sent me down a more distant corridor than intended.

I had found the Asian porter entering with the exaggerated care of the subservient through a fire door and then greeting my presence, in what must have been a staff-only refuge, with horror. In a flash of constructive thought I told him I required a clock and he looked a little thrown, probably at my rare lucidity, and assured me he'd get one. I found my room eventually, and in the void my thoughts drifted to the black girl and where that took me once again.

So there I was, done with that and still no Tony. It wasn't the money, the eighteen grand, that was generating pressure. It would be available but I wanted it done as soon as humanly possible. To not alarm Brewster, I knew we'd have to stay in the city until the payment was made. But there was no Tony and I realised that I was hungry.

I fastened my trousers and investigated my scattered clothes until I located a relatively clean jacket. Leaving the room, I looked down the corridor to see the Asian porter running towards me with his feet battling the ground in scuffing, sliding interactions. He slowed and held up a surprisingly cheap, electric clock. His shirt was spattered and streaked with liquid.

'Is it raining?' I asked him and he answered, bizarrely, 'I don't know,' but I had no time for this and thanked him, flung the clock into the room and departed with increasing vigour to find some food.

It was raining, and raining properly too. Stretched bullets of water scaled down in vast swipes, pinging and poking my shoulders while I walked fast down the darkening street past the bar where I had met the journalist for the interview. At least *she* had gone, I thought in consolation.

I crossed the road, through parping cars that were starting to spark lights in response to the unexpected dulling of the daytime. I jumped the streaming gutter and headed for the likeliest looking cluster of commerce, a line of awnings that would also provide some temporary shelter.

When I got there I wasn't alone, with a small grouping of caught-out travellers shaking their heads and peeking upwards for signs of abatement. I stood with those people and saw something else. In response I took out my phone and called Tony once more. Again he didn't answer but this time there was a marked difference in circumstances because it was Tony that I had seen.

Maybe twenty yards to my left he stood, well along the line of others but projecting slightly while looking exasperated to the sky. When I called, he ejected his mobile phone from a trouser pocket that was tightened by the demands of his demonic thighs. I looked coldly down the chests of strangers to see Tony regard his phone and then replace it with greater ease. He looked ahead in thought and then slipped away into the rain. After no great debate, I followed him.

Twenty-nine

Through the rain we went, Tony walking with his head bent in protection and me maintaining space and bodies between us with a fair collection of concern. I didn't mind his unresponsiveness, I could hardly mind that. Our relationship was steeled by my lack of respect and a rare display of open neglect from Tony in response had to be grudgingly allowed.

The real worry, which flamed while I skulked behind him, was that Tony was going somewhere and he didn't want to lie to me about where that was. Tony didn't mind lying to me, not at all, even though he wasn't very good at it and he knew that he wasn't very good at it. His theft from me meant that those lies came often. Usually, he would tell me that he was going to go for a drink or for sex but there would be only caution in his delivery. I would ignore the lie and he would go and see to his stealing.

But now Tony was going somewhere and to do something that not only did he not want me to know, he didn't even want to speak to me before doing it. He didn't want the risk of me reading him or testing him. This unnatural precaution, together with the fact that Tony was taking a measured path through these foreign streets, created a beating fear.

He was approaching, *we* were approaching, a rendezvous. For a rendezvous, you need someone at the other end. I was arrested by the danger. I quickened, going round and over the springing puddles and closing on Tony's steady advance while he continued past doorways filled by spectators of the deluge, watching the onslaught that Tony and I continued through.

The rain had made it to my skin. My body warmed the liquid and dragged my clothes into a lashed, slick outer layer that tightened around me and disrupted my breathing that was already shortening with the unexpected demands of the chase. I got within yards of Tony and was distracted by whether his leather jacket was shining with rejected rain or was similarly overrun when he turned sharply into a narrower street that was floored with gleaming cobbles.

He picked his way over the stones and up the steps of a small bar, the name of which he openly checked, with a flick of the head and a sheltering hand over his eyes, before entering. He had checked the name because it was where he had to go. He had to go there because he had to meet someone.

The bar was busy, because it was small and swollen with refugees from the passing punishment of the weather. There were men in suits and female shoppers ill at ease in their chosen escape but doing the best they could, drinking wine and gin and tonics and looking through the window in grim hope of release. And then there were the regulars, tricky specimens both excited and put out by the interlopers and clinging to usual perches in increasing desperation.

Beyond this unlikely gathering there was a space at head height five yards deep before the back wall where I guessed some tables lay. I teased my way past the steaming jackets and fractured conversations until, through breaks in the bodies, I caught a snatch of Tony's right shoulder and his hair matted and clinging to his neck like that of an old lady.

I eased a man to the side with a strained smile and a gentle palm on his arm and I got a little more. Tony's hands were clasped together and he talked with a grave disposal. I couldn't see the other side of the table until a stationary woman swung round to address her friend and a gap opened. I sidled into the pocket that she'd left and the scene emerged.

Before Tony was a fresh pint of beer and then a drink that looked neutral, non-alcoholic. Then there was another pair of hands and I knew, I already knew, but I kept going. I kept moving into the space that the woman had created while my eyes travelled up two arms and then I was looking, through the smoke and confusion, at the face of my father.

After Birmingham, that first tour was a shuddering delight. The process itself was repetitive – train, hotel, venue, all as basic as they could be – but my future was opening up in front of me with the blaring suggestion of upward spirals. I got better, quickly. My handling of the crowd, my handling of my talent, everything toughened together.

In the afternoons, during my work on my reawakened calves, I would devise another dozen pieces of work that I could throw in if needed during the evenings. My mind became busy but ordered and when a man or woman in those dingy crowds offered a crashing negative, I would thrill myself with how rapidly I could counter it.

Tony was exuberant and there was a shared level to our achievement back then. We'd sit up late, at the venue or lying, drinking, on our hotel beds and I'd push him for more details, more projections, of where we went from here. He'd talk of bigger shows, longer tours and higher prices. More than anything, he talked of television.

'But that's all bollocks,' he'd say, about anything, 'compared to TV.'

Getting on TV, Tony told me, was *the ticket to a different world*. I was flattered and exhilarated, a twenty-year-old who had come from what I'd come from to these promises of so much more. There was no doubt that Tony was a liar but that was OK. Liars operated low down on my understanding of human failing. So I didn't mind when the tour ended, and the lies came.

Liverpool had been the last night – a buoyant session in a faded nightclub near the docks – and the following day we were on the train home to London. There was pleasure in the finishing. A contentedness, better than relief, and yet on the train Tony was edgy and unresponsive, checking his watch with awkward regularity.

Finally he braved discussion and I knew immediately what was happening. He asked if I had enjoyed the tour, and if I was excited about what was to follow. Once again he drew out scenes where the venues, the hotels, everything, were lifted in standard and opportunity. I decided to ambush him.

'And what about the money?'

He looked attacked, scanning the carriage and holding a hand unwittingly to his chest.

'Yeah,' he said, 'the money, I was just getting to that.'

I had roughly formulated the financial mechanics of the tour. In Sunderland, I had heard the club owner tell his barman that Tony was on half the ticket money. Outside the club a blackboard had said:

COMEDIAN

MEDIUM (MINDREEDER)

FREE DRINK WITH TICKET (DRAUGHT,
HOUSE SPIRIT)

£8

There were perhaps one hundred and fifty in that night. £600 for Tony. The hotel had been £80. Throw in taxis and trains and the sickly meals that Tony made a show of paying for and stowing the receipt, and I reckoned Tony was making an average of £400 a day. Fourteen nights, £5600.

Tony sandwiched his hands, holding them on the train's table in a kindly gesture before slinking into a ramble of further preparation. Transport costs, accommodation, taxes, booking fees, promotion, deposits. A monotonous stream of stuttering justification. He used the word miscellaneous at one point, like this: waving his hands about, looking at the train roof and saying, with his voice pulled and hopeful,

'Then you have... miscellaneous.'

For me money was rooted in the corrupt and illegal, now I saw it was to stay there. I wanted money, needed it, but there was no panic attached. I had upwards of forty grand in the flat in Earl's Court, had found a way of making more, and was about to be given some more by Tony. Though, it was becoming clear, not too much more.

'Anyway, Nicky, I pushed those bastards as far as I could on the tickets and so on.'

From his jacket he pulled an envelope and held it out. It felt thick but then I looked in and saw the tens. I was expecting £2800. In fact, no, I was expecting £1500 and for him to tell me that it was half of the profits.

'It's £750, half the profits.'

His face was pinched and not holding the smile well. I felt that I should at least resist, if only to protect myself from increased mistreatment in the future.

'Is that it? Fourteen nights? That's what? Fifty quid a night or so?'

'No, there's more, Nicky, there's more, but I'm doing your taxes for you, remember.'

The point was eager and prepared.

'Unless you want to do them yourself, get down the tax office, get the forms?'

He arched an eyebrow. That was the only resentment, the fact Tony thought he could blackmail me over the filling out of a form. Or maybe it was because I knew that he could. I had never strayed too close to any serious piece of administration.

I had to give the appearance of mild outrage and I did, staring him down and going through the sums I had constructed myself. Tony seemed remarkably hurt, offering conflicting figures that emerged with wild spontaneity and didn't stand up to much study. We bounced about like that for a while before I took the envelope.

The theft was a flaw, certainly, but Tony was so weak that I felt it could be rectified in time. Or perhaps I didn't. Perhaps I was scared of facing theft because I would be facing myself. Either way I let Tony's stealing go, drifting away to nothing on the train from Liverpool.

'It's fine, Tony, don't worry about it, I just thought it would be more.'

'It will be, Nicky, much more. Next time.'

I hesitated for a moment, looking out the window at the landscape that was flattening while London neared.

'It had fucking better be.'

We laughed. This easy descent into the childish was becoming the best way to handle Tony and my relationship with him. Ultimately it wasn't, because the failings it ignored were allowed to develop. The end result was always going to be disastrous.

At the train station, Tony was picked up by a wasted old blonde who smiled at me but not at him. I caught the tube back to Earl's Court and my flat. The accomplishment of the tour was already starting to move away and I didn't enjoy that at all. In the flat, however, distraction waited.

The cash payment of my rent and the absence of any logistical normality to my life meant that I received no mail. Anything that came bore the names of other, mysterious figures who had lived there before and gave glimpses into unattractive lives. Credit card offers for strange sounding banks and doctor's appointments. Unpaid council tax and endless junk mail tailored to the desperate.

But when I pushed through the door on my return that day I had received my first, and last, delivery of mail. It was a package of forwarded letters from Soviet Street, in a startling piece of professionalism by the building's owner. There was a rubble of invoices and receipts from my advertising, a couple of plaintive notes from former clients and a newspaper article, framed on one side by a jagged parting from the rest of the paper.

I read it right there – standing in the flat with the door hanging open. It was a solitary article ranked above and to the side of an advertisement for a trouser press. At the top was the paper's name. the *Soho Star*, the paper that had carried the scoop of Java Joe's teeming shelves of porn.

The words swarmed around a photo of Java Joe when he

was a few years younger. He was with a woman and small boy. Java Joe was smiling off to the side of the camera, sitting on a low wall with his legs splayed and in front of what looked like a cage. London Zoo, I presumed. It was hard to look at the photo when at the foot of the page – in writing lined with a ruler, small capitals etched with feeling – there was the casual observation –

YOUR FAULT NICK

I walked through the cold rooms holding the article and finished it sitting on my bed that felt firm and foreign.

Tragic Death of Local Shopkeeper

The Metropolitan Police have confirmed that there were no suspicious circumstances in the sudden death of well-known local shopkeeper Mr Joseph Yakari (43), who operated Soviet Street News and whose body was found in another commercial property in Soviet Street last week...

And on it ran below the photo of Java Joe (I couldn't take his surname seriously) and his former wife and kid. The paper meekly referred to its previous scoop – delicately talking of Java Joe's shop having *recently been in the news*. That sense of shame ran through the coverage and the glowing testimonies they had seemingly rounded up from unnamed *regulars* of Soviet Street News. Nothing from the family.

I wasn't overly concerned. The accusation could have come from anyone, and if all it had driven them to was to slip this through my old letterbox at Soviet Street then that wasn't going to damage me.

I was exhausted from the tour's demands and my mind was still placed determinedly in the future and the promised action to come. This stealthy arrival of the past struggled for attention. I took the article, with the written addition, and put it in a drawer in the flat's limited kitchen. When I moved out, to Fulham and a richer life before that final tour, I left it behind.

Life had shifted and I had a new understanding of what I was doing. The poverty of my days was fine, because it wasn't permanent and I enjoyed the temporary lack of commitments. I didn't mind either about the flat's taps choking, or the radiators lying silent for hours then launching clanging furies at night that woke me terrified and long seconds from knowing where I was.

What I minded was that my own money from Soviet Street, those fees arranged and stretched by Tiffany, had only been lightly inflated by Tony's £750. Java Joe's money, the forty thousand that I had stolen, was waiting. I felt it approaching, the feeling I would have when I had to reach into the detergent box for the first of the poached notes. I was surprised how little I wanted that moment to arrive.

Most days I spoke to Tony and he told me that a tour was being put together, I was to buy more *stage clothes* ('and keep receipts,' he stressed, in a manner that I was supposed to see as generous) and what did I think about corporate parties? Everything was vague until he called and battled through some worthless conversation before moving to his revelation.

'You ever been on a boat, Nicky?'

'Yeah,' I lied, I don't know why.

It was a two-month cruise and I was to join the entertainment staff. It was spring – Earl's Court was struggling with deceptive blue skies and sudden, triumphant rain – and the invitation was instantly appealing. Even before Tony's hyperbole about life at sea, which he pitched as an assault of sex, sunshine and free booze, all involving him. And even after.

'We're flying to Spain in a couple of days, hooking up with the boat in Barcelona. What do you think about that?'

'Sounds good, Tony.'

'Then it's Mallorca, south of France, Italy, Sardinia and, hold on I can't read my writing, Tunisia.'

'Great.'

'Evening show, every night, third from the top of the bill and all food and drink on the house. Sea-view cabin.'

'OK.'

'I've done us a decent deal,' he said and this was a new approach. 'I'm going to advance you three grand for the trip.'

'Fine.'

'Have you got a passport?'

'Yeah.'

In the Jock's Lodge days, my mum had got me a passport for a much anticipated trip to France. We never went. Dad had found another, less constructive, use for the money and only told us on the morning of the planned departure. Mum had screamed and thrown the contents of a frying pan – oil and bacon – at his chuckling departure from the pub's kitchen.

Two days after we spoke, Tony picked me up in a minicab. I was pleased to see him and the tangible link to possibilities he brought.

'Ready for this then, Nicky?'

He laughed aimlessly and prattled away about the ship while we gradually freed ourselves from London. Tony knew the ship's entertainments director, a man that he called a *right dirty bastard*. He'd got me on as a favour, Tony claimed, as the spot was really beyond my development.

'Usually they'd want you to have done more, but I told them you'd tear it up. You'll love it, Nicky, I'm telling you.'

'I was thinking, Tony, it'll be the same people every night will it not?'

'Nah.' He shook his head and enjoyed the authority. 'People come and go, they hop on and off and the boat keeps going. Plus there's a lot happening and if the boat's docked then most of them fuck off for the night. You won't get many of them twice, let alone more than that.'

Tony had booked us on a budget flight that was two hours late so we went for drinks and were in decent spirits when we boarded the plane past the sullen, budget attendants. He pulled a pile of newspapers from a plastic bag and retreated into one, scorning his way through the front page revelation of a footballer's affair.

I took a paper and moved into the television pages. I read the reviews with the plane starting to move under us and then looked for a long time at the schedules. At what was there and what might be there. Tony's hand touched mine and I expected consultation on the footballer story. Instead he grinned and pointed to the schedules.

'We'll get there, Nicky. You'll get there, guaranteed.'

It was one of the times when I appreciated Tony. He may have already started taking from me but I needed him because he understood ambition. And I, having only just found it, did not.

The docks in Barcelona were a barren, industrial complex. We walked, hot and struggling with our bags, past warehouses that were vast blasts of corrugated iron towards a row of cruise ships. There were around half a dozen of them and I was only disappointed and not surprised when Tony phoned his contact and was guided to the smallest and most faded of the lot.

While the others gleamed above well-ordered ramps – floored with carpet and with ribbon snaking through the rails – our brave craft was another matter entirely. It seemed a little thin, almost rectangular in design, to maximise the rooms that could own one of the squat balconies that ringed it. The shell was functional grey and the staircase to it looked like it had been deployed as an emergency measure. The ship was a cheap building, slung on to a hull and pushed sheepishly out to sea. We approached with our hands shielding the sun.

'Fuck me,' I said.

'Christ, it's not the best is it?' Tony conceded, though clutched back some optimism with, 'Still it's the view from up there that's important, you know?'

We clambered up the stairs, giggling a little when the staircase swayed and we took turns to swear and grip the handrails in alarm. On the ship's cramped deck a woman in a uniform too big for her jogged to greet us. Only her top lip had been bothered by the lipstick that was still in her hand.

'Welcome to the SS *Victory*, gentlemen.'

I thought that she was joking. Tony was more interested in her.

'Not quite ready for us?' He pointed at the lipstick and she gave him a brittle smile and not much else.

'So, what tour are you from?'

After we revealed our heightened status the woman took us into the ship through slender passages, framed with whining pipes that ran shamelessly outside the plasterwork. Our room, which she called a suite, was a tight and unsettling arrangement. The ceiling was low and had a block of neon set within it that gave a deafening glare.

Picked out in the choking light were two single beds sitting alarmingly close, two chairs round a tiny table and then a sliding door to a balcony where two people could just about stand side by side.

'Jesus,' Tony shouted from beyond a small door.

I tried to join him but he was on his way out and I had to wait until he had freed himself before entering the bathroom that was hunched into a cupboard. A single pace separated the sink, shower and toilet. If you were driven to do so, you could use them all at once.

The woman left us to our dismay. I was interested in how Tony would attempt to redeem this but he couldn't even manage that, turning instead to saving himself.

'I think I'll just do the first week, Nicky. Get you settled in.'

'I can't blame you, let's go for a walk.'

The entertainments director found us in one of the ship's bars – a Hawaiian-themed affair with plastic fruit hanging in unlikely combinations from what was supposed to be a straw roof.

'Does the boat ever go to Hawaii?' I asked the entertainments director after our initial introductions faded into silence. He was an evasive character, who shook my hand firmly while talking to Tony.

'It's never been out the Med.'

I followed his gaze to the barmaid whose despondence clashed with the jollity of her flowery uniform. She was perhaps two feet away, her face flushed in discomfort through awareness of his fierce study.

He didn't give us too much after that, only that I would be starting in two night's time when we left port. After more drinks and a grim meal, Tony and I endured a trying night in our room. The beds were stern and bolted to the ground for security against the waves. Mine felt like it had a spine, with a curious extra tightness running down the middle. I lay awake for a long time while Tony groaned.

The next morning we found a terrace loaded with deckchairs and settled in to watch the arrival of the ship's other passengers. In relatives' cars, taxis and on foot they would come marching proudly down the concrete. Tony and I would already be off – chortling and whispering encouragement,

'Not that one, not that one, not that one,' during their hopeful checking of the SS Victory's prettier neighbours.

When the people finally clocked the monstrosity on which we sat they launched into huddled consultation, with hands going to heads in shock or over faces in a refusal of acceptance. Tony and I would laugh in our deckchairs at their reluctant journeys on to the shaking stairway.

That killed off the morning and in the afternoon we were summoned to a gathering of the ship's staff. It was held in what was called the ship's ballroom. The ballroom at Glendoll College had been a gaping hall with a floor of polished wood and walls hung with Highland hunting scenes. We had learnt Scottish country dancing there, boys dancing stiffly with other boys while the teachers shouted instructions and music played from a tape deck raised on a chair.

The ballroom on the SS Victory was a long room with brown carpet that ran up and over a stage at the end. One wall bore windows glazed in reinforced vacuums that left the view blurred with trapped smudges and condensation. Light got through, but not much else. The other wall had framed calendar shots of various, better ships.

Other than the rows of uncomfortable seating – chairs of metal and sticky leather that hooked together into lines – that was the ballroom. This, Tony confirmed, was where I would be working for the next two months.

On the stage an angry woman with a clipboard was reading out various disciplinary points. Her instructions, and her broken and deliberate speech, were aimed at the muddled foreign majority of those in attendance – glum Eastern Europeans and Spanish-looking clusters who sat whispering while she spoke.

Also on the stage was the entertainments director. He was a couple of yards behind the woman and stared, with little subterfuge, at her arse. When she had finished he approached the microphone with his hands in his pockets.

'My lot stay here. The rest of you can fuck off.'

The woman stiffened at his language but he was busy watching a group of female cleaners make their way out. Soon there were only around two dozen of us left. They were unremarkable other than one middle-aged couple with dyed hair that hung in blonde eruptions. The man had his feet lifted to the top of the chair in front and the woman was sending a text message, causing clinking from the plastic hoops round her wrists.

'Not bad, eh?' said Tony. 'Apparently a real goer back when they were big.'

'Big?'

'"Christmas Ain't For Me". Christmas number two, 1979?'

'I wasn't born.'

'Fuck me, I'm old.'

'Right then,' announced the entertainments director, 'welcome to this shithole. Two months, one show a night, two on Fridays and Saturdays. Piece of piss. Any problems then come to me as a last resort. Don't come to my room. Ever. That's a sackable offence. There's tomorrow night's programme,' he pointed to a whiteboard that was gridded and marked with red. 'All shows are in here, God help us. Best of luck.'

He hopped off the stage, winked and walked out of the room.

'What a boy,' said Tony, with something that sounded suspiciously like respect.

When we got to the board, my name had 21.00 scrawled beside it. After me came a man called Goodtime George and then a word that looked like it was supposed to appear foreign but probably wasn't and, in brackets beside it: ('Christmas Ain't For Me,' 1979).

'What are they called?'

'I could never pronounce it to be honest. Look at you, third from the top of the bill. Not bad eh?'

'I suppose not.'

A few hours later, the SS Victory bravely edged out into the Mediterranean with the decks full of passengers nervously watching land creep away. Tony and I left the forlorn crowds and retreated to a bar where we drank alone and then with Goodtime George who was a Canadian former television presenter. He hadn't yet recovered from the fall from grace that had led to his unheralded appearance on the SS Victory.

'I'm a victim of fashion,' he urged in that strange accent – a floating pitch that you keep waiting to identify itself. 'It seems that if you want to be a comedian on the TV these days then you're not *actually* allowed to be funny.'

Tony and I sighed and agreed with this critique of Canadian light entertainment until Goodtime George became flummoxed by the fishbowl cocktails and elected for an early departure.

'Showtime tomorrow,' he said, smiling and pointing at me. 'Showtime all round.'

'Can't wait,' I told him.

When Goodtime George left Tony asked me what I was going to do during my shows on the ship. It was a curious question and I couldn't decide whether he felt he should ask or was looking for involvement. Either way, I decided to keep the division.

'It'll be fine, Tony, don't worry.'

There was a trace of hurt in his silent acceptance.

I shouldn't have said, when discussing Birmingham and my first tour, I never failed at another show because the first show on the SS *Victory* was a disastrous affair. The experience was some distance from success, but I would argue that I was hopelessly handicapped by the ship's ballroom.

I arrived early to find a magician on, laughing a lot more than his thin crowd and working achingly slowly through basic stuff. The only real addition to the ballroom was a plywood screen to the side of the stage, allowing some cover for the transfer of acts. It was getting dark and for some reason the room's main lighting had been turned on to join the stage lights that were weaker and therefore redundant.

The chairs were pushed back a full ten yards from the stage. This, I would find out later, was to accommodate the night's cherished climax when the blonde couple sang 'It Ain't Christmas For Me.' During their headline moment they would embark on loping forays into this space of carpet, an act of audaciousness that would see middle-aged audience members leap to their feet in glorious abandon.

For me the room was impossible. I needed proximity for the audience to foster the feeling of involvement, and comfort that was removed by the brightness. I walked on to the stage with little confidence. It was a lacking that was fully merited.

I tried some low-rent comedy which got hopeful smiles but when I moved into what was starting to pass for my act it was unworkable. There was some attempted assistance from a few appreciative figures but I struggled to even hear their responses, called out from beyond the void at the front. The lights and the paltry spread of bodies gave proceedings an artificiality that I could not afford.

After a tough half hour I was delighted to see Goodtime George standing behind the plywood screen, drinking champagne and looking at me with pained solidarity. I dwindled to a close, eliciting a desperately weak applause, and introduced George as a man who *needs no introduction*. I skipped down to the shelter of the screen and Tony appeared round the corner before George muttered, 'Into the valley of fucking death,' put down his glass and walked stiffly on to the stage to not much reaction.

Tony, I could see, wanted to laugh. It was hard to see another response, there was no one in the room who had any hold over us. The entertainments director certainly wasn't about. Tony kicked his feet on the carpet, his mouth itching at the corners until it triggered me and the two of us were laughing, into our hands and in gulps of containment so it wouldn't carry to George.

'Fucking disaster,' I gasped.

'*SS Victory*,' replied Tony and that set us off again. In the background, Goodtime George spoke into silence.

The next morning I left Tony sleeping and went to find the entertainments director. He was in the main breakfast saloon, not the staff one, but holed up on a single table amongst the passengers.

'Morning.'

'Morning,' he answered with suspicion.

'I need to move the room about a bit before my act. Is there anyone that can do it, then get it back together after? I think there's a break between Goodtime George and the band?'

'There's fifteen minutes.'

'So, is there anyone?'

'You know what?' He looked thoughtful. 'I think there is. Two Polish guys, we took them on for that kind of stuff, I've not seen them about.'

'Right, so I can use them?'

'If you can find them.'

I found them playing cards in a room that I hadn't been aware of. It had sweating brass pipes running through it and the Poles sat on deckchairs, tossing cards on to the upturned base of a cardboard box. They were disappointed when I told them their positions were about to be activated, clearly they had so far not been charged with a single task. If I hadn't hunted them down, then they would have played cards amongst the pipes for two months.

They followed me to the ballroom where I gave my instructions. From that evening's show onwards, I was going to have the magician buy me five minutes at the end by doing tricks and posing for photos at the door with his departing audience. While that went on, the Poles were to remove about half the seating, stacking it to the side, and push the rest into crowded intimacy round the stage.

They would then wait until whatever crowd arrived were seated in the new arrangement, turn all the lighting off, and the one with the best English was to announce me in an adaptation of the speech I had handed to Keith in Birmingham and to many others since. They enjoyed that sign of involvement and on the way back they asked me about my act.

'Is bollocks though?' asked one. 'All bollocks?'

'Hard to say, lads,' I told them. 'See you tonight.'

That evening, I roared back to form. The Poles were an unexpected success – organised and talented while they whipped the seating into place and then announced me and started the clapping the moment I emerged from behind the plywood on to the lit stage.

I felt eased and, crucially, so did the audience. It was still paltry but they were bunched and I quickly got things going. I decided to use the move that I had abandoned amidst the failure of the previous evening.

I had been nervous about using it because it was the one point of my act that left me truly, powerfully vulnerable. It would be a talking point in the contained environment of the ship, and that could be devastating if it did not go as planned.

First there was a woman for me to trip through some basics with. I was sensing she had been feeling a bit down recently, which she agreed to with some welcome surprise.

Who doesn't? Who doesn't feel down on occasion? And yet that's the kind of thing that stayed with me to the end.

I frowned, froze and I did the move. They had been warned, in the Pole's halting introduction, and reacted differently to the cautious, silent appreciation of the club crowds. There was a lot more cheering but that wasn't cynicism, it was a catch-all reaction, given to me as it was given to the other acts.

Straining in apparent possession, I waited for the cheering to end before speaking to the woman on behalf of a man who turned out, to her surprise, to be her late father. And from there things strengthened and achievement built around me.

The following night was even better. There was random luck in my selection of a couple who identified themselves as foster parents in some pocket of urban warfare in the north of England. It became obvious, through their fear and hand-holding, that they had seen dozens of wounded youngsters pass through their care, and I was off conjuring every specimen of youthful failure you can imagine – drug addicts, boozers, gamblers, thieves.

I would sketch out these wasted lives, the couple would give me the names and I would pass on gratitude for the brief shelter that the young dead had been given. They cried and so did affected, unconnected others.

By the end of the show the crowd were so supple that I launched into a parting shot at modern society that had people doggedly staying at the end until Tony and I were forced, through the most basic level of decency, to emerge from behind the plywood so I could hug and shake hands and frown and agree.

I found a bearable routine – resting or wandering during the day, peaking in focus for the show and then drinking with Tony and Goodtime George afterwards. When we approached Mallorca, my evening's company was swiftly halved.

'Well, it's going brilliantly,' said Tony repeatedly over breakfast.

We were docking in Mallorca that afternoon, and I knew that he had spotted an early escape.

'You want to go back to London?'

He launched into a covering of sighs and shrugs that ended with:

'It's just if I don't get off that's me for another week, you know? You seem settled in and I've got a lot I could be doing in London, for you.'

'It's fine, no problem.'

It was OK to show that I meant it. The remainder of the two months would be precarious and extending Tony's frantic presence wouldn't do much to help that. He was delighted and produced what he had reluctantly valued my sacrifice at.

'Here you go, Nicky, a little bonus,' he said grandly and I took the envelope. 'You deserve this.'

That evening, while we toyed with his last minutes on the ship's deck, he announced that his absolute priority on returning to London would be constructing a new tour for me.

'You're ready, Nicky, I can see that now. Do these two months, have a week off when you get back, then we're going back out there. On the road.'

'Sounds good, Tony.'

It was hot and Tony wiped his face with his hands and peered longingly at the staircase until I moved towards it so he knew that he could go.

I had forgotten what Tony's departure meant, the instant relegation back to solitude. It was hardly a new sensation, but being alone in the trapped atmosphere of the ship was much harder. The only real diversion came from watching the entertainments director.

At breakfast he ate alone in a corner, constantly evaluating the room. When he roused himself it would be to set off on a wandering tour of targets. Mothers with their families would be surprised by his sudden presence, his face appearing beside their own with a manic smile and his hand pressed against their backs. He would work the table – a joke to the children, earnest conversation with the father and all the time I would watch his hand while it pressed and circled and the woman straightened and looked in question at her befuddled husband.

During the day he marched the deck, throwing arms round

shoulders and pulling women of all ages to him for intense snatches, forcing them to battle politely free. After the matinée, the plump showgirls would barricade themselves in their dressing room and turn up the music to cover his heated pounding. His dedication stood out amidst the apathy of the SS *Victory*, and at least offered something to watch.

Everything else was work, and it began to fill my uncontested days as they became preparation for the shows. With my act smoothed through nightly exposure, I concentrated on the rise within my battery of the value of information. The more I could make the audience offer me, the quicker I'd have them with me, and the quicker I could move my work in amongst them.

On the first tour this had been peeking from behind curtains or surveying from shadows during their arrival. Looking for something, anything, that rose above the normal. On the ship this process grew more studied because it was too easy and I had nothing else to do.

The croupiers were the best. They had no professional concern in detailing the major winners and losers of the ship's troubled casino, where the felt was crumpled and the roulette wheel was known to jam and cause hysteria. The barmen, too, would help by telling me of witnessed scandals, fighting couples and the men who ghosted in for sunken double measures with one eye on the door. They would tell me too about the ageing women who sat on the stools, drank wine and dropped their room numbers into the conversation.

Every related piece of an individual's shortcomings I would match to a face and store it, waiting and hoping for an appearance at my show. The ship's limited alternatives would send along at least a few each night and I would go to them with flattery and suggestion and what they didn't know that I knew.

Word carried of my nightly wonders and the crowds grew. The Poles were leaving all the seats out in their changeover routine, and then they were adding more and thinning the passages at the room's flanks to cram the rows tighter. One day the staff's whiteboard announced that my show had joined the singers of 'It Ain't Christmas For Me' in demanding advance booking.

Advance booking offered something else. I told the women at guest reception that I'd had a troublesome heckler and wanted to ensure he wasn't returning. They showed me where the sheet lay with my show's bookings, and from then on I sidled in each afternoon to read the personal information for the passengers I would be seeing hours later.

I was back in Glendoll College, forcing the stuff in, and the result was just as impressive and altering as it had been there. The shows became unstoppable. I'd race through my jokes and the move (which had started to get a cheer that built from seconds before it came. It was a catchphrase, warmly reprised) and then I was conjuring up the dead in haunting droves.

I'd pull someone from the crowd and ask for their name. I'd be looking, at least initially, for any honeymooners or a couple who had made the questionable decision to mark their retirement on the SS Victory. This information was on a helpful noticeboard at guest reception.

'I'm sensing this is a new beginning,' I would tell them. Then I'd find a wise, dead ancestor to tell them that they were, 'Doing the right thing' (for the honeymooners) or, 'You deserve it, and have a drink for me!' (for the retirement couple).

In the end, inevitably, I created a core of regulars. This had once been my worry, but it was in fact a gift. The same befuddled old women, simple families and excited kids would arrive sharply and sit smiling from the front rows, hoping for recognition for their nightly vigils. My duties after the show – signing and grinning into cameras – thickened with their demands. Santini leant itself easily to autographs, with a row of vertical lines and jaunty dots that I sketched as minute circles.

Late at night in dark corners of the quietest bar, and early in the morning while I lay next to Tony's empty bed, I ran through the latest show for signs and spaces for improvement. Ambition was being fed, and I wanted to return to London, and Tony, prepared for elevation.

I had been speaking to him regularly and, as always, it was to receive a barrage of positive responses with the slightest of news hidden within. He had been speaking to theatre owners and comedy clubs, he still wanted me back on the road a week after I returned, there was a chance of something in Ireland.

There was more lying too. Tony would mention that he had been having *good reports* from the entertainments director. I enjoyed the suggestion of the entertainments director interrupting his all-consuming hunt for grubby satisfaction to offer regular, rounded feedback to the representatives of the ship's acts, who he never watched. I told Tony to get something set up and that I didn't want any delaying when I got back.

'Yeah, yeah, hit the ground running sort of thing, that's the spirit, Nicky.'

The passenger attention was rapidly drained of enjoyment. Their gasping questions on the previous night's shows had become an irritation, coming when I was sat sweating waste in the sauna, or during my hurried journeys to and from the ship's reception, or while I was having a piss in a bar toilet (and once while I was having a shit – a pound on the door and 'Excuse me, I was in the other night, is that stuff all real?' I looked in disbelief at the plastic that was between us).

They abandoned me as the end approached. Audiences dropped to the truly desperate while the rest stayed on decks that became static. People didn't walk any more, just stood with arms hooked over the edge while they stared relentlessly at distant coastlines and wished away their remaining time. When I left the *SS Victory* in Tunisia I was delirious with the liberation. I called Tony from an expensive phone at the airport and he shouted through the fuzz.

'It's all done, Nicky, another tour, all set!'

'Great, thanks Tony. That's great.'

I think that I was happy then, at the airport in Tunisia.

Thirty

The rain eased during my walk back to the hotel. People's movements slowed with departing urgency and above us the sky split and lightened. On the way, briefly, I saw the journalist who had been there at the very start of this and who I had hoped had now gone.

She was sitting in a café studying a newspaper. My only concern, which came and went very quickly, was that it was strange the way she was reading it. It was held up stiffly and she was peering with little connection. She was reading it the way that people read newspapers, but I wondered if I would expect her to read it differently, with at least a sense of familiarity.

Seeing her was just something that broke up the journey and the main, thundering issue at hand. If it hadn't been for my dad – what he was and, now, where he was – then I would have had more time. But as I made it back somehow, one foot following another through the flooded streets, I was only enlisted by Dad's face through the heat of the bar, with Tony sitting traitorously beside him.

Until my hotel room there was movement to take the edge from the unwelcome energy. Inside that windowless place I slipped into an insane run of activity. I packed, emptied and repacked my bag. I ordered drinks then cancelled them. I ran a bath that I didn't use and then shaved myself with a shaking, angry hand. I cut myself as I knew I would, a small curve under my chin that I pressed aftershave into and my eyes watered with the fiery response. I walked the carpet and spent a long time looking at the phone until it rang and Brewster was there.

'Any luck with that cash, I want to put an offer in on those houses by the end of play?'

I was remarkably polite, explaining to Brewster that I should have news for him in the morning if the deal could wait until then. I spoke in quiet, helpful tones and he was as unnerved as I was.

'Right,' he said. 'Well, first thing tomorrow then. Have a nice evening.'

'Same to you, Brewster, cheers.'

There was a lot coming to me now. Early days in the Big Apple, Mum's silent protection. Jock's Lodge and the OK Corral with Dad laughing, or angry, or silent, and each time working determinedly against me. Ayako and that scene of shock and betrayal.

My head tightened around my mind and I found myself in the bathroom, gasping and throwing water into my face. The phone in the room began a cautious ringing and I waited in the bathroom, watching it from the door until it stopped.

So Tony had gone from me. He'd been attracted by Dad's amoral fearlessness and it was just me left. Tony was with Dad and I was here, in a hotel where a girl had died, maybe murdered, and with a bent policeman chasing me for eighteen grand. I couldn't even go because Tony had my money. Even if I did, there would be nothing to go to other than a decent flat with a few months left on the rent. Tony had my future and now it looked like Dad might have it with him. It is hard to convey how forcefully that thought affected me.

The hotel phone sounded again and I looked at it until it ended. My mobile rang. Tony.

'Hello.'

'Nicky my man, fancy some dinner?'

'Who with?'

'Well, with me.' He was confused as I supposed he would have to be.

'OK, sounds good, when?'

'It's seven now, meet me downstairs at half past?'

I had been in my room, back from the rain and Dad, for three hours. Half an hour later, I walked through the corridors, ready, but not really ready, to see Tony and Dad standing by the hotel's doors. Tony would be cowed and hanging back, Dad would start shouting from the moment he saw me. He would be grinning angrily and would take my hand quickly and release it slowly, saying something to Tony about me that left me switched immediately back to his control.

This was what was going to happen and I was going to have to let it happen because, right then, there was nothing else that I could do. I got to the final bend and when I walked round it only Tony was waiting for me, smiling and waving without needing to.

Thirty-one

Tony was nervous walking me to a restaurant. He spoke about the afternoon's rain, asking me if I'd been caught out by it. He'd been soaked, apparently, at the end of a wasted shopping trip.

'There's nothing in this city, Nicky, it's a load of bollocks. We've got to get back to London.'

'Brewster wants eighteen grand.'

'He what?'

'To buy a couple of flats. Or so he says. But he wants eighteen grand. He's got this note, Tony.'

I looked at Tony. He looked at me. He was comfortably lost.

'What kind of note?'

'A note that means I have to pay him eighteen grand. How quickly can you get it?'

'Maybe in the morning, if you're sure.'

'Yeah, I am.'

He just nodded at that and I presumed that he had more pressing worries. Dad, for example, who was surely waiting for us in the restaurant – already with a half a bottle gone, lifting a hand but not rising from the table. He wasn't there though, and Tony asked for a table for two.

It was a downstairs Italian, with red and white checked tablecloths and plastic hams hung on imitation wooden beams. Tony ordered drinks and I waited, unsure of how to react to the continued hiding of what I had seen that afternoon.

'He's a fucker, that Brewster,' said Tony with unlikely conviction, 'and dangerous too. We have to be careful with him, Nicky, if there was even a suggestion in the press that you could be linked with something dodgy about that girl, then you'd be fucked. Totally fucked.'

'Well, yeah, it wouldn't be good. Let's get him the cash then get out of here.'

'We'll take a bit of time off,' said Tony thoughtfully. 'There's only three dates left, I'll cancel them. We'll get back to London, meet the TV lot, see what they're saying, you know?'

As things stood, perhaps it would be manageable. There was certainly a chance that things could keep grimly growing. If Brewster could be bought off, if Dad was never mentioned and never appeared, then maybe I had been wrong to guarantee disaster. It wasn't really optimism, there wasn't enough behind it for that, but it didn't last long anyway. After we finished our starters, Tony coughed a bit, drank a bit, and then slipped his eyes round the restaurant.

'Nicky, I've got something to tell you mate.'

'Right.'

'The thing is, Nicky, I've been thinking of what we can do next. I think we need something good for the TV people, something that can show that you're safe and that they can use for the press.'

'OK.'

'And for you too, Nicky, something that will make you, well, happier.'

'Yeah.'

'The stuff with,' he peeked around once more, 'Java Joe. There's nothing we can do about that, we just have to take the chance, you know?'

'I know that.'

'Yeah, and I think we've got through it. But there's something that we *can* do something about, that we can sort. And it would be good for you, Nicky, as well, I'm sure about that.'

'My dad?'

There was no point in delaying this. It wasn't his arrival into the conversation that was going to be the issue, it was Tony's presentation.

'Ah, yeah, yeah, your dad. I tried to talk to you about it the other night, in the honesty bar.'

Tony starting to speak and me, drunk and saying *no, no Tony*, until he stopped. It was the memory that I'd been unable to position, back when it mattered.

'The thing is, Nicky, I've been talking to him. If we could do a big piece, one of the nationals, a reunion sort of thing, it would play very well for the TV boys. I've not told him that yet, but he just wants to see you.'

'Is he here?'

'Here?' And there went his eyes. 'No, he's in London. But I think he should come up in the morning, meet us for lunch. We've talked over the phone a lot. He seems a lot different to how I expected.'

'How?'

'He's just very, sort of, normal. He says he doesn't drink any more, that he works in an office for the brewery, and he thinks about you all the time. Every day, that's what he said. And your mother too. He says he wants to give you all the money that he got from the newspapers that time. He reckons that's when he packed in the booze.'

I laughed. That run of devious claims wasn't a problem. The problem was that Tony had lied about Dad not already being here, in the city, but as far as I could see, and I would be surprised if I was wrong, he hadn't been lying about anything else. All that meant was that Dad had been lying to him. Now that he was here, and in the conversation, I accepted my needed course.

'OK fine, I'll meet him, not lunch though. I'll meet him in the morning, I'm sure he can get the first train.'

Maybe I just wanted to meet him. Tony was delighted, this was close to the culmination of something he had long hinted at, and he wanted to form some unlikely celebration around it. I told him I was tired and we settled for a final drink then a quiet journey back.

'Tony,' I asked him outside the hotel, 'do you know the last time I saw my dad? Apart from in the street a few times, the last time I properly saw him?'

'With the Chinese girl, he told me.'

'Japanese.'

'That's right, Japanese. He said something about that, about the way you looked at him.'

Tony was embarrassed and he was happy to leave me when I told him I was going to bed. I kept going though, up through the floors, until I reached the honesty bar. I took a bottle of wine from the fridge before I noticed her, the journalist, sitting at a table in the corner. She had her back to me and her hand on a drink, and I walked quickly away.

At best, she was stretching an unlikely expenses allowance. At worst, she thought she was on to something with the black girl. That was a worry, tying with the grey understanding that had settled over the black girl's death. The bruises on her arms, Brewster and that fucking note.

It didn't work for a clearly limited journalist with a local London paper to be staying in that hotel, so she was obviously looking for me. I moved carefully back through the room and round the corner. The Asian porter was coming towards me, before he saw me and stopped, with a strangely sudden caution.

'OK?' I nodded, thinking that perhaps he was going to muster the responsibility to mention the wine in my hand.

'Yeah,' he said, and seemed to be trying to look beyond me, back into the bar. I wasn't going to delay my escape so I walked on, leaving the porter and the journalist behind me.

Thirty-two

Back when the OK Corral was Jock's Lodge, there used to be a tape that played in the toilets. It was Scottish comedians on a loop, telling stories. There was Chic Murray and Billy Connolly and others. Billy Connolly had a joke he told. It was about a man who went to the doctor. He had various complaints and the doctor looked him over for a while before announcing that he couldn't find a definitive answer to the man's symptoms.

'It must be the drink,' he told him in the end.

'Oh, well, don't be embarrassed, Doctor,' said the man, 'I'll come back when you're sober.'

And from the tape in the toilets came laughter, though over time I realised it was the same laughter that followed all the jokes on the tape.

Sitting with Dad the next day, I thought about that joke. Almost from the moment we met, and he shook my hand steadily, and guided me with a touch on the back into the café, and sat down and looked nervous and a little lost, I thought about that joke. Everything had been taken from him, left absent or replaced. His voice was slow and quieter, and he moved like an old man. He had crept into his fifties since I last saw him, but you would have taken anything up to seventy.

His skin was slightly greened, and his cheeks hung in pallid drapes. Within the flesh, a swarm of blood vessels had popped in silent, internal protests. Tiny zigzags and dots, exclamation marks and pairs of eyes, ran across his face. All I could think, looking at Dad and answering his questions, was that it must be the drink. The removal of the drink. Only that could have done this, only that could have possessed the power and the shock. Although I tried monumentally not to do so, I wondered what else the drink might have taken away.

'I don't really know where to start, Nicky,' he said, once our teas had arrived and he had lifted his with a strong hand. 'I've been thinking about what to say to you for more than a year, every day.'

'Since when?'

'Since I did those newspaper stories. You know, Nicky, I never even cashed their cheques. It was when I opened the envelopes, that was when I, you know. That was when I stopped, Nicky. Stopped everything. The booze, obviously, was the start.'

'Where have you been?'

'Working in head office, at the brewery. Living in town, a little shithole down in Pimlico. Near the Big Apple, the Marquis of Granby, do you remember that place, were you too young?'

'I remember it,' I said and he nodded in general apology.

'That's all I do really, Nicky. Go to work, go home, go to meetings, you know, for the drink.'

'Ayako,' I said, 'remember her?'

I wanted it to be a piece of devastation, something that might break this ludicrous reunion entirely, but in saying it I lost my nerve. I looked out the café's window and the silence grew. When I finally turned, Dad was staring with intensity at his tea. His concentration, I could see, was to stop himself from buckling in one way or another. I stood up.

'I've got to go,' I told him, feeling a weakness that I didn't understand.

'OK, Nicky.' He offered me his face's battered geography. 'Thanks for coming. If there's anything I can do, anything that might help. Tony said, he said I might be able to help?'

I left him there with that.

Thirty-three

Out in the street I managed to wrestle my feelings round to anger and called Tony.

'Well?' he answered hopefully.

'What's going on with this eighteen grand?'

'Eh?'

'Have you got the eighteen grand? I told you we needed it this morning.'

'I've got it, Nicky, I've got it here, don't worry.'

'Right, I'm coming to get it now.'

'Fine, no problem. So what happened?'

'With what?'

'With your dad?'

'I don't want to talk about that, Tony, just get that fucking money ready, let's pay that prick Brewster and get out of here.'

'OK, OK.'

I called Brewster who told me he'd meet me round the corner from the hotel in ten minutes. 'Oh, it's yourself,' was how he answered the phone, and he'd hung up sharply at the end. This riled me further and I was ready to take what I could out on Tony. He'd seen that coming though. When I got to his room he handed me the money and exited at the same time, pulling the door carefully behind him.

'Listen, Nicky,' he said, 'I'm going out for a few hours this afternoon, well this evening really.' He looked at his watch far too deliberately. 'To be honest with you,' he smirked without much confidence, 'I've got a little thing on, a woman from round here. I know her from way back.'

He was going to meet Dad and someone had to suffer apart from me.

'What's her name?'

He swallowed. 'Jane.'

'Has she got any mates, maybe I'll join you?'

'Ah, yeah, well, let me speak to her and get back to you. I'll text you.'

'Where will you be, I might just pop out later?'

'Not sure, Nicky, not sure, I'll text you.'

He was walking backwards from me, hands out and pleading. He was going towards the stairs, which showed his desperation.

'Alright,' I surrendered. 'Have a good time.'

I pushed the envelope into my jacket and went the other way, taking the lift right down to the hotel's car park and leaving through the service door for my rendezvous with Brewster. He came swinging round the corner in a branded police car. When he saw me he activated the lights and gave the siren a quick blare. The few people that were around stirred and he made it worse by braking in a squealing angle to the kerb.

'Thought you'd like a ride in one of these,' he laughed.

'Not particularly,' I replied, getting in. 'Here's your money.' I held out the envelope and his face tightened.

'Put that away, for fuck's sake,' he said, spinning the wheel and taking us back out into the road. 'Christ, how do you think that would look?'

I wasn't going to apologise to Brewster and he didn't have much to say so it was a calming journey down to the city's docks. They were a mix of rust and development. Abandoned warehouses and cranes faced vast follies of apartment buildings that managed to look expensive and cheap.

'Used to just be hookers and dealers down here,' said Brewster. 'Now look at these flats. The ones up there,' he leant forward and jutted his face up and towards the tops of the buildings, 'the penthouses, they're going for half a million.'

'Brewster, I've got your money here, I need to get back.'

'Let's go for a pint,' he said. 'Just one, I need to get this car back soon anyway.'

He parked on a side street and made us walk some distance to a bar. There was a decent afternoon crowd that Brewster sidled through and ordered us two pints of Guinness. We went to a table and he scanned the others while he lit a cigarette. I presumed he was checking for any familiar faces before the handover of the cash but he was looking for something else, which arrived when a woman came over and tapped me on the arm.

'I'm sorry, are you Nick Santini?'

'I am, yes.'

'Could you sign this to Sarah, please? That's my mum. What are you doing here?'

'Just a quick drink,' said Brewster, 'with a friend.'

I enjoyed the fact that the woman didn't even turn to him, just stood loyally while I signed the napkin and handed it back.

'Tell your mum to keep believing,' I said solemnly and the woman went back to her friends, where they giggled and looked back over.

'Must be great that,' said Brewster.

'Come on,' I replied, 'let's get this done. I've got your money.'

'I got a call today,' he told me. 'Someone said it was all bollocks about you and that girl. That it was all a set-up for the papers.'

'Who called?'

'A woman.'

'A journalist?'

'I don't know, just a woman,' he sipped his Guinness and the foam was left in balls of white amongst his beard.

'That's irrelevant, what's that got to do with the police?'

'Because those bruises, Nicky, there's a problem. I got a report back this morning. They've come back with the size of the hands that caused them.'

'Whose were they?'

'I don't know, Nick, you're the fucking psychic,' he laughed, the foam dancing about his mouth. 'But I'll tell you this, they weren't her hands, that's for sure, too big.'

'So what are you saying?'

'I'll tell you in the car.'

On the way back to the hotel Brewster smoked and talked about the woman in the pub, about how those situations might, somehow, lead to sex. He told me about traffic policemen, how they were always *at it* in the car parks of motorway service stations, and how there were women who hung about the station reception, with bubbling fantasies of interrogation by detectives much like himself.

'But, you know, Nick, I've been married nearly twenty years and I've never touched another woman. Never even touched one.'

'That's the deal though, is it not?'

'Yeah, but, fuck me, Nick, it's not easy. I can't take chances, I've got responsibilities, Nick. Two kids, you know, to put through school and everything else.'

And now I could see it coming again. He talked about his mortgage, his established buy-to-let ambitions and how his car needed replacing. 'I mean, you've seen it, Nick, it's a goner.' I started to hope, perversely, that the figure would be big, much bigger than before. Then I could at least hope that this would be over.

'Nick,' he said, pulling the car into a road near enough to the hotel, 'I want four hundred grand, now I know you're not going to like that,'

'No chance,' I said simply.

'I thought you'd say that. But listen, Nick, I'm putting my job on the line here. And I promise you, right now, on my kids' lives, that four hundred grand and we're done. Permanently. I'll get rid of the note and I can do a job on the bruises as well. I've spoken to the main man down there. He's getting a piece of the money and those bruises are going to disappear. Like fucking magic, Nick.'

'You've not got anything on me, Brewster, nothing that could get me done.'

'Nick, you know that's not true. If the papers got hold of the bruises on the girl's arms, then that would be you finished, even if we never do anything on it. Now, I know that things are going OK for you right now, you're on the way back. Four hundred grand is a fair price for a career.'

He was on top of it. I suppose, for four hundred grand, he could afford to have put in the research and his day job clearly offered flexibility.

'Maybe,' I told him, 'but I don't have that money.'

'You're going to have to get it then.'

On that point, his confidence was hopelessly misplaced but it was at least keeping him from threats.

'Call me later tonight, any time, and let me know how you get on. And I'll take this off the balance,' he pointed to the envelope, which I left in the plastic shelf below the dashboard.

I muttered some sort of agreement, got out the car and found my way back to the hotel. Asking Tony for four hundred grand was a laughable proposition but it was going to have to happen and the money was going to have to come from somewhere. Tony's flat maybe, given as security.

Brewster's threat was definite and I could see he had approached it with more conviction than I had previously realised. This was a singular, troubled hit of pure corruption he was aiming for. I believed him when he said that the money would end things, because I think he wanted that as much as me.

The black girl and the bruises I didn't even want to think about. I suspected that Brewster's female caller was the journalist, taking a chance and looking for an angle. If that was why she was still here then that was fine with me. She was running on close to empty if she only suspected that the black girl and I weren't as close as we'd suggested.

I had a price for escape from that city. Tony and Dad could keep talking if they wanted and I had seen all that I wanted to see of him. Maybe in London, maybe in time, there could be another haunted session but for now I would leave his reappearance with everything else the city had hit me with.

Four hundred grand though, and I didn't know if Tony had it. I didn't know what Tony had. But I should have, because what Tony had was largely mine. Sitting in my hotel room, this angered me far more than it had done for a long time. It was the pressure of the situation, and the not knowing, but maybe it was also the fact that Tony was currently with my dad.

Whatever the motivation, the conclusion was that, after a couple of hours of these poisonous thoughts, I left my hotel room. I walked to Tony's, checked the corridor in each direction and then kicked it, hard and pointed, over the lock. It flung open, leaving the frame softly damaged, and I walked in. It was dark in the room, so it took me a moment to find the light and then a little longer to adjust and appreciate what it was that was lying on Tony's bed.

It was probably halfway into the second tour that the TV people came for me. I'd only had a few days after my return from the SS *Victory* before the tour began and, by the time the TV people turned up, we were seven or eight successful nights down.

I was playing theatres, not big ones but theatres all the same. It was still a mixed bill, usually a vague cabaret in large towns or small cities, but there was the definite air of the professional. The crowds were decent and, more importantly, welcoming. The acts weren't seen as intruders with their presence to justify, rather the audiences veered towards appreciation that we were there to be watched.

Fresh from the SS *Victory*, I was irresistible. I didn't have the embarrassment of information I had enjoyed on the ship but I had found new practices on that front. First, I realised that there was another, forgotten factor – the area itself, the home of the people that sat waiting for me. When we arrived at a train station in the morning I would buy local papers, when we arrived at the hotel I would badger the staff for the town or city's unique touches.

The more I knew the place, the more I knew the people. In later, bigger tours Tony would take this job from me and, to his rare credit, he approached it with surprising care, picking out everything from local industries to any event that would have touched a fair slice of locals.

For now, Tony's job was to creep amongst the crowd from the moment they came through the doors. He would listen to conversations, pick up dropped ticket receipts for surnames and seat numbers and speak to the tour-bus drivers while they smoked in the car park to discover the groups they had ferried to the theatre. He'd arrive backstage, red-faced and proud to tell me what he had learned in unnecessary whispers.

This all went into the show's crucial opening where I built the interest and the trust. Then came the move – the snapped calves and the shock – which stilled every room it saw, before I moved daringly to conversation with the dead, safely cushioned on goodwill against any minor faults.

Tony told me most nights that he was expecting *a couple of TV people* to be amongst the crowd. I didn't believe him because I generally didn't believe him but also because it would do me little good to do so. And then one evening, after a show that had reached new heights, I was waiting backstage for Tony's late arrival when he came through the door with two other men.

'Nick, these are the guys I was telling you about, from TV.'

'Oh right, hi.'

'Nick,' they both said, smirking and shaking my hand in turn. They spoke quietly, with unaffected smoothness, and told me how much they'd enjoyed the show.

'Let's speak over lunch, can you two do sometime in the next few days?'

He was, presumably, the senior but it was hard to tell. They looked nearly identical, with tightly cut clothes and light tans, and their ages were impossible. They looked like they were on the television *now*, I remember thinking, and Tony and I were left meek and wondrous.

'Tomorrow would be good,' said Tony.

We were still in southern England at this point, and the tour had a couple of nightly gaps, including the following day.

'Great,' said the other one, who might have been the senior after all. 'See you there.'

They shook our hands again and ducked clear of the room. It was strange, once they had gone, Tony and I didn't talk about them again that night. When we went into the bar next to the theatre, Tony very deliberately ordered a club soda.

On the train to London, Tony brought out a tiring list of instructions.

Only he was to talk to them about any *terms* or *logistics*. I was allowed to deal with *the creative side*. My only concern was Tony's ability to guide this further. There had been a natural division between him and the men. He represented something older and more basic, and I could see this causing an ugly clash.

In hindsight, I should have thought about the mixed extraction of those I had grown up amongst in the pubs. I had forgotten the common attraction of corruption. In this case, it was cocaine that drew Tony and the two men together.

I don't know which of them instigated matters but when I went to the bathroom I returned to find the three of them falling silent in conspiracy. From then on they laid siege to the toilet in rolling visits, with busy hands swapping something under the table in between. The position of the two men moved from loose enthusiasm to definitive guarantees.

'We'll get you screen tested,' said one, his face active after another eager return from the toilet.

'Let's get a pilot in the diary,' said the other, slapping his palms on the table in decision. Tony stared back and said,

'That would be brilliant, yeah that would be brilliant.'

'That thing you do,' said one of them suddenly, 'when you kind of jump in the air, that's fucking amazing,' and the other added, 'Yeah, that's the grabber. That grabs them by the balls,' and they both nodded.

By the end of the meal the three of them were going to the toilet in pairs and, eventually, all together. I sat waiting for a while, alone amongst their empty glasses and untouched food, and then decided to leave. I turned off my phone and returned to my flat, where I watched TV on the small screen and thought that I should really be looking to move.

The following morning I switched on my phone and returned one of Tony's many messages to find out the train time. At the station, he looked hunted, still operating at a different level and struggling with the containment of the train. He talked rapidly about how the offer of a pilot had been firmed up during the night and then again this morning in a phone call.

'Those boys are back at work, they sound like nothing happened.' He had an ugly sweat on him. 'Christ, I wish I could say the same.'

'So the pilot's happening, for sure?'

'Guaranteed, as soon as the tour's finished. This is it, Nicky, this is it.'

By the time of the pilot, I'd moved onwards again. The rest of the tour had been constant accomplishment and brought a range of interest in me. Women's magazines, radio stations, individuals looking for private sessions and more TV companies all sent Tony scurrying to find me with an excitement that I should probably have found worrying.

None of these parties were as impressive in what they offered as Tony's coke partners. The two, it emerged, were senior figures at a proper TV channel, not one of those hidden away in the hundreds. For two weeks I travelled daily to their studios where I sat with a small, enthusiastic team to plan the pilot. What we really had to plan was how we were all going to get round the most delicate area. There had to be an understanding and I was relieved when this was managed for me.

'We're here to help,' said the executive producer on the first day, with heavy significance. 'Just tell us what we can do to *help*.'

I designed the studio for them. The chairs were organised into a circle and I found a pitch of lighting that would leave the seats dimmed but accessible, with me picked out during my prowls over the round stage. For the audiences, I suggested they found me certain people.

'Old or unemployed if possible.' The confused and the desperate, I could have said.

'That's who we deal with,' they answered.

Seats for the pilot were allocated in advance and, after a quiet word with the executive producer, I was given a copy of the names. On the day itself, despite the cameras and the false walls, the pressure of the occasion sent me fully employed with what I had to do. It was ludicrously easy. Sitting in a studio, peeking goggle-eyed at the wires and the crew in headphones, gave people a new submissiveness. When I started deducing names at speed they gasped and clapped. And then I did the move.

We didn't want to miss the move with the cameras so, to disguise the suddenness, I constructed an introduction and warned the director. He primed the relevant cameraman and soon they were all listening for the new words.

I became deliberately coy and, mostly because of the lights and the closeness of the people, I put my fingers to my temples to frame my face with cover. I circled the skin slowly and spoke. I'm not sure why I went for this phrase, to get the cameraman pulling out to capture my leap, but it encapsulated something.

'Let them come through,' I said and seconds later I was in the air while a woman in headphones lifted up a card with written instruction and the audience rose in acclaim.

That evening, the two men from the TV channel took Tony and me to a private club in Shoreditch. I presumed from the champagne that we were celebrating but it took a few hours of vacant conversation before the pilot's success was accepted.

'We'll start shooting next month,' said one of the two. 'We're thinking sixteen shows.'

'Great,' said Tony. 'And where do you see this fitting into the schedules?'

When Tony spoke like that I only ever assumed he was pretending, that he had heard these words from other people and stolen them.

'Afternoons, you'll be a housewives' favourite.'

'OK,' I said.

'What about a name, what's the working title?' Tony, pretending again.

'Well it has to be, doesn't it?' The two men nodded in confirmation. 'Yeah, it has to be.'

Tony was nodding also but that wasn't an indication of anything.

'What?' I asked.

' "Let them come through".'
'Perfect, absolutely perfect,' said Tony, reaching for his glass.

The weeks before filming began were active and anxious. Tony was wilting under meetings with lawyers and the TV station. I was signing forms on demand, trying not to think about what they meant and avoid the strange sense of responsibility.

I plotted relentlessly with the executive producer and the director, both of whom displayed a charming and needed corruption. They told me they could get junior members of staff to mix with the crowd, listening to conversations and reporting back.

'Yes, OK, that would help,' I said, sticking to the code.

I worried a little about the dangers of exposure. The drinkers, for example, of The OK Corral and its predecessors. It wasn't difficult to identify individuals who would look to end my rise if they saw me, with confusion, on their televisions. It wouldn't be through any traceable animosity, I was popular and pitied by them all, but those people operated in a gaping absence of values. Success was not to be trusted, and certainly not encouraged.

It was hard to shape this concern for the executive producer.

'What do you think that they might say?'

'Well, you know, that maybe I'm full of shit.'

He laughed and put a kindly hand on my shoulder.

'Most people are going to say that.'

That was the attitude. No one cared about anything apart from the show, and making it work, and that was all right with me. I had my own, personal hopes for what the show might do for me. I didn't, I don't think, ever really consider Dad. It was hard to imagine him even conjuring interest if he saw me there before him on the TV. It was Mum that I wanted to tell, maybe once I was there in the schedules.

For now it was about generating material. The great advantage was the editing. With that impregnable guard behind us, it was a case of keeping the audiences as long as they would stay and letting me probe and harry them into something. Only when failure became uncomfortably common in my speculative runs of discovery would I end matters and sign autographs while the cameras drooped and lights were killed.

The information from the team members in the crowd and my bank of easy hits from the crowd's personal details, loyally given in reward for tickets, combined to create a lot more than we eventually needed. The executive producer and director called me into the edit room where we drank warm beer and they told me that they wished the series was longer. The channel, they said, was *really going to get behind this one*.

When we finished recording the series, the channel threw a party that the chairman came to. He had expensive hair thrown back and a long-established tan and held the room with a funny and graceful speech.

'I've seen the tapes,' he said, picking me out at the end. 'And I think that Nick Santini is our new star.'

Everyone turned and looked, clapping when I smiled and raised my champagne glass because I didn't know what else to do.

'I could tell you stories about that guy,' said Tony from my side, 'that you wouldn't fucking believe.'

The series went out while I was on a new tour, because Tony had said something about striking while the iron was hot and I had agreed. It was large venues and a shared bill with someone who called himself a modern magician. He was billed as Outrage, looked like a teenager and may have been one, was covered in tattoos and did a lot of stuff around fire and stuff stuck on the venue's roof.

Because of Outrage the audiences were younger, tougher and less easily mystified. For the first couple of weeks that made my routine trickier than it had been in a while, but when the series approached, with coverage around it, a switch was flicked.

I was called almost every day by the shrill publicity team to tell me of another interview or appearance. Journalists came from London to wherever the tour was to speak to me about my talent and, sometimes, about me. I was careful, telling them my parents were living abroad and I had been *a bit of a loner as a kid*. I would say that thoughtfully, stumbling over it, and every journalist would dwell on it happily, having found their angle. Then I'd be handed to photographers who would frown at sheets of papers and say,

'It says you've got to look mysterious, does that sound right?'

Tony was a disastrous companion for these engagements – with comments such as 'I don't think that's something Mr Santini would like to comment on,' or, 'Can we have him looking a bit more serious, he's a serious act' – until I told him I didn't want him there anymore. 'I'm sure there's more important things you could be doing instead,' I told him, kindly.

One evening I walked past Outrage's dressing room and saw him reading an interview I'd given to a newspaper. He was leaning back towards the door with the paper facing me. A photo showed me looking distant with my hands clasped and fingers pressed to my chin. Outrage shook his head at the paper held in his tattooed arms, those weapons of youthful magic.

Everything seemed to be on the rise apart from one area. There was no great arrival of money, which still came from Tony in sudden bursts. Anything from five hundred to a couple of grand, handed over in envelopes as if in afterthought. He would give it to me at moments that defied further discussion. Through taxi windows pulling away or at the close of evenings when I was tired and silent, or chucked like grenades into dressing rooms in moments when he knew I needed to be left to my preparation.

And this was money that I needed. The money from Java Joe was still there, still in the detergent box, still unused. But I hadn't even considered taking any of it with me on the tour or, before that, using it for any purpose. The only money I wanted was money that I earned and was given to me in exchange for my talent. Unfortunately, it had to get through Tony first.

It was the T-shirts that forced me to speak to him. During the hectic closing of a show, a woman darted round the seats and made a playful grab at me. I palmed her off and turned to see her T-shirt.

NICK SANTINI – *LET THEM COME THROUGH*

The words were below a shadowed image of a man with his fingers held at the sides of his head. I laughed at the woman's inventiveness. By the time I reached the dressing room I had glumly arrived at the alternative. Tony.

The next day I waited until half an hour before I was due to take the stage, pulled on a woollen hat and walked out the side door and round to the main reception. I never ventured into these areas, it would have looked to anyone with an open mind that I was doing the information gathering that Tony was doing. And doing well, I should say. Amongst other initiatives.

He was in the corner of the theatre's lobby, giving stern instructions to a couple of young girls who stood behind a stall. I walked closer and saw those same T-shirts, some CDs and books.

'Business good?'

Tony frowned at the floor.

'Yeah, going well, Nicky, going well. Did I tell you about this?'

'No, you didn't.'

I left him there with his secret stall. When I got off stage later he was waiting in the dressing room with drinks and an envelope.

'Great show, Nicky, brilliant. Sorry about not filling you in on the merchandise by the way, just something I'm trying out. Going great guns, here you go.'

It was the thickest envelope I'd had yet.

'And plenty more to come,' he said proudly.

'OK, Tony,' I said. 'No problem.'

The first time it happened was at a supermarket. We were still touring, a few nights to go, and I had left the hotel to buy a newspaper. The woman in the queue turned, saw me, turned away, then sharply back, and opened her mouth to speak. There was a moment's confusion and then she looked away again. She stole quick, flushed looks at me while she packed her bags and when I left the shop she was there.

'Here,' she said, harshly, 'were you on the TV the other day?'

'Ah, right, yes.'

'I thought so, what was it called?'

'Let Them Come Through.'

'That was it, well, thanks.'

And then she walked away.

These scenes arrived all over the place. I would be approached in the street, in restaurants and in bars. Taxi drivers would swear they knew me and on the train there would be at least one person resolutely watching me pretending not to be watching them. Even though the programme was doing well (we hit a million viewers. 'That's fucking *outstanding* for the afternoon, Nicky,' Tony told me), I still found it hard to make the connection to this new awareness.

I watched the shows when they went out, seeing the glorious reworking that left me looking fearless in my accuracy. Over the closing credits, the audience wept gratefully and spoke of amazement and boundless gratitude that their *wounds had been healed*.

With the tour finished, and the series nearing the end of its run, the two men from the TV channel took Tony and I for lunch at a restaurant in a cavernous room near Trafalgar Square. Only a dozen tables sat in pockets of isolation under a roof that lifted to a glass dome. Waiters appeared for individual tasks and weren't seen again. They ordered slim bottles of wine and we were there for five hours. Tony told me later, with a strange excitement, that the bill had been over three grand.

During the meal the men promised me a second series. They said they were going to build their daytime scheduling around it and that it was to be extended to twenty shows.

'Same director, same producer, they can't wait to work with you again, Nicky.'

'Great. Same set-up?'

'I'll speak to you two separately about that,' interrupted Tony quickly.

'I mean the studio and so on,' I said, not looking at Tony.

'Whatever you want,' said one of the men. 'You're the star, Nicky, you decide.'

The most dramatic of the headlines, of the three papers that Dad managed to sell the same story to, was:

HE CAN TALK TO THE SPIRITS BUT HE CAN'T TALK TO ME

There was Dad holding a phone and staring boyishly at the camera.

They ran it the week after the first series finished, when as many people as possible might have at least seen my name before. I got a call from the TV channel to say that he'd done it, gone to the papers and sold this drivel.

He told the papers that he was living in *poverty*, that he was *disabled*, and that he was *proud of me* but that he didn't know why I had *cut him off*. That first story was the biggest, then he managed to punt much the same again to two lesser papers the following weekend.

I wasn't surprised and I was beyond being hurt, I was only worried about the TV channel. They couldn't care less. The executive producer suggested chummily that I didn't speak to Dad for a while. I told him that wasn't going to be a problem.

Tony suggested I do a story telling the truth, but I had no interest in prolonging it. I considered contacting Mum but it would have been a weak excuse to do so. I think I would have forgotten about Dad's newspaper appearances pretty quickly anyway, but in the end something far more important arrived shortly after.

Tony saw it first, on the Internet. We were about to start filming the second series and I had the morning off while they readied the studio. When he called I was sitting on the stiff furniture in the flat in Earl's Court and looking through the property rental pages, edging finally to escape.

'Are you on the Internet?' he asked.

'No.'

'Right, well you'd better come round to mine. You got a pen?'

I'd never been to Tony's house before. At the end of evenings in London we'd shake hands and take different taxis, but I knew he was somewhere in the richer northern districts. I expected a decent set-up but on arrival at the road near Hampstead Heath I found a demanding, detached residence. There was no obvious further division into flats and the main door had just one bell, which brought Tony out in a pair of shorts.

'How you doing, Nicky? In you come.'

'Some place, Tony.'

'Mortgaged to the fucking hilt. Come and see this.'

He led me through rooms that were overly bare, stripped with commitment, and to a computer raised on a table that was surely a cheap replacement for something else.

'I've been looking on the Internet, seeing what people are saying about you.'

'In emails?'

'It's not just emails, Nicky. Message boards. People talking like they were in the fucking street or something. Sad bastards, but look at this. It's a message board about you.'

The screen was an unattractive grid of type. I could see my name, and that of the show, but it was hard to follow the rest. Tony clicked a couple of times and a ladder of short comments came up. At the top it read:

Who here knows the REAL Nick Santini?

I saw the date, two weeks ago, and since then there had only been a few replies, mostly extractions from the diluted biography that I had given the TV station's website.

'Looks OK.'

'No, Nicky, look at the name.'

The name of the person who had left the questions was Soviet Street, or **SovietStreet** as it said on the screen. I walked away from the computer, found another room and sat on a couch. Tony clicked things off and came and found me, standing with his hands in his pockets and rocking on his heels.

'How much did you pay Tiffany?' I asked.

'What do you mean?'

'Was it enough?'

'You think that's her?'

'Well, unless my dad's got himself a fucking computer.'

Or the estate agent, I thought. But wouldn't he be bringing himself down with me?

'Right, yeah, it would have to be Tiffany,' said Tony, nodding. 'Could be anyway.'

'Can we find her?'

'I don't know, might make it worse.'

'OK.' Tony wasn't going to make a decision, so I had to. 'Right, keep an eye on that thing for me Tony, every day. Let's see what happens.'

'I will do, Nicky. I wouldn't worry about it.'

I stood up. I wanted to be out of Tony's big house. It was another irritation and, together with the computer's anonymous threat, it gave me a rare anger.

'When am I getting my next money, Tony?'

'You need some now?'

'No, but I shouldn't have to always fucking ask. Why don't I ever just get *paid*?'

He knew how unusual and fleeting this confrontation was, which is why he scarpered off, shouting back through the large, empty rooms,

'Stay right there, Nicky.'

He came back with what he had and announced, 'You're right, Nicky, you're spot on. It should be regular. I'll give you ten grand a month, how about that?'

All that did was make me wonder how much he would be keeping from me, and he never stuck to it anyway.

'OK, cheers Tony.'

For the second series the seats ran deeper into the dark and the stage's circle was widened. The lighting was all new, a vast rig that hung above us, and there seemed to be twice as many people calling me Nick and stopping for short technical conversations about things I didn't really understand.

The taping of the shows went well and it would have been difficult for it not to. The production team kept the assistance coming to me, in whispered revelations and sheets of stolen information, and the audience were now firm supporters rather than the curious. With no natural resistance, I had just to guide the people along for them to commit and confirm, while their excitement on being chosen would lead to an outpouring of appreciation and tears.

'Get them crying,' the director would flatly instruct in my earpiece and I never let him down.

It is an important moment to consider, when the second series arrived on TV a couple of months later. This, without doubt, was my peak. I had hurriedly moved into a two-bedroom new-build near the river in Fulham, amongst angry locals and middle-class arrivals from the country. Three grand a month and people washing their cars on Saturday mornings. I hadn't taken much from the flat in Earl's Court, just enough for one taxi. Amongst the bags and boxes had been a resealed, ageing box of detergent that the driver had passed to me with puzzlement.

'Fulham? Bit fucking boring down there isn't it?' Tony had said.

The last of the new furniture had arrived in the days before leaving for the biggest tour I had done, and the biggest I would do. I had unwrapped and arranged it all, then sat on the balcony and looked at the river. On my last morning I had gone for a walk along the water that slid in flat, grey plates towards the distant sea. I had a pint in a bar that had menus of sharing items, wine lists on the tables and smelt of cleaning.

The tour was a headlining romp around the country with three or four thousand at every show and there was a new success that ran alongside. The TV channel released a DVD of the first series that, Tony told me and anyone else who would at least listen, was *flying off the shelves*.

I was being taken from the tour, by car and plane, and pushed on to television shows where I would smile and be modest and try a little something on the host – usually a safe stab at the closing months of their grandparent's lives, followed by a bland message from the latter.

There was one other thing I did, when there was a question or the sense of a question that I would not have welcomed. I shifted the interview away from where it was with a short, worthless but distracting anecdote that I had concocted for the purpose. It was about a Catholic wake, a dead uncle, and a hilarious misunderstanding with the man from the gas board.

While all this unravelled I was recognised everywhere. I couldn't walk in public without being stopped, questioned and sometimes abused, which I enjoyed if Tony was there because of how it rattled him. There were some ludicrous points. We had a meeting with a publisher, who got the train from London to somewhere on the tour and took us for lunch. He wanted to sign me up for:

Letting Them Come Through: The Nick Santini Story

Obviously, Tony wanted to do it. Obviously, I didn't.

I slept with a lot of women around this time, thanks to Tony, who called it fucking, no matter the company. We would have a night out with people from the TV channel, or journalists, or tour companies, or corporate clients wanting me for their Christmas party. Tony would whisper in some woman's ear, wink at me and soon after she would approach with manufactured interest.

On the tour it was even more concentrated. When women stayed behind at the end of the shows, Tony would come into my dressing room with panting evaluations and I would swagger out to make jokes and pose for photos with busy hands around shoulders and waists.

There were some grubby endings. Reckless women awoke with me around the country and cried about husbands or, surprisingly equally, the fact that they should be at work. Other mornings I crept from strange accommodation and flung a hand for a taxi, before calling Tony for directions as my skin crawled with the night's lingering dirt.

There was one night, or one morning, in the lost hours when I was behind a woman who had her skirt up and over her back while she was tricked and thrown by my soulless urges. It was a living room with an old bar heater and a television with plastic wood panelling. There were photos of children on the mantelpiece and a bookcase of brightly jacketed novels with their titles picked out in raised gold. On the carpet was a bottle of vodka and two glasses. Only mine was empty. The woman turned round without stopping, her face reddened with something.

'I'm only doing this because you're on the telly,' she said in a local accent.

'Why do you think *I'm* doing it?' I said, not meaning to be cruel.

The fall began in Southampton when the phone rang in my hotel room. A female voice.

'You killed Joe.'

A click. I stared at the ceiling. I was drunk, it was halfway to morning. I hoped I wouldn't remember it when I woke up but I did. I didn't tell Tony, tried to forget.

Cardiff.

'You killed Joe.'

I hung up before she did. I was going to tell Tony. I read the time, five. I was going to tell Tony. When I woke up again I decided not to.

Dundee, the phone rang.

'Nicky?'

'Yep, I thought we said six?'

'Come round to my room, you'd better see this.'

'What?'

'The Internet.'

Tony had a new computer set up in his room and wired to a setting on the wall. It had come from a box on the bed that was ripped open and flung aside. On the screen was the same grid I had seen in Tony's house. He'd already opened it on one of the conversations. The title was

SANTINI SECRET?

Below it the entry read:

I've heard a worrying rumour about our Mr Santini.
Anyone else heard this? Apparently he had some client
who used to visit him for personal sessions. The client
killed themselves. Right there in Santini's office.

It had been written by someone who called themselves LTCTFAN123. There were a few responses, people expressing surprise and disbelief, and then there was a contribution from SovietStreet.

Heard that too. Santini was nicking money off the
guy. Love the show but always thought NS was
dodgy. Something to do with a shares scam?

That apparent reinforcement darkened the mood and the messages continued. Most began with the cover of If *this is true* before moving into betrayal and anger. The last person to comment, a women who had a photo of her dog beside her contribution, announced she had *had enough*. She didn't believe the story but she felt it should be checked with the station. Which, she said, was what she was about to do.

'We're fucked.'

'We might be,' Tony answered, pathetically.

'If they hear about Java Joe at the channel then we're fucked Tony.'

'Probably. What's this about shares?'

'No idea.'

It was only an hour before a show that we stood looking at the screen in Dundee. I went ahead and got through it and at the end

Tony and I left through a delivery entrance. We went straight back to his hotel room, as if being near the computer would help us find an answer to what it had told us.

There were few options available. Tony suggested he went on the messageboard himself and gave the story a chummy dismissal, but that would risk extending the attention. Our solution, not that it was one, was this: the station received a rush of strange calls after every show went out, and this one would surely get lost in the muddle. It wasn't great, but it at least let me return to my own room and sleep. For a while anyway, until the phone went again to bring me that same voice.

'They know,' she said.

'Tiffany?'

'They know you killed Joe,' and she left me breathing hard and trying to remember how Tiffany had sounded. Not like that, I wearily concluded. It took me a long time to find a version of sleep and then I was woken again, by Tony slamming at my door until I opened it. He was sweating and wearing clothes thrown on without thought.

'They've seen it, the TV lot, they want us to fly down this morning.'

Thirty-four

They were documents. Papers, folders, contracts and what were clearly statements of accounts. After a first, rough, look I started to see the pattern. The two names, together. Tony and mine. And the two signatures with them. Tony and mine. My signature, over and over, except it wasn't mine. It was close, but it had been written by a foreign hand.

For over an hour I was in Tony's room, looking through what I'd found. I sorted it slowly by date, building piles of years that started when Tony and I first met. Everything was there, or at least what I presumed was everything and there was no reason to doubt it. That very first contract, the fifty per cent carve-up that he had made me sign in a bar near Soviet Street just after Java Joe's body was carted off, was available and I started with that.

It was a stern affair, with a vast tract of protection against its central charge that Tony would receive half of everything I earned, in any fashion, at any time. And then there were the additions. He could pilfer my share for any number of eventualities and measures that were called *Exceptional Expenses*. Some of this I could follow, some I couldn't, but what was clear was that there were constant opportunities for Tony to take from me.

The early stages, the club tours and the cheap hotels, showed a little more than I expected. There were a couple of new contracts that I didn't recall and where the first of the false signatures arrived. Percentages began to be paid to companies that sounded strange until I found their accounts. All had two directors, myself and Tony, and all had that same signature where mine should have been.

While time passed through the paperwork, the sums increased rapidly. By the arrival of the theatre tours, signalled in glossy contracts with promotion and ticket companies, there were tens of thousands slipping from one account to another. When the TV money arrived, in great bulks of advance, I was startled at the money that had been juggled through the growing system.

Hundreds of thousands would arrive suddenly and be immediately splintered into several other accounts and then slowly drained. It wasn't hard to see where most of the money ended up – lost to an invasion of withdrawals, large and small, that had Tony's name ranked defiantly alongside.

A few of the contracts I recognised. These must have been unavoidable exposures for Tony but he'd crudely given me cover sheets to sign and then initialled the attachments himself.

It was in the six months before the abandonment of the second TV series, and the restarting of the final tour, that Tony had really gone to work. It was, I recognised sinisterly, the point of his divorce and it appeared that I was the real victim of the judge's ruling. Nearly a million had gone. The tour, the TV, the DVD. Sliced and chopped over six months and run clumsily through a few of the companies before reaching Tony's grasp.

It was hard to get a confident picture, but it appeared that there was about five hundred thousand left across the board, clubbed together from the dozen or so accounts that could be found in the most recent print-outs. It was more than I would have expected before I came into the room, which was the reason I was in that position.

'Everything OK?'

I sprung from the bed, turning with unnecessary guilt and a handful of paper.

'Yeah, fine thanks.'

The Asian porter was looking at the door frame in confusion.

'Don't worry I'll pay for that,' I said, 'I just had to get something from my manager. An emergency.'

'No problem.' He smiled easily enough and moved away.

I lifted a piece of paper and pen and wrote:

Tony, I need four hundred grand of <u>what's left</u> for Brewster ASAP. Discuss tomorrow

I left that on top of the now ordered files, pulled the door as tightly as I could and headed back to my own room. I was happy enough that the money was there not to have to worry about Tony too much for now. It would have to be dealt with tomorrow, but it was going to have to be dealt with at some point anyway.

I texted Brewster, too tired to speak to him, telling him that I had the money and I'd be in touch in the morning. I ate all the snacks from the minibar and then I undressed, turned my phone off and climbed with unusual gratitude into the hotel's bed. It was only early, still within the evening, but I didn't want any more of what that day had to offer. I pulled the blankets round me. Somewhere in that city was the suitable pairing of Tony and my father.

Thirty-five

Sleep felt unusually convincing so I was confounded by the Asian porter's cheap clock telling me it was three. I turned on my phone and revealed that it had gone ten and I'd slept unbroken through the night. The phone's messages arrived in a relentless line of beeping. All Tony. We need to talk, he said, we need to talk. I called him from the hotel phone, which he had clearly lacked the courage to try, not wanting to wake me with this needed confrontation.

'Nick, thanks for calling. Listen, Nick, we've got to go over this, it's not what you might have thought it was.'

'Fine, we'll go over it. But I need four hundred grand, today if possible.'

'I've already called the bank, Nick. I've authorised a cheque for you. You just need to countersign it.'

'You can't do that for me this time?'

'Nick, honestly, you don't understand...'

'Forget it, just meet me in the reception in an hour, bring the cheque.'

'OK. Nick, it's just investment all that stuff, that's all it is.'

'See you in an hour, Tony.'

I phoned Brewster and was surprised how willingly he agreed to the cheque. I thought that would be a worry for him, with the needed involvement of his bank account at the other end and the likelihood of a swift cancellation from myself, but he happily agreed to receive it in the hotel's reception in an hour.

'And then that's us finished,' he promised me again.

I readied myself and prepared my loose plan. I was going to pay Brewster, fire Tony, though not tell him yet, go back to London and approach the TV people directly. I would tell them that I was worth the risk. That the devastating truth about Java Joe and me could remain trapped between us forever. This was the main thrust of my thinking. There was the secondary thought, that of Dad, but I knew more or less what I wanted to do there.

After a torturous period with my mobile phone, locating and then practising the photo option, I left for the reception where Tony greeted me warmly.

'Bet you thought I'd been nicking from you, eh Nicky? The way it looked?' He laughed and slapped me on the back. Unusually, there was someone behind the desk, the blonde who had checked us in less than a week before, when we thought we had a few days of trudging normality ahead. She looked up in case we required her reluctant assistance, which I did.

'Excuse me. The clock I got from you has stopped.'

'Oh, there aren't clocks in the rooms yet, sir.'

'I know, I got one from you, but it's stopped.'

'I do apologise sir, here, let me get you another.'

She turned to a cupboard behind the desk. Inside was a stack of boxed clocks with their image on the side. They were slim and steel, more like what I would expect from the hotel. She pushed it across the desk.

'That's better, the one the porter brought me was a joke.'

The woman frowned. 'These are the only ones we have, sir. Who brought you the other one?'

'The little Asian guy, the porter or whatever he is?'

'Asian?'

'Yeah, nice guy.'

She was entirely lost.

'I'm in charge of recruitment, sir, I really don't know who you mean.'

I didn't have time for this confusion. I thanked her for the clock, which felt light and expensive in my hands. I thought about the Asian bringing me that other clock and how he had the rain all over him yet denied he'd been outside. Perhaps he was a cleaner who had felt compelled to act on my request, but it rang oddly that this woman wouldn't know him.

There was a more immediate concern, when Brewster came slinking through the hotel's doors.

'Do you want me to stick around?' asked Tony.

'Yeah, you might as well.'

He wouldn't have asked if he wanted to, that was my only reason for making him do so. Brewster shook our hands, offering a polite greeting to Tony and a stronger one to myself.

'Let's go upstairs,' I suggested. It would save time and I was interested to see if the Asian was about.

We talked in the lift about the weather outside, which had looked entirely neutral but Brewster insisted was *a little on the nippy side*, and then he said, just as casually, despite Tony's presence.

'You're doing the right thing, they were going to have another look at the girl's body this morning but I put them off. I'll get the case closed this afternoon, no problem, just a case of dropping off a few envelopes.' He smiled wolfishly and I looked at my feet while Tony breathed beside me.

After we got out the lift, Tony gestured Brewster towards the honesty bar and then stole back a yard and whispered to me,

'By the way, your dad called, he's in the Royal Hotel down the road, in case he hasn't told you.'

Tony knew he hadn't told me. I nodded, and felt the beginnings of fury at Tony's deception and choice of timing.

'It's not a hotel,' he clarified thoughtfully, 'just a bed and breakfast really.'

'Shut up,' I told him and quickened to take Brewster to a table in the empty bar.

'Right,' I said while the two sat down as far apart as they could manage. 'Tony has the cheque here, Brewster. Tony?'

He handed it to me with inappropriate eagerness. I signed it and passed it on to Brewster.

'No hard feelings on my part, you've made a few quid, but I want one thing.'

I took out my phone and managed to retrieve the photo option.

'I'm going to take a photo of you with it. I think that's fair, I've got no reason to ever use it, and if I did then I'd be fucking myself over and you know that. But it's just so I know that we're done.'

Caught unguarded, Brewster looked at Tony. As if Tony had a decision to make in this.

'Hold it up,' I commanded. Brewster lifted the cheque in silent rage and I took two for good measure.

'Perfect, thanks.'

I started to enjoy the scene. Brewster managing to appear defeated despite holding a route to four hundred grand and Tony looking on the verge of some sort of breakdown. He knew that once Brewster left we were going to have to discuss his own crimes and he knew that the money, which he clearly needed badly, had now all gone. I delayed both their discomforts.

'Excuse me for one moment please, gentlemen, quick piss.'

The honesty bar was a cluttered affair, and being raised on top of the original building meant there were a series of pillars. I had almost reached the bathroom at the opposing end of the room when I decided to instruct them to get drinks. I wanted one and liked the thought of those two working awkwardly together.

In my newly lightened mood I doubled back. It was just luck, or a lack of luck, that meant I returned to them hidden behind the line of one of the pillars. I was only yards away when I heard them.

Brewster's voice first, flattened and hissed when he whispered to Tony:

'You'd better get that fucking phone off him.'

And Tony, back to him:

'I will. Don't worry, I will.'

Thirty-six

I slipped back across the honesty bar and into the bathroom with my head ringing. Some of it was there already when I stood by the taps and the mirror. Tony and Brewster and the money.

It had to have been Tony, delighted with a new, external means of robbing me, who had directed this. All Brewster had wanted me for was a guest turn at the retirement party. That, I saw now, was the start and finish of Brewster's plans but Tony had plotted out this ragged extension of Brewster's involvement. For a share of the money, the detective had slotted into the scheme and Tony's bed had been coated with the documents while he worked out what they could ask for. Brewster could trust a cheque because the cheque was to pay them both.

It was a perfect system for Tony to squeeze the last of my money from me. I would have accepted we were skint, without any request for evidence, once I had seen the powerful handover of such an amount. Without that distraction, Tony could never tell me the pot was empty without rousing me into some examination. I didn't understand the scale, why Tony needed this grand move rather than the measured theft that he'd perfected, but that was largely irrelevant.

It had all been very easy for them and most of my anger was for me. The note with the blood. *Nick Santini is a murderer.* I'd seen the fact that it came on the hotel's paper as a slick piece of warning but it was just laziness from Tony, or Brewster, or both. The phone calls to Brewster revealing that the black girl and I had duped the paper.

The police form identifying the blood, liberated and utilised from a department's cupboard. All bullshit. Easy supporting evidence for the two of them while they drew me in.

There was one way to check this and to ensure that it was all built on nothing. I left the bathroom and walked back to the two of them.

'Cheers, boys, I'm going to head back to my room. Brewster, nice to meet you, best of luck,' I held out my hand and he took it with an unconnected smile. 'Tony, I'll call you in a bit.'

I jogged to my room. I hoped I still had it and after a wild search I found it. The card had the local police insignia and the name and rank of that other policeman. The policeman that Brewster had fought against me meeting and had been so disturbed when he gave me his card. He answered on the first ring, as someone sitting at their desk would.

'Oh, hi there, it's Nick Santini, I hope you don't mind me calling like this.'

'Oh hello, Mr Santini, this is a nice surprise.'

'Yes, I just thought I'd give you a quick call as we're leaving today for London.'

'OK.'

'I just wanted to check you didn't need me for anything else, any paperwork or anything?'

'With regards to?'

'Well, the girl.'

'Oh, right, right. No, Mr Santini, that case is closed.'

'Closed?'

'Yes, I think,' there was some tapping at a keyboard, 'yeah, the body was released back to the family a few days ago. You're not going to the funeral?'

No body. No bruises. How had I let them do this to me?

'I'll call them now, yes of course, I'll be going. Well thanks very much for your help.'

'Not at all, and thanks so much for the demonstration the other day. I'm a big fan, it was a bit naughty of me I suppose, to ask to meet you, it wasn't really necessary.'

'No,' I said and meant it, 'I'm very glad you did.'

I thought of the two women who had stopped me with the evening paper, with the account of the press conference and the quote from the local police confirming the absence of suspicion. I saw also where this had started. The morning I had gone with Brewster to the retirement party. He had come for me early and Tony and I had been up late, but when I called Tony beforehand he was already alert and outside on some anonymous journey. Tony only got up, and only got up early, when he had something to do.

That morning what he had done was intercept Brewster and go to him with his alliance against me. In accepting this I had a strange thought. That Tony and Brewster weren't bad men. They were just thieves.

The hotel phone rang and, to stop me thinking, I answered.

'Mr Santini, I interviewed you the other morning, for the *Soho Star*?'

The journalist, the forgotten and diluted menace.

'Right, hi, I really can't talk just now.'

'No problem, it was just that, and I meant to ask you when we met, about Joe Yakari?'

I hung up the phone, then picked it up again, hitting the button for the reception. When they answered I asked,

'Can you put me through to the Royal Hotel, please?'

Thirty-seven

I told Dad in halting bursts of disbelief the run of outrage and revelation that the city had given me. He sat and nodded, asked questions only when he had to, and stirred his tea in the same café as before.

'I knew Tony was dodgy,' he told me, 'but I didn't think he'd screw you over like that.'

'You should know.' It had been nearly an hour and that was my first slip. He almost welcomed it. It showed I was genuine, that this wasn't some bluff or an angled piece of charm. In fact all I wanted was to put Tony and him together. That way it would be easier to leave them both, which made some sense against the pressure.

'Exactly,' he confirmed. 'I'll deal with Tony. Tell him to meet you here and bring all the documents, I'll deal with him.'

'No.'

'It's up to you, Nicky,' he replied. 'I'm just trying to help.'

I told him about the journalist and, vaguely, about Java Joe.

'The *Soho Star*,' said Dad. 'Fuck me, are they still going?'

'Unfortunately, yes,' I told him.

'If this guy was a client of yours, and the *Soho Star* did something on him at the time, then they already know that you know him don't they? I wouldn't worry about them.'

'Yeah, I suppose so.'

'She didn't say anything else about it?'

'No.'

'Well then, she's got fuck all on you, Nicky. What happened with the guy anyway?'

'He topped himself, in my office.'

'Fuck me, were you there?'

'No.'

'Well then there's not much you can be blamed for. The important thing is to sort Tony out and get you back to London. You're right about those TV boys, go and see them on your own. You're the star, kiddo.'

His look was, possibly, pride. I was enjoying the conversation too much, telling him too much.

'When did you last see Tony?'

'Last night, he wanted to know how it had gone with you. I told him I didn't know, to be honest.'

'Right, Dad, if I get Tony to meet you, you think you can sort that stuff out?'

He was delighted and banged his cup down.

'Of course, Nicky, of course. Anything you need done, I'll do it.'

'Right then, I'll get him to come here in an hour. Call me when you're done.'

Outside the café I checked the name and the address and phoned Tony. He was in the hotel. I had considered he might have gone but then remembered that he still thought I was with him.

'Nicky, good to hear from you, listen, we have to go over all the paperwork, the companies and so on. I should have explained it all before really but let's get it done now,' he urged, weakly trying to shape it into his decision. I didn't want to see him and I didn't want to see what he called the paperwork. I just wanted to leave. To get away and plan a revenge from some distant, hidden point.

'Listen, bring it all and meet me in this café in an hour, here's the address.'

I caught a taxi back and, in fear of bumping into Tony, went straight up to the honesty bar. It was in the usual state of emptiness and I planned to sit out an hour, grab what I needed from my room and leave that hotel and that city. I was trying to pull together my plans when the Asian appeared, hurriedly and in a jacket.

'Hello sir.' He smiled. 'Can I get you a drink?'

'Why not, yeah. Vodka please, large, with tonic.'

I sat on an uncomfortable couch. I had a couple of days to cancel Brewster's cheque and would do so from London. Dad and Tony were soon to be together, and therefore would soon be plotting against me, but that was something else I could deal with once I was free from that city. The weak threat of the journalist hardly registered. My outlook held loosely together. Back to London, straight to the TV people, with Tony cut off and Dad to be dealt with separately.

The Asian brought me my drink, along with a beer.

'I thought you could do with two.' I thanked him and drank the vodka quickly. It stung a little on the way but I needed it and so down it went.

'Here,' I said to the Asian, 'how come they don't know you at reception?'

He sat opposite me, still in his jacket.

'I don't know.'

'And where did you get that clock?'

'From a shop.' He was watching me. He seemed to be waiting.

'Why are you wearing your jacket?'

It was getting hard to talk, my voice was different and forced, and I was swept by a sudden heat. I landed on the time I had seen the Asian sneak in the fire door at the back of the hotel. Because he couldn't come in the front. Because he didn't work there. He'd brought me those papers, after the press conference, and the one that spoke blindly of Java Joe was folded and ready at the top.

'Because I've been following you and it's cold outside,' answered the Asian, then looked away and said, 'Here he is, I've given him it, in his drink.'

I turned to the side, which was a lot harder than it should have been, and saw the journalist come and join us.

Thirty-eight

She sat beside the Asian, lifted a hand and rubbed his back.

'Hello, sir,' she said.

'Hello,' I replied, and giggled.

'That's what Joe used to call you isn't it,' she asked. 'Sir?'

They were moving a bit in front of me but if I pulled my eyes together I could focus. It took a while for me to hear the phone, it was only when the Asian lifted it from my pocket that I realised what it was. The ringing stopped and then there was a beep. The Asian pressed some buttons and my answer service played over the speaker. Dad, speaking from a phone box with traffic in the background.

'Nicky, the *Soho Star*'s not going any more, I didn't think it was and I just checked with a pal. They went bust a few months back so Christ knows what that woman's playing at. Anyway, I'm waiting for Tony, I'll call you later. Don't worry, I'll sort it out.'

The Asian turned my phone off and the journalist, no, she wasn't a journalist, produced something from her bag. It was the article from the *Soho Star*, after Java Joe had died. In the photo he sat at the zoo with his family. The woman and the boy. The journalist and the porter.

'You two,' I said, pointing at the page. I only felt happiness when I made the connection. I tried to say something else but I couldn't. The air was there, going through my throat, but there was no sound. I stopped, startled, and tried again.

'Diazepam, Mr Santini,' she said. 'There was some other stuff in there for your muscles but right now you're feeling the Diazepam. Valium.

Dissolves in alcohol but not in water. That's one of the reasons I met you the other day, to see if you drank alcohol and to see if you had much protection around you. Lucky for us that you're a degenerate and that other man is as well. He heard you two talking that first night,' She pointed a thin finger at her son. 'To that poor girl, giving her the money. No wonder she did what she did.'

'I know,' I said, 'I know,' but neither her words nor mine seemed to be having any effect.

'And that man's a thief, isn't he, Mr Santini? Just like you with Joe's shop and the money he gave you for the stock market. What happened to the money?'

I grinned back.

'That's him under,' she said, not to me. 'They gave me Diazepam when you killed my husband, Mr Santini. When they took me away and locked me up, that's what they've given me ever since. Do you know why they gave it to me?'

I shook my head, I felt bad that I couldn't answer properly.

'Mania. That's what they said I had, Mr Santini. Mania. They said they had to protect me from the mania so instead I got what you've got now. Somnolence it's called. It feels like you're about to fall asleep doesn't it? Well you're not. That's how I've felt for three years. Can you feel your heart?'

I looked at my chest. My shirt quivered. I could feel my heart. It was drumming against my chest.

'That's called tachycardia. It'll keep like that for twenty minutes. It's amazing, Mr Santini, what nurses will tell you in the middle of the night. About control and dosages. I could do their job for them, I honestly could.'

She was English and a long way from Soviet Street and I wondered how Java Joe might have met her. I decided, between slipping in and out, that she was a nice woman. She wasn't pretty, her face was uninteresting and she was a little boxy in body, but she was nice.

'They said I was a danger to myself and others, Mr Santini. That's when Joe here, Joe Junior,' the Asian was regarding me with staggering intensity, I pointed happily back, 'that's when they took him into care.'

'He left this in your office,' she waved the article in front of my possessed face, 'and he got a computer to talk about you on the Internet. I called you then, after dinner before they made me take my pills. You were in hotels, do you remember?'

I nodded. Dundee.

'But I told him to wait, you see, until I got out. So we could do it together. I only got out last week, Mr Santini.' She leaned into me, her eyes existing only with insanity. 'They let me go to the shops. Half an hour they gave me, that's all I needed.'

She had a plastic tag on her wrist. I'd never been to hospital. Twenty-three years and I'd never been to a hospital. Apart, I presumed, from my arrival, but I didn't know anything about that. Where it was, who had been there. Just Mum and me, surely.

'Come on,' she said to the Asian, Joe Junior.

Joe Junior told me to get up and I found myself doing so with their help. We walked to my room down those corridors. They held an arm each and my mouth opened and closed in silent, burning screams.

From arriving at Dundee's cramped, provincial airport I was resigned to disaster. Tony did his best during the flight and then in the car they had sent for us, going over again and again the fact that the TV channel had *only* said that their press department was *aware of certain allegations* on the Internet.

'That doesn't mean anything, Nicky.'

It wasn't much of the story that had seeped on to the Internet, it was far less than had been carried in the *Soho Star* at the time, but there were two reasons that Tony failed to calm me. The first was the idea that I would accept reassurance, on anything at all, from Tony. The second was the fact that only I knew the deepness of the threat that any mention of Java Joe could possess.

In London, it was the most impressive restaurant yet. We had our own room that was walled in padded leather and cut with a hatch that Oriental staff ducked through to deliver small plates of small food that no one seemed to have ordered. Half a bottle of champagne had already gone when we got there and the two men, the same two men as it always had been, greeted us warmly and handed us glasses.

We drank and talked, and sometimes laughed, while they discussed the tour and the DVD – which they also said was *flying off the shelves* – and then one of them, still smiling and without breaking the pace, said,

'We're going to have to pull the series though guys, as I'm sure you can imagine.'

I nodded. Tony said,

'What? Come on, lads, because of that shite on the Internet?'

'It's not shite though, is it?' said the other man, he was smiling as well. 'We checked it out, our lawyer did. This guy died in your office, Nick, it doesn't look good.'

I nodded. Tony said,

'How the fuck is Nick to blame for that?'

One of the men stood and pointed to the door.

'Tony,' he said, 'can I have a quick word outside?'

Tony left muttering. The other man pulled some papers from his pocket and pushed them across the table to me.

'The lawyers did a few searches, Nick. Standard stuff, property, you know?'

The paper showed the sales records of an address in Soviet Street. Java Joe's shop. And there I was. My old name, before Tony and the arrival of Santini. The buyer and then the seller. On the same date. Quite a margin too, the estate agent had done well. Better than me.

'A short career you had as a newsagent, Nick, not to your liking?' He was smiling, drinking as he spoke. I watched him as the words came out very easily. 'The lawyers say the only way you'd not be charged for that is if all the paperwork is in order and the guy's family is happy with it. Otherwise, it looks like extortion. Diminished responsibility, you see, considering what he did?'

'OK.'

I wondered what else he might have, I hadn't caught up to realise that he had everything that was needed.

'You know, don't you, Nick, that we have to pull the series?'

'Yeah.'

'You need to go away for six months, no public appearances, nothing. The press can go with the guy topping himself in your office, we'll help you with the quotes on that. But they'll hold off for a month, it's only one paper that has got enough to worry about and we'll sort them out.'

'We've got another story for the series being pulled. We'll look after you, Nick, because this...' He flicked a finger at the damning figures beside my old name. It felt appropriate that this humiliation was being represented by that name, handed down as it had been by my father. 'This would hurt us as well as you.'

My main thought was how much I would miss this man and the others like him. The professionals and the efficient. They were going to go and I would be left with Tony.

'Tony?' I asked.

'He's out there being told the cover story of why the series is being pulled. And he's being compensated for the next six months. A decent cheque, for you obviously.'

There was no profit in letting this man know that I would be fortunate to even hear about the cheque.

'OK.'

The man looked at me as he pulled the evidence away and I struggled with the silence, the first opportunity for judgement. It was welcome to see Tony and the other man return. Tony was arguing and trying new angles, probably for my benefit, but either way it was already done.

We ate and drank and the men produced an illicit load that this time was just passed over the private table between them and Tony while they took swift shifts in the bathroom. Our driver appeared through the hatch, nervous amongst the decadence, and suggested we had to leave in order to catch our flight back. I had a show that night.

'The last one,' announced the man who had spoken to me while Tony had been outside hearing lies from the other. 'Go out with a bang, Nick, you deserve it.'

We shook hands with the men and they wished me luck. With Tony, they insisted that they would be in touch and one said,

'Oh, and the DVD. We're going to have to pull that as well. But it's done brilliantly so far, congratulations again.'

'Yes,' said the other one to me. 'Congratulations Nicky.'

'Thanks,' I said, heading for the hatch.

At the end of that last show I waited on the stage far longer than usual, until the applause was nearly ended. After that we cancelled the tour citing my *exhaustion* and the TV station cancelled the series with a decent cover story – they explained to anyone who asked that there was a lurking legal problem due to the wrong type of disclaimer being used for audience members in the series' later shows.

It worked, with minimal coverage in the press. The channel's PR department had already run through my quotes for the approaching story on Java Joe. One of the tabloids had it and they had promised us a month's delay. I spoke of my devastation, about how Joe Yakari had been *a troubled man*, about how I *think every day if there was anything more that I could have done.*

Back in London we waited. Tony in his big house in Hampstead and me in my new Fulham residence where the soft, sunny streets helped with the trauma.

We didn't get our month. Two weeks of waiting led to Tony calling me late on a Saturday night.

'They're running it tomorrow,' he said. 'The channel just called me.'

I struggled through a night of short, broken sleep and then walked to the petrol station round the corner. The tabloid I was looking for didn't have me on the cover. I took it from the display and read it there in the forecourt.

Through the pages I went with delight to find myself a fair journey in. A picture of me, a picture of Java Joe. Those quotes of mine, offered without question. It was a *tragedy*, a *secret tragedy*. And a blameless one. I didn't even buy a copy, just left the petrol station and called Tony during the joyous walk home.

A few days later we met for a long dinner. He had been watching the message board and reported with relief that the only reaction to the series' collapse was dismay, and some spirited denigration towards the show's legal team for such an elementary error. The story on Java Joe had only collected a handful of comments. There was little people could add to my, and Java Joe's, obvious misfortune. Soon my former supporters had moved on to nostalgia – long discussions of their favourite moments of the programme they were already missing greatly.

We both knew that something had finished and there was little conversation until I, with sudden decision, asked him how much money I had made.

'Up till now. All together, minus what you've given me.'

'I'd have to check the accounts, Nicky.'

'OK, but guess. In the last year, say, with the TV, the tour, the DVDs and all that. How much?'

'About half a million,' he tried, and when I didn't react badly added, 'minus what I've given you. And before tax. And, obviously, my cut.'

'Which is half?'

'Yeah.' He could see that I was about to answer that so clapped his hands,

'More than that actually, Nicky. Seven hundred grand probably. I'd forgotten about the DVD. Seven hundred grand, minus all costs.'

A million, that's what I thought, it must have been at least a million.

'Alright, well, I want forty grand please, for now.'

'What for?'

'To live.'

He had to agree to that so he had to agree to the money. He wasn't happy with the ambush. When the bill came, he fidgeted and sighed until I paid it.

It took a week and a couple of reminders before Tony got the money together. We met at a café in town, near Soviet Street as it happens, though neither of us seemed to notice. Tony handed me a rucksack and I looked inside to see the tight piles and rubber bands.

I had a bag of my own, which had roughly the same load but was heavier and more awkward. My money was a loose charge of notes large and small. It was disordered, stuffed still inside the detergent box and the total would have been a rough one, somewhere near the forty thousand, if I had ever bothered to count it. The bags sat together at my feet as Tony talked.

'I spoke to the TV lot again. They're delighted with how the paper handled it. They said they'd be in touch, at some point.'

'OK.'

'And I'm going to start putting together a new tour soon as well, get it ready for when the six months are up, you know?'

'Well, let's see.'

Tony didn't even react to that, he was as shaky in his view of our future as I was and he didn't know, as I did, that the TV station would surely never be in touch again. We walked together to the door. I wondered, without bias, what Tony was going to do with himself.

'Stay in touch, Nicky,' he said. 'It'll all blow over. We'll be back in the game.'

'I hope so, Tony.'

'You can keep the bag,' he smiled and I did too and made what I said next sound as light as I could.

'Don't call me, Tony, I'll be in touch.' I left him there, near Soviet Street, and started to walk towards Tottenham Court Road with both the bags.

I wasn't entirely confident that Mervyn would still be gainfully employed but, sure enough, there he was in Atlas Electronics. And promoted too, chatting gently to customers at a bank of screens. I waited for him to finish before rounding a basket of reduced-price headphones to get to him.

'Nicky!'

He was happy and so was I while he took me through to the same room in the shop's cluttered rear. Mervyn didn't mention my TV breakthrough, he just apologised for the mess and pulled out some chairs. I wasn't surprised that he had missed it but it made it harder when I told him I had something for him.

'That ten grand you gave me, Mervyn. I've got it for you, plus interest.'

'No, Nicky, no way, you deserved that money.'

'I know I did but I know that you're not a thief, Mervyn.'

'What's that got to do with it?'

'The ten grand you gave me. It wasn't the pub's money was it? He'd never have had that lying about. It was yours. It must have been about all you had?'

He hesitated just enough.

'Yeah, I knew it. Listen Mervyn, take this. I promise you I can afford it.'

He placed the bag on a table and unzipped it. He pulled out the detergent box, opened it and peered inside.

'Jesus, Nicky, how much is that?'

'It doesn't matter, Mervyn, it's yours. I don't want it.'

'No way,' he said, 'You deserve everything you get, Nicky, after what happened.'

'Mervyn,' I said, 'I promise you, I don't want it.'

He looked at me, still holding the detergent box with Java Joe's money in his hands. Where had he come from, Mervyn? How had a good man ended up in my life?

'Please,' I told him. He looked at me for a long time. There was something about seeing him like that. Unsure, and in the shirt and tie he would never wear easily. I felt close to a collapse. 'Please Mervyn.'

'I've got this bird now,' he said tentatively, 'she's got two kids. It's not easy, so maybe...'

'Exactly,' I said, smiling. 'You can keep the bag.'

At first the call to Mum went well. She had been watching my show, after being tipped off by a forgotten cousin, and had called the station a few times trying to get a message through. That might have been true. She didn't mention Dad's newspaper appearances. Her new life clearly didn't include the calibre of paper that had carried his regrettable exclusives.

When I told her that I wanted to visit she panicked a little and asked for my number to call back. It was later that evening when she did so. She was still scared – she was speaking with that same slowness she had used when frightened or angry, with Dad in both cases – but told me *they* would love to have me down for *an evening*. The directions were to a town in a green county one out from London.

I saw her from the train. It was drawing into the small station and she was standing in the car park. Even without seeing me, she looked terrified. I tried my best to calm her, walking to her with a smile and going for an embrace. Her hands shook while she drove us along roads that grew smaller and she told me she lived with a man called Toby, who managed a bank in the town.

Mum took us into a drive that opened into a broad garden and then a whitewashed cottage. I knew she would feel guilty if I complimented the setting, so we got out of the car and walked in silence through the porch and into a large kitchen.

'Do you want a drink?'

'Yeah.'

'Good,' she laughed and walked to the fridge. In the laugh and the quick smile back, I saw her as I remembered her from before she left. There was something shielding that memory though, and I saw it when we took a bottle of wine to a table in the cottage's garden. She looked better than she had ever looked back then. Time and money had gone into her appearance and she had lost the view through which she had seen the world. Fear.

'The TV show, Nicky, it's amazing.'

'Thanks, Mum, I'm glad you like it.'

'What's happened to it?'

'Just a legal thing, it'll be back soon enough, you should come to the studio one time.'

'I should do, yes.'

She picked at her drink and the words were drawn and vague.

'This place is nice, Mum.'

'It's Toby's.'

'Do you work?'

'No, I did when I first came down here. I got a job in town. Administration, in an office, Nicky.'

She laughed again and I did too. Then I asked where and she stumbled a little bit.

'Just an office, in town.'

'What kind?'

'A bank.'

'The bank this guy manages?'

She smiled uneasily, but she didn't have to. I would have made it clear how little I cared that she had transferred her ruined affections from Dad, but a saloon car came creeping up the drive. A tall man with little hair climbed out and walked over with his jacket slung stiffly over an arm.

'Nick?' he asked, and introduced himself by his full name and then the name of his bank.

The three of us had a decent dinner, where Mum panicked and drank and Toby and I largely ignored her and talked about the intricacies of television mediumship and provincial bank management. Afterwards they showed me round the cottage. Upstairs I shied away from the bedroom and walked into the room next door.

'That's just my little study,' said Toby. Sheets were stuck evenly along the bookcase. Colour-coded graphs and stickers on paper headed with titles.

HOLIDAY NUMBER ONE
HOLIDAY NUMBER TWO
DINNER PARTY ROTA
BILLS (HOUSEHOLD)
BILLS (EXPENSES)

Order and application, responsibility and security. I couldn't blame Mum. Who could? Back in the garden, we had a final glass of wine. When the conversation grew quiet there was perhaps a quarter of the bottle left. Toby rose, said,

'Well, that was a lovely evening,' put the cork back in the bottle and carried it through to the kitchen.

In the morning, at the train station, we sat in the car.

'Nicky, you know that first time I left? For a few months?'

'Yeah.'

'I only went down to Tooting. I worked in a nursery down there. It was a good job, and I finished early in the afternoons.'

'Right.'

'Then I'd get the tube into town. I'd go and sit in Carol's.'

Carol's was a café around fifty yards up the road from the OK Corral. It was vegetarian and therefore untouched by anyone connected with the OK Corral.

'Why?' But I knew.

'To look for you. Sometimes I saw you and sometimes I didn't, but I saw enough to see that he was taking you to the bookie's with him. That's when I came back.'

'Yeah, I remember.'

'I came back for you, Nicky, but I hope you can see that I couldn't stay.'

'I know, Mum, it's OK.'

I didn't mean it. I was thinking of Ayako. If Mum had stayed, then there wouldn't have been Ayako. There would have been though, or something else, maybe worse, but I was struggling to see that, fiddling with the lock on the door of the car that Mum had been bought by another man.

'Do you mean it?'

I looked at her. Her skin was smooth and coloured, her hair thicker than I remembered.

'Yeah, I do.'

I had to jog for the train that came sliding round a corner. If I hadn't had to run, then I might have looked back.

Mum and Mervyn, and that was me done. I thought about Dad, now and then, but it was never going to lead to action. He was a blocked presence, and not just from me. Neither Mum nor Mervyn had strayed close to discussing him for long. He had just floated around us, probably laughing.

I didn't see Tony again for six months and Fulham wasn't a bad place to be bored and rich in my understanding of the word. I bought more stuff for the flat, lived well and paid the bills with the clean, deserved money that Tony had given me.

I watched a lot of television, particularly in the afternoons, particularly in the slot that I had once filled. I walked along the river in both directions and stopped for lunch and to read newspapers.

I found a library, hiding down a side street and showing little action. From then on I would be in there most days, prowling the aisles and enjoying the search. At first I went for enjoyment, clutches of crime and biography, but it turned to something else.

Medical books. A complete collection of diluted versions, meant for the home, where ailments were identified and lightly assessed. The other books I had read in pubs or on my balcony, but I read the medical books at a table in the flat's ordered lounge with the TV inactive in the corner.

I read them in a different way, with a notebook open and pen ready. I made notes, checked one book against another and a pile of findings built on the table beside me. I knew why I was doing this but pretended to myself that I didn't.

After a few months of study I had exhausted the library's medical section from every angle. Baby health, psychology, alternative medicine and, more than anything, terminal illnesses had all been and gone. It was those major killers that I had mined with the greatest commitment and they dominated my block of scribbled notes, which now became the object of my daily examination. I would spend a week travelling steadily through them and then the next week I would start again at the beginning for my mind to fill once more.

When Tony phoned me I was distant and non-committal. But the truth is that if he hadn't called, then I probably wasn't far away from calling him.

He came to Fulham to see me, in a taxi that must have taken an hour. I had been impressed by the hidden will power that had made him wait six months before troubling me. In fact, he had been suitably distracted by the final conclusion of his divorce, which had dragged and crept all the way from Soviet Street. He told me he'd moved.

'A one-bedroom flat, Nicky, round the corner from the house which is what really fucking hurts.'

'Rented?'

'No, I bought it but still, she's fucking cleaned me out. All I've done is talk to lawyers and sign cheques.'

'What about my money?'

'That's fine,' he said. 'Don't worry, it's safe, but I had to stick it away somewhere, so it didn't get seen as my assets, know what I mean?'

He was walking a fine line and I could see his aim – to convince me the money was there, but demonstrate that accessing it was somehow complicated. That wasn't my main concern though, and neither was it his.

'I've been speaking to people Nicky, it's time to get back out there. People want to see you back.'

'Who?'

'The tour lot, they want me to put something together, starting in a few weeks.'

I wanted to do it.

'I don't think so, Tony. What about that stuff, Java Joe?'

'It's only the TV boys that ever knew about that stuff, Nicky, everyone else has been asking why we're not out there. They don't give a shit. It's only TV that can get turned over by the papers for anything dodgy, not a tour. We'd start small,' he continued quickly when I didn't speak, 'then we wouldn't have to advertise and we'd crack on from there, just keep the thing going.'

'No press, no interviews, that would be vital,' I said. I didn't want to antagonise the TV channel and I didn't want any attention that would link to Java Joe. But I wanted to get back. Tony beamed.

'No problem. Word of mouth, that's all we'd need.'

'Alright. I've got some stuff I want to try out anyway.'

That final tour began in small halls where I would be on a variety bill (*TV's Nick Santini*) and dealing with other people's audiences. There would be some recognition, which would sometimes help and sometimes wouldn't, but I created each evening's workings from those basic propositions and my devastating medical backing.

This is how people die:

For ages fifteen to twenty-nine, mortality rates are highest for injury and poisoning. Injury tends to mean car accidents and poisoning tends to mean accidental drugs overdoses.

For ages thirty to forty-four, it's still injury and poisoning for men but for women it's cancer. There's a one-third chance it's breast cancer, then the others.

For ages forty-five to sixty-four, cancer has taken over all round. Here's the best and worst cancers you can get, from the best downwards – testicular, breast, prostate, cervix, bladder, colon, stomach, oesophagus, colorectal, lung.

For ages sixty-five and up, cancer loses out to circulatory diseases (dominated by heart disease and strokes), then respiratory diseases (pneumonia and smoking-related lung disease).

I knew how people died and I knew what happened before – the symptoms, survival rates, and treatments both traditional and alternative.

As well as my new, perfect understanding of how people died, I also knew what happened *after*. Organ donation, the trade that arrives when your body becomes a body, and that was a staple on the final tour.

There are fifteen million willing adults on the NHS organ donor register. That's not far off half of all those trusted to fill in the form, though there's something else. Up and down the country, while families grieve and the nurse arrives and shows them the signature of the dead, nearly half of them tell the nurse that they want the deceased intact and the knives should go back in the box. That means pride or guilt for those left behind, and those were the people and those were the feelings that I needed.

This mix of insight and education confused the audience. The switch from the tangible to the speculative became lost in their minds and they followed me loyally through. I was infused with a newly manic appreciation of the stakes. I had seen how temporary success could be and I was keenly aware that this tour was our last chance. What made me most aware of it was the fact that, several times a day, Tony would say to me:

'This is our last chance.'

Against his normal outlook, that was cataclysmic, and as a result I was more aware of everything that came with the tour's building buzz. For the first few weeks I sought out attention, catching eyes around the theatre and gratefully stopping for conversation and autographs.

Tony grew in confidence with me and the tour developed in scope through his cajoling and bribing. He was thrillingly dedicated to the task I had given him – the local facts, figures and anything else that could help me in the evening's show – and enjoyed the involvement.

I knew that Tony's new sense of responsibility came only from the financial pressures of his divorce, but that was fine with me. Now he needed this to work as much as me, maybe more.

He checked his computer regularly for any adverse coverage. The message board that had been such a threat was now deserted. Days, weeks passed between entries. The flitting interest of the people there had moved away from me, and that was fine.

After a couple of months we were using larger theatres and Tony was once again employing students, backpackers and confused others to work around us. He told me that he was going to get in touch with the TV people.

'Let them know you're back in the game, see what they're saying, Nick, you know? They might want to chat.'

'Might they?' Tony would be fortunate if they even took his call. I felt responsible, and almost guilty, for his pointless enthusiasm.

'Yeah, yeah, I do. Why not, eh?'

I can't think what happened in the days before we arrived in that last city. It wasn't supposed to be the last, but it was. I presume that we were in a fair state of mind. The tour was naturally enlarging, Tony was buoyant about the planned reunion with the TV people, and everything seemed as normal as it could be while we moved through hotels that were more comfortable each time.

There was the arrival of the black girl. Tony had talked me through her band's success, assuring me that she and I together would be enough of a story to help convince the TV channel I could come back with a more positive *media profile*, away from Java Joe's suicide, my dad's outbursts and the cancellation of the series. It could, he suggested, be the kick to *get them back on board*.

I didn't see many of those aims as possible, especially when the black girl joined the tour and no one, literally no one, seemed to recognise her. Tony said this was lucky because we didn't want the story to *slip out*. When I countered that it was also slightly worrying he insisted, with a desperate piece of conjuring, that she had *done something with her hair* since her glory days a few years before.

He regained some control with the sly suggestion that he'd been forced into such a move.

'It doesn't look like you're going to get *yourself* a bird, Nick, does it? Not one that we can use for this anyway.'

In the testy silence that followed I thought without meaning to of Ayako.

On the first night in the city where everything ended, I felt little option but to join Tony and the black girl for the execution of his plan. Into the city's limited centre we ventured. Tony paid the waiting photographer who took photos of the black girl and me exiting various bars, always with that same shock when we saw him rear up before us.

Later, in the hotel's honesty bar, Tony gave the black girl her money. She smiled when she took it. I still can't see why she did what she did, and why existing the next day had been impossible for her.

After he gave her the money, Tony turned to me.

'A journalist wants to speak to you.'

'Well, he can't.'

'It's a she and I think you'd better.'

'Why?'

She was from the *Soho Star*. The paper that had splashed on Java Joe's porn range, then sullenly reported his death shortly after. The paper that had somehow come to me in Earl's Court with the scribbled blame for Java Joe's brutal ending.

'You'd better see her.'

'OK, I'll meet her in the morning. But it's a one-off, just to check her out. Make sure she knows that.'

'I will. It won't be a problem.'

That's what he said, sitting in the honesty bar framed by ignorance and optimism. That it wouldn't be a problem. As I said a long time ago now, that interview with the journalist is where it all began.

Thirty-nine

The drugs make what happened next an uneven experience. The support was removed from my arms and I collapsed on to the bed in my room. My eyes twitched open and closed while the two of them continued their movements. Their hands were around me, my shoes and socks were teased off, and then they began to construct the scene in the middle of the room.

All I had with any firmness was who they were and my brain, cheated and humiliated, did its best to draw for me what had happened. I saw the journalist leaving the press conference that day with Joe Junior at her side. From there and elsewhere I thought of his walk, that struggling shuffle, and of Java Joe, walking with increasing difficulty up and down the Soviet Street stairs. Java Joe had told me that he had inherited his weak legs from his father and I had seen, but missed, where he had passed it downwards in turn.

Joe Junior held the chair in place. He was too young to have worked in the hotel, he was only a kid, but he'd pulled up something to disguise it. The belief and the bravery of the injured. Pain. He looked like an old man. He looked like me, like I had looked when I was his age and when I was him. If I could have spoken freely then, and I don't know if it was the drugs that made me want to do it, I would have told Joe Junior that it was OK.

Java Joe's wife stood on the chair. The plastic bracelet on her wrist dropped out of sight when she lifted her hands to tie the rope. There was a hook banged professionally and recently into the ceiling. They were lucky that the hotel was so barren of activity, if any of this could still just be luck. I knew what they wanted me to do but I couldn't see how it would work. I looked at my hands and told them unsuccessfully to move. My muscles were only controlled by what she had given me.

They pulled and dragged me to the edge of the bed and then, in one lift, on to the chair. I wondered if it was always going to be like this. If when Java Joe had silently turned to me in the failed air of Soviet Street, if he had been plunged within me and gripped me and led me always to this. The rope was around my neck and tightening.

'No.'

I spoke in a breaking croak and Joe's wife said, 'He's coming back,' and her son was around me. He tied a cloth round my mouth, then my hands and feet were pulled and bound in turn.

'Stand up.'

Java Joe's wife gestured upwards. She was entranced, her face lightened over the creases and faults when she arrived at a moment that had been long imagined. The rope dug within my skin and made me stand. My legs were only just coming back under my control and they shook when I stood on the floor and then the chair, with the rope being pulled downwards and lifting me upwards. If I hadn't moved higher then what was going to happen would happen lower.

Joe Junior was hidden while he guided the rope so it was her that was before me, directing the chair under my feet until I moved to the edge. She looped another piece of rope round the end of the bed and said, 'Do his hands.' Joe Junior untied my hands and pulled them round to take the rope that his mother placed in them. Then the chair was pushed some final inches from beneath me. The rope round my neck stopped moving and I could see what they had done.

Now that I was perched with vibrating feet on the chair's thin brim, I had to hold on to the other rope to keep my balance and this precarious arrangement in place. Joe Junior untied my legs and then stood on the bed, leant over and yanked away the cloth from my mouth. They didn't need to leave me any more contained than I was. My legs couldn't move from their needed position and the rope meant I couldn't call out. I needed to concentrate only on breathing. It would be a suicide.

I held the rope that held my life. If I let it go, then before I fell I would maybe have a second to try to grab the hook. That offered only a brief space of clinging on with my mistrusted arms until the fall would surely come.

'Hold on to the rope,' she told me sternly, kicking the chair and making my toes shake on its curved side. The rope in my hands and round my neck sharpened in response and I realised how temporary and how quick this would be.

Joe Junior was at the door. He never even looked at me at the finish, just stood with his hand on the handle while his mother spoke.

'Alone,' she said, 'like Joe.'

She walked to the door and they left me there.

Forty

I held on. Maybe seconds. Or an hour. It wasn't time like I had ever known it, just a crashing awareness that it was passing. Every section of my body groaned protest at what was happening and what was to come.

When I let go of the rope I did so without any thought. It was only my fingers moving and my body falling. I cracked to a halt with a force that stole my awareness before it returned in a gagging rush and the rope braced and cradled my head to face the wall of the room. There was no sound.

My view switched from what is normal to a dulling bowl with my eyes tightening and bloating in their sockets while, from behind, came twitching emergency. In the corner of the departing vision a dark block flashed white then dark again, and a new shadow arrived through the dimming yellow and brown.

He lifted me from my knees, leaning the log of my choking body on to his shoulder. Sound punched its way through in uneven bursts of primal fury. I was moving, lifted then lowered. Rises and falls. It was just him and I knew that if it was to be anybody then it would have to be him.

This was the only way he could do it, try to flip the rope back over the hook. When he managed, and the rope slipped into space, I was released and sent down for an ugly landing on the hotel's carpet. I began my wretched return. My fingers jutted and worked between the rope and my neck, tweezing and scissoring in the heat of the blood while Dad said,

'Fuck, Nicky, speak, Nicky.'

The rope gave way and I breathed and breathed and soon I could see without the panic. The documents from Tony's bed lay scattered from Dad's rushed approach. My hand looked ancient when I pointed.

'I've got them all, Nicky, we'll sort it out. He's not a bad guy, he's just a thief. He gave me the documents straight away. Said to say that he's sorry. But he was calling the other one, the copper, when I left. I can't see him letting us just walk away, Nicky. We've got to get out of here. Right now.'

My throat was opening and closing by itself. My neck was just rings and rings of pain. Dad had a hand on the back of my head and it felt like my whole body was resting on it. His face was dark with the effort and the world shrunk while I watched. I realised that I had never seen him scared before, as great beats of connection travelled between us.

Forty-one

That was a little more than a year ago, when I lay on the floor of the hotel room and he held my head. The pain dominates the memory. It was there, constantly, while I managed to stand and we left the room, striking out down the corridors with Dad hopeless in the lead but me unable to voice directions from behind.

My neck moved out of synch with my body, the vicious contractions uncontrollable and not linked to my movement. I tried lifting my head, lowering my head, moving slower and then, briefly, not at all. There was no way to influence the erratic arrival of the jolting twitches that closed my throat and left me lashing with my palms and trying to stay calm and extend how long I could wait for it to open.

Dad spun busily around me, opening doors and urging me onwards. In one fist he gripped the documents. We had made it outside the hotel, staggering past the woman at the desk who managed mild interest, and battled fifty yards down the road when the siren became too loud to ignore. Dad told me to keep going but I turned, my throat drumming with spasms, and saw Brewster's car slide ungraciously to a stop outside the hotel with a temporary blue light attached to the roof.

They'd have seen us if they'd looked but they were too busy – Brewster with the anger that sent him bounding up the steps, Tony with the shame that saw him lurk behind, walking stiffly and with unbearable reluctance. The fury of Brewster's sprint for the hotel's door, and the corrupted importance of the abandoned car and its spinning blue light, confirmed we had to go.

We carried on with our ragged escape, Dad a nervy presence and me managing a dozen paces to one gasping, suffocating stumble. He knew a route and it took us to the train station where he had arrived after his invite from Tony. The sound and activity of the station didn't help. Dad levered me on to a bench and told me to wait, that he would sort the tickets.

'We're in luck, Nicky,' he said on his return.

It must only have been a few minutes, but he'd had to wake me. We made it to the train, where we sat side by side facing south. I pushed my head into the seat's frayed corner to stretch my throat open. After a period, there was no new tightness and I gave in to horrific sleep, crammed with ghoulish appearances and speculation of further disaster. I woke many times but finally in London, with Dad tapping and saying,

'That's us here, Nicky.'

I breathed and already the process felt secure. I touched my neck and it flamed in response but there was no pain from the air passing through it. On the table the documents had an order to them. That was how Dad had spent his empty hours. I lifted them and he reacted only by standing and waiting for me to pass.

London felt like victory, a long way and separate from the other city and everything that had been created there. King's Cross had hushed after the evening charge and Dad and I walked almost alone along the platform. He was perhaps a yard in front when I turned to the side.

There was no purpose to my doing so, it was probably a movement dictated without reason by my neck, but I looked at the window of a shop closed for the night. With no light behind, and the glass relatively cared for, the window gave a rough reflection and in it I saw Dad react to me looking away by glancing back. He watched the documents in my hand until I turned again. It could have been anything. A check, a complete irrelevance and devoid of intent. It didn't matter. It didn't change anything.

'You're in Pimlico, right?' I asked weakly at the taxi rank.

'Yeah.'

'Can you meet me tomorrow?'

'Yeah, of course. You don't want me to drop you off? You're going to Fulham are you not? Tony said that you're down there.'

'No, it's fine. I'll see you tomorrow.'

I took the first taxi, instructed the driver and pulled down the window.

'Let's meet in Parliament Square. One o'clock, OK?'

'Of course, Nicky, of course.'

He hadn't expected to end there and he was trying to keep things lightened.

'I'll see you tomorrow then,' he said in lilting question.

'Yeah,' I replied, with the taxi slipping away from him and my neck burning. I knew that Dad was wrong on two counts of what had happened to me in the hotel room. He thought I had done it to myself and he thought I had done it, at least partly, because of him. I left him with that understanding, as a start.

Forty-two

The morning brought further improvement. In bed in Fulham all I felt were defined aches from my body and tenderness from my neck. They were forgotten by the time I had started with my tasks. I began by calling a travel service and making the booking, arranging to pay at the airport for an outrageous supplement. I was going to have to grow familiar with bank accounts, debit cards, the arriving of normality into my financial affairs. From the Yellow Pages I selected a lawyer's advert. They were in Victoria, near enough to Parliament Square, and their advert was large and boastful.

There was no great ceremony in leaving the flat in Fulham. I packed what was needed and left. At the end of the street, where I had enjoyed living, I posted the keys to Mervyn at Atlas Electronics. The note told him there was two months on the lease, the furniture was mine and he should take the lot and drop the keys back to the agent.

I stopped a taxi on the New Kings Road and gave the driver the lawyer's address. It took a while for someone to see me at the office but it was worth the wait, with the lawyer rapid and impressive in his reading of my situation. There were no complications with my unorthodox requests, just clarifications at his end.

I gave him all the documents, those hidden companies and secret accounts, and did my best to explain what they meant. It was the lawyer who cancelled Brewster's cheque, putting me on the phone to confirm my identity and then bullying the bank swiftly into submission while they panicked at the obvious fraud.

He photocopied my passport, had me sign a few forms and declared that he didn't see any great obstacles. And that was before I told him that Tony could keep half the money, which we both agreed would make him easy to deal with. When I revealed where the other half should go, I could only tell him what I knew. The lawyer said that he had a relationship with a private investigator but there was no guarantee that they could track *the party* down. I pointed out that there couldn't be too many Yakaris kicking around.

The lawyer was to deliver the second cheque personally. I was clear on that. Tony's reaction to this settlement was of fleeting interest. The reaction of Joe Junior tugged fiercely at me in anticipation. He was to be told that this was an initially overlooked insurance payout from his father's death.

When I left the lawyer, with all the secret money despatched, I had only what was in my immediate possession. There was a decent amount of cash, enough for what I was going to do, but there was other value. My notes. Six years of learning and investment, tucked into a bag amongst some clothes and pitifully little else. I walked to Parliament Square.

Forty-three

Mum took me to Parliament Square once. She guided us all the way from Marylebone to show me Big Ben. We crossed over the traffic and on to the vast grass and I stared for a long time at the big clock in the sky. Other families had been taking photos, with the parents hunched and the children holding out a hand to give the effect of patting the tower. Mum looked at them and I knew that she was wishing we had a camera so I made faces to make her laugh, to distract her and let her know that I didn't mind that we didn't have a camera like the other people.

Parliament Square had seemed shrunken ever since, and I had never been back on the grass. The traffic was bad when I arrived. Buses and cars were lashed round the square and only taxis were moving, edging and swivelling to buy a yard. At the top of the square, the Parliament end, war protestors drank from flasks in front of their tents and sloganed bedsheets.

I stayed at the other end. Instead of cutting through the traffic to reach the square, I moved into the people gathered outside Westminster Abbey. There were enough lingering tourists to give me safety and provide the needed spot. I could see him easily enough, he sat alone on a bench, and the distance and the other people meant that he couldn't see me.

Over the next few hours there were two interesting touches in Dad's behaviour. The first was that he didn't look for me. Almost entirely, he sat with his hands on his knees and his eyes on the ground.

The second was that there was no surprise. There was no anger, but that tied with his new, flattened manner. I thought there would certainly be surprise. Instead he just sat, still and waiting even though he seemed to know what was happening. As if he needed to be there for me to punish him and to let me know that I had.

I'm not sure where that scene in Parliament Square came from. Mum leaving is a likely start. The evening my taxi pulled away outside the OK Corral to carry me and Mervyn's money to Victoria is another. But perhaps it was the day just a week before, following Tony through the rain to find my father at the other end. He had come back different but that hadn't altered what had to happen. This was a cheap return of what he had done to me, and I knew that he knew that while he sighed and waited.

When I finally left, walking back towards Victoria and then a taxi to Heathrow, it was only my body's stiffness from the standing that decided my exit. In the taxi, I wondered if Dad would cash those cheques now, from the newspapers who had carried his flimsy accusations against me. I still wonder that.

Forty-four

When the lawyer called, I was in Nassau, staying in a hotel near the port and already scouting the cruise ships. The lawyer told me that he and his wife would be in The Bahamas for Christmas, but I said that I didn't expect to be there that long. Tony hadn't been hard to deal with. He had tried 'many, many times' to get some contact details from the lawyer, or a message passed through to me. I laughed thinking of Tony battling unevenly with the lawyer's cool dismissals, trying to appeal to a matey logic that didn't exist.

It hadn't been hard to find the Yakaris. She was back in care and he was working at a chain hotel near Oxford Street. It hadn't been a great leap, the uninvited role that he'd taken at the hotel where we had met. When the lawyer talked to Joe Junior in the hotel's staff room, and told him of the long-forgotten insurance payout, Joe Junior stopped him to ask if I was OK.

'I did my best, Mr Santini,' the lawyer told me, 'but he caught me somewhat on the hop.'

That phone conversation with the lawyer was the last time that anyone called me Santini. I was staying in the hotel in Nassau under my own name, my father's name, but it would also be abandoned after my first meeting with the new, very different entertainments director.

I had seen the frequency with which the American cruise ships roll in and out of Nassau's port so there was no pressure in the interview. The American entertainments director wore a suit and had an earpiece, white teeth and immaculate arrangements of paperwork stacked on shelves behind his desk. He spoke about *customer expectation* and *adding value*.

I told him I had worked in Britain with some success and moved quickly to my glorious period on the *SS Victory*. I jettisoned everything else – the tours, the TV, Nick Santini, *Let Them Come Through*. This man was American, so was the company and so, I had checked from their brochures, were their passengers. That wasn't an accident on my part.

There was no gamble in giving him the contact details of his spectacularly inferior counterpart on the *SS Victory*. I knew that he'd fail to get hold of him, though it would have been an enthralling conversation if he had, with professional structure meeting studied corruption. Anyway, I had said enough to merit a trial and he called the hotel afterwards to invite me on to the ship for two weeks. The reception staff were confused by the call, with the requested name not matching my room number.

In the air-conditioning of his office, after my speculative arrival, he had asked for my name while reaching for a form. Only then did I realise the chance to escape Santini and the benefits of doing so. I have been restricted to my answer ever since. It's delivered to me daily by dozens of unknowing lips and I'm no longer sure who the joke is on. When the American entertainments director called the hotel, he asked for Nick Brewster.

Forty-five

The two-week trial led to a contract and constant work, hopping between the company's fleet that harasses the Caribbean in endless, looping routes. At each stop, more Americans arrive or depart and everything starts again.

My show is in the afternoon. It's a slower and chattier affair. I don't do most of what I used to. No jump into the air, no real dramatics. I've never said *let them come through* or directed someone with a microphone or camera. There's no intensity and the shows pass me by like they do most of the audience. I walk, smile, joke and then poke about gently with possible voices from far beyond. The audience laugh and clap and some of them probably believe.

The only similarity between the ships I work on and the *SS Victory* is that they all float. Right now, I'm enchanting the learned inhabitants of the *SS Royal Crusader*. There's no connection to any royalty, but the passengers like it. The ship has a coat of arms that's stamped everywhere it could be, and the suites are named after *Great English Castles*, one of which is called *Edinburgh* and another simply *Wales*.

I still don't have a suite, but I'm not far behind, with a one-bedroom cabin that sweeps out to a terrace. The ship is slick and expensive, full of once-in-a-lifetime couples who walk around wearing T-shirts that announce where they've come from. Des Moines, Iowa. Charleston, South Carolina. Laredo, Texas. I move unhindered amongst them and fill days with the ship's many Attractions and Activities. Mostly the library, and the restaurants and bars.

It's easy for time to pass without any great study, which is what has happened until this morning. Overnight we arrived in Bridgetown and that meant newspapers. I had breakfast on my terrace, eating the strange bacon and leaving the fruit, with the *Barbados Advocate* spread before me. The room's phone rang and the guards told me there was a man asking for me at the gate.

Tony, of course.

Forty-six

I thought, I mean I was absolutely sure, that the first thing Tony would say when I opened the door to my cabin would be:

'It's hardly the fucking *SS Victory*, is it?'

He didn't say that. He started talking while the door was still turning.

'Nick, I'm so sorry, I really am. Let me tell you what happened, let me tell you, Nick, just listen, please.'

'In you come.'

I offered Tony my hand but he didn't take it, too desperate to display his regret. He was wearing clothes that suggested he had flown in naked and desperate from London. Straw sandals, enormous shorts, a T-shirt that read *Wet 'n' Wild in Barbados* and a cap that declared the wearer had *Survived* a beach bar. He sat on a chair that was coated in velvet and embroidered in gold with the ship's crest. His legs were burnt, red smears that stopped in a sudden line at his shorts, with white flesh beyond.

Tony talked about that city and the situation he had been in when there. Mortgage payments and child support, credit cards and overdrafts. All neglected and demanding urgent replenishment. But the money was there, I pointed out.

'Why didn't you just keep nicking it like you had been?'

He didn't flinch, he was well beyond that.

'I panicked, Nick, I think I panicked. That money wouldn't have lasted long. One day you were going to turn round and ask for it and it would be gone. When Brewster turned up I thought it was a way out. I didn't want you to be angry with me, Nick, I didn't want to let you down.'

He couldn't even sell that logic to himself, grimacing at his own words and rubbing at his face.

'Why did you give me the money, Nick?'

'To keep you away and to make sure you gave up the other half.'

'OK.' He puffed out his cheeks.

'What if I'd got back on the TV though, after you'd gone with the money? What would you have done then?'

'You weren't going to get back on the TV, Nick.'

'But that email they sent, it sounded like they wanted me, that they were interested?'

He flushed and I knew but my anger was only with myself.

'That wasn't from them, was it?'

'No.' He shook his head, his eyes on the room's majestic carpet. 'I made that up. I called them, the morning of the black girl and you in the papers. They said there was no way, that there was no way back for you whatever we came up with. And that was before she, well, you know. Before she topped herself, the poor bastard. They said to wish you all the best, but obviously I couldn't pass that on, could I?'

'Obviously not, Tony, no.'

'Without the TV, we'd have had to stay on the road all year. You could have done that, Nick, I know you could, but I couldn't. I'm a lot older than you. It just seemed like a way to end it.'

He shook his head with regret and surprise at his own decisions.

'You know, Nick, when we got to your room and I saw that rope,' his fear wasn't affected, 'Jesus, Nicky, I nearly had a heart attack. Then the woman at the desk said you'd left with your dad. I'm glad, Nicky, that you and him sorted things out. I meant what I said when I brought him up from London, I thought it would be good for you.'

'Good for me?'

'Because I was going to, you know, I was going to leave. I didn't want you to be alone.'

'That wouldn't have been a problem, being alone.'

He didn't look hurt, I didn't mean for him to be. He was unaware of so much. The Yakaris, who had been in the middle of everything but it had only ever been between them and me. And that was how it would stay.

'Anything else, Tony?'

'What do you mean?'

'Is there anything else I don't know?'

He pursed his lips in decision before speaking.

'I fucked Tiffany.'

He looked at me with care and I couldn't stop myself from laughing.

'Good for you, Tony. Right, let's have a drink.'

I sent him to the terrace and got beers from the room's fridge. Outside, Tony stood with a steadying hand on the parapet, his grey hair active in the breeze. I handed him a bottle and he looked suddenly hopeful, taking it and saying:

'It's hardly the fucking *SS Victory*, is it?'

'No, it's not. What's going on with the clothes, Tony?'

'I know,' he said, smiling down at his shorts and scorched legs. 'I've been here a week waiting for you. I found you on the Internet eventually, some American couple with photos from their holiday and talking about the English medium called Nick, but the company wouldn't tell me what ship you were on. They told me your name though.'

He wanted to laugh, but had to wait for me.

'What happened to Brewster?'

Tony shrugged.

'Fuck knows, he was angry and threatening all sorts, but what could he do? He didn't even bother trying to cash the cheque. He kept the eighteen grand and that was that.'

The past left us while we drank on the terrace. Tony described his recent project, a group of precocious teenagers who he had just sold to a record company. He said that he hated them and hated their music more but that they ticked the demographics. I smiled and wondered from where he'd liberated the phrase. He asked me about my work and I told him about the success and the boredom.

'Do you need a good manager?' he asked, but I think it was only another joke.

'Yeah,' I answered, 'do you know any?'

Tony laughed and lifted the bottle to his lips, his face red and older in the sun.